MANDASUE HELLER

Forget Me Not

HODDER

Copyright © 2003 by Mandasue Heller

First published in Great Britain in 2003 by Hodder & Stoughton
A division of Hodder Headline

This paperback edition published in 2003

The right of Mandasue Heller to be identified as the Author
of the Work has been asserted by her in accordance with the
Copyright, Designs and Patents Act 1988.

A Hodder paperback

17

A CIP catalogue record for this title is
available from the British Library

ISBN 978 0 340 82026 1

Typeset in Plantin Light by Palimpsest Book Production Limited,
Grangemouth, Stirlingshire

Printed and bound by CPI Group (UK) Ltd, Croydon, CR0 4YY

Hodder Headline's policy is to use papers that are natural,
renewable and recyclable products and made from wood
grown in sustainable forests. The logging and manufacturing
processes are expected to conform to the environmental
regulations of the country of origin.

Hodder & Stoughton Ltd
A division of Hodder Headline
338 Euston Road
London NW1 3BH

problem was, how could she explain it to Debbie:
Everyone knew there was only one reason women went
down Westy Lane.

'Where we going?' Debbie asked.

'The Lane,' Lisa admitted, hoping she'd leave it at
that.

'The *Lane*?' Debbie stopped dead, her eyes wide
with alarm. 'What for?'

Sighing heavily, Lisa turned back. ''Cos me mum
might be there, all right?'

Debbie was confused. 'But why? That's where the
prozzies go, isn't it?'

'So what you sayin'?' Lisa demanded, giving her a
fierce glare.

By the same author

The Front
Tainted Lives
The Game
The Charmer
The Club

About the author

Mandasue Heller was born in Cheshire and moved to Manchester in 1982. There, she has found the inspiration for her novels: she spent ten years living in the infamous Hulme Crescents and has sung in cabaret and rock groups, seventies soul cover bands and blues jam bands. She still lives in Manchester with her musician partner, three children and a tarty squirrel-tailed cat.

The Family
(Past, present and future)

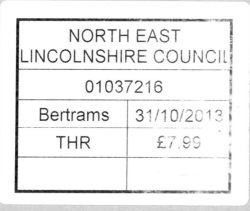

Acknowledgements

Apart from sincerely thanking all those within the business who have helped me along the way, I'd like to thank the following once again for their untiring support (despite driving some of you crazy along the way!):

WINGROVE WARD, my partner – as strong as ever – and still growing.

JEAN HELLER, my mother – I never thought I'd live up to your faith in me.

MICHAEL, ANDREW & AZZURA, my children – such wonderful talents. Can't wait to see where you end up!

My gifted (if she did but know it) sister, AVA, and her children, AMBER (& KYRO), MARTIN, JADE and REECE.

NANA, Auntie DOREEN, LORNA, CLIFF, (CHRIS & GLENN) PETE and ANN.

DANIEL & NATALIE.

KAINE BROWN – glad we're not on the wrong side of you!

Again, many thanks to my agents: CAT LEDGER &

FAYE WEBBER. (Talkback) Great to have you on side!

NICK AUSTIN: So glad I lived up to your expectations second time around.

Everyone at HODDER, as always, especially:

My dear friend, BETTY SCHWARTZ – a lovelier woman you couldn't hope to meet.

And (always last, but forever first in excellence): WAYNE BROOKES, editor supreme!

Prologue

She looked at her watch and decided to make a move. At four in the morning it was highly unlikely that there'd be any more passing trade. Just in case, she stepped forward into the dim pool of light at the pavement's edge and checked up and down the Lane one last time. It was dead. Silent. No cars passing by at either end, and no drunken stragglers to tempt out of their last tenner. Still, she had the thirty quid she needed for her morning hit and a bag of nappies for the nipper. There was no reason to stand here freezing her tits off any longer.

Turning, she climbed over the trodden-down section of fence into the field. She didn't usually take the short cut alone but as there was no one about she figured she'd be safe enough. It only took five minutes to cut across to Stanley Road this way, whereas walking around took at least twenty. No contest.

Little more than fifteen feet in she was plunged into pitch darkness, the street lamp she'd left behind too weak to cast even a glimmer of light into the tall grass she was wading through. The sensation of blindness unnerved her and for a moment she was tempted to turn back. But tiredness won out and she carried on, stumbling in the numerous small pits and rabbit holes that seemed to have sprung up all around her.

Halfway across, her heel caught in the mangled wheel of a long-abandoned bicycle. Cursing as her ankle twisted painfully, she wrenched her foot free of her shoe, then dipped down to wrestle the heel clear. That was when she heard a rustling in the bushes behind her. Her heart leaped into her throat. Was it the breeze? A startled rabbit?

A *rat*?

Ripping the shoe clear, mindless now of the new patent leather, she rammed it back onto her aching foot, all the time peering fearfully around in the darkness. If it was a rat, it would be from the sewers at the far end of the field. It would be big and dirty – and *hungry*.

Seeing nothing, she half hopped, half trotted on, dreading with every step the sharp yellow poisoned rat-teeth sinking into the back of her legs.

And she had no doubt it had seen her – whatever it was. She could feel its eyes following her. And the more she was aware of this, the more she panicked, sure it would smell her fear and know exactly where she was – exactly where to bite.

And it was definitely following her. She could hear it rustling through the grass. Stalking her.

'*Saaandraaa.*'

She stopped dead, not breathing, unsure if she'd actually heard the voice or only imagined it. Straining to hear above the whooshing of her own blood rushing through her ears, she heard the breeze whispering through the undergrowth, and the distant rumble of traffic on the Mancunian Way. But nothing more.

'Stupid cow!' she muttered to herself, trying to stop

the shaking in her legs by chiding herself. 'Freaked out by the bleedin' wind! Get a grip, girl!'

Pulling her jacket tighter around herself she set off once more. She hadn't taken three steps when she heard it again.

'*Saaandraaa.*'

There was no mistaking it this time. It had whispered her name. Its tone was low – male. Mocking. Hissing through a smile. She could hear it in the sing-song inflection.

'Who is it?' she called out, peering blindly into the pitch dark. 'I know you're there, I can hear you!'

'*Remember me, Sandra?*' The voice was close behind her now.

She spun around but there was no one there. Then, behind her again, a twig snapped and she was sure she heard a tiny laugh. Whoever it was, he knew her name, she thought, slightly relieved. It was probably one of her regulars, playing games.

'Who is it?' she called again, her voice stronger now. 'You can stop messin' about 'cos I—'

He moved so quickly that she saw nothing but a blur in the darkness. She was too surprised to defend herself as his arms enveloped her in a vicelike embrace, his breath hot and heavy on her face. And then she was flung around so that her back was against his chest, her arms pinned to her sides by his grip.

She had just about recovered her wits and begun to struggle when she felt the tip of a blade piercing her stomach. Icy fear mixed with scorching, searing pain as he wrenched it upwards, slicing easily through the material of her jacket, her dress and the flesh beneath.

As her flesh gaped and her guts began to spill from her abdomen, she gave way to unconsciousness, only vaguely aware of the knife withdrawing, then re-entering – cutting horizontally now.

Then nothing at all.

Jeff was ten minutes late, as per. Mike lit another roll-up and shifted his heavy work-bag onto his other shoulder. He wished he'd stuck to nights now. It was a pain in the arse leaving the house at half-five in the morning. Especially on days like this – struggling to dawn and ball-numbingly cold.

'Oi! That you, you tosser?'

Mike turned in the direction of the voice. In the half-light, he could just about make Jeff out.

''Bout bleedin' time!' he called back. 'I've been waitin' ages.'

Jeff laughed. 'Aw, shaddup! You're worse than Yvonne for naggin'! Subject of,' he went on, coming alongside and giving Mike a playful punch on the arm. 'Should have seen the gob on it last night!'

'What you done now?' Mike grinned, following him through the gap in the fence into the field.

'Wouldn't go to bleedin' bed, would she?' Jeff flipped back over his shoulder. 'Thought we was gonna get all cosy-cosy on the sofa. But I soon sorted that little game out.'

'Yeah?'

'Yeah. Shoved the bluey on, didn't I? Does the trick every time, that. She gets well narky.'

'You're a right wind-up merchant.'

'S'right, though, innit? Should have heard her kicking

off. I said don't bleedin' watch it, then, if you don't like it! Jeezus! It ain't like I got it for her benefit, the dozy bitch! Like I'd splash out forty quid to look at her pulling her mush!'

Mike laughed at his friend's indignant expression. 'So what's she say?'

Jeff gave him a lopsided grin. 'Exactly what I knew she would. Told me to go fuck meself, then pissed off to bed with two sleepers. Well sorted! Snuck that little Hannah one in the back door and shagged her rigid.' He yawned exaggeratedly. 'Didn't get a wink of kip all night.'

Mike shook his head. 'I don't know how you keep it up, mate. I'm too knackered to give Sharon one half the time, never mind taking on another one.'

'The secret's in variety,' Jeff told him quite seriously. 'You get bored with the same old same old. I mean, I've been with Yvonne for – what – six years? I'd get less for bleedin' murder!'

Mike laughed. 'You want to watch yourself, mate, or it'll be *you* getting murdered!'

Jeff opened his mouth to answer, then let out a howl of surprise as he tripped. Mike laughed as his friend fell flat on his face in the rubbish-strewn grass, but he soon stopped when Jeff immediately leaped to his feet, his face white with shock.

'What is it, mate? What's up?'

Jeff pointed to a bush. 'That! Shit . . . *Shit!*'

Mike peered down to where Jeff was pointing and felt the blood leave his own face as he made out the shape of a foot sticking out from beneath a bush. It was wearing a shoe – a patent-leather stiletto, half on, half off, its gleam dulled by streaks of dried blood.

'What is it?' Mike muttered stupidly.

'It's a bird,' Jeff croaked. 'Oh my God, Mike! It's a bird, and she's dead to fuck!' Turning away, he threw up violently.

Mike watched Jeff's heaving shoulders for a moment. Then, overtaken by a sudden morbid urge, he dipped his head to take a look for himself.

He immediately wished he hadn't.

'Better call the dibble,' Jeff said when he had recovered. He dry heaved as Mike emptied his stomach beside him. 'Make sure you don't splash none of that on . . . on the shoe, mate.'

Digging his mobile out of his pocket with wildly shaking hands, it took Jeff four attempts to tap in the three digits.

Detective Inspector Seddon closed his notepad and looked down at the two men huddled together on the tree stump. Big and scrappy as they looked, he pitied them. They were shocked now, but there was worse to come. Nightmares. Flashbacks. They would never forget what they had seen beneath that bush. Seddon himself found it hard enough to shake off the brutal images of death and destruction he saw day after day, but a case like this stayed in the minds of even the most hardened operators for the longest time. And these men, who right now looked more like frightened little boys, weren't equipped to deal with it at all.

'Look, lads, the café's open down the end of the Lane,' he told them kindly. 'Why don't you go and get yourselves a cup of tea, eh? I've got your details, so I'll contact you later to make a full statement at the station. Okay?'

'Yeah, sure. Thanks.'

Getting to their feet, Mike and Jeff picked up their work-bags and headed for the gap in the fence, grateful to be escaping the now-crowded field.

Seddon watched them go, then walked back into the field to the bush. Dipping beneath the scene-of-crime tape posted all around it, he sidestepped the white-suited forensics team and made his way over to the attending pathologist, Lynne Wilde, who was on her knees beside the body, making notes.

'The same?' he asked, knowing full well what the answer would be.

She peered up at him and nodded, saying quietly, 'Neater. Look.'

Seddon crouched beside her, shifting slightly to make way for the official photographer. The flash of the camera in the dawn light accentuated the blood that seemed to have drenched every inch of the area. It also highlighted perfectly the vertical and horizontal slashes to the victim's stomach that Lynne was pointing out to him. He saw immediately what she meant.

This was the fourth killing of its kind in the past two months, but these incisions were almost professional in comparison with the jagged, frenzied cuts that Lynne and Seddon had first encountered.

'Seems our friendly neighbourhood whore-slayer has honed his skills somewhat,' Lynne said grimly. 'Makes me wonder if there aren't more we haven't discovered yet.'

'You don't think it could be a different guy?'

Lynne shook her head, pursing her lips emphatically.

'No chance. Everything's identical. No panties. Exact method of cutting. The *gift*.'

Seddon leaned forward slightly and peered at the inner organs protruding from the ruined stomach. Lacerated beyond repair and drained of all blood, they reminded him of the chicken giblets his wife boiled for the cat. He quickly shook off the disturbing image and looked deeper.

And there it was, its delicate petals barely visible. The trade-mark forget-me-not, nestling innocently in the wreckage of Sandra Foggarty's remains.

'Why does he do it?' he muttered, saddened by the incongruity of it all.

Lynne shrugged. 'No good artist leaves his work unsigned.'

Finished with her examination, she stood and motioned Seddon aside as the team moved in to bag the body.

'Raped?' Seddon asked, lighting a cigarette and pulling on it hard, releasing a great stream of smoke from his nose, making his eyes water – his way of erasing from them the sight of the mutilated body.

'Yep . . . and before you ask, no, there's no semen deposit. This guy covers himself so well he could be one of my team.'

'Don't suppose you've any freaks with a fetish for cross-cuts and flowers?' he asked then, jokingly.

Lynne smiled. 'Not that I know of, but I'll keep my eyes open.' She checked her watch. 'Look, I've got to go, Ken. I've four autos to get through before I'll get a chance to look at Lady Bush. I'll call you if I find anything, okay?'

'But don't hold my breath, yeah?'

'Not unless you get a kick out of self-asphyxiation.'

Seddon grinned, then said seriously, 'He'll slip up sooner or later, Lynne. And when he does, I'll be waiting for the bastard.'

'Me too,' she agreed. 'Nice sharp scalpel in hand! Speak to you later.'

'Yeah, bye.'

Seddon waved Lynne off, then turned to look back at the bush. He stared at it for a moment, then let his gaze wander over the surrounding area. It was fully light now and the field looked exactly what it was – a rubbish-strewn piece of wasteland, with next to no chance of it holding clues to this latest murder.

But he'd meant what he had said. He *would* find his man – hopefully sooner rather than later. Especially now that the bastard seemed to be getting so good. There was no telling what he'd turn his hand to once he'd perfected his art. This kind of killer rarely stayed satisfied for long. The ones who felt a compunction to sign their work craved recognition and would vary their style to achieve it.

Seddon just hoped that the fucker slipped up before he moved on to bigger and better things.

I

Pat Noone rolled over, sending her quilt sliding to the floor. An icy draught assaulted her exposed backside, waking her. Groping for the missing duck-down warmth, her groggy gaze fell on the bedside clock.

Ten past eight. She'd slept right through the seven-thirty alarm.

'Oh, shit!' Completely awake now, Pat leaped from the bed and grabbed her dressing gown from the back of the door. Dragging the gown on, she yanked the door open and rushed to the bathroom, banging on her daughter's bedroom door as she passed, yelling: 'Move it, Lisa! We're late!'

Groaning, Lisa pulled her quilt up around her face. She'd been awake for a few minutes already, but she didn't relish the thought of getting out of bed. It was too warm in here – and too cold out there, where the radiators didn't work and you had to boil the kettle to have a wash. The council should have fixed the heating weeks ago but as usual they hadn't shown their faces, and her mum had been too idle to chase them up.

Dragging herself from the bed when she heard her mum thundering down the stairs minutes later, Lisa threw on the clothes she'd been wearing for the past three days and shivered her way to the bathroom. Plonking herself down on the freezing-cold toilet seat, she thought it was a good job that piss was warm or there'd be icicles hanging down her legs by the time she'd finished.

In the messy living room below, Pat was trying to do everything at once: put on make-up, fasten her too-tight blouse, find her shoes, and light a cigarette.

Squinting at her mirror image through a blue haze of smoke, she misdirected the loaded eyeliner brush and let out a wail of despair at the resulting panda-eye. She looked like a raddled old slapper now – definitely *not* the right impression to give the magistrates.

Reminded of them, Pat rushed across to the TV and switched it on to check GMTV's time-dog. She gasped when she saw that it was now almost eight twenty-five. She was due in court at nine, and she couldn't afford to bollocks this one up. Three pulls in one year was taking the piss as it was, but turning up late would be a definite step too far.

'Lisa!' she screeched at the top of her voice, running back to the mirror to swipe at the smudged eye-liner with a spit-wet tissue. 'Get a bloody move on, will you!'

Already on her way down the stairs, Lisa ground her teeth in annoyance. *Just who was doing who the favour here?*

'All right, I'm coming!' she grumbled, pushing through the door, a scowl on her face.

Pat recoiled at the sight of her daughter: dirty blonde hair – dark with grease and not so much as *licked* by a brush; filthy socks sagging listlessly around her skinny, mottled ankles; scruffy coat inches too short at the sleeve, exposing her bony little wrists and accentuating her bitten-down nails.

'What you staring at?' Lisa demanded sulkily.

'You!' Pat snapped. 'Put another coat on, will you? And sort your bloody hair out, for gawd's sake! You look a right tramp.'

Pulling a face, Lisa snatched up a brush from the sideboard and raked it through her hair, muttering, 'It don't matter what I look like. It ain't *me* getting done.'

'Course it matters!' Pat said, shrugging into her jacket and throwing her cigarettes and lighter into her handbag. 'The judge is supposed to take pity on *me*, not *you*. He'll do me for bleedin' neglect if you turn up like that! Now shift your backside and sort yourself out or we'll miss the twenty-to!'

Still muttering under her breath, Lisa swapped the coat for a not-much-better jacket. Buttoning it up, she suddenly remembered that she hadn't told her best friend that she wouldn't be walking to school with her today.

'Oh, sugar!' she muttered, popping her head around the door. 'I forgot to tell Debbie where we're going, Mum. D'y' think I should knock on before we go?'

Rooting for her purse now beneath a mountain of discarded clothes strewn across the couch, Pat said, 'No, you bloody well shouldn't! It's no other bugger's business, this.'

'I don't mean tell her what f—'

'You'll tell her nowt!'

Finding the purse, Pat rammed it into her pocket. Then she reached for the half-bottle of vodka she'd brought home the night before. Unscrewing the cap,

12

she slugged back a hefty mouthful and shuddered as the liquid burned its way into her stomach.

'God, I needed that!' she murmured, tipping the bottle up for a second shot.

Watching in dismay, Lisa said, 'Mum, don't! You can't go to court drunk!'

'*Drunk*?' Pat snorted. 'On that little drop? Do me a favour! That'll just about take the edge off, that. Anyhow, stop fussing. I've got more to worry about than getting a bit pissed.'

'You think they'll let you out?' Lisa asked quietly as her mum swiped on another layer of lipstick.

She didn't know what she'd do if her mum was sent down. She'd never been away from her for any length of time before. And then there was the problem of who would take care of her while her mum was away. There was no one she could stay with, and she was too young to look after herself. But one thing was for sure – there was *no* way she was going into a children's home. She'd run away before she'd let that happen. Where to, she'd deal with at the time.

Taking a deep breath, Pat gave her daughter a tiny nervous smile.

'I honestly don't know, pet. I'm just banking on you swaying the balance.'

Screwing the lid back on the bottle she slipped it into her bag, determinedly shrugging off the feeling of impending doom.

'Anyhow, there's no point looking on the bad side, eh? Let's just go and show 'em how much we need each other.'

Then, with a grin that made her look far less nervous

than she felt, Pat headed for the door, calling back over her shoulder: 'Shove Monty in the kitchen, will you? He'll only start eating me shoes if we leave him out.'

Lisa looked down at the cross-bred Alsatian with sympathy. He hated being locked in the kitchen, but there was no alternative. Left to his own devices he would cause havoc. Reaching for his collar, she hauled him up from his hiding place behind the couch and dragged him towards the door.

'Sorry, boy. I'll have to feed you when I get back,' she said, herding him into the kitchen and closing the door on his mournful face.

Making their way to the back of the crowded bus minutes later, Pat ushered Lisa onto the seat next to the window. Plonking herself down beside her, she rooted through her bag for her cigarettes. Completely ignoring both the 'No Smoking' signs posted on every window and the disapproving stares of the other passengers, she lit up and settled back in her seat in a cloud of smoke.

Pat was dreading the outcome of today's hearing, but she felt better now that they were actually on their way. They'd still have to run to get to the courts from Deansgate, but a few minutes late was better than the half-hour they would have been if they'd had to wait for the next bus.

Noticing how badly her mum's fingers were shaking as she sucked the life out of her cigarette, Lisa nudged her and asked if she was all right.

Smiling, Pat pushed a stray strand of lank hair behind Lisa's ear and said, 'Course I am, pet. I just want to get this over and done, that's all.'

'Are you gonna stop working now?'

Pat snorted softly. 'What do *you* think? You don't reckon I want to go through this again, do you?'

'And you're not just saying that?'

'No. Now stop going on with yourself and just keep your fingers crossed, eh?'

Satisfied, Lisa settled back in her seat and looked out of the window – the fingers of both hands firmly crossed between her thighs.

Michaela Dunne paced the entrance to the Magistrates' Courts with a frown on her pretty face. Anxiously smoothing down her smart black skirt for the fiftieth time, she glanced back at the clock on the wall and tutted loudly. If Pat Noone didn't get here soon the magistrates would take a very dim view of it – and the stupid woman had little enough going for her as it was.

Blowing out an agitated breath, she mentally cursed Malcolm Waverley for having dumped this case on her – and herself for accepting it without a fight. How pathetic was that?

She'd almost convinced herself that it was his status of senior partner at Waverley-Fitch Solicitors that had made her unable to refuse his 'request', but she knew it wasn't really that. It was his year-round tan, his immaculate suits, and his perfect teeth. He was just too damned attractive to resist!

Clutching the social worker's report tightly Michaela made her way outside, mentally rehearsing what she would say to both the magistrates *and* Malcolm should her client fail to appear – which was all too likely given

Pat Noone's apparent refusal to take the laws of the land seriously.

Five anxious minutes later, she breathed a sigh of relief as Pat hurtled around the corner with a child in tow. She was gratified to see that at least the foolish woman had the grace to run. Maybe she had finally realized the precariousness of her situation? Then again, Michaela very much doubted that Pat Noone had the intelligence to realize any such thing!

Seeing Michaela hovering like a crow at the top of the wide bank of steps fronting the courthouse, Pat felt a sinking in her stomach. She'd met her at the solicitors' offices a couple of times and hadn't been impressed by her snooty, disdainful attitude – or her obvious inexperience. She thought that she probably knew more about law than Michaela did – and, given how many times Pat had been to court, she was quite possibly right.

Fearing that her chances of escaping a custodial sentence would be next to nothing without the arrogant Malcolm Waverley to defend her, she hissed, 'Shit!' under her breath.

Running beside her mother, Lisa caught the underlying fear in her voice and looked up at her with concern.

'What's up, Mum? Have you forgotten something?'

With a sick smile that was intended to reassure, Pat said, 'Oh, it's nothing, really. I was expecting Mr Waverley, that's all, but he's sent his lackey instead.'

'Is that bad?'

'Well, the magpies don't really like women briefs,' Pat explained. 'They might say women are equal nowadays, but it's still an old farts' club when it comes to law. Just *wait* till I see that bleedin' Waverley!'

'Can't you just make them wait till your proper solicitor comes?'

Pat shook her head. 'Nah. He can send anyone he wants, so long as they're qualified. But never mind, eh? At least I've got you on my side.'

'Too right,' Lisa agreed, giving her mum's hand a reassuring squeeze.

Smiling gratefully, Pat looked up at the young solicitor and sighed. It might not be who she wanted, but it was all she had so she'd better make the most of it.

'Sorry we're late, love,' she called in a determinedly friendly voice. 'Missed the bus.'

Resisting an urge to roll her eyes when she saw the dark roots screaming out from the approaching brassy blonde head, Michaela smiled tightly.

'At least you made it,' she called back, cringing inwardly at the cliché. 'That's what counts.'

Reaching the top of the steps, Pat pushed Lisa forward to where Michaela was now holding the door open for them.

'This is my Lisa,' she said. Then, nudging Lisa: 'Say hello to Miss . . . ?'

'Dunne,' Michaela said.

''Lo, Miss Dumb,' Lisa muttered, slipping through the door.

Following them inside, Michaela gave the child a furtive once-over. She thought it a pity that the girl was so plain, and very much doubted that her scruffiness would engender much sympathy from the magistrates. But without her, the mother was surely doomed.

As Pat joined the queue for the metal-detector arch, Michaela cast a worried glance at Lisa who was standing to the side now, gazing around the busy reception area. There were things Michaela needed to go over with Pat before they went into court. Sensitive things of a sexual nature that Michaela felt awkward enough about already, without being responsible for traumatizing the child by discussing them in front of her if she were clueless.

Tapping Pat on the arm, she said quietly, 'Lisa is aware of why you're here, isn't she?'

'Oh, yeah, we've no secrets, us,' Pat replied airily. 'So, who've I got?' she asked then, holding up her arms in the hope of being frisked by the well-built security guard.

Ignoring her obvious desire for the hands-on approach, the guard waved her through the arch into the bag-searching bay.

Sidestepping a second guard with a flash of her official pass, Michaela said, 'Bennett, I believe. But they haven't posted all of the allocations yet, so I'll have to check.'

Grinning flirtatiously now at the unimpressed guard as she relinquished her handbag, Pat said, 'Yes! I was hoping I'd get him!'

Michaela raised a neatly pencilled eyebrow. 'I hope he's as pleased to see you, Mrs Noone,' she muttered, without adding that she very much doubted he would be. Justice Bennett's reputation for leniency was fast disappearing of late. The recent 'three-strikes-and-you're-out' campaign had seen many a seemingly mild magistrate's attitude harden beyond recognition.

Pat didn't hear Michaela's last remark. She was too busy trying to stop the guard from confiscating the bottle of vodka he'd found in her handbag.

'Aw, just give us a quick swig, luv,' she pleaded, watching with hungry eyes as he stashed it out of sight in the official 'bin'. 'It's nearly finished anyhow. I won't tell if you don't!'

The guard shook his head firmly. 'Sorry, no can do.'

Michaela grimaced, wishing with all her heart that the ground would open up and swallow Patricia – common tart – Noone whole.

'We'll sit there, shall we?' she said through clenched teeth, motioning towards a row of empty chairs lining the wall beside Courtroom Three. Turning on her heel, she marched on ahead.

'Snotty bitch!' Pat muttered conspiratorially, linking her arm through Lisa's. Giggling together like a pair of schoolgirls, they followed Michaela to the seats.

Michaela had the report folder open on her knee.

'Now, I just need to go through this quickly with you,' she said as Pat and Lisa sat down. Rifling through the contents, she handed a couple of pages to Pat. 'If you could just read through from subsection seven, paragraph three . . .'

Blah, blah, blah, blah, thought Lisa, as Michaela droned on in words she couldn't understand. Folding her arms, she let a loud breath vibrate out through her lips. God, this was boring! She wished she hadn't agreed to come now. She'd much rather still be in bed dreaming about Jamie Butterworth. Or at school, snatching the odd glimpse of him at break.

Sighing heavily, she closed her eyes and lapsed into one of her increasingly frequent daydreams.

Within seconds she was in the Head's office at school,

being told – in a most gratifyingly grovelling way – that the school secretary had just discovered a mistake in her records.

'*It seems,*' Mr Lennox was saying, '*that your stupid mother made a bit of a cock-up when she registered you here, Lisa. She gave us the wrong year of birth for you, so all this time we've been thinking you were twelve going on thirteen you were actually thirteen going on* fourteen *and should be in year nine already! I can't apologize enough, Lisa. Can you ever forgive me?*'

'*Can I get you a cup of tea, Lisa?*' Sheila, the secretary, asked then. '*And how about some biscuits from Mr Lennox's special stash?*'

'*Yes, you must have some,*' Mr Lennox insisted, patting Sheila's fat bum – making Lisa want to laugh out loud because everyone in school thought the Head and his secretary were shagging, and now she knew it for a fact!

'*Get her the choccy ones, Sheila,*' he went on. '*In fact, give her anything she wants, to make up for this awful mistake.*

'*I blame myself, you know?*' he said to Lisa then. '*I really should have sussed that you were older 'cos you're so mature, and that.*'

'*Yes,*' Sheila chipped in, '*but we just thought you were really brainy . . . Didn't we, Lenny?*'

'*Indeed we did,*' the Head agreed, slipping his hand up Sheila's skirt to stroke the backs of her orange-peel thighs.

'*Anyhow,*' he went on. '*Now that we know, we can put it right, can't we? So, Lisa, I'm sending you straight to year nine! In fact, you'll be going into Jamie Butterworth's class, because he's asked for you to be placed with him, and—'*

'Oi!'

Lisa's dream dissolved as a sharp nudge jerked her back to the here and now.

'What was that for?' she demanded, glaring at her mum, who was in turn frowning at her.

'Here!' Pat said, shoving the fifty-pence piece she'd scrounged off Michaela into Lisa's hand. 'Go and get yourself a drink if you're bored. I can't concentrate with you sighing all over the place. You're doing me head in!'

'Fine!' Lisa grunted, snatching the money. 'But you didn't have to break me ribs!'

Escaping before she earned herself a backhander, Lisa went to the vending machine and bought a can of cola. Ripping the tab off, she took a long drink, then wandered over to the large windows overlooking Crown Square. Pushing herself between two small, noisy children who were using the bench as a play area, she kneeled on the seat and peered out at the people milling about in the Square.

Directly opposite, a team of builders were well into their half-naked stride, shifting huge trays of bricks about as they catcalled to the pretty young secretaries making their way to and from the numerous office blocks surrounding the Square.

To their left, a ratty-headed old woman – complete with the obligatory Tesco trolley full of bulging plastic bags and filthy blankets – jealously held sole possession of her pigeon-surrounded bench by wildly waving her arms every time anyone walked by.

Lisa watched the nutty old bat for a few minutes, but quickly lost interest. Her gaze became unfocused – unseeing now, her thoughts were on Jamie once again.

Gorgeous, fit Jamie, with long, floppy blond hair, sexy blue eyes and kissable lips.

One day . . .

'Lisa! *Psst*! Lisa!'

Disturbed yet again, Lisa turned around and saw her mum waving frantically from across the crowded room.

'She's just checking, but she reckons we're up next,' Pat whispered when Lisa joined her. 'Now, I want to get it straight with you before we go in, yeah?'

'Yeah, all right.' Nodding, Lisa sipped at the cola.

'Good girl,' Pat said, reaching out to fiddle nervously first with Lisa's hair, then her collar. 'Right, it's deffo Bennett,' she went on, licking her thumb and rubbing at a spot of dirt on Lisa's cheek, 'so when I give you the nod, just do like I told you and we'll be laughing. You listening?'

'Aw, Mum!' Lisa moaned, pulling her head back to escape the annoying ministrations. 'I can't do it just like that!'

Jerking her own head back, Pat gave her an incredulous look.

'You do it quick enough when you're set for a belting! Anyhow, you'd better if you want me home today. And make it nice and loud, and all. If there's one thing Bennett hates, it's skriking kids in his nice quiet court. Got that?'

'Yeah.'

'Patricia Anne Noone . . .' the usher called. 'Courtroom Three . . . Patricia Anne Noone . . . Courtroom Three.'

Pat blew out a nervous breath. 'Here goes! Wish me luck, kid.'

Clutching at Lisa's arm, she made her way into the court to answer for her sins.

The magistrates were taking for ever. Huddled together behind the high plinth, they reminded Pat of a coven of witches, and she wondered what they were cooking up for her.

Whatever it was, she had a horrible feeling she wasn't going to like it. And glancing at Michaela sitting stiffly beside her, she felt no better at seeing such a grim expression on her brief's face.

'What they doing?' she hissed from the corner of her mouth.

'Reading through the social worker's report,' Michaela whispered back without looking at her.

'But they already did that. What's so interesting about it, anyway?'

'Ssshhh!' Michaela hissed, adding in a whisper: 'It can only help. It must mean they're undecided. Don't annoy them by kicking up a fuss.' With that, she resumed her study of the very interesting clock above the magistrates' heads.

Ten forty-five. They're certainly dragging this out.

Pat sighed heavily. Never mind not kicking up a fuss, she'd like to kick this patronizing bitch of a solicitor up the arse!

Turning her head as far as possible, she saw Lisa sitting near the back of the room. If ever there was a need for a bit of courtroom drama it was probably now. If the magistrates *were* undecided about the report it meant they were considering the best way to deal with Lisa's welfare, and a good show of distress from that direction might just tip the scales.

Seeing Lisa staring blindly up at the ceiling, Pat glared at her across the rows of seats, willing her back down to Earth to get on with her part of the bargain. Lisa dreamed on obliviously.

Little cow! Pat seethed to herself, turning back around. *If I get out of here today, I'll give her a walloping she'll never forget!*

'Please stand, Mrs Noone.'

Pat didn't realize she had been addressed until the solicitor nudged her and motioned her to her feet.

'Oh, sorry,' she spluttered, jumping up. 'I was just worrying about my—'

'If we may proceed?' Bennett cut her short coldly.

'Yeah, sure . . . sorry.' Pat gulped at the uncharacteristic harshness of his tone. This didn't bode well at all.

'Prostitution, Mrs Noone,' Bennett intoned in a doom-and-gloom voice, 'is a heinous offence for which, in our opinion, there is no legitimate excuse. In plying your nefarious trade, you and your ilk have made a mockery of the system by which those of us who are decent and lawful abide. And in doing so, you degrade and harm not only yourselves but all women in general. You have created an untenable situation, making it impossible for innocent females to go about their legitimate business without fear of approach or attack from the sick individuals who roam the streets looking for your sort.'

Pausing, Bennett reached for his glass of water and took a leisurely drink. Pat hardly dared to breathe, she was so sure they had decided to send her down this time. Digging her nails into her palms like miniature daggers, she watched as he replaced his glass on the bench with agonizing slowness.

'As this is not the first but the *third* time you have been brought before this court on this charge,' he went on at last, 'we feel that it is quite within the bounds of reason to inflict a custodial sentence—'

'No, you can't!' Pat interrupted with a squawk. 'What about me—'

'*However*,' he cut across her protests sternly, 'taking into account the somewhat *favourable* social report . . .'

Pausing again, he raised a shaggy grey eyebrow as though he couldn't quite believe that the report had contained a single good word about the trollop standing before him.

'We have reached the conclusion,' Bennett continued after clearing his throat, 'that this action would not be in the best interests of your child, and have therefore decided upon a suspended sentence, with—'

'Oh thank you, your honour!'

'*With*,' he repeated, 'a period of probation and a fine, which shall not exceed five hundred pounds.'

'Oh, that's fantastic!'

'This is not for *your* benefit, Mrs Noone,' Bennett told her frostily. 'And please do not labour under the misapprehension that I will tolerate a single moment's fall from grace.'

'No, sir!'

'Because I assure you I will not hesitate to invoke the full three-year sentence if you do!'

★   ★   ★

Rushing outside a little while later, the paperwork detailing the conditions of her probation screwed up in her hand, Pat grinned triumphantly.

'Well, that was a doddle!'

Frowning disapprovingly, Michaela said, 'I hope you took stock of what they said? Because I assure you the magistrates were serious. This really *is* your last chance.'

Sneering derisively, Pat popped open the top three buttons of her blouse and shrugged her ample cleavage into view.

'They'll have to catch me first, love. And I'll tell you now, they don't stand a cat in *hell*'s chance!'

'They've managed it three times so far,' Michaela replied tartly.

'Yeah,' Pat agreed, giving her a cold look. 'Three times lucky! They caught me off guard, that's all. They won't get me so easy next time.'

'Mum!' Lisa frowned, her childish angst almost laughable in its intensity. 'You promised you wasn't gonna do it no more!'

'I'm only joking, kid!' Laughing, Pat threw an arm around Lisa's shoulder and hugged her expansively – all thoughts of punching her lights out for drifting off at the crucial moment forgotten in the euphoria of being free.

'Really?' Lisa asked, not overly convinced by her mum's display.

Planting a wet kiss on her cheek, Pat said, '*Really!*'

Michaela's nose wrinkled with distaste at this common display of affection. Averting her gaze, she eased the cuff of her sleeve back to check the time, dismayed to see that it was now eleven thirty-five. As if she didn't have better things to be getting on with!

'Well, I've got to get back to the office now,' she said. 'So I'll say goodbye.' Without adding *until next time*, she gave Pat a curt nod and began to walk away.

'Here, you can tell that boss of yours I'll be having words with him,' Pat called after her. 'Standing me up in me hour of need! Just tell him I'll be expecting preferential treatment next time or he'll get *you-know-what*!'

Just as Pat had intended, Michaela bristled visibly at the implication behind the words. With shoulders as stiff as a *Dynasty* dress, she turned back, her nostrils twitching with indignation as she ground out between clenched teeth: 'Let's hope there *isn't* a next time, shall we? Goodbye.'

'Yeah, *see ya!*' Sticking her fingers up at Michaela's back, Pat turned to Lisa, grinning maliciously. 'Stuck-up bitch! She's well after getting a grip of Waverley, but she's got more chance of farting "Edelweiss" in tune! Anyway, forget her. We've got a date.'

'Who with?' Lisa asked.

'A pint of lager at The Hopscotch,' Pat said, linking her arm through Lisa's. 'We've got some serious celebrating to do!'

Grinning widely as her mum propelled her towards the road, Lisa said, 'You getting me a pint?'

Pat laughed out loud.

'In yer dreams! You'll have a Coke, and like it!' Smiling at Lisa's disappointment, she added: 'But if you're really, *really* good, I might let you have a puff of me fag.'

'*Honest?*'

'Behave!' Pat snorted. 'And let me catch you smoking before you're sixteen and you'll know about it, lady!'

2

It was only just gone twelve noon, but The Hopscotch was packed out already, the air blue with smoke and raucous laughter. In the corner, the ancient jukebox blared out country-'n'-western for the motley crew of regulars, whose voices rose and fell in direct proportion to the volume of whichever song was playing, creating an endless cacophony of noise.

The barmaid, Rita, was running back and forth like a headless chicken, trying to keep up with the demands of the two-deep line of baying customers. Lunch was the pub's busiest time but, as the landlord was nowhere in sight, she was having to cope alone. Claiming a migraine, Dec had told her to get on with it – and warned her in no uncertain terms not to disturb him. *Cranky Irish bastard!*

At the least busy corner of the bar, two men were chatting quietly. The larger of the two, Elvis, was a mild-mannered man, with a mass of dyed black hair, and a once-good-looking face that was now well past its sell-by date. The other, Happy, was the complete opposite of his drinking buddy. He was a skinny little man with a huge bald patch, which he tried – and failed – to disguise by draping a greasy chunk of side-hair over it. He also had one of the most miserable faces ever to be allowed out in public.

Decent enough blokes, Elvis and Happy were usually pretty obliging in the free drinks stakes. Which was exactly what Pat was thinking when she spotted them from the door. That was the good thing about having a local like this, in her opinion. You might not have a penny in your pocket when you came in, but someone would always be pleased enough to see you to buy you at least one drink.

Nudging Lisa, she motioned her to follow as she made her way over to her mark.

Squeezing in between them, she treated them both to a pinch on the backside, saying cheerily, 'How you doing, me little luvs? You gonna buy a couple of good-looking girls a drink, then?'

Before either man had a chance to answer, Rita rushed over to them with a harassed look on her pinched face.

'Sorry, Pat, but the kid'll have to go. Dec's been in a right one today. He'll go off it good style if he sees her.'

Flapping a dismissive hand, Pat said, 'Aw, she won't be no bother, Rita. Anyhow, we're celebrating. I've just got off with a fine and a suspended.'

'Congratulations,' Rita said, genuinely pleased for Pat but nervous of being caught letting a child in nonetheless. 'But she'll still have to go. Dec'll do his nut.'

Grinning lewdly, Pat said, 'Tell him I'll do his nuts if he lets her stay for a bit.'

'Aw, don't be such a spoilsport, Rita,' Happy chipped in. 'She's just a wee scrap of a thing. Dec won't notice her if she slips into a corner.' Reaching out a bony hand, he squeezed Lisa's shoulder. 'Look, she's tiny – nearly invisible, ain't you, darlin'?'

'*Gerroff!*' Lisa grunted, wrenching herself free and looking Happy up and down with the undisguised disgust only a child can successfully pull off.

Despite the glare, Happy good-naturedly continued to fight her corner.

'Come on, Rita. We'll keep an eye on her, see she don't get into no bother. Just let her have a drink with her mum, eh?'

Sighing heavily, Rita glanced at the door to the land-lord's private lounge, then nodded.

'All right, she can stay for one – and I *mean* one! But if Dec comes out, I didn't know she was here, right?'

Snapping the top from a bottle of Coke, she handed it across to Lisa, throwing in a packet of crisps as a goodwill gesture.

'Ta, babe,' Pat said. 'I owe you one.'

'So what you having, Pat?' Happy asked, adding with a gummy grin: 'Elvis is buying!'

'Oh, I am, am I?' said Elvis, raising a heavily dyed eyebrow. 'Cheers, mate.'

Pat gave him a playful dig in the ribs. 'Now then, Elvis! You don't have to make it sound like you begrudge me. I'll have a B and G, thank you very much – a *double!*'

Elvis shrugged. 'Sorry, love, I'm boracic. It'll have to be a single.'

'That'll do nicely!' Pat said, pleased that her ploy had worked. Men were so stupid sometimes.

'By 'eck, you're looking well today, Pat.' Leering, Happy stepped up onto the foot-rail snaking around the bar and peered down her cleavage. '*Mighty* fine, I must say.'

Grabbing his ugly little head, Pat crushed his face to

her breasts, saying, 'There you go, Happy – no point
beating around the bush, eh?'

Blushing furiously, Lisa said, 'Mum! Stop it!'

Pushing Happy away, Pat chuckled at Lisa's scandalized expression.

'Oops, sorry, love, I forgot you were still here. Look,
why don't you go and grab a seat over there.' She
motioned towards an already crowded booth beside the
door. 'I'll come over in a bit and make sure you're all
right, okay?'

Lisa shook her head in despair when her mum immediately turned her attention back to the men. It was one
thing knowing what she did, but another altogether
actually seeing her in action. Still, that was her business,
Lisa supposed.

As long as it wasn't business *business*.

Making her way to the booth, she plonked herself
down beside an ancient slapper who was wearing a worn
leatherette miniskirt and a low-cut flowery gypsy blouse.
As the woman sang merrily along to the latest jukebox
offering, Lisa looked her over from the corner of her eye,
taking in the mottled thighs that were spread grotesquely
across the seat, the dimply old tits jiggling precariously
close to escape, and the blood-red lipstick leaking into
a hideous web of wrinkles around the woman's mouth,
making it look like a chunk of raw meat.

Shuddering with disgust as the woman turned and
winked at her, Lisa edged as far into the corner as possible
and began to slurp noisily on her Coke – determined
to avoid unwanted conversation with the woman, or
with any of the other equally revolting characters in
the booth.

It worked a treat as no one so much as uttered a word to her for the next hour, by which time the Coke and crisps were long gone. Having waited patiently for her mum's promised visit, Lisa began to bounce around in her seat, trying in vain to attract her attention. It was useless. Her mum was far too wrapped up in flirting with the ugly, desperate-looking old men surrounding her.

Pat had in fact forgotten all about Lisa stuck away in the corner. She was having a whale of a time entertaining the men. It had always been her forte, and so far today it had earned her five brandies, a pack of cigarettes, and the promise of twenty quid for a blow job. The latter, unfortunately, not until the following Thursday, when she could have really used it today. But it was still a good take by anyone's standards – even if the punter *did* smell like a skunk in heat!

It was all in the way you treated the suckers, and Pat prided herself on her ability to get what she wanted. Build them up till they think they've got the hottest dick in Christendom, then watch them fight to get their hands in their wallets. It never failed.

She'd just downed the fifth brandy when someone put 'Stand By Your Man' on the jukebox.

'Aw, God, I love this!' she squawked.

'Whyn't you give us a turn then, Pat?' Happy suggested.

'Yeah, come on, Pat,' some of the other regulars joined in, knowing from past experience that she would give them a belting show if she could be persuaded. Someone set up a chant that was immediately taken up all around the room: 'On the table . . . On the table . . .'

Flapping her hands, Rita tried desperately to shut

everyone up before they brought Dec out from his lair.

'For gawd's sake, Pat, just give 'em a song, will you?' she begged when it proved ineffectual.

Grinning happily, Pat said, 'All right, but someone better get us another in there, 'cos I ain't doing it for nowt!' Slamming her empty glass down on the counter, she climbed unsteadily onto a nearby table.

Heads turned as the regulars settled back to watch the show, and she didn't disappoint them. Singing in a surprisingly sweet, if drink-slurred voice, she gave it her all in a heartfelt way. All around the room, old tarts began to sigh and gaze mistily into their old men's drink-ruined eyes, and one couple even got up and began to waltz on the spot.

Lisa watched it all with a mixture of shame and pride. Her mum could sing, there was no denying that, but did she *have* to climb up on a table and make an exhibition of herself in front of these old farts? She breathed a sigh of relief when the record finally came to an end, but before her mum could hop down from her makeshift stage the next tune was blaring out and, gee'd-up by the whoops of encouragement, Pat began to pout and pose along to 'Hey, Big Spender!' Lisa wanted to die.

Suddenly, the door to the private lounge flew open and Declan Donnelly appeared. A pot-bellied, truculent Dubliner, Dec could look miserable for Ireland at the best of times, but today he was in a particularly foul temper. Being woken by all the noise in the bar hadn't eased his migraine any, but seeing Pat cavorting on his table top crowned it with thorns.

'Get away down from there!' he bellowed at her across

the bar. 'Ruining my feckin' wood with them clod-hoppers!'

Turning at the sound of his voice, Pat grinned drunkenly.

'Dec, me darlin'!' she trilled, hopping down and making her way to the bar. 'Giz a kiss then, you grumpy auld sod! I'm celebrating!'

Giving her a murderous look, Dec turned on Rita who was hovering beside him anxiously wringing a bar-cloth between her fingers.

'Can't you keep order for one fecking minute?' he yelled, decorating her cheeks with a fine spittle-mist. 'I've a head on me like a hurricane, so I have! I've hardly slept a tick all day!'

'Sorry, Dec,' Rita mumbled, not daring to wipe her face in case he took it as an insult. 'I was just gonna tell her, honest I was, but—'

Dec wasn't listening. He'd just spotted Lisa trying desperately to melt into the back of the fake-leather booth seat.

'What's *she* doing here?' he boomed, completely over-riding Shirley Bassey's lung-busting crescendo as he pointed accusingly at Lisa. 'Out of it, you . . . *Out!*'

Lisa wanted to shrivel up and die as every pair of eyes in the room turned to stare at her. Her cheeks flamed, the hairs on her neck bristling with humiliation.

Pat turned too, then suddenly remembered that Lisa was with her.

'Aw, she's all right, Dec. It's only my Lisa. She ain't doing no harm.'

Again, Dec ignored her and turned his wrath on Rita, his cheeks wobbling with fury, bubbles of spit exploding from the corners of his flabby lips now as he bellowed: 'Get her out, quick smart! And let me catch you at it again, lady, and you'll be out the fecking door on yer arse!' With that, he turned and stormed out the way he'd come.

Sticking her fingers up as the door marked *Private* banged shut behind him, Pat said, 'Ah, go on with yer, y' miserable auld shite-face!'

'Leave it out, Pat!' Rita hissed, the blood draining from her face. 'Just get the kid off home, eh?'

'He wants putting down!' Pat muttered angrily. 'What's up with him, anyhow? Someone swapped his dick for a toothpick while he was asleep or something?'

'Just belt up and get her out, will you?' Rita insisted. 'You've already got me in enough trouble, all's I need is for him to come back and find her still here. You heard what he said. You want me to lose me job, or what?'

'Aw, quit panicking!' Pat snapped back at her. 'He'd never oust you. He wouldn't know what to do with himself.'

Rita wasn't so sure. She started to say something more but was stopped by Pat slamming an angry fist down on the bar.

'Aw, for God's sake! All *right*! I'll send her home. *Satisfied?*'

Curling her lip at the injustice of it all, Pat turned and made her way towards Lisa, pausing at each table she passed to tap money from the occupants.

'Just a couple of bob so me kid can get some chips . . . And she'll need a few pence for bus fare . . .'

Dying of shame, Lisa ran to the door. Yanking it open, she rushed outside, squinting painfully in the bright light of day. Seconds later, Pat followed her out and thrust the handful of scrounged change towards her.

'Here you go, pet. Get yourself something from the chippy on the way home. I'm just stopping here for a bit. You don't mind, do you?'

Shrugging, Lisa pocketed the money. 'Suppose not.'

'Ah, you're a good girl, you,' Pat said, staggering towards her with open arms. 'Giz a kiss, then!'

Embarrassed to be hugged in the street in broad daylight, Lisa wriggled free, saying, 'Leave it out, Mum! Me mates might see!'

Stepping back a pace, Pat chuckled. 'My, we're growing up, ain't we? Here, I bet you'll be glad of a few hours away from me, won't ya?'

Shrugging again, Lisa said, 'What time you coming back?'

Pat gave her a sly grin. 'Why, what you got planned? Got a lad coming round, have you?'

'Don't be daft!' Lisa snapped. She hated it when her mum teased her about lads. 'I just want to know, that's all.'

'Yeah, right!' Pat gave her a mock-suspicious look, then abruptly lost interest in the game. 'Oh, I don't know. Dinner time-ish, I suppose. Why?'

'I need some money for the youthy disco.'

'I've just give you some!' Pat snorted. 'You think I'm made of money, or something?'

'That's for *chips*!' Lisa argued. 'They cost eighty pence now, you know.'

Rolling her eyes, Pat said, 'Jeezus! They was only tuppence when I was your age!'

'Yeah – about a hundred years ago!'

'Oi, you!'

'Well, give us some more now, then you won't have to bother coming back, will you?' Lisa reasoned, smiling now.

Pat tapped her empty pockets. 'Sorry, kid, I'm flat broke, but I'll see what I can do, okay?'

'You'd better not do anything stupid.'

Pat spread her arms wide in a gesture of innocence. 'Like what?'

Folding her own arms, Lisa gave her a stern look and said, 'You know exactly what I mean.'

'Oi, you!' Pat admonished her again, snorting. 'Who's the mum here? . . . Aw, come here, you dozy bat!'

'Get *off*!'

Struggling free as she was pulled into yet another bear-hug, Lisa was smiling as she made her escape.

Pat watched until her daughter had turned the corner, then made her way back into the pub. She was ready for another drink or two – or *ten*. It wasn't every day she had reason to celebrate, and she planned to make the most of it.

Around the corner, Lisa pulled the change out of her pocket and counted it. Two pounds and twenty-eight pence! Enough for ten cigs and a box of matches.

Who needs a bag of fattening chips when you can have a smoke instead?

Grinning happily at her good fortune, she ran the rest of the way to Moss Side's crumbling shopping centre, not stopping until she'd reached Murphy's Newsagents – the only shop in the area guaranteed to serve her without the usual inquisition.

Ripping the cellophane off her precious smokes a

minute later, she lit one and took a long, luxurious drag before setting off home at a trot.

She had things to do before going to the disco tonight – like finding something decent to wear to attract Jamie's attention, and washing the filth out of her hair. There was *no* way she was letting Jamie see it in all its greasy glory!

Monty was barking when Lisa opened the communal landing door fifteen minutes later. Remembering that he'd been locked in the kitchen without food since the morning, she hurried inside to free him – then spent a good two minutes wrestling him down as he tried to lick her to death in a post-lock-up ecstasy.

'All right, all right!' she laughed. 'Let me in so I can feed you then, you dozy mutt!'

Taking a huge tin of Cheap'n'Nasty Doggy Shite from the cupboard, she emptied it into Monty's bowl, then turned to fill the kettle. Before she'd even switched it on, Monty had wolfed down every scrap of the meat she'd given him.

'You greedy get!' she scolded as he lolloped to the door. 'You'll make yourself sick! Chew, not spew . . . *remember?*'

Letting him out onto the landing to empty his bladder in his favourite spot – *all over the prize blooms in next-door-but-one's flowerpots* – Lisa waited for the kettle to boil, then carried it up to the bathroom and washed her hair, humming to herself in anticipation of the night ahead.

With a grubby towel wrapped around her apple-scented head, she went to her bedroom to find something decent to wear. But after a quick sift through the clothes heaped on her bed, she gave up. There was nothing even remotely good enough. It was all either stained, ripped, or too small. Pushing the heap aside, she flopped down onto her back with a despondent sigh. What was the use of having clean hair when your clothes smelled like shit?

There was only one thing she could do, Lisa decided after a moment. She'd just have to borrow something off Debbie – providing Debbie had the balls to smuggle something out past her bitch of a mum! She'd catch her on her way home from school – give her plenty of time to stash something away.

Satisfied that she'd solved the clothes problem, she reached for a comb and raked it through the tangles in her hair, flipping through a magazine as she did so, imagining herself in all the latest gear.

Wouldn't Jamie just fancy the tits off me if I had my hair done like that – and had that nose stud – and that top – and those boots – and . . .

It was almost three-thirty when Monty's barking woke Lisa. Remembering that she'd left him outside – and that she'd meant to catch Debbie on her way home from school – she leaped from the bed and ran down the stairs.

Letting Monty back in *en route*, she rushed into the living room and pushed the half-drawn curtains back to get at the window. Opening it, she leaned out as far as she dared to scan the road below. It was deserted, which meant she'd either missed Debbie already, or Debbie hadn't got back yet. Hoping it was the latter, she drew her head back in and went to get her cigarettes from her jacket in the hall. If she had to keep vigil at the window, she'd do it with a smoke in her hand.

Halfway across the room, something on the TV her mum had forgotten to switch off that morning caught her eye. Turning to take a proper look, a thrill of recognition ran through her when she saw a shot of Westy Lane.

Plonking herself down on the couch, she turned up the volume with the remote and listened as the grim-faced *Granada Today* presenter gave his all too brief account of the local news.

'In the early hours of this morning, the body of a young woman was discovered beneath bushes on an area of wasteland adjoining Westy Lane in Hulme.

'The gruesome discovery was made by two men who were on their way to work at the nearby Thornton Engineering plant. The men, who wish to remain anonymous, are said to have been deeply traumatized by the horrific nature of the injuries sustained by the as yet unnamed victim.

'Earlier, a spokesman for Greater Manchester Police refused to confirm whether the woman is the fourth victim in a series of vicious murders that have occurred in Manchester in recent months, but did admit that there are "striking similarities" between this and the previous murders. We'll bring you more on this story as we have it.

'"Stop-'n'-Go" Bus Company executives have today—'

Totally uninterested in the rest of the news, Lisa switched the TV off.

So, there had been another murder . . . and closer yet!

Too close, given that Westy Lane was one of her mum's regular patches.

Lisa wondered if her mum had heard about it – and hoped that, if she had, it would make her think twice about working again. It was all very well her making a joke of it for the solicitor, but Lisa had her suspicions. She might only be twelve, but she'd long ago learned that what people said and what they did were entirely different things. Still, now that it had happened on the Lane, surely Pat wouldn't risk going back there again?

No, of course she won't, Lisa told herself firmly, getting the cigarettes and going back to the window. *She isn't that stupid!*

Is she . . . ?

'Shut up, you stupid cow!' she scolded herself, aloud now.

'Psst! *Lisa!*'

Hearing Debbie's voice drifting up from the road below, Lisa forced her mum from her mind and looked out of the window.

'About time!' she shouted down.

'*Sshhh!*' Debbie hissed back at her, glancing nervously towards her own house at the other end of the block. 'Open the door quick before my mum sees me.'

Rushing in a couple of minutes later, her clothes, as usual, clean and neat, her thick black hair glossy in its ponytail, her pretty face red and sweaty, Debbie dropped her bag and slumped into an armchair.

'I ran all the way back,' she gasped. 'Had to go and pay Mrs Kent for the trip, and you know what she's like for prattling on with herself. Oh, and she asked where you were, by the way. I had to tell her you were ill.'

'Thanks.'

'It's all right. But don't make a habit of it, 'cos I'm a crap liar. Where were you, anyway?' Debbie went on accusingly. 'I was late this morning, thanks to you. You could have said you were going out.'

'I just had to go somewhere with me mum,' Lisa told her evasively. 'So what's this trip you're on about?'

'*Duh!* Tatton Park!'

'Oh, yeah. You deffo going, then?'

Reaching down to pat Monty who had shuffled over to lie by her feet, Debbie said, 'Yeah, it should be a laugh. Which reminds me . . . Kenty says to tell you if you're planning to come you'll have to get the money in by tomorrow morning or there'll be no seats left. And she'll be really, *really* pleased if you do!' she added with a smirk. 'As long as you're *better*, that is.'

Lisa snorted derisively. 'Huh! She must fancy me, the old lezzer!'

'Come off it, she's married! She just thinks you're – how did she put it now – *wasting your abilities*!'

'Bull!' Lisa scoffed. 'She's after getting in me knickers! Anyhow, I ain't going to no poxy park. It'll be dead boring.'

'Aw, Lisa, please. It'll be dead boring for *me* if you don't. I'll get stuck with Smelly Kelly!'

'Tough!' Lisa grinned. 'Anyhow, I couldn't if I wanted to. No dosh.'

'Thanks!' Debbie tutted, slumping further down in the chair. 'I thought best mates were supposed to do everything together.'

'Well, no one told you to go,' Lisa retorted, refusing to be made to feel guilty. 'Just say you've changed your mind and get your money back.'

Debbie shook her head miserably. 'Can't, can I? My mum would kill me.'

'*Duh!* Like you'd *tell* her!' Lighting the cigarette she was still holding, Lisa took a couple of hard pulls and blew the smoke out of the window before offering it to Debbie. 'Want some?'

'Yeah, just a quick puff.' Getting up, Debbie joined her at the window.

'Seen Jamie today?' Lisa asked casually.

Giving a little shrug, Debbie made great play of waving the smoke away. 'Just for a minute at lunch.'

'Did you talk to him?'

'Not really.'

'So what was he doing?'

'What he's always doing – keeping the mongs in line.'

Lisa made a face at the mention of Jamie's imbecilic mates, Steve Lunt and Andy Green. You couldn't get within two feet of Jamie without one or other of them popping up like a bad smell.

'What they done now?' she asked.

'Nicked my bag and tipped everything out,' Debbie told her. 'It took me bloody ages to find my pens and that under the lockers.'

'Muppets!' Lisa sneered, taking the cigarette back. 'Anyway, forget them . . . how much have you got for the disco?'

'Nothing,' Debbie admitted gloomily. 'My mum reckons she's skint.'

'Yeah, *right*!' Lisa snorted disbelievingly. 'She's just

a tight-arse! Tell her you'll do the dishes for a quid, or something.'

Debbie rolled her eyes. 'Yeah, like she's gonna *pay* me for that.'

'Well, you'd better think of something,' Lisa said sharply. 'I'm not going on me own, and you promised.'

'I said I'd *try*,' Debbie protested. 'But you know what she's like, and she's already pissed off with me 'cos she tried to rope me in to babysit for stupid Kyle this morning and I said no.'

'Do it. At least you'll get a couple of quid for it. I'll come with you if you want?'

'Duh – *tonight*! Anyhow, forget it. I can't stand the little pleb.'

'So what we going to do?' Lisa moaned, dismayed that she might not get to see Jamie – again.

Debbie thought for a moment, then said, 'Hang about . . . how much have *you* got? I could give it you back on Saturday if you paid me in.'

'You're joking, ain't you?' Lisa flicked the cigarette butt into a patch of flowers in the garden below. 'I'm counting on me mum getting back in time as it is.'

'Oh, right.'

Depressed at the prospect of yet another boring night in, they slumped onto the window sill and stared out at the road together.

'What you wearing if you *can* go?' Lisa asked after a minute.

'Jeans. You?'

Smiling slyly, Lisa said, 'Dunno. Depends what you've got for me?'

Debbie gave her a funny look. 'What *I*'ve got for you?

I've got nothing. Only me jeans, and I'm wearing them.'

'Get lost! You've got tons of stuff.'

'Yeah, and it's all in the bag to go to the launderette tomorrow.'

'Except your jeans?'

'Yeah, and *I*'m wearing them,' Debbie said. Glancing at her watch, she tutted. 'I'd better get off. My mum's going to go mad.'

'Tell her Benty Kenty kept you back,' Lisa said, pushing herself away from the window and heading for the door. 'I need you to help me pick something nice to wear – seeing as you won't *lend* me nothing!'

Debbie hesitated for a moment, then gave in and followed Lisa up the stairs.

'All right, but you'd best hurry up 'cos I'm going in ten minutes – max!'

Twenty minutes, and a parade of totally unsuitable outfits later, Debbie jumped at a loud knocking on the front door.

'Oh, shit! I hope that's not my mum, she'll kill me! Tell her I'm not here.'

'I'll tell her to piss off!' Lisa muttered, struggling to wrench a bright red Lycra miniskirt up over her thighs. 'Don't see why you're so scared of her, anyway. She can't stop you coming round.'

'She doesn't like it, though, does she?'

'Doesn't like *me*, more like,' said Lisa, pulling her dressing gown on over the skirt and going to the door.

'It's not that,' Debbie lied. 'It's just—'

Cutting her short with a dismissive tut, Lisa left the room.

It was *exactly* that, and Lisa knew it. Sue Morgan

couldn't stand her. She'd always thought Lisa was a bad influence on her precious daughter, and had tried everything to stop them seeing each other – to no avail. Even *she*'d had to admit it was impossible in the end, seeing as they lived on the same block and went to the same school. And seeing as Debbie *liked* Lisa, no matter what her mum said.

'Is it her?' Debbie hissed from the top of the stairs as Lisa reached the door.

'Sshhh!' Waving her quiet, Lisa peeped out through the spyhole.

It wasn't Debbie's mum, it was Sam – her own mum's Wednesday-night 'regular'. And he looked decidedly nervous, Lisa thought, his piggy black eyes flicking every which way as he waited for the door to open – obviously afraid of being seen by anyone he knew.

Smirking to herself, Lisa decided to make him wait a bit. Serve him right for coming round in broad daylight if it was supposed to be such a great big secret!

When she eventually opened the door, she gave Sam a sweet smile, then frowned and peered at his sweaty face as if concerned.

'You all right, Sam? You're looking a bit . . . *flushed*.'

'I'm fine,' he snapped irritably, noting with disapproval the dressing gown she was wearing – in the middle of the day!

'Is your mother home?' he asked then, making to enter but having to step back when Lisa stayed put in the doorway.

Amused by his discomfiture, Lisa folded her arms and shook her head. 'Nope. But she wasn't expecting you today, was she?'

Squirming beneath her mocking gaze, he said, 'Er, no, not exactly, but . . . Look, where is she?'

'At the pub,' she said, adding in a low voice: '*Celebrating.*'

Remembering that Pat had said she was going to court today, Sam nodded. 'Ah, yes, of course. How did it go?'

Stepping out onto the landing now, Lisa pulled the door to behind her. There were some things Debbie definitely *didn't* need to know.

'She got a fine and a suspended,' she told him, half whispering.

Sam smiled, pleased that his plans wouldn't be scuppered by the jail sentence Pat had been expecting.

'Ah, good, very good. So . . . will she be coming back soon, do you think?'

Shrugging, Lisa said, 'She's supposed to be, but you never know with her, do you? She might meet someone down there, and, *well* . . .'

Letting the words hang in the air between them, she gazed innocently into Sam's rapidly darkening face. He was a jealous old git, that was for sure. Not for the first time, Lisa wondered why her mum bothered with him when she could find herself a really decent-looking bloke if she wanted to. Anything would be better than this fat, slimy creep!

Smiling as a glimmer of an idea struck her, Lisa reached behind herself and pushed the door open.

'Look, why don't you come in and wait?' she suggested. 'I don't reckon she'll be all that long. Better *not* be, anyway,' she went on slyly. 'She's got to give me some money for the disco, or I'll be stuck at home *all* night.'

Stepping inside, she paused and looked back at Sam

thoughtfully. 'Un*less* . . . ? I don't suppose *you*'ve got a couple of quid going spare, have you?'

'*What?*' Sam snapped, then quickly tempered his tone – the last thing he needed was to be seen arguing over money with a half-dressed child! 'No, I'm sorry, I haven't. I didn't bring my wallet.'

'Yeah, right!' Lisa muttered, not believing him for one minute. She felt like telling him he shouldn't have bothered coming, then – that her mum wouldn't entertain a sweaty old oink like him if he didn't have the readies. But, knowing her mum wouldn't thank her for chasing her best punter away, she held her tongue.

Giving himself a mental kick for allowing this wretch of a child to wind him up, Sam checked his watch. He didn't have much time to waste, but he really wanted to see Pat tonight.

'Look, can you just tell her I called?' he said. 'And I'll, er, come back later.'

'Sure you don't want to wait?' Lisa asked, sure that if she could just get him to take his jacket off and sit down she'd get lucky with his pockets. 'I could go and get her for you?'

Sam shook his balding head. 'No, that's all right. I've something I have to do, so I'll come back in a while. Goodbye.'

'Yeah, *see* ya.'

Frowning, Sam headed for the stairs. That girl needed a lesson in respect! If he ever caught *his* daughter talking to a man like that . . . But then, she wouldn't, because she was a good, decent girl.

'Was it her?' Debbie asked apprehensively, coming down the stairs when Lisa came back inside.

'Nah, it was only Sam. I tried tapping him for a couple of quid but he reckons he's skint, the tight-fisted git!'

Relieved that it hadn't been her mum, Debbie went through to the living room and picked up her bag.

'I'd better go. I'll give you a knock if I get any money.'

'You'd *better* get some,' Lisa warned her. 'Even if you have to nick it.'

'No chance of that!' Debbie snorted. 'She'd notice if a *tea bag* was missing, her.'

'Well, you'd better try,' Lisa told her. 'And hurry up, 'cos I don't want to get there dead late.'

Opening the door, she stuck her head out to scan the landing. Seeing no sign of Debbie's mum, she waved Debbie out, hissing after her as she went: 'Tell her you'll babysit for stupid Kyle all next week if it makes her happy. *Anything*, so long as you get out.'

Down below, Sam climbed into his car, which, as usual, he'd parked around the corner out of sight of Pat's nosy neighbours. Closing the door with a heavy *thunk*, he took his mobile from his pocket and switched it back on. He always turned it off when he was busy being unfaithful. He considered it less deceitful somehow than lying to his wife should she decide to call him mid-fuck.

Dropping the phone onto the passenger seat, he tapped his nails agitatedly on the steering wheel and wondered what to do. If he waited for Pat, she might never show. But if he went home now, he'd stand no chance of getting out again. His wife would see to that.

'But it's our tenth anniversary, dear! What do you mean,

you're going back out? You can't! Mummy and Daddy have travelled all this way . . .'

He shuddered at the thought of his in-laws. The dreaded Conroys. Elsa's pompous, boring, ever-so-English parents, who would by now be imposing themselves on his home for their annual week-long visit. It was a ritual he should have culled at its birth – and probably would have, had he not been so eager to please his lovely new bride back then.

Back then . . . before his pleasure-giving lover/wife mutated into the practical-minded mother/super-housewife that she was today.

Startled out of his reverie when the mobile began to ring, Sam snatched it up and looked at the screen. It was Jessica, his secretary. Annoyed by yet another potential disruption to his plans, he answered the call more brusquely than he'd intended.

'Yes? What do you want?'

'Mrs Rashid has called twice since you left,' Jessica informed him – in as clipped a tone as possible to convey her disapproval of his sharp manner.

Sam sighed, fully aware that he took the patience of this capable woman for granted. 'What did she want?' he asked, more evenly.

With a tiny huffing sound that spoke volumes, Jessica said, '*I* don't know, I'm sure. I'm not in the habit of asking my employer's wife for details of personal calls. She just said I was to tell you to call her back – *urgently*.'

Sam rolled his eyes and ran a sweaty hand across an equally sweaty brow. *Urgent*, indeed! She was probably under orders from *Mummy* to summon him home.

'And the flowers you had me order arrived just after

you left,' Jessica went on frostily. 'What would you like me to do with them?'

Sam slapped his fist down on his thigh in exasperation. The bloody flowers! He'd forgotten all about them. Two ridiculously overpriced displays – a lavish bouquet for his wife, to show her parents how utterly devoted their precious daughter's husband still was after all these years; the other, more modest basket arrangement, for Mother Conroy, to prove what a kind, considerate son-in-law he truly was.

Catholics and their ridiculous pretensions! Why did I ever stray into their territory?

Cupping the phone beneath his chin, he reached down and started the engine.

'Right, I'm coming back. Don't leave until I get there.'

'I wasn't intending to,' Jessica retorted tartly. 'I don't finish until six, do I?'

'And call my wife,' he went on, ignoring the dig – if he wanted to leave his own office early, then he bloody well would! 'Tell her I'm . . . Just tell her I've been held up and I'll call her as soon as I can!'

Snapping the phone shut, he threw it back down and roared out onto City Road. If he put his foot down, he stood a slim chance of fitting everything in. He could pick up the flowers, then call in at the jeweller's – for the other symbol of devotion he knew he was expected to produce. Then he could nip to the bank and, with luck, still make it back to check if Pat had shown her face before going home to face the family.

Turning left onto Chorlton Road, Sam found himself caught in a long queue of traffic. Crunching into reverse, he tried to back-up into a side street, but a furious horn blast from the car behind forced him to stay put. Well and truly stuck now, he checked the time, and was further irritated to see that it was only four-thirty. If the rush-hour traffic was building up already, he was going to have a hell of a time fitting *anything* in, never mind everything.

But fit it in he would! His balls felt as if they were about to explode, and that was an unhealthy state of affairs for a virile man like himself. Elsa might be a superb housekeeper and mother, but she had a lot to learn from the likes of Pat when it came to being a woman.

As if on cue his mobile rang again, this time displaying the warning: *Elsa.* Biting his lip, he contemplated ignoring it – but he knew it wouldn't work. His wife was a very determined lady, and she would just carry on ringing until he answered. Reluctantly, he did.

'Hello, dear, I was just about t—'

'I've been trying to get hold of you for ages!' Elsa cut him short tetchily. 'I do wish you wouldn't switch your phone off. There's been a change of plan.'

'Oh?' Sam felt his heart sink in his chest.

'My parents can't get here,' she went on, oblivious to the sudden joy her words gave him. 'Not tonight, anyway. There's been some sort of crisis with the trains out of London so they've had to reschedule. They'll be coming by coach now, but not until tomorrow.'

'Oh!' he said again, much brighter now. Then, more sympathetically: 'Oh, dear. You must be disappointed?'

Ever the martyr, Elsa sighed softly. 'Oh, well, they can't be held responsible for the shortcomings of the rail service, can they? Still, that's not why I'm calling. It occured to me that I'll have time to do a duck now, so I want you to go to the Deli before they close and pick one up.'

Sam dropped his head back against the seat and groaned inwardly. The Deli was on the other side of town, on Cheetham Hill Road – an absolute swine at the best of times, never mind rush hour. He'd never make it there and back in time to see Pat.

'Or I could call them – arrange for them to deliver?' Elsa was suggesting now. 'They'll charge a delivery fee most likely, but it shouldn't be too extortionate, and Jessica *did* say you had a lot on at the moment.'

Sam smiled to himself. *Good old Jessica! . . . Paving the way for my devious pursuits with her efficient cover-all excuses.* He'd have to remember to get her something nice for her loyalty. Not that she knew *what* she was covering for, he was certain of that.

'And,' Elsa went on, 'you wouldn't have to rush back if I did that, which would make things a little easier for you, wouldn't it?'

'Yes,' Sam agreed, adding hastily: 'Not that I wasn't looking forward to getting home, but as Jessica said, I *am* rather busy. In fact, I've a couple of appointments I was just about to cancel, but I'll be able to fit them in now – thanks to you. You always manage to find the right solution,' he finished, congratulating himself for making the praise sound so genuine.

'Mmm, well, it's not always easy,' Elsa admitted with a modest sigh. 'But I must say, I'm pleased with the way things have come together this year. Now, you won't be too late, will you?' she went on. 'Tonight's dinner was well under way before Mummy called, so we may as well have it anyway. It *is* still a celebration, after all.'

A spark of guilt threatened to engulf Sam at these words, but he quickly brushed it back beneath his thick skin where it belonged. What she didn't know wouldn't hurt her. And she *had* been the one who'd lost interest in the physical side of things. She wasn't entirely blameless.

'It certainly is,' he agreed. 'And, actually, it'll be quite nice to celebrate alone for once. Have the children gone to Louisa's yet?'

'Yes, she picked them up from school.'

'Good!' Sam sighed contentedly. He loved his children dearly, but what *bliss* to spend one anniversary without squabbling kids or interfering in-laws to destroy it.

Inching forward as the lights changed, he used the revving of his engine as an excuse to cut the call short.

'Well, I'll see you when I've finished everything, okay?'

'What time do you think you'll be back?' Elsa asked quickly.

Sam did a rapid mental calculation: *flowers, jeweller's, bank, duck, fuck.*

'Around nine, I imagine. Bye, dear.'

Smiling to himself, Sam switched the CD player on, flooding the car with the haunting strains of Streisand at her melancholy best. Now that he had a reprieve, he could afford to mellow out – and to spend a little longer with Pat, if she ever decided to go home.

As the traffic began to flow at last, Sam eased his cherished Lexus forward, singing along with Barbra at the top of his lungs.

Things were definitely looking up.

Meanwhile, things were looking decidedly down for Pat at The Hopscotch. She needed money, but one by one the men who'd so obligingly supplied her with free drinks throughout the day had left.

Elvis was the only one left, and he was proving a hard nut to crack – insisting that he had no money, when Pat knew for a fact that he had a fair few bob tucked away. But he could plead poverty as much as he liked, she had it on good authority that he was well minted. His own wife had spent enough time bragging about his bank account. Everyone in *Manchester* must know about the massive redundancy pay-out he'd received by now.

The problem now was how to find a way over the wall of stinginess he'd built up around himself. After a day of not-so-subtle hinting that had got her precisely nowhere, Pat decided it was time to stop beating about the bush and start climbing the trellis.

Bluntly, she said, 'So, come on, Elvis . . . how about it?'

'How about what?' he answered warily.

'You know full well what!' Dropping a hand onto his thigh, she raked a path towards his crotch with her nails. 'Stop playing the innocent!'

Sighing, Elvis looked down into his pint, unsure how to deal with such a full-frontal assault. If he wasn't such a gentleman he'd tell her where to get off, but he hadn't been brought up to be rude to women. He'd already tried playing the ignorance card – pretending not to understand what she'd been angling at all day in the vain hope that she'd give up and try someone else. But all the 'someone elses' had left, and now she was getting physical.

It wasn't that he didn't like sex – he liked a good fuck as much as the next man. But he was buggered if he was going to do it with a pissed-up tart like Pat! There was no telling what nasty surprises lay in store in that well-used hole of hers.

Still, for all that, wished to God she'd keep her hand still . . .

Shifting his leg to hide the bulge that was rising in his pants despite himself, Elvis said, 'You're wasting your time, Pat. I'm skint.'

Pat narrowed her eyes. 'Aw, come on! We both know that's not true. And this –' she grabbed his mutinous hard-on '– says you want it!'

'Cut it out!' Shoving her hand away, Elvis crossed his legs. 'You're giving me ball-ache!'

'And I know just how to relieve it,' she persisted, pressing her crotch up against his thigh. 'Oh, come on, big guy, just think about it, eh? A blow job and a shag for twenty little squids. You wouldn't get better than that nowhere!'

They both almost jumped out of their skins when Dec suddenly appeared as if from nowhere and slammed an enormous fist down on the bar, scattering the contents of an over-full ashtray every-which-way.

'Out of it, y' feckin' *hooer*! I'll have none of that filth in here! And me with the hooer gards in here just the week since! Go on with yer . . . Out! *OUT*!'

'You *what*?' Recovering quickly, Pat thrust her battle-ready jaw forward and gave him a belligerent glare. 'What did you say, y' paddy bastard?'

'I said *OUT*!' Dec snarled, his face beetroot with fury. 'And you've got ten seconds!'

'Or you'll *what*?' she snarled back, slapping her palms down on the counter, facing him off.

Rushing over to them, white-faced, Rita said, 'Leave it, Pat! Just go home and sleep it off, eh?' She knew what both Dec *and* Pat were capable of, and didn't fancy spending the night picking up broken glass – or making statements to the Murder Squad if things got totally out of hand.

'Shut it, you!' Pat hissed without taking her eyes off Dec. 'No one calls me a whore and gets away with it – *no one!*'

'Seven!' Dec snarled. 'And no one comes in my pub hustling their stinking cunts to my punters! Six—!'

'She wasn't,' Elvis chipped in lamely, hoping to avert disaster as his hopes of a peaceful night's ale-supping looked about to disappear. 'She was just asking for the lend of a few quid, that's all.'

'Don't you be trying to bail her out now, Elvis, or you'll be following her out the door!' Dec warned through clenched teeth. '*Five . . .*'

Holding his hands up in surrender, Elvis decided to do the sensible thing and mind his own business.

Sneering at Dec across the bar, her eyes ablaze with malicious challenge, Pat hissed, 'So what you gonna do when you get to one, Dec? 'Cos I'd like to see you lay your filthy hands on me, you ugly bastard! I'll rip the bollocks right off you and eat the fucking pair of 'em for dinner, you see if I don't!'

Dec's cheeks quivered and flamed as he fought down an urge to batter the face off the foul bitch standing before him. But fight it he knew he must. The last thing he needed was a run in with the Gardai – he had way too much to lose if they got him on another assault and battery charge.

Like a trip back to Dublin to answer for far worse.

Tearing his stare away at last, he turned on Rita again, telling her in a low, mean voice, 'If she's not out that door in one minute flat, call the po-lis and have her picked up for hooering!'

Pat gave a triumphant jeer as Dec slammed his way out of the bar again. But her euphoria was short-lived. Mention of the police had cut through the drink-rage and given her a nasty jolt back to earth. She couldn't afford to get picked up again – not on the very same day she'd been given her last chance.

'I think you should go, love,' Rita told her quietly. 'He's right about the Vice. They was in here twice last week, and you don't need picking up again, now do you? Think about your little lass, eh? Won't she be waiting for you back home?'

The mention of Lisa reminded Pat that she'd promised to be home by dinner time with some money. She glanced at Elvis to see if he looked of a mind to come with her, but he was suddenly deeply engrossed in the apparently fascinating bubbles in his beer.

'All right, I'm off,' she declared, with all the pride she could muster. 'And I won't be coming back to this shite-hole neither! There's plenty more pubs to drink at, I don't need this dump! Fuck the lot of youse!'

Flipping the room a victorious 'V', she stomped out, head held high.

It was almost completely dark outside, and the rapidly cooling air hit Pat in the face like a hammer blow, sending the whole world into a sickening spin. Leaning against the wall for support, she gulped at the saliva flooding her mouth. But she was too far gone and, before she could stop herself, she was throwing up, splattering the pub step with a chunky red mess of vomit.

Wiping her mouth with the back of her hand when she'd finished, she pushed the door open again and yelled: 'And there's your fucking drinks back, an' all!'

Cackling loudly, she finally staggered away, pride intact.

Strolling drunkenly through Moss Side and Hulme, singing snippets of her favourite songs and paying no attention to where her feet were leading her, Pat was more than a little surprised to find herself turning onto Westy Lane a short while later.

Stopping at the corner, she looked around herself as if waking from a dream. Then, as the mind-fug began to clear, she chuckled softly to herself. Wasn't it amazing how your body marched to its own drum when you stopped conducting? Shrugging at the undeniable forces of fate, she decided that now she was here, she might as well stay for half an hour or so.

If Lisa needs a couple of quid, then Lisa will get a couple of quid!

Peering into the darkness up ahead, she could just about make out the trademark stance of a pro leaning against the old factory gate. At least she'd have someone to chat with while she waited for a punter. There was nothing more boring than doing it alone.

Gloria Witherspoon was so preoccupied with thoughts of the murder of one of her workmates that she didn't notice the approaching figure until it was almost upon her. Her heart leaped into her throat.

Oh God! This is it!

Turning in dread anticipation, she saw Pat and gasped with relief.

'Oh, thank God it's only you! You scared me half to death!'

Pat laughed. 'Nice to see you, an' all!'

Gloria was immediately annoyed with herself for being so jumpy. If Pat Noone could carry on as normal after what had happened, why did Gloria have to go showing herself up by freaking out like some big kid?

Shivering as she felt herself sobering up, Pat said, 'So, how's it going, kid? Done much?'

Affecting the lack of nerves she presumed Pat to be feeling, Gloria shrugged her bony shoulders and wiped her incessantly dribbling nose with the back of her hand.

'Nah. It's been dead like I don't know what. I wouldn't have bothered staying, but you know how it is.'

Pat sighed wearily. 'Still not kicked it, eh?'

'Nah. I was gonna start on the Methadone last week, but I had a run-in with me ma and it set me back a bit. Old bitch! I'll never get off the gear with *her* hanging round me neck like a pair of cheesy bollocks!'

Pat didn't bother responding to Gloria's complaints. With junkies there was always a bloody good reason why they had to delay giving up. It was always someone else's fault, and nothing anyone said or did made a scrap of difference. They either kicked it off their own back, or carried on until they couldn't find any more veins to torture.

'How come it's so dead?' she asked instead, changing the useless subject.

Gloria looked at her as if she were an alien that had just landed in a pod.

'Don't tell me you haven't heard? Where've you *been* all day?'

'In the boozer. Why, what's up?'

'It's Sandra.' Gloria shook her head sadly. 'Only went and copped it last night, didn't she? Poor cow! I thought everyone knew?'

Pat was shocked. 'Sandra? *Our* Sandra – with the kiddies?'

'Yup.' Sniffing loudly, Gloria wrapped her arms tightly around her skinny chest. 'It's been *mad* down here this arvo with the coppers swarming all over the show. Thought they'd never piss off.'

'*Here?*' Pat spluttered. 'It happened here?'

'Yeah, over there.' Gloria motioned with a nod to the field opposite.

Turning to look, Pat noticed for the first time the strips of blue and white police tape flapping listlessly in the breeze on the other side of the Lane. The one that had been placed across the gap in the fence was now trailing along the pavement – one end still attached, the other ripped free by local kids before the last police vehicle had even disappeared around the corner.

'No way!' she gasped.

'*Way!*' Gloria said, smirking – unable to mask the perverse delight of being the one to impart the tragic news. 'Two blokes found her this morning. Sticking out from under a bush she was – ripped to fuck!'

Shaking her head, Pat let out a loud breath. 'So what are the pigs saying?'

'The usual bullshit,' Gloria told her scornfully. 'Don't

work here for the time being – or at least not alone. Like they give a toss! I'm surprised you hadn't heard, though. It's been on the news all day.'

'Well, no wonder it's dead, then,' Pat said matter-of-factly. 'The punters must have seen it and all.'

'Not all of them,' Gloria sniffed. 'I've had one, but that's it. *And* the cunt ripped me off! I was just thinking of going down Patton Street when you come.'

'I wouldn't if I was you, kid,' Pat told her grimly. 'They're a right load of psycho bitches down there.'

'*Safe* psycho bitches,' countered Gloria.

'Yeah, from the punters, maybe,' Pat agreed. 'But not from each other! You'd be better off trying Deansgate.'

Just then, a car turned slowly onto the Lane at the far end. Spotting it, Pat stepped forward, all thoughts of danger gone in an instant.

'Here, what you doing?' Gloria demanded. 'I've been here ages. It's mine, this.'

'Yeah, and you said you've done one already,' Pat retorted sharply. 'So I reckon it's mine.'

Gloria gave a soft moan. 'Aw, have a heart, Pat! I got ripped off on that one, and I'm gonna turkey any minute. Just let me do this one to get meself a score an' I'll take off. You can have the rest for yourself.'

Pat looked at her hard. She did look iffy, clutching at herself in that fold-yourself-in-half way junkies on the come-down have, teeth chattering like old bones.

But she'd promised Lisa.

'Sorry, kid!' Stepping forward again as the car came alongside, she gave Gloria a no-point-arguing-about-it look. 'I just need this one, but I promise I'll let you have the next.'

Gloria wasn't happy about having the job nicked from under her nose, but she knew better than to push it – Pat was a rough bitch when she was pushed.

'Go on, then . . . but you owe me!'

Amused by Gloria's attempt to make it look as if she'd *allowed* her to take the job, Pat was smiling as she leaned in through the driver's open window.

'Looking for business, sweetheart?'

3

Sam arrived back in Hulme at just gone six – more than a little pleased with himself for getting almost everything done. He'd missed the bank, but that was all right. He'd just call there in the morning instead. Everything else was in perfect order. The flowers were on the seat beside him. The small velvet jewellery box was snug in his pocket. And he'd even managed to set up a meet with a new, high-paying client for the next day.

All he had to do now was fuck the tension out of his bollocks, and he'd be all set to entertain the in-laws when they descended.

Picking up the bottle of brandy he'd bought from the local Happy Shopper on the way, he got out of the car, activated its alarm and locked it, then made his way up the communal stairs to Pat's maisonette.

Lisa answered on the second knock – her lips painted a bright shade of red to match the ridiculously short, tight skirt she was wearing. Taken aback, Sam looked her over with disgust and had to fight an urge to slap her and send her up to the bathroom to wash the muck off her face – exactly what he'd do to his own daughter if he ever caught *her* tarted up like that.

Lisa smirked as she watched the thoughts flitting across Sam's face. She didn't give a *damn* what he thought of her. Disapproval from a sad old git like him just confirmed what she already knew: that she looked hot! Old people always had a shit-fit when they were faced with someone younger and sexier. It reminded them that *they* were well past *their* sell-by.

Sticking her head out to peer past him down the landing, she said, 'Me mum isn't back yet. I thought that might have been her, but it looks like I'm going to have to go and find her now, doesn't it? Here, you don't fancy giving me a lift, do you?'

Sam blanched.

What? And risk being seen with this sluttish child in my car? Never!

'Er, no. I don't think that's a good idea,' he said. 'Anyway, what if she turned up while we were out? She wouldn't know I'd been and might decide to go out again.'

'Suppose so.' Sighing, Lisa stepped back into the hall. 'You'd better come in and wait, then. I'll just *walk*.'

Sam followed Lisa to the living room, but stopped dead in the doorway when Monty, who was sprawled out on the couch, spotted him and let out a long, low growl.

'Could you move him, please?' he asked, keeping a nervous eye on the demon hound.

Lisa gave him a scornful look. 'Didn't know you was scared of dogs, Sam? Thought you ate 'em where you come from?'

Shaking his head, eyes peeled for signs of sudden movement, he said, 'No, we just shoot them! Dangerous, disgusting things.'

'*That*'s disgusting!' Lisa snapped, reaching down to

smooth Monty's raised hackles. 'He wouldn't hurt a fly, would you, boy?'

'Could you just put him in the kitchen, or something?' Sam begged. '*Please?*'

Lisa rolled her eyes and tutted loudly. 'No, I can't. He's already been locked in there nearly all day. I'll take him with me if you're gonna be such a wuss about it!'

Grabbing Monty's collar, she hauled the dog off the couch and pulled him towards the door, giving Sam an evil glare.

Stepping neatly around the hateful creatures, Sam lurched into the room. His face fell when he saw the state of the place – every surface was littered with clothes, discarded newspapers and used cups and plates.

As he fussily cleared a space for himself on the couch, brushing the cushion down briskly before committing his enormous rear to it, Lisa watched with amusement from the doorway. Snobby sod! Why did he bother with her mum if he wanted tidy?

'So *sorry*,' she apologized sarcastically. 'If we'd known you was coming, we'd have cleaned up.'

Sam gave her a tight smile. 'That's okay. I don't mind a little disorder.'

'Yeah, *right!*' Snorting softly, Lisa turned on her heel and flounced out with Monty in tow.

Yanking open the front door, she found Debbie about to knock.

'I've got two quid!' Debbie exclaimed happily. Then, spotting Monty, she tutted. 'What you doing with him? Don't tell me you're not going now?'

'I've got to fetch me mum first,' Lisa said, pulling the door shut with a window-rattling slam. 'And I've got

Monty with me 'cos Sam's in there and he's shit-scared of dogs. All right?'

'Great!' Debbie muttered, folding her arms. 'Then what we gonna do with him? We can't take him to the youthy.'

'I'll get me mum to bring him back, stupid! Now quit moaning, or we'll never get there.'

Going down the stairs, they headed out onto City Road. It was completely dark now, and a brisk wind was developing. As they passed the open field at the side of their block, a strong gust licked the hem of Lisa's unbuttoned coat, whipping it back to reveal her too-short skirt and far-too-tight top.

Debbie raised an eyebrow in surprise. She could see not only the tops of Lisa's tights, but also the goose-bumps pushing up through the nylon. Warm in her own sensible jeans and jacket, she suddenly remembered what she had meant to tell Lisa.

'Oh yeah!' she said, turning to her friend excitedly. 'Guess what? . . . There's been another murder! It was on the news just before I came out, an—'

'I already know,' Lisa cut her off, affecting boredom at the old news. 'I saw it this arvo.'

'Getting a bit close, isn't it?'

'Mmmm. Just a bit.'

Debbie pursed her lips disapprovingly. 'My mum reckons they're all prozzies, anyway.'

Lisa shot her an evil look. '*And* . . . ?'

'And, I'm just *saying*,' Debbie replied defensively, wondering why Lisa was such a moody bitch at times. 'She reckons they deserve everything they get, that's all.'

'Bollocks! *No* one deserves that!'

'I'm just telling you what she said.'

'Well, *don't*, 'cos you don't know what you're talking about – and neither does your mum! Stupid cow!'

Debbie frowned at the fierce attack on her mum, but didn't bother protesting. Lisa was obviously in a volatile mood.

Ten silent minutes later, they reached The Hopscotch.

'Here, hold him while I find her,' Lisa said, thrusting Monty's lead at Debbie.

Scowling, but obeying the command, Debbie looped the lead around her wrist and slumped against the wall, arms tightly folded. She'd had just about enough of Lisa's shitty temper!

Opening the door just a crack, Lisa peeped inside to check if the dreaded landlord was about. Seeing no sign of him, she nipped inside and made a dash for the bar.

Spotting her, Rita abandoned the pint she'd been pouring and rushed over to her.

'What you doing back here? You'd best just—'

'Don't worry,' Lisa interrupted. 'I'm not staying. I'm just looking for me mum. Is she still here?'

'No, love, she left a while back. And you'd better get yourself off, too. My boss and her had a bit of a fall-out.'

'Where's she gone?' Lisa demanded, a sinking feeling in her stomach.

Rita felt a twinge of pity for the white-lipped child. Sighing, she said, 'I don't know, sweetie. Didn't she come home?'

Lisa shook her head, her face clearly displaying her worry.

'Look, don't fret,' Rita went on kindly. 'She probably got home while you were on your way here, eh?
I bet she's sitting there now, wondering where you
are.'

'When did she go?'

'About an hour since, but I don't think—'

'Thanks!'

Not waiting to hear the rest, Lisa pushed herself
away from the bar and cut through the crowd to the
door.

Rita frowned as she watched her go. The poor kid
was worried to death – and with good reason, in her
opinion. Pat was well out of order, taking off all the time
without letting the girl know where she was or what she
was doing.

Outside, Lisa snatched Monty's lead from Debbie and
stalked away.

Trotting to catch up with her, Debbie said, 'Where's
your mum?'

'Gone.'

'Gone where?'

'How the hell should I know?' Lisa snapped. 'Just shut
up prattling and let me think, will you?'

It didn't take much thinking about. She knew exactly
where her mum would be. The problem was, how could
she explain it to Debbie? Everyone knew there was only
one reason women went down Westy Lane.

'Where we going?' Debbie asked.

'The Lane,' Lisa admitted, hoping she'd leave it at
that.

'The *Lane*?' Debbie stopped dead, her eyes wide with
alarm. 'What for?'

Sighing heavily, Lisa turned back. ''Cos me mum might be there, all right?'

Debbie was confused. 'But why? That's where the prozzies go, isn't it?

'So what you sayin'?' Lisa demanded, giving her a fierce glare.

'Nothing. Well, not about your mum, anyhow. I just wondered why she'd be down there, that's all.'

''Cos she's got a mate who lives down there,' Lisa lied. 'You want to make something of it?'

'*No.*'

'Good job an' all!'

Reluctantly following as Lisa set off again, Debbie tried to make amends.

'Look, I didn't mean anything, Lisa. It's just that – well – that's where it happened, isn't it?'

'Yeah, so it'll be safe now, won't it?' Lisa said, as if explaining something really simple to a child. 'Look, there's no way the bloke who did it is gonna show his face down there again the next day, is there?'

'I suppose not,' Debbie conceded unhappily. 'But I still don't want to go there – it's dark!'

'Well, stay at the top end then, mardy arse!' Lisa shouted. 'I'll go by meself!'

Pat was fuming. The punter, despite his nice car, had turned out to be a real cheapo. He'd only wanted a quick hand job, and to add insult to injury, he'd only had a fiver on him when she'd specifically told him ten. And she knew he wasn't lying about how much he had because she'd made him open his wallet and show her. She could have kicked herself for not getting it up front!

What was wrong with her? Was she losing her bloody marbles, or what?

Still, at least he'd brought her back to the Lane. He could have been a complete cunt and left her to walk back from the Arches, like some of the other jokers they got down here. Motioning him to pull in by Gloria, who was still standing at the factory gate, she tucked the fiver into her shoe and opened the door.

'Can I see you again?' the punter blurted out before she'd had a chance to climb out.

'You *what*?' Incredulous, she turned back to see if he was for real and found him grinning at her like the village idiot. 'I don't fuckin' believe this!' she snarled.

'Please?' he simpered. 'I really enjoyed it.'

Feeling as if a blast of steam was exploding from her head, Pat screeched, 'Get to *fuck*, you shit-stabbin' little *twat*!' And, hopping out of the car, she slammed the door and aimed a vicious kick at it as the alarmed man quickly pulled away.

Shivering more than ever, Gloria watched the scene with a nasty smirk on her pinched face.

'Get ripped off an' all, did you?'

'Fucking ponce!' Hawking up noisily, Pat spat on the floor in disgust. 'Twenty minutes for a bastard fiver! Don't know why they bother paying for a wank when they've got two fuckin' hands of their own! Cunts!'

'Should have let me take it if you're that fussy,' Gloria sniped. 'You knew I needed it.'

'So did I – and not for meself, neither!' Pat retorted, folding her arms and stamping her feet against the increasing cold. 'Anyhow, I'm not arguing over a poxy bloke, so shut it!'

Gloria sniffed, and stayed quiet – giving Pat a chance to calm down. A couple of minutes later, she did.

'Sorry for shouting, kid. He just pissed me off.'

''S all right.' Gloria smiled nervously. 'I'm glad you're back, to tell the truth. I was getting a bit spooked on me own. Thought I heard a noise in there.' She motioned with a nod to the derelict factory behind them.

Pat glanced back at the dark, hulking building with its broken windows and boarded-up doors. It had a stillness about it that screamed of years of disuse and neglect.

'Daft cow,' she snorted. 'You're just para 'cos of Sandra. No one's been near that place in yonks. Anyhow, he ain't likely to come back, is he?' she added, hoping to allay Gloria's obvious fear with a dash of common sense. 'He'll be expecting the pigs to still be here, won't he?'

Gloria shrugged uneasily. 'S'pose so. But I deffo thought I heard something. Freaked me right out, I can tell you.'

'Not enough to make you piss off home, though, eh?'

'Can't, can I?' Gloria murmured with a hint of accusation. 'I haven't got enough for a bag yet.'

Saddened by the knowledge that Sandra Foggarty had only worked to feed *her* habit – and look where that had got her! – Pat sighed.

'You want to give it up while you still can, kid.'

Hugging herself even tighter, Gloria said, 'I will – if me ma will stay off me back long enough!'

'Any excuse,' Pat said softly. 'Just don't leave it too late, eh?'

'I won't.'

For a moment Gloria had the grace to look ashamed, but her expression immediately hardened when another car turned onto the Lane and came slowly towards them. Before Pat could make a move, she rushed forward to the pavement's edge, staking her claim.

Having had no intention of going for it herself, Pat laughed at Gloria's determination and said, 'You don't have to fight for it, kid. I said you could have it.'

'Yeah, well,' Gloria muttered. 'You never know with you. You might take it into your head to nick this one and all.'

'Nah, I'm having a fag.' Taking out her cigarettes, Pat lit one and stepped back to lean against the factory gate. 'See you in a bit . . . and be careful, yeah?'

Gloria nodded, half-smiling as she hopped into the waiting car.

Pat shook her head as she watched it drive away. The stupid bitch hadn't so much as *looked* at the driver to check him out before getting into the car with him – something Pat did every time, without fail. You got an instinct about punters, and all it took was that one momentary glance at their face to know if they meant you any harm. Still, why should she be bothered about Gloria, when Gloria obviously didn't give a toss about herself?

Sighing, she decided she must be getting old – it was the only explanation for all the worrying she was doing lately.

She just hoped to God it wasn't the menopause. That would be all she needed!

★   ★   ★

Safely concealed in the shadows of the abandoned factory's canteen area some feet behind Pat, he narrowed his eyes and shifted onto his other knee.

It never ceased to amaze him how stupid these women were. He'd heard every word the two outside had said, and could have laughed at their ignorance – if he weren't so disgusted by it.

What made them so sure that the perpetrator didn't return to the scene of the crime? In his experience it was exactly the opposite. There was no better time to see the aftermath – especially now the police spent as little time as possible on a case. It was imperative to return soon after – or risk seeing nothing.

It was fun watching the idiotic authorities crawling all over the place looking for the one elusive fibre that would wrap the case up for them – however short the duration of that futile search.

Fun to know that they could never succeed against such a vastly superior intelligence.

Still, even knowing the lack of care employed these days, he had to admit that the police had disappointed him even more than usual this time. They hadn't even posted anyone to guard the scene for one lousy night! Were they really so confident that lightning could not strike twice in such close proximity?

Or had they somehow guessed how he relished the challenge their presence provided?

But no! They could never be so sophisticated as to employ such devious methods to frustrate him. A disappointment in itself.

The women, however, had not disappointed him. Just as the police should have been more vigilant, so should the women have stayed away, rendering his ambitions victimless. But, as he had anticipated, they had come – whores to the slaughter. Far too greedy and stupid to understand that he would predict just such a flaw in their worthless characters.

But then, how could any mortal hope to aspire to his level of guile? Did he not have the guidance of the unequivocal Master?

Smiling to his blessed self, he took the hood from his pocket and eased it over his head, concealing all but his dark, glistening eyes as he tucked it deep inside his collar. Then, carefully pulling the latex gloves he favoured for his work – so much more sensation! – over his long, slender fingers, he extracted the small, clear plastic bag from his inside pocket. Holding it up to the dim glimmer of light filtering into the shell of a room from the street lamp outside, he traced a fingertip gently around the petals of the tiny flower within.

It was time.

Repocketing the bag, he raised himself slowly to his feet, his hand curled around the hilt of the blade as he breathed deeply through the mesh of the hood.

Through the pane-less window he could see her quite clearly now. Oblivious to his gaze, she loitered against the gate, amusing herself by blowing a series of smoke rings into the icy air.

Closing his eyes, he savoured a sudden vision of her startled gasps escaping the 'O' that her mouth would become when he began the process.

Those last earthly breaths that would appear so like the smoke rings that were even now dissipating into the atmosphere as though they had never existed.

As though she *had never existed.*

Feeling the familiar surge of life-giving blood to his member, he vowed to make an extra-special effort to record these details he had previously overlooked.

The precious last breaths . . . The frantic, rhythmic jerking of the body-shell as the spirit fled its earthly confines . . . The humiliatingly shameful, and oh, so uncontrollable release of bowels that every woman would rather die than succumb to . . . The clean-up . . . The entry . . .

Pure joy.

And what joy to see what the thoroughly inept police force made of this second body appearing in the exact same place as the last – the very next day! Wouldn't that just confuse them all – blow their little theories sky high.

And this woman waiting so unwittingly before him was a deserving case if ever there was one. The language he had witnessed spewing from her filthy mouth on the occasions he had watched her was cause enough – not to mention the disgusting display of flesh she flaunted so blatantly.

Oh, he knew all about Pat *. . .*

'Mum? Is that you?'

As the shrill voice echoed around him, he instinctively dropped back down to his haunches.

Damn! Who was that? And why had she chosen now to appear?

Pushing herself away from the gate, Pat peered ahead at the silhouettes of Lisa and Monty running towards her.

'What you doing here?' she called out.

'What *you* doing, more like?' Lisa demanded when she reached her. 'Don't you know what's happened?'

Pat sighed. 'Yeah. It was one of me mates, actually. Well, not exactly a *mate*, but you know what I mean.'

'So if you knew, what you playing at?'

'I didn't know till I *got* here, did I?' Pat folded her arms defensively. 'Anyway, never mind me. What you up to?'

'I'm looking for you,' Lisa retorted sharply. 'I knew you'd do this!'

'Oi! Less of the lip!'

'Well!' Lisa stood her ground. 'What d'y' expect? You do me head in, Mum! You promised you wasn't gonna do this no more.'

'Stop going on with yourself, for gawd's sake!' Pat laughed softly. 'You're like a bloody old woman with your nagging! Anyway, I was just coming, if you must know. There's nothing doing down here.'

'Good!'

Amused by Lisa's annoyance, Pat linked arms with her and walked her towards the main road.

'So what's the emergency?' she teased. 'The house burnt down, or something?'

'No, I needed that money for the disco,' Lisa said, snapping at Monty's lead to stop him running on ahead. 'Oh, and Sam's at ours.'

'*Sam*? What's he up to? It's not Wednesday, is it?'

'No, Tuesday. And *I* don't know what he's up to, he hardly talks to me, does he?'

Smiling, Pat said, 'That's 'cos you're too gobby.'

Lisa gave her an incredulous look. 'And *you*'re not?'

'Oi! Shut it!' Pat started to laugh, then abruptly stopped when she spotted Debbie waiting up ahead. Jerking on Lisa's arm, she hissed accusingly, 'What did you bring *her* for, you stupid cow?'

'She's coming to the youthy,' Lisa said. 'But don't worry, I told her you had a mate living up here.'

'In what?' Pat snapped. 'The bleeding factory?'

'Well, I had to say *something*,' Lisa snapped back. 'Anyway, she won't know there's no houses, will she? She don't exactly come down this way a lot!'

Pat gave her a hard look. 'You'd better not have told her why I'm here, Lisa. 'Cos if her mum gets hold of it, your arse'll be in care!'

'Don't be daft!'

'Hello, Mrs Noone.' Debbie greeted Pat nervously. You never knew with Lisa's mum – one minute she could be really nice to you, and the next she'd be threatening to kick your head in.

Ignoring Debbie, Pat said, 'I've only got a fiver, Lisa. You'll have to come to the offy while I get some change.'

'Aw, Mum! That's nearly back home! The youthy's only ten minutes this way.'

Pat shrugged. 'Not my problem, is it? Anyhow, there's no shops open down that way.'

'Just give me the fiver, then?' suggested Lisa. 'I'll bring you the change – honest! Come on, Mum. We're gonna be dead late.'

Pat frowned at her persistent daughter for a moment, then reached down and took the hard-earned note from her shoe.

'All right, take it! But I want the change as soon as you come in, and no messing about!'

'Ta, Mum!' Grinning, Lisa snatched the money with one hand and held Monty's lead out with the other. Pat looked at it with disgust.

'What do you expect me to do with that?'

'Take him home.'

'Oh, no! No way! You brought him, you take him back, lady!'

'Aw, Mum!' Lisa complained, then grinned slyly. 'He'll protect you if that nutter comes after you!'

Tutting at Lisa's guile, Pat snatched the lead from her hand. 'All right, smart-arse! Now sod off before I change me mind!'

Lisa didn't need telling twice. With a wave, she grabbed Debbie's arm and hustled her away. She turned back when her mum shouted after her asking what time she'd be home.

'Ten all right?' she called back.

'Make it eleven,' Pat said, 'and you can keep the change from the fiver.'

'*Yeah?*'

'Yeah!'

'Cool! See ya later!'

Sliding out from behind the bushes at the corner where the factory wall ended, he watched as Pat went one way, and the girls the other.

He felt unsettled – needed time to gather his thoughts. He hadn't expected this at all. It changed everything.

Surely it had to have been intended? But if so, why had it never even occurred to him that the whore had a child? He should have guessed a woman her age would, but somehow she hadn't looked the type.

But then, it wasn't the first time he had got it wrong. He obviously still had a way to go.

Closing his eyes tightly, he waited for inspiration, whispering: 'Master, don't fail me now. Lead me to your bidding as the rain leads the root to its succour.'

Frustrating seconds passed as he fought his impatience – surely one of the vices to be conquered. Then blessed relief flooded him as he heard and understood.

He had only to wait and watch.

Checking that there was no one around, he slipped off the hood and gloves and pushed them back into his pocket, then dusted himself down, hopped over the wall, and stepped out onto the road. Head down, he set off after the girls at a casual pace. As he walked, he felt a tingle of excitement in his gut.

This had been no chance encounter. He knew that now.

4

Feeling magnanimous with a whole fiver in her pocket, Lisa paid Debbie in to the disco, then impatiently pushed her through the double doors into the main hall.

Kicking tunes were already pumping out from the resident DJ's huge system, and a bank of coloured lights swirled above the dance floor, painting the faces of the heaving mass of teenagers below as they gyrated their bodies in all the latest sexy moves.

Scanning the crowd, Lisa was disappointed not to see Jamie among them.

'Oh, God, he'd better come,' she moaned.

'Who?' Debbie asked, waving to a couple of girls she knew.

'Duh! *Jamie!*'

'Oh, right.'

'Aw, he'll come!' Lisa declared then, confident that Jamie wouldn't miss the once-a-week disco. 'Come on, let's get a drink while we're waiting.'

Shrugging her coat off, she rolled it up and stashed it behind a row of chairs set against the wall, telling the group of younger girls sitting there to make sure it didn't go walkabout – or else!

Debbie cringed as she saw the full effect of Lisa's

outfit. Everything was so *tight*. She looked like a prostitute who'd outgrown her clothes. And as for the garish lipstick . . . No wonder everyone in the room seemed to be throwing dirty looks their way. Lisa was going to get herself a right reputation if she wasn't careful!

'Not taking yours off?' Lisa asked, fluffing up her hair – which was already looking stringy, despite the washing.

Folding her jacket tighter around herself, Debbie said, 'No. I'll leave it on for now. It's a bit cold.'

With a suit-yourself shrug, Lisa gave her hair another tweak, then set off at a strut towards the bar. After buying their drinks, she led Debbie to the far wall opposite the door.

'Aren't we gonna dance?' Debbie asked.

'Later,' Lisa said dismissively, staring fixedly at the door. 'I don't want to miss Jamie when he comes in.'

'Oh, thanks a lot!' Debbie griped, leaning back against the wall with a sigh. This was going to be fun – *not*!

'If you're just gonna start moaning,' Lisa snapped without looking at her, 'you'd best just pay me back and get lost! I'll let you know when I want to dance – all *right*?'

Tight-lipped, Debbie glared at her but said nothing. There was no point.

Lisa doesn't want to dance – so we don't; Lisa wants to dance – so we do! Lisa wants to do this . . . Lisa wants to do that!

It really annoyed her how Lisa always had to be in control of everything, but she knew from experience that it was best not to argue about it. Lisa was great when she was getting her own way but she could be a complete bitch when she wasn't, and though it galled Debbie to have to put up with it, she thought too much of Lisa to tell her to piss off. Anyway, left alone Lisa never stayed in one of her moods too long, so it was just a matter of biding your time and keeping shtum.

Fifteen minutes – and a number of tunes Debbie would have loved to dance to – later, she had almost resigned herself to this being it for the whole night when Lisa suddenly brightened up and began to wave at someone over by the door. Turning to look, Debbie's heart sank when she saw that it was Linda Parry. This was just getting better and better!

Debbie didn't like Linda. She was loud, rude and aggressive – and she obviously didn't think too much of Debbie either. Debbie had never figured out why, but Linda had taken against her from the first and felt nothing about dragging Lisa away from her when they all got together. In fact, Linda and Lisa usually ended up forgetting that Debbie was even there.

'Lin!' Lisa was shouting now. 'Lin . . . Over here!'

'Shit!' Debbie muttered under her breath as Linda spotted them and came towards them, using her enormous tits to force a path through the dance floor.

'Did you see it?' Linda asked, her face a mask of excitement.

'See what?' said Lisa, peering over Linda's shoulder to see if Steve was with her. As set on Steve as Lisa was on Jamie, Linda only usually went where she knew he would be. And if Steve was here, Jamie would be too.

'Mark Dean just got jacked outside!' Linda explained. 'Three lads were supposed to have pulled a knife on him!

I can't *believe* you didn't see it!' she added, disappointed that they hadn't.

'No way!' gasped Lisa, equally disappointed.

'*Way!*'

'Is he all right?' Debbie asked.

Casting her a contemptuous side-glance, Linda said, 'Yeah – apart from crapping himself, the little wuss! But he ain't *hurt*, if that's what you're worried about. Seen Steve?' she asked Lisa then.

Shoulders drooping, Lisa shook her head. 'No, I thought he'd be with you.'

Linda made a little huffing noise. 'Huh! He reckoned he was already here when I rang him on me way. He's a right bleeding liar! Don't suppose you've seen Jas, either?'

'No.'

'That's bleedin' typical, that is!' Linda tutted. 'She'd better bleedin' came – she owes me for her half of the bottle.'

'You got booze?'

'Ssshhh!' Linda shoved Lisa's shoulder, almost knocking her over. 'Tell the whole bleedin' world, why don't you! Yeah, I've got cider, but I had to leave it outside, didn't I? They was searching everyone on the door.'

'So what we standing here for?' Lisa demanded, rubbing her hands together at the prospect of getting into party mode before Jamie arrived.

'Don't know about you,' Linda said, 'but I'm waiting for Jas. And she'd better hurry up, 'cos I ain't waiting all night!'

'Ah, she probably won't even bother coming,' Lisa

said. 'You know what's she's like. But we'll help you drink it, won't we, Deb?'

'Yeah,' Debbie muttered sulkily. At least Lisa was including her.

Linda thought about it for a second, then said, 'All right, but it'll cost you. Got any fags?'

Lisa tapped her pocket. 'Yeah, six – but I'm keeping one for on the way home.'

'That'll do!' Grinning, Linda linked her arm through Lisa's and pulled her towards the door.

Following them out, Debbie checked her watch to see if it was too early to take off. But it was only twenty past seven. If she went home now her mum would think she'd fallen out with Lisa – and wouldn't *that* just make her happy! No, she'd just have to stay and hope that Jas or Steve got here soon to take Linda away.

Outside, Linda ran ahead to retrieve the bottle she'd stashed behind a pile of bricks at the entrance to the alley.

Shivering as the cold night air bit straight through her skimpy clothes, Lisa linked arms with Debbie and pulled her towards the low wall that faced, and ran the length of, the youth club side wall. Sitting down, she huddled up against her for warmth and shouted at Linda to hurry up.

'It's slipped down!' Linda yelled back, her loud, rough voice bouncing off the alley walls. 'I can't reach it! . . . Ah, just a minute . . . *Got* the little fucker!'

Directly opposite the front door of the youth club, in the recessed doorway of a closed-up-for-the-night office block,

*a cigarette glowed red in the dark, then fell to the floor
and died.*

*Grinding the butt out with venom, he glared across at
the girl – the whore's daughter.*

*She wasn't wearing a coat now, and with eyes that were
fine-tuned to adjust to the dark he could clearly see the
outline of budding nipples straining against the ridiculously
tight T-shirt material. The sight infuriated him – made him
wonder if it wasn't already too late.*

No! *he reprimanded himself angrily.* Of course it isn't.
It's exactly the right time.

Exactly right.

*Shifting his focus onto the larger girl as she rejoined the
others at the wall, he saw that she was waving a bottle
above her head – obviously alcohol. His eyes narrowed to
furious slits.*

*Oh, what evil influences circulated around this child he
had been led to!*

How timely, then, that he had been . . .

Celine Dion had never sounded as bad as she did right
now, issuing tinnily from Pat's cheap stereo. Tuning the
sibilant whining out as best he could, Sam poured himself
a second glass of brandy in the flickering light of the silent
TV and settled back to wait for Pat to return from the
bathroom.

In the half-light, with a drink warming his stomach
and the mess he'd encountered when he arrived now
relegated to a heap behind the couch – out of sight, out
of mind – Sam thought the living room looked almost
inviting. The smell of the filthy dog still pervaded the air,
but it was bearable – he had long since learned to breathe

through his mouth instead of his nose when visiting this house. And at least Pat had been good enough to lock the thing in the kitchen when she came back, saving him the unease of having it stare at him as if it were just waiting for an opportunity to tear his throat out.

Reaching for the remote control, he flipped idly through the TV channels, hoping to find one of the soft-porn films the people of this country enjoyed so freely. But it was not to be. The seven-thirty schedule for Tuesday night was, as ever, predictably boring. Soaps, soaps, and more soaps.

For a moment he toyed with the idea of getting Pat hooked up to Sky, but immediately discarded the notion. That wouldn't do at all! God only knew which Tom, Dick or Harry would be reaping the benefits of cable porn in his absence – at his expense!

'Oi, you . . . where's mine?'

Turning at the sound of Pat's voice, Sam saw her standing in the doorway brushing her hair with a large, round brush. Lit from behind by the dim hall light, the dark roots he had meant on a number of occasions to point out seemed almost invisible, and the brassy bottle-blonde tone he so disliked seemed softer and more golden than in the harsh light of day.

Noticing too that she had changed into a scarlet satin dressing gown through which he could clearly see her large, unfettered breasts, his dick sprang to immediate attention.

'Well?' she asked again. 'Have you poured me one or not?'

With a teasing smile, Sam tucked the bottle safely out of reach down the side of his cushion, then took a leisurely drink from his glass, watching Pat's face all the while. She liked her brandy, did Pat!

'Tastes good,' he said, smacking his lips exaggeratedly. 'But I think you've had enough today already, so I'm going to keep this all for myself.'

With a sly half-smile, Pat moved slowly into the room. 'Oh, so that's your game, is it?'

Sam took another sip. 'It's no game, Patricia. You've been a very naughty girl, and you need to be punished!'

'And you think you're man enough to do that, do you?' Snorting softly, Pat smacked the side of his thigh with the hairbrush. 'We'll have to see about that, won't we?'

Sashaying across the room, she turned the stereo volume up then came and stood before him, just out of reach. Swaying to the music, she dropped the brush and slowly unwrapped the dressing gown. Watching as beads of sweat began to form above Sam's fleshy lips, she cupped her freed breasts in her hands and began to knead them, rolling her nipples tantalizingly between fingers and thumbs.

'Well, if you're keeping all that for *your*self,' she said, motioning towards the glass he was clutching more tightly by the second, 'you won't mind if I keep *these* all for *my*self, will you?'

Sam groaned lustfully. 'You are very bad, Patricia. Very, *very* bad.'

'Yeah, but you love it, don't you?' she murmured huskily. 'You *dirty* little man! I bet you're just *dying* to get your little soldier out, aren't you? Bet you can't wait to slip your little bayonet right up my wet trench?'

Sam gulped at his drink, both to cool himself down and to prolong the game – as long as he could, given that he had to get home soon.

Pat had other ideas. Launching herself at him, she straddled his hefty thighs, pinning him to the couch as she thrust her breasts into his face.

'Want a suck of Mummy's big titties, do you, Sammy Boy? What's it worth then, eh? How much you gonna give me for a taste of paradise?'

'Not here!' Struggling against her, Sam lashed his head from side to side to avoid the monster nipples. 'Your daughter might come in!'

'You big soft git!' Pat scoffed. Snatching the glass from his hand, she drained it triumphantly.

Seizing the opportunity to push her off, Sam fussily adjusted his trousers – to cover his hard-on should the child suddenly appear. It was one thing *starting* the game down here – quite another to go all the way. He could never do that outside the privacy of Pat's bedroom.

'I don't see your problem,' Pat said, handing him back the empty glass. 'She'll be ages yet.'

'It just wouldn't be right,' he replied, in the lecturing voice she despised. 'She's only a child. She shouldn't see these things.'

'I ain't exactly doing it in front of her, mate,' she protested. 'But it ain't like she don't know what we get up to. She's a bright kid, my Lisa.'

'Well, she shouldn't know *any*thing!' he told her reproachfully. Dragging the bottle out from where he'd stashed it, he poured a couple of glasses, muttering under his breath: 'That's the problem with this country – no morals! And they wonder why their under-age children have children of their own!'

Pat was getting pissed off now.

'Not my Lisa!' she retorted frostily. 'She's no slag, I'll have you know! Anyhow, *you*'ve got room to talk. What is it they do in your country? Marry 'em off the minute they bleed? Eleven, twelve – younger than that sometimes? Dirty bastards!'

'At least they are *married* before they are touched by a man,' Sam countered stiffly. 'Legally sanctified. Pure!' Purse-lipped, he thrust her glass towards her.

Snatching it, Pat said, 'Bollocks! It's still just dirty old men having it off with kids – married or not!'

Sam shook his head, saying quietly, 'You'll never understand our ways. But I don't want to talk about this any more. We've obviously got different views on these matters, so let's just agree to disagree, shall we?'

Pat watched as he threw back his drink, immediately pouring himself another. She shook her head, her lip curling with contempt. He was such a sanctimonious prick sometimes! All she wanted to do was get him hot and horny – into bed, and out with the dosh. Left to his own devices he would waste half the night arguing and worrying, and she'd have to work doubly hard to get him stiff enough to do the dirty deed. It was obviously down to her to get things moving.

Getting up, she headed for the door, calling back over her shoulder in a no-nonsense voice: 'Right, you! Upstairs – now! And bring that bottle with you.'

Between them, Lisa and Linda had polished off almost half of the litre bottle of White Lightning and, more than a little tipsy, had to keep reminding each other to be quiet as their laughter grew more raucous.

Linda had the bottle now. Tipping it up, she completely missed her mouth and spilled the liquid down her chin. Thinking it was the most hilarious thing she'd ever done in her entire life, she slid to the floor in silent hysterics.

Debbie, who was still sober – having neither wanted nor been offered any of the cider – jumped down from the wall and set about patting her heavily on the back, sure that she was choking.

Gulping and spluttering, Linda slapped her hand away.

'Pack it in, you dozy cow! You nearly fuckin' killed me!'

'Sorry!' Debbie muttered. 'I was only trying to help.'

'Well, help your fuckin' self and keep your hands off me before I smack you one!' Cackling at her own joke, Linda hauled herself up from the ground and sat back on the wall, wiping her weeping eyes on the back of her hand. 'Jeezus, I love this shit!'

'Yeah, we noticed!' Grinning, Lisa snatched the bottle and took a slug.

'Spark up,' Linda said, rubbing her hands together. 'I could do with a puff after that!'

'Go back in, then,' Lisa squawked, pointing towards the youth club. 'There's enough puffs in there! I bet Mark Dean would give you a ride – if you paid him!'

'Get to fuck!' Linda yelped, then burst out laughing again. Clutching at her stomach, she gasped, 'Aw, shit, pack it in, man! I'm gonna piss meself!'

'Aye, aye . . . what's all this, then?'

All three girls jumped at the sound of Steve Lunt's voice. Linda nearly fell off the wall again.

'Stupid bastard!' she shrieked, righting herself. 'You nearly gave me a fuckin' heart attack.'

Andy Green leaped over the wall then, making them all jump again. Grinning stupidly, he said, 'Looks like a right slags' meeting, this! What say we give 'em a bit of action, Ste?'

'Oi you!' Linda bellowed, cuffing his ear. 'I ain't no slag!'

'Could've fooled me,' Steve said, laughing.

'Yeah,' Andy agreed, dodging another slap. 'Me an' all!'

Craning her neck to see where Jamie was, Lisa smiled with relief when she saw him strolling out from the alley. Her heart began to beat faster and a warm glow spread through her stomach.

God, he was gorgeous!

'Oi! What's your game?' she squealed when the bottle was suddenly wrenched from her hand.

'It's called jacking,' Steve told her sarcastically, taking a drink, then passing the bottle to Andy.

Passing it back after swallowing a huge mouthful, Andy flicked the end of Lisa's nose with a dirty fingernail and said, 'Yeah . . . you've got it, we jack it off you! See how it works?'

'Get lost, you mong!' she snapped, watching in despair as they drained the rest of the bottle.

Tossing the empty bottle over the wall, Steve said, 'Is that it?'

'Yeah,' Linda said, throwing a hefty punch at his arm. 'And it was mine, you thieving twat!'

'Yeah,' Lisa chipped in, 'so buy your own next time!'

Dodging another punch, Steve laughed. 'No can do – no dosh!'

'Oh, yeah?' Linda folded her arms. 'So how you gonna get in there, then?'

Sidling up to her, he put his arm around her shoulder. 'You're gonna pay me in, ain't you, babe?'

'In y' dreams!' she snorted, grinning broadly now – and making no effort to remove his hand as it fell onto her left breast.

Andy decided to try his luck with Debbie. Jumping up beside her, he nudged her with his shoulder and gave her a cheesy grin.

'All right, Debs?'

'Fine, thanks.' Embarrassed, she shifted a couple of inches away from him. Andy Green was a grade-A moron!

Smiling up at Jamie as he reached them, Lisa said simperingly, 'Hiya, Jamie.'

Giving her a brief nod, Jamie put his hands in his pockets and looked down at the floor, kicking at invisible stones as he waited for Steve. Glancing up from beneath his floppy blond fringe after a moment, he caught Debbie's eye and gave her a tiny smile.

Blushing furiously, she dropped her gaze – hoping to God that Lisa hadn't seen the exchange. Lisa wasn't the only one who thought Jamie Butterworth was gorgeous.

When Steve still hadn't stopped messing about with Linda after a few minutes, Jamie said, 'You planning on stopping out here all night, or what? 'Cos I'm off in, so I'll see you later, yeah?'

Breaking away from Linda, Steve tucked the two

pound coins he'd scrounged off her into his pocket alongside his own tenner.

'Nah, I'm right,' he said. 'See you later, girls!' Waving over his shoulder, he followed Jamie towards the door.

'Yeah, see you later, *girls*!' Jumping down from the wall, Andy followed his friends at a run, shouting: 'Here, Steve, wait up, man! You said you'd pay us in . . . *Steve*!'

'Knob-head!' Linda yelled as Andy lurched out of sight around the corner. Then, turning to Lisa, she said, 'Here, we'd better get in before they cop off.'

Panicked by the very idea of some other girl getting a grip of Jamie, Lisa hopped down from the wall, yelping, 'They'd better not! Jamie's mine! Come on, Debs.'

'Yeah, come on, misery guts,' Linda sneered. 'You can have Andy.'

'No way!' Debbie retorted, but Linda was already halfway to the door, dragging a still-tipsy Lisa along behind her.

Back inside, they looked around for the lads but couldn't see them anywhere. Disappointed, but by no means defeated, Linda declared that she wasn't wasting the night looking for Steve.

'He'll come crawling soon as he wants something,' she said, hauling Lisa along behind her to the middle of the dance floor.

Left out again, Debbie watched from the sidelines as Linda and Lisa pretended to be having a good time, when all they were really doing was craning their necks to peer around the room for Steve and Jamie. It was pathetic!

Sighing, she made her way back to her original spot against the wall. Surprised to find that her Coke was still there, she picked it up and took a sip.

Linda's vigilance paid off after a few minutes. Spotting Steve coming onto the dance floor, she was about to tell Lisa she was getting off to dance with him when she realized he wasn't alone. Zoë Clayton was with him. The bitch!

'What the fuck's *she* doing?' she bellowed in outrage as Zoë looped her arms around Steve's neck.

Lisa wasn't watching. She was too busy looking for Jamie.

'Where is he?' she moaned. 'I can't see him anywhere! He'd better not have copped off!'

'Who gives a fuck about *him*?' Linda roared. 'That slag's trying to get off with my fella! Right, she's had it! I'm gonna mash her up!'

'No!' Grabbing Linda's arm just in time, Lisa forced her to stay put – no mean feat given that Linda was built like a brick shithouse and stood a good two inches taller than her. 'Wait till she goes outside. You'll get us barred if you kick off in here!'

Linda shrugged her off angrily. '*Okay*! But she's dead when I get my hands on her!'

Going into a stiff dance of fury, Linda glared across at the couple with ice-melting intensity. Two tunes later, her eyes lit up when Zoë leaned up to whisper into Steve's ear then headed out of the room.

'She's going to the loo!' she yelled, almost wrenching Lisa's arm out of its socket as she dragged her towards the door. 'Come on!'

Debbie saw them rushing out and was about to go and

see what was happening when Jamie suddenly appeared. Smiling, he rested his shoulder against the wall beside her.

'Hi, Debbie. I hoped you'd be here tonight.'

'Oh?' Blushing again, Debbie stared intently at the bottle clasped tightly in her hands – hands that had suddenly become very sweaty.

'Yeah, I wanted to apologize for Steve and Andy tipping your bag out at school earlier.'

She flicked him a tiny smile. 'It's all right.'

'No, it's not. They do my head in when they mess about like that. Did you find everything?'

'Yeah, thanks.'

Jamie nodded and took a drink from his bottle, wondering what to say now. It had taken him this long to get to talk to Debbie Morgan alone, he wasn't about to give up after three sentences.

'By the way,' he managed after a minute. 'I've told them to leave it out in future, so just let me know if they give you any more hassle, yeah?'

'Yeah. Thanks.'

Clutching her bottle even tighter, Debbie breathed in deeply, suddenly aware of the scent of Lynx. It surprised her. Most of the lads their age couldn't be bothered *washing*, never mind using deodorant.

But then, Jamie wasn't like the others. He was much nicer. Nicer-looking, nicer-mannered – nicer everything.

Not that she'd ever admit this to Lisa.

'So where's your mate?' Jamie asked, as if reading her mind.

Shrugging, Debbie said, 'I don't know. She's just gone out somewhere with Linda.'

'Good,' he murmured, smiling. 'I was starting to think youse were joined at the hip, or something.'

Debbie returned the smile guiltily, telling him almost apologetically, 'She's my best mate. We live on the same block.'

'Shame,' Jamie said. 'It's kind of nice seeing you on your own.'

Debbie's heart began to thunder in her ears. What was going on? Was she imagining this?

'I was, er, sort of wondering,' he went on, sounding shy himself now. 'Do you fancy a dance?'

'No!' The refusal shot out instinctively. Lisa would skin her alive! Blushing furiously again, she said, 'No, I, er, don't feel like dancing. I'm sorry.'

Jamie shrugged, an amused smile playing around the corners of his mouth.

'It's cool, don't sweat it. How about I get you a drink instead?'

'No, I'm all right,' she said, showing him her half-full bottle. 'But thanks, anyway.'

Gazing down at her, Jamie sighed. 'You don't make it very easy for a guy, do you?'

'W-what do you mean? Easy to what?'

Piercing her heart with a twinkle of blue eyes, he said, 'Easy to get to know you.'

Debbie bit her lip as a mixture of joy and guilt swept over her. Joy, because she had liked Jamie for ages and had had no idea until now that he had even noticed her. Guilt, because Lisa had the biggest crush on him.

Still, he wasn't going out with Lisa, was he? In fact, he'd never even spoken to her, as far as Debbie knew.

'Can I walk you home?'

Forget Me Not

'Pardon?' Debbie looked him fully in the eye now, unsure if he'd actually said it or if she'd imagined it.

'I said, can I walk you home?' he repeated softly.

She felt like yelling: *Yes! Yes! Yes!* Instead, she said, 'I can't. I've got to walk with Lisa. We came together.'

Jamie pulled his head back and gave her a strange look.

'Funny . . . I wouldn't have thought she was your type.'

'What do you mean?' Debbie asked, frowning.

'I don't know.' He shrugged. 'You just seem . . . *better*, I suppose.'

'*Better*?'

'Well, I mean . . . doesn't her mum bother you?'

'Her *mum*?' Debbie said, wondering how he knew Pat. 'Not really. She's a bit moody sometimes, I suppose, but she's all right. Why?'

Jamie peered into her eyes, trying to assess if she were deliberately playing the innocent or genuinely didn't know the rumours about Lisa's mum. Judging by her confused expression, he guessed it was the latter, and felt like kicking himself.

What kind of idiot was he? He'd nearly broken rule number one: *Never slag the best friend off if you want them to think you're nice.*

'Look, I guess I'm doing this all wrong,' he said. 'I'm not trying to diss your mate, honest I'm not. It's just that . . . Oh, shit!' He slapped a palm to his brow, grinning sheepishly. 'How's about we get off this subject and talk about us instead?'

'*Us*?'

'Yeah, us – me and you. I really like you, you know. Have done for ages.'

'Have you?'

'Yeah. So what do you say?'

'About what?'

'*Us!*'

Debbie gave a helpless shrug. 'I, er, don't know what you want me to say.'

'How about yes?' he said quietly, moving towards her.

'Yes to what?'

'To this . . .'

Pulling her gently towards him, he kissed her, softly at first, then harder as he felt her resistance give way.

Skidding to a halt just a few feet away, Steve almost knocked Andy flat on his back by flinging a stiff arm across his chest. They had been about to haul Jamie away to come and see if the rumour that Linda Parry and Zoë Clayton were scrapping over Steve in the loo was true but, seeing that Jamie was otherwise engaged, Steve decided not to disturb him.

'Leave 'em to it,' he said, pushing Andy towards the door. 'We'll tell him later.'

In the girls' toilets, the fight was well under way. Linda, who was by far the harder of the two, was winning hands down. Egged on by the shouts of encouragement from the girls who'd managed to squeeze themselves into the small space – the loudest coming from her best friend, Jasmine Kelly, who'd arrived just in time for the kick-off – she dragged Zoë down to the floor by her hair, then jumped on top of her and set about bouncing her head off the piss-wet tiles, screaming at her the whole time that this was what she got for messing about with other girls' men.

Crying hysterically, Zoë begged her to stop. She swore she hadn't known that Steve was Linda's boyfriend and promised she'd never look at him again. But nothing she said made any difference, because Steve wasn't the real reason behind the vicious attack – any more than he was really Linda's boyfriend.

Linda *wanted* to beat her up, it was as simple as that. Zoë was everything Linda wasn't, and Linda loathed her for it. Not only a natural blonde, Zoë was also slim, pretty and feminine. And she had something Linda would never have: the ability to make boys *want* to be with her without having to give them something in return.

Standing guard at the door, Lisa was almost sent flying into the thick of the action when someone suddenly shoved at it from the outside. Calling another girl to come and help her hold it shut, she shouted through to whoever it was that they couldn't come in.

'It's me and Andy,' Steve called back. 'Let us in!'

'Get lost!' she hissed. 'You'll have the bouncers onto us!'

'Come out and tell us what's goin' on, then.'

Realizing that he wasn't going to give up, she said, 'All right! But you'd better back off, or you'll land us all in it.'

Waiting until she'd heard them move away, Lisa slipped out, pulling the door to behind her. Steve and Andy were waiting for her by the entrance.

'What's going on?' Steve demanded with a huge grin. 'They really scrapping over me?'

'Like you don't know,' she retorted sourly.

'Oh, *yes*!' he crowed and, turning to Andy, held his palm up for a high-five. 'Who da man?'

'You da man!'

'Ah said *who* da man?'

'An' ah said *you* da man!'

Watching them, Lisa almost laughed but stopped herself. She didn't want these idiots to think she found them amusing.

'You want to be ashamed, you pair of plebs!' she said instead.

'Fuck that!' Steve snorted, thoroughly pleased with himself. 'So come on, then . . . who's winning?'

'Who do *you* think?' Giving him a withering look, she folded her arms and glanced casually around the corridor. 'Where's Jamie?' she asked after a moment.

'How should I know?' Shrugging, Steve pushed the door open. 'Coming for a fag, And?'

'He's not gone, has he?' she called as they made their way outside.

Turning back, Andy grinned nastily and said, 'Ask your mate!'

'And tell them two in there there's a shag in it for the winner while you're at it!' Steve said.

Ignoring him, Lisa shouted, 'What you talking about, Andy? Ask me mate what? Which mate?'

'That Debbie,' Andy said, trotting backwards now. 'The one whose neck he's got his tongue down!'

Lisa felt the blood drain from her face. It wasn't true! He had to be winding her up?

But there was only one way to find out.

Marching back to the main hall, she barged through the door and scanned the room. Suddenly, the music faded to nothing, and the lights merged into one giant, rainbow-coloured spotlight shining directly down onto Debbie and Jamie . . . The only two people in the room . . . In the world!

Debbie, the two-faced, back-stabbing bitch . . . Kissing Jamie!

Oblivious to the despair she was causing her best friend, Debbie broke away from Jamie's lips and leaned her hot face against his chest.

Four times they had kissed – each one better than the last. She couldn't believe it was happening.

Opening her eyes at last, her euphoria dissolved as a shard of ice slithered down her spine.

Lisa was staring at them from across the room. She'd seen them!

'Oh, *God*,' Debbie groaned.

'What's wrong?' Pulling his head back, Jamie looked down at her and frowned when he saw how pale she was. 'I haven't upset you, have I?'

'No, it's not you,' she said, pulling herself from his arms. 'It's just . . . you've got to go!'

'Didn't you like it?'

'It's not *you*,' she said again, shaking with guilt and apprehension as Lisa made her way towards them. 'Look, I can't explain right now – can you just go, please?'

Jamie took a step back. 'You're sure it's not me?'

'No, I swear it's not!' she insisted, panicking now. 'Just *go*, will you?'

'All right.' He backed off with his hands up. 'But I'll see you in school tomorrow, yeah?'

'Yes, okay!' She was practically pushing him now.

Lisa reached Debbie just seconds after Jamie had gone. 'You *bitch*!' she cried. 'How *could* you?'

Reaching out to her, Debbie said, 'Lisa, please . . .'

'Don't "*please*" me, you slag!' Slapping Debbie's hand away, Lisa glared at her. 'You're supposed to be my friend, so how could you get off with me fella like that?'

Debbie frowned. 'Aw, come on, Lisa, he's not *your* fella. And I didn't get off with him, he came to me and—'

'Save it!' Lisa spat, swiping at a rogue tear with the back of her hand. 'You know what? If you wasn't me best mate, I'd kick your bleedin' head in for what you've just done!'

'But I haven't *done* anything!'

'And I still *might* if you don't shut it!' With a last furious glare, Lisa turned on her heel and marched away.

'Lisa,' Debbie called after her. 'Wait, please . . .'

'Get stuffed, slag!' Sticking a finger high in the air, Lisa pushed her way through the dancers and dragged her coat out from under the chairs.

She ran outside then, not stopping until she was around the corner out of everybody's sight. Leaning her face against the wall, she finally let loose the tears that were choking her.

'Oi! What you skriking about, nappy butt?'

Jumping at the sound of Andy Green's jeering voice, Lisa gulped back the sobs still flooding her throat and quickly wiped her eyes on her sleeve. She'd forgotten they'd come outside for a smoke – hadn't noticed them lounging against the wall just feet away.

'Yo!' Steve said when she didn't answer. 'We're talking to you. What's up with you?'

'Nothing!'

'Don't give me that shite!'

'Get stuffed!'

'Charming!' Andy said, spluttering with laughter.

'Here,' said Steve, nudging Andy to shush. 'Come here a minute.'

'What?' Lisa sniffed, cursing herself for showing herself up in front of these morons.

'Come here and I'll tell you.'

'Oh, get lost!'

Still shaking, she reached into her pocket for her cigarettes. Realizing that they weren't there, she kicked out at the wall in frustration. Steve and Andy burst out laughing.

Turning on them furiously, she screeched, 'Someone's nicked me fags, all right? I don't see what's so funny about that!'

'Y' give me joke, man!' Andy jeered in a passable Jamaican accent. 'Ro-ad rage!'

'Anyhow, never mind that,' Steve said. 'Who won?'

'Won what?' Lisa grunted sullenly.

'The *fight*, you thick bitch!'

'How the fuck should *I* know?' she barked. 'Stupid pair of cows anyway, if you ask me, fighting over a tosser like you!'

'*Oooohhh! Bitchy!*'

'Aw, just go and die!' Lisa said and, pushing herself away from the wall, began to walk off.

'Here, don't go,' Steve called after her. 'We was only havin' a laugh. Come here, we'll give you a fag.'

'Yeah, we'll *give* you one,' Andy joined in, sniggering.

Lisa stopped in her tracks – her need for a cigarette greater than her need to escape these idiots. Turning back, she said, 'You gonna stop taking the piss, then?'

Steve gave her a sincere look. 'Yeah, course. We're sorry. Here you go. Come on . . . Take it.'

Still sniffing, she went towards him, reaching for the cigarette he was holding out.

Dangling the bait, Steve slowly backed up into a deep recess.

'You'll have to come in here for a light,' he said, sparking his lighter. 'It's too windy out there.'

Stepping into the recess after him, Lisa took the cigarette and leaned in towards the flame. Instantly, Andy was behind her, his breath hot on her neck as he tried to stick his hand up her skirt.

'Oi!' she yelped, twisting around to shove him off. 'What's your game?'

'*We* ain't got one,' he said, giving her an ugly sneer as he herded her back against the wall. 'But we know all about *yours*, don't we, Steve?'

'We sure do,' Steve agreed, closing in from the side with an evil look in his eyes. 'Bet your mum's got you well trained up, eh, Lisa? Shown you how to give head, has she? Told you the going rates, and that?'

'Not that *we*'d have to pay for it,' Andy added nastily. 'She'd give us a freebie – couple of studs like us!'

Pushing out at them, Lisa said, 'What you on about, you pair of dickheads?'

Steve grinned menacingly. 'Aw, come on, don't play

the innocent! We know all about your mum, don't we, Andy?'

'Too right!' Andy sneered. 'How *is* Pat the fat twat, anyway?'

Lisa felt the anger churn up in her stomach.

'Don't you *dare* talk about my mum like that, you pair of filthy bastards!' she hissed.

Steve laughed out loud. 'That's rich coming from a slag like you!'

'Yeah,' Andy agreed. 'You're a proper slag, you, ain't you, Lisa? Gonna give us a gobble for that fag, then?'

'Get off me!' Lisa squealed, struggling to hold them back as they advanced on her, their hands groping and grabbing at anything and everything. She was on the verge of screaming when Andy was suddenly wrenched backwards through the air.

'Oi! What you playin' at?' he yelped, thrashing wildly to free himself from whoever had a grip on his jacket. When he realized he couldn't get away, he yelled, 'Steve . . . get him off me, man!'

Still holding Lisa by the arm, Steve looked at the man who had Andy by the throat now. Bigger than both Steve and Andy, he completely blocked out the faint light coming from the lamp at the end of the alley, making it impossible to see anything of his face but the piercing malevolence of his eyes. Steve instinctively didn't want to get into anything with him, but knew he had to say something before he strangled Andy.

'Hang about, mate,' he managed. 'Don't be doing that!'

'Don't call me *mate*,' the man hissed, and something in the low quietness of his voice assured Steve that he wasn't messing about when he went on to say: 'Now let her go, or I'll have to hurt your little *friend*.'

Doing as he was told, Steve dropped Lisa's arm and stepped back, holding up his hands in a gesture of surrender.

'All right, calm down. We was only messing about . . . Tell him, Lisa.'

'Lisha,' Andy gurgled, flapping his hands feebly against the steely arm constricting his throat. 'Pleash . . . Tell 'im y' know ush!'

They all looked at Lisa then, waiting for her to condemn or confirm. Eventually, she nodded.

'Yeah, I know them, it's all right.'

Andy was dropped as suddenly as he'd been grabbed. Rubbing at his throat, he gave the man a baleful glare.

'There was no need for that, man! I could have the law on you for that!'

Flicking him a warning glance, Steve said, 'Shut it, Andy.'

The man looked at each of the boys in turn – turning their knees to water with the dark intensity of his eyes. Rooted to the spot with fear, they didn't dare move until, suddenly, he dismissed them with a flick of his head.

'Go! *Now*, before I change my mind!'

With more sense than either had displayed all night, they sidestepped him and rushed away. But Andy couldn't resist turning back when they reached the youth club door. Brave at a distance, he yelled: 'We'll have you for that! *Wankeeeer*!'

The man made to lunge after them and smirked with satisfaction when they nearly fell over themselves in their haste to get inside. Turning back to Lisa, who was still in the recess, nervously biting her nails now, he asked if they had hurt her.

She shook her head. 'No, they was just messing about.'

'So why have you been crying?' he asked, peering down at her.

'I haven't,' she lied, embarrassed by his scrutiny. 'I'm all right.'

In a gentler tone, he said, 'I don't believe you. Tell the truth.'

Lisa shrugged, unsure how to handle this. She didn't want to tell her problems to this stranger. And she didn't like the way he was making her feel vulnerable as, in no apparent hurry to unblock her path, he gazed down at her, patiently waiting for an answer to his question.

'All right, I was,' she admitted at last. 'But not about them. They was just winding me up.'

'What was it, then?' Still looking down at her, the man took out a twenty-pack of Benson and Hedges and lit one, blowing the smoke out above her head.

In the momentary flare of the lighter, Lisa saw that he was wearing gloves – black leather to match his jacket. Her heart began to thud against her ribs.

Oh, God! Please don't let him hurt me!

'Well?'

His question had been softly spoken, but Lisa jumped as though she'd been cattle-prodded.

'It was n-nothing really,' she stammered. 'Just something me so-called m-mate did.'

'I see,' he murmured. Then, as if realizing that he was making her nervous, he added kindly: 'Don't worry. I'm not going to hurt you.'

Lisa stared at him for a moment, then slowly relaxed.

Surely if he was going to do anything, he'd have done it by now?

The man smiled when he saw the tension leaving her shoulders. Remembering his manners, he held out the cigarettes to her.

'Smoke?'

'Thanks.'

Holding the lighter towards her, he said, 'So, this friend of yours? What did she do to upset you?'

Inhaling deeply, Lisa blew a fierce stream of smoke out – barely noticing that he had begun to walk out of the recess and that she had begun to follow.

'She got off with my fella,' she told him.

Stopping at the entrance to the alley, the man leaned back against the wall, casually crossing his legs at the ankle as he regarded her, one eyebrow raised.

'She stole your boyfriend?'

'Yeah.' Lisa felt the blush colour her cheeks as the lie tumbled from her lips. 'Well, no, not exactly,' she admitted. 'But she knew I liked him!'

'Ah, I see,' he murmured understandingly. Then: 'How old are you, Lisa?'

The fear she'd felt in the recess returned with a vengeance the instant he said her name. *How the* hell *did he know that?*

'What's the matter?' he asked, his voice gently mocking. 'Have I frightened you again?'

'How . . . how did you know my name?' she demanded with as much courage as she could muster.

Chuckling softly, he shook his head. 'Calm down. Those boys said it when I rescued you. Remember?'

Remembering, Lisa nodded mutely. She felt ridiculous. How could she have thought he meant to hurt her when he'd gone to the trouble of helping her out in the first place?

'Sorry,' she mumbled. 'I'm just a bit freaked out.'

Smiling softly, he said, 'You don't have to apologize, Lisa. You don't know me, and if you weren't suspicious I'd think you were stupid. But I guess it's safe to assume you're not.'

'Thanks.' Pleased by the compliment, Lisa returned the smile.

'No problem,' he murmured, putting his head back to release his smoke into the air.

Lisa gave a tiny, involuntary gasp as the light fell fully on his face. He was absolutely gorgeous! A million times nicer than Jamie the two-timing bastard could ever hope to be!

As dark as Jamie was fair, the man had long, black eyelashes framing his sultry eyes, and equally black hair that rested on the collar of his jacket and gleamed like jet. His nose was perfectly shaped, and his lips were neither too full nor too thin.

Lisa thought he looked like a god. And that he appeared to be about twenty certainly added to the appeal.

Me with a gorgeous older man! Debbie will shit a brick!

As if deciding that he'd given her enough time to become captivated, the man flipped his finished cigarette onto the floor and pushed himself away from the wall.

'I'll walk you home if you like?'

Lisa was startled – and more than a little tempted by the unexpected offer. If she could spend just one hour gazing at his gorgeous face she would die happy.

Then she remembered that she'd promised to stay out late – and her mum wouldn't appreciate being disturbed on the job. But maybe if it wasn't too early . . .

'What time it is?' she asked.

The man pulled his sleeve back and checked his watch.

'Quarter to nine.'

'Oh.' Disappointed, she sank back down onto the wall. 'No, it's all right. I'd better just wait for Debbie. You go, though, if you want. I'll be fine.'

'Debbie? . . . Your "so-called friend"?'

'Yeah.'

'And you're going to *wait* for her?' He arched an eyebrow again.

Lisa shrugged. 'I should, really. She's dead soft. She'll get well scared on her tod.'

'Whereas you aren't scared of anything, I suppose?'

'I do all right.'

'You didn't look all right when I found you,' the man said. 'What if those lads come back?'

'I doubt that!' Lisa grinned. 'You scared the shit out of 'em!'

Sensing a flicker of disapproval, she muttered an apology. The man accepted it with a nod, then told her that the offer to walk her home was still open. But before she could answer, the youth club door opened. For a moment loud music flooded out, and then it was quiet again.

Turning to check who had come out, Lisa saw that it was Debbie – alone, which cheered her up no end. But when she noticed how forlorn Debbie looked standing on the deserted pavement glancing both ways up and down the road, she felt a sudden desire to rush over to her and make up for the fight.

'Debbie, I presume?'

Turning when the man spoke, Lisa nodded sheepishly.

'So what's it to be?' he asked, as if sensing what she'd been thinking. 'Do you go to her, or come with me?'

Lisa dithered a moment too long. When she looked back, Debbie had gone.

'Guess that's decided it for you,' he said, heading into the alley with the absolute confidence of one who knows he'll be followed. 'At least you'll be safe with me.'

Catching up with him as he turned out of the alley onto the road, Lisa said, 'You didn't tell me your name?'

Smiling to himself, the man studied the cigarettes in his hand as if contemplating whether or not to tell her.

'You know mine,' she persisted. 'It's only fair.'

'True,' he agreed, inclining his head slightly. 'All right, it's Benny.'

'*Benny*?' she snorted.

Giving her an amused side-glance, he said, 'Oh, you find that funny, do you?'

She grinned back at him cheekily. 'No, not funny. Just a bit . . . well . . . *gimpy*!'

'*Gimpy*?'

'Yeah, you know. A bit daft, like.'

'Ah . . . I see.' Smiling, he continued on his way.

And Lisa walked beside him in silence, paying no heed now to the icy wind that was eating at her bare legs. It just felt so nice to be with this man who had taken the time to protect her and talk to her.

When he walked straight past the turn-off they should

have taken, she reached out and tapped him on the arm, blushing as a tingle ran through her fingers.

'We're going the wrong way,' she told him shyly. 'It's that way.' She pointed across the road. 'I cut through behind the church and go up Chester Road. My house is just through the park on the estate.'

'Whereabouts?' he asked.

'Southern Ave,' she said, adding with a giggle: 'Me and cow-bag *both* live there – on the second floor.'

'Ah,' he said. 'The maisonettes?'

'Yeah.'

Raising an eyebrow, he said, 'Posh, eh?' Then, smiling his half-smile as Lisa puffed up with pride, he said, 'Off we go, then.'

As Benny set off again, Lisa had to half skip, half run to keep up with his long stride. But she didn't care. He'd asked where she lived. He must like her to want to know that. And he'd said it was posh. He must be well impressed with her now.

5

S am climaxed with a loud, prolonged grunt. When the spasmodic seed-pumping had stopped, he flopped onto his back like a marooned whale, his breathing heavy and noisy in the dark.

More than a little irritated, Pat reached out and switched on the lamp. Glancing at the clock, she was further annoyed to see that it was now almost nine o'clock. Forty minutes it had taken to get him going after their little 'disagreement'. And *then* she'd had to endure another twenty minutes of him humping away at her. Precisely fifty-eight minutes too long, in her opinion!

Snatching up her cigarettes, she lit one and pulled on it hard.

Sensing her mood and misinterpreting it, Sam grinned sheepishly. 'I'm sorry, but I did tell you I was in a hurry.'

Annoyed more by this than his taking too long, Pat snorted angrily. 'Yeah, yeah! The great bloody anniversary dinner! How *could* I forget?'

Pulling herself upright in the bed, she studied her nails, then began to chew them. She wasn't sure why being reminded of his anniversary had made her so angry, but that was exactly how she felt – angry and cheated. And not because the sex had been so naff – the shorter and naffer the better, as far as she was concerned. It was more the knowledge that she was just a stopgap.

She knew it was ridiculous, given her line of work, but she couldn't help it. Sam was the only punter she had ever allowed into her home – her bed. And what did he do to repay this special privilege? He treated her like she didn't matter – pushed her to one side to keep his spoilt bitch of a wife happy! God, she hated that!

Chewing even harder, Pat scolded herself for feeling this way. She must be going soft in the head, letting a *man* get to her! Then a far more horrifying thought struck her. Maybe she really *was* getting old? Maybe her knackered old body was telling her it wanted to settle down? Shuddering at the very idea, she wrenched half a nail free and spat it out onto the quilt.

'I wish you wouldn't do that!' Pushing the quilt back, Sam heaved his bulky body up and dropped his feet down to the floor. 'It's disgusting, and very unhygienic.'

'*And* . . . ?' she challenged, biting even more exaggeratedly. 'So's farting, but I don't complain when you're letting rip all over the show, do I?'

Peering down at her livid face, Sam frowned. 'Have I done something to upset you, Patricia?'

'Nothing you need worry yourself about, *Samir*!'

'Oh, I hate it when you're annoyed,' he whined. 'I can't help it if—'

Interrupting angrily, Pat said, 'If you've got more important things to do? Well, don't let me keep you. I'm sure Mrs Frigid is climbing the walls by now. Off you go, there's a good boy!'

'Don't talk about my wife like that!' Sam snapped.

'She's a fine woman, and any problems she may or may not have are none of your business!'

'The only problem she's got is you!' Pat retorted, hauling the quilt up to cover her breasts. 'She's got to be a fucking moron if she don't know what you're up to. No wonder she's all dried up like an old Weetabix!'

Sam shook his head, regretting that he'd ever discussed Elsa's lack of sexual interest with Pat.

'What I choose to do in my spare time has nothing to do with Elsa's . . . *women's* things,' he said primly. 'I thought *you* of all people would understand that.'

Pat glared at him. 'I'm nowhere near the big M, matey, and don't you forget it! Anyhow, that's just an excuse, that is. Something women like *her* pull to keep blokes like you from laying their grubby paws on 'em!'

Sam gave her a hurt look. 'You can be very cutting sometimes, Patricia. Exactly what have I done to deserve this?'

'It's what you *haven't* done,' she sniped. 'Shit sex is bad enough, but you're just a joker, you!'

'*Why*?' He held his hands out in a gesture of confusion.

'All right, I'll spell it out for you, shall I? Seeing as you're too thick to work it out for yourself! First off, you turn up when it ain't your night—'

'I thought you'd be pleased to see me!' he interrupted miserably.

'*Stopping* me,' she carried on regardless, 'from going out and finding a decent punter. Then you tell me you're fucking off early, so I can't even make a good wedge on you! And *then* you've got the nerve to tell me you ain't even coming when you're *supposed* to!'

'But I'm here now,' he said, a confused frown creasing his brow. 'What difference does it make?'

'The difference is, *mate*,' she snarled, balling her hand into a fist and slamming it down on her thigh, 'that if I'd known you weren't coming tomorrow I'd have fixed myself up with another punter!'

Sam's face darkened two shades. 'You know I don't want you to do that. Not on *my* night.'

'*Your* night?' She snorted incredulously. 'That's ripe, that is! So, let me get this right . . . You come a night early, but you still expect me to keep myself free on *your* night as well, yeah? Even though you ain't coming?'

'All right,' he snapped. 'I'll pay you for tomorrow, if that's what you want.'

'*And* tonight!'

'Yes, okay.' He hissed out a resigned sigh. 'Happy now?'

She held out her hand. 'Show me the green, and I'll let you know.'

'But I haven't got it all at the moment,' he told her indignantly. 'I wasn't exactly expecting to be paying *double*, was I?'

'But you expect *me* to wait till next week?'

'You can trust me – surely you know that by now?'

'Trust is nowt to do with it, mate! It's a question of me having to make do in the meantime. Nah, sorry.' She shook her head emphatically. 'I'm no mug! I'll just do what I've got to do.'

Sam ran his hands through his hair in exasperation. 'You know I don't like to think of you with other men. It isn't right! You should be satisfied with me.'

Smiling slyly at his display of jealousy, Pat rolled

onto her side and propped her head on her fist. In a satin-smooth voice, she said, 'So what you saying, Sam? You want to set me up somewhere nice and pay all me bills? Or maybe you want to make it proper and decent, eh? . . . You thinking what I'm thinking, Sammy boy?'

'What?' Sam didn't know where this was headed, but he didn't much like her expression or her tone of voice.

'Dump wifey and move me in, of course!' She shrugged casually. 'Makes perfect sense to me. Get moany-hole off your back for good – and sexy old me *on* mine whenever you want!'

Looking at her as if she'd grown two heads and asked him to cut one off and walk round town with his cock in its mouth, Sam squawked, 'Are you *crazy*? I can't do that! What kind of man do you think I am?'

'The kind who wants it all his own bleedin' way!' she snarled, turning instantly nasty at the rebuff. 'Mrs fucking Never-give-it-up sat up there with them spoilt brats in the lap of bleedin' luxury, while me and my Lisa are stuck in this dump waiting on your once-a-bloody-week visit! You're a joke!'

'You're being unreasonable.' Reaching for his underpants, he hauled them on. 'All this because I care about you and don't want to share you with those . . . those *filthy* men!'

'You mean you don't want no one else shagging what you see as yours!' Pat retorted angrily. 'You think you bleedin' own me, don't you? Think you've bought the exclusive rights? Well, that's where you're wrong, mate! I can shag *who* I want, *when* I want – got that!'

'Stop shouting,' Sam hissed, glancing nervously at the wall. 'Do you want your neighbour to hear?'

'I don't bleedin' *care*!' she bellowed. Then, screeching at the connecting wall behind which, she had no doubt, the old lady next door was glass-up: 'D'y' hear me, Ada bleedin'-nosy-hole Baker?'

Seconds later, someone knocked on the front door.

Leaping from the bed Pat made a dive for the window and, without looking to see who was calling, threw it open and yelled '*FUCK OOOOFFF!*' at the top of her lungs.

'That might have been Lisa!' Sam gasped, appalled by her behaviour.

'She's got a bleedin' key!' Pat snapped, hopping angrily back into bed. '*Jeezus*, Sam! What kind of mother do you think I am?'

Sam was beginning to feel ill. A thin sheen of sweat gathered along his fleshy top lip. This woman who held him captive sexually was the complete antithesis of everything he admired in his wife. Loud, rude, aggressive, dirty – oh, so dirty! Admittedly, Elsa was less than accommodating in bed, but in every other respect she was the model wife – clean, tidy, elegant, a good cook, a fabulous mother. How could this harlot ever have nurtured the notion that she might replace her?

'And where d'y' think you're going?' Pat demanded as, naked but for his Y-fronts, Sam got up and made for the door.

'To the toilet,' he told her quietly. 'And then I'm going home.'

'Not before you pay me what you owe, you're not. You know the going rate for a suck and fuck!'

At the door, Sam paused and turned back, his face reflecting his misery at her attitude.

'I really thought we were past all that?'

Staring back at him, Pat said coldly, 'If we *was* you wouldn't go down the Lane when I'm not there, picking up any old bit of tat, would you? And don't say you don't, 'cos the girls talk.'

Sam felt as guilty as if he'd been caught cheating by his wife. It was a strange sensation but, having no defence against the truth of her words, he could only shrug and grin boyishly.

Pat continued to stare at him accusingly.

'Look, okay, so sometimes I do – but it's *your* fault,' he told her defensively. 'Sometimes I look for you, but you're nowhere to be found. So what do you expect me to do? . . . Wait a week? I'm a man, for God's sake! I have needs – *rights*!'

'And what about *my* rights?' she demanded. 'My right to make a decent living for one?'

'You're a *woman*!' he retaliated – as if that explained everything.

'*So?*'

'So it's not right to do what you do!' he said, adding fiercely, 'And it's *dangerous*! There has been another murder, Patricia – on the *Lane*!' He emphasized this last with a manly glare.

Raising a defiant eyebrow, she said, '*And . . . ?*'

'And so you should stop being stubborn, take what I offer and leave it at that!'

Satisfied that he had laid down the law according to Samir Rashid, Sam trounced from the room, pulling the door sharply to behind him.

Pat waited until she'd heard him lock the bathroom door, then leaped from the bed.

She'd give him *rights*, the selfish bastard! Oh, it was fine for him to go with any old pro he felt like, but *she* was supposed to live like a bleeding nun! Well, sod that!

And sod Mrs Elsa-bloody-perfect-Rashid too!

Pat hated that woman with a passion – despite never having laid so much as an eye on her. She was the enemy, as far as Pat was concerned – all women of her type were. Giving nothing and taking everything, as if they had some divine right to riches and happiness. Sitting in their ivory towers like goddesses. Protected from the harsh realities of life, while their men screwed the very heart out of women like Pat – picking them up and dropping them back down at will, leaving them to scrape by as best they could. *Putting* them in danger, never mind saving them from it, as Sam would have her believe was his noble intent!

Well, just for once, Patricia Anne Noone was going to take action against the whole bloody lot of them. And she'd start by making that untouchable queen of Sam's wake up and smell the Nescafé!

Rooting through the heap of clothes she'd pushed onto the floor when she'd brought Sam upstairs, she quickly found what she was looking for. Peeling the minuscule, slightly soiled G-string panties from the tights she'd been wearing earlier, she looked around for Sam's suit jacket.

She'd like to see him explain this one away!

She was back in bed, casually blowing smoke rings, when Sam finished his fifteen-minute washing ritual and came back to the bedroom. He looked at her questioningly and was relieved when she smiled at him.

Forget Me Not

Sitting down on the side of the bed, he said, 'I don't want to fight, Patricia. But you do understand why I can't come tomorrow, don't you?'

Still smiling, she replied, 'Not really, but I'll have to accept it, won't I?'

Patting her hand in a grotesquely fatherly fashion, he said, 'Good girl. Now just promise you won't go out looking for men, and I'll leave happy?' Smiling, he looked down at her expectantly.

'Just make sure you pay, and we're sweet,' she replied.

'Next week, I promise.' With another fatherly caress, Sam stood up and began to get dressed – whistling to himself now that the storm was over.

Benny, too, was whistling – a low, sweet melody that Lisa didn't recognize but thought really nice.

They had been walking for a while now, in companionable silence but for the whistling. Lisa glanced up at him every now and then, drinking in his profile, committing his image to memory for future fantasies. She was fascinated by the way he frequently clenched his cheek muscles. And the way he narrowed his eyes as if he was thinking deep, secret thoughts. She blushed when he suddenly turned and gave her a knowing smile.

'You never answered my question,' he said.

'Which one?'

'I asked how old you are.'

'Oh, that.' Grinning, she cocked her head to the side. 'Guess?'

After a moment's appraisal, he said, 'Sixteen?'

Lisa's face split into a wide smile. 'You really think so?'

Smiling himself now, Benny said, 'Now don't tell me you're *older*?'

'Wow!' she squeaked, flooded with pride. 'You really think I look that old?'

'Yeah. Sixteen – maybe even seventeen, at a push. Am I right?'

Grinning with delight, she said, 'I'm nowhere near! I'm only twelve.'

He gave her a disbelieving look. '*Never*!'

'I am!' she insisted, adding quickly, 'But I'll be thirteen in a few weeks.'

He shook his head. 'Well, I never would have guessed. You're very grown-up, aren't you?'

Lisa pulled herself up to her full four feet eleven, feeling for the first time in her life like a real woman. She was so glad she'd decided to wear her sexy clothes tonight. Debbie wouldn't have stood a chance with him the way *she* was dressed. All *she*'d have needed was a hat and scarf and Benny would have thought she was his granny! But obviously Lisa looked hot, or he wouldn't have wanted to spend time with her, would he? So much so, in fact, that he'd taken a much longer route than she normally took!

Watching from the corner of his eye, Benny smiled to himself. She looked so proud of herself, and all because he'd said she looked older than he'd known her to be all along. He found it incredible how these young girls just couldn't wait to add on the years – and how quickly they tried to reverse the process when they reached the cherished goal.

Turning onto Chester Road, Lisa saw the lighted *Fish and Chips* sign halfway down the block of otherwise darkened shop units. Embarrassed by a sudden loud rumbling in her stomach, she hugged herself tightly, wishing that she had bothered to eat before coming out tonight.

'Fancy a bag?' Benny asked.

Fingering the coins in her pocket (she didn't want to count it out in front of him and look like a tramp if she didn't have enough) she felt a twenty-pence piece, a couple of tens and a five. The rest was copper. She didn't even have enough for a small bag of chips.

Shaking her head, she said, 'Nah. I'm not really hungry.'

By now, Benny had stepped into a doorway to light a cigarette. Taking a pound coin from his pocket, he held it out to her.

'Well, I'm starving. But I can't stand going into chippies – I hate the smell of vinegar. Would you get me a bag, please? Just salt.'

'Yeah, sure.' Taking the money, Lisa ran to the chip shop, glad to be doing something for the new love of her life – even though she knew she'd suffer when he ate the chips in front of her. She just hoped her belly would stay quiet.

Coming out a few minutes later she ran back to the doorway, but Benny had disappeared. Stepping back, she turned in circles looking all around the deserted road. He was nowhere to be seen.

Shoulders drooping with disappointment, she looked down at the neatly wrapped chips in her hand and realized that he had tricked her. He'd probably been scared off when she told him how old she was and had used the chippy as a means of escape.

Sighing heavily, Lisa set off towards the park. She felt very alone now without Benny's presence, but at least she didn't have too far to go. Only problem was, once she got home she'd have to sit outside till Sam left – and that was bound to be ages yet.

Shivering at the prospect of sitting on the cold wall for God only knew how long, she hugged the warm chips against her stomach and cursed herself for wearing skimpy clothes.

'Stupid cow!' she muttered through chattering teeth. Then: 'Fuckin' bitch!' This was aimed at Debbie, whose fault it obviously was for ruining a good night out in the first place.

Halfway through the park, she decided she might as well eat the chips seeing as Benny had deserted her. Popping one into her mouth, she groaned with pleasure. It was deliciously greasy and hot, warming her entire body as it slid down into her stomach.

Smiling now, she said, 'Thanks, Benny.'

Debbie had almost shit a brick when Lisa's mum had shouted at her through the window, and couldn't have run away any faster if she had been being chased by a machete-wielding maniac! She just thanked her lucky stars the woman had been in her bedroom and not right by the front door. She dreaded to think what would have happened if Pat had been downstairs!

Back in the safety of her own home now, Debbie was still shaking like a leaf, and finding it hard to convince her own mum that she was perfectly all right.

'For the fourth time, Mum, I am *fine*. Stop fussing, will you? I'm just tired, that's all.' Backing out of the living room, she said a final goodnight and closed the door firmly on her mum's concerned face.

Running up the stairs, longing for the sanctuary of her bedroom, she closed her door and turned the lamp on. Undressing quickly, she folded her clothes into a neat pile, then pulled her nightdress on over her head. As the faint strains of the *Crimewatch* theme music drifted up from down below, Debbie thought it was no wonder her mum had thought there was something wrong. It was still only nine-thirty, and she'd said she'd be at the disco until ten. Even when she stayed home, she never went to bed this early.

Switching off the lamp when she'd finished, she sat on the bed and looked out of the window, praying that Lisa wasn't home already – that she hadn't already told her mum what Debbie had done to her, and that that wasn't the reason Pat had shouted.

Why, oh why did I let Jamie kiss me like that?

Even though she knew how much shit she was going to cop for what she'd done tonight, just the thought of Jamie caused a warm glow to spread through her traitorous stomach.

Did he really say he'd liked me for ages?

Did he really kiss me four times?

Yes, he did! She could still feel his soft lips on hers – could still smell the Lynx.

Could still feel the shock of seeing Lisa staring straight at her.

And she had seen everything, so there was no point trying to deny it. Poor Lisa . . .

Poor me! Debbie thought bitterly. *Why* shouldn't *I go out with Jamie? He asked me*, not *her. He'd have asked* her *if he wanted her.*

Still, it didn't excuse what she'd done, and Debbie

knew that. No matter what, you were *not* supposed to go after the lad your mate fancied. And Lisa had fancied Jamie like mad for ages.

Racked with guilt, she dropped her chin onto her arms and resumed her scanning of the road below. But Lisa was nowhere to be seen, and after a few minutes she gave up. Closing the curtains, she switched the lamp back on and made a decision.

There was only one thing to do if she ever wanted Lisa to speak to her again. She'd have to tell Jamie it was off.

Not that it was ever really on, but it could have been really nice.

As the sharp sting of tears built up behind her eyes, Debbie reached beneath the mattress and pulled out her secret diary. Tomorrow, she would go and make things right with Lisa. But tonight, she would write down every detail of her brief time with Jamie so that she'd never forget how nice it had felt. With tears dripping onto the back of her hand, she began to write.

Jamie kissed me at the youth club and it was fantastic! I love him so much, but . . .

Letting himself out of Pat's block, Sam hurried across to his car, deactivating the alarm and the central-locking system with the key-fob remote as he neared it.

Climbing in, he felt himself relaxing immediately – a combination of the warm leather smell he so loved, the subtle quality of the expensive CD player compared to Pat's cheap stereo, and the soothing red glow of the dash-board clock showing nine thirty-five p.m. It was only a little later than he'd promised. Elsa would understand.

Smiling down at the flowers on the seat beside him – the stem-ends of the bouquet encased in a sealed pod of preservative the florist had kindly supplied – he started the engine and pulled smoothly out onto City Road.

Fifteen minutes and he'd be home. A nice hot shower was in order, followed by a glorious meal, a few glasses of excellent wine, and a nice big – and spotlessly clean – bed. Bliss!

Seeing the tail lights of Sam's fancy car disappearing around the corner as she emerged from the park, Lisa almost cheered. She'd never been so glad in her entire life to see him go. It wasn't that she hated him, as such – nor particularly liked him, either – but it was a pain in the arse having to hang around outside while he screwed her mum.

Flinging the last of the chips to the floor, she ran the rest of the way up the road and wrenched open the heavy door at Debbie's end of the block. Running up the stairs – tiring to a near-crawl before she reached the top – she opened the landing door wide, then gave it a good hard yank as she passed through it. As it slammed back into place behind her she imagined Debbie and her mum jumping out of their skins with shock inside their house. Smiling nastily, she stuck her fingers up as she passed their kitchen window.

'Mum?' Lisa shouted, going quickly into her own house. 'You still up?'

Popping her head into the living room, she saw that the TV was still on – volume down. Switching it off, she went back into the hall and called up the stairs.

'Mum? . . . You in bed?'

Behind her, Monty whimpered and scratched at the kitchen door. Letting him loose, she went up to her mum's bedroom. Peeping in, she saw the empty bed and wondered for a moment whether her mum had actually been back at all. Then Monty nudged the back of her thigh with his snout, and she remembered pawning him off on her mum earlier. He was here now, so her mum must have been too. She'd probably gone out with Sam.

Satisfied that her mum was safe, Lisa closed the door and went to her own room. Undressing quickly in the icy air, she leaped into bed, calling Monty to come and share his warmth with her.

Within minutes, she'd fallen into a deep, dream-filled sleep.

Pat, who had missed Lisa by seconds, having left from their end of the block as Lisa was entering at Debbie's, was at that moment stalking furiously through the park, cursing Sam with every step.

He was a bastard! A low-life, cheating, *cheap* bastard!

Not only had he managed to oil his way out of paying the two nights' money tonight, he'd also conveniently *forgotten* to leave tonight's. And since she'd given Lisa her last fiver, banking on Sam's usually generous 'tip', she now didn't have a brass farthing to see them through the rest of the week.

Emerging from the park, she clopped noisily along the street with her hands swinging beside her in balled fists and her shoulders rigid – defying anyone to come out and complain about the noise her heels were making. If anyone was foolish enough to try it on with her tonight, they would get what Sam deserved!

Bastard!

So much for him saying he wanted her all to himself. He'd left her with no option but to go out and find a punter, even though it was the last thing she'd wanted to be doing tonight. She had changed into indoor night-mode gear for that fat, slimy Arab git, and certainly hadn't expected to have to dress up to go out again.

Inconsiderate to the max!

Pat stomped all the way down Chester Road, not even pausing for breath until she reached the traffic lights at the Mancunian Way roundabout. Stopping there, she looked around and tried to decide which direction would be best to go. There was no point going down the Lane – it had been dead enough earlier, but it'd be riddled with rigor mortis by now! So she had three options: Regent Road to the left, the flyover to the right, or straight ahead to Deansgate.

Regent Road led to the M62. You could get good pickings there, but there was always the risk that some nutter would cart you off to Blackpool or some other godforsaken shite-hole and dump you on your arse for a laugh.

If she took the flyover, she'd end up with the psycho bitches behind Piccadilly station. Again, good pickings, but too much hassle to make it worthwhile. You could be flush one minute, with a couple of ton stashed down your bra. The next, some cunt's jumped you and you're staggering to hospital to get your face sewn back on – without so much as a penny left on you to catch a bus home! And hard as Pat was, even she didn't rate her chances against a knife.

Deansgate was best – especially since the recent boom in wine bars. The only drawback was that you had to spend all your time dodging the police, who also seemed to have got it into their heads that Deansgate was the place to be after nine p.m. Still, if you could get past them, you were guaranteed at least a couple of punters. There was no end of lonely, bulging-walleted men down Deansgate at night. They seemed to gravitate to the wine bars like lemmings – searching for a decent woman to call their own, but somehow only ever managing to pick up tarts like Pat.

Having decided, Pat was about to set off when she heard a car coming up behind her. Sticking her chest out, she turned and bent low to smile at the driver – a white-moustached old man with a curved spine. He glanced at her fleetingly as he sailed past, his gnarly hands gripping the wheel at exactly the right ten-to-two position all old duffers seemed to adhere to for grim death.

Seeing him looking back at her in the rear-view mirror, his eyes gleaming with both disgust and fascination, Pat stuck her fingers up angrily. This hypocritical longing/loathing scenario pissed her off even more than Sam's possessive/non-committing nonsense.

She was luckier with the next car. It went by but then stopped just a few yards ahead. Seeing the driver leaning across the seats to unlock the passenger door, she plastered the professional smile back on her face and trotted towards it – making a mental note of the licence plate as she went.

Not that it would help if anything happened, but it made her feel safer somehow.

'Business, darlin'?' she cooed, looking in through the now-open door.

The driver nodded, his face almost indistinguishable in the dark interior. Pat climbed in, her intuition telling her that he was non-threatening. She was immediately grateful for the blast of warm air fanning out from the heater vents as the driver eased away from the kerb.

Relaxing as she thawed, she did a quick scan of the car's interior. It was classy. The upholstery felt plush and smelled clean, and the dash glowed with a bank of muted lights, at the centre of which was an expensive CD system. She was impressed. And the bloke wasn't too bad-looking, either, which was always a bonus. A bit younger than she liked, but she was sure she'd be able to cope with him if anything kicked off.

You always had to be wary with the young ones, as Pat had discovered to her cost on more than one occasion. They had more hang-ups than the older blokes. The worst were the ones whose sweet little wives wouldn't give them what they really wanted – low-down dirty sex. And it was amazing how many went on the hunt before the honeymoon was officially over. They'd drive around with their insistent hard-ons, pick up a tart and do the deed, then go on a guilt trip about the bride back home and start cutting up rough.

Pat had learned the hard way. But a lesson learned like that was a lesson never forgotten, and she knew that a sharp, no-nonsense twist of the old bollocks in the confined space of their cars where they couldn't easily manoeuvre to retaliate usually sorted *that* little game out!

The man suddenly spoke, interrupting her thoughts as he asked politely: 'Is there some place we can go? Or do you usually do it in the car?'

Pat smiled to herself. His voice was soft, nicely modulated – and nervous. This was no aggressive beast on the hunt. It would be a doddle. And she might even get a lift home at the end.

'Whatever you want, sweetheart,' she said, settling back in her seat. 'It's your money, you choose.'

6

*H*e pressed himself back into the shadows as the magical moment arrived. Ten o'clock. Time for the teenage sluts and Lotharios to exit the noisy meat market and wend their foolish ways home.

As the crowds began to pour out onto the pavement, he peered at them intently, determined not to miss the one he had come for.

He tensed when he spotted her, the coil of excitement nestling in his gut springing to vibrant life. She was easily recognizable. So very fat, her breasts obscenely large.

At first he thought she was alone, but then another girl joined her, closely followed by three boys. They stood to the side of the doors for a while, apparently discussing what to do next. Then one of the boys left, going one way up the street as the remaining four teenagers went the other.

He waited until the road was clear before setting off after them.

He spotted them immediately he turned the corner. In no apparent hurry, they were walking slowly, laughing coarsely in response to jokes he could not hear but whose content he knew without having to guess. Filth.

Before too long, they reached their apparent destination: Alexandra Park.

A few seconds after they had climbed through a gap in

the mangled fence, he followed. Slipping silently into the shadows cast by the huge, stooped trees surrounding the dark pathways within, he crept stealthily along, parallel to the group as they headed towards the small, foul-smelling lake on the far side of the park.

At one point, he stepped on a thin dry branch and had to keep deadly still for a moment as the noise of it cracking underfoot rent the air. But the four carried on without pausing so much as a beat – far too caught up in their adventure, apparently, to register something as insignificant as a snapping twig.

As they climbed over the small, wrought-iron fence that enclosed the darkly glittering waters, he scanned the pathways to the left and right. Then, satisfied that there was no one else around, he darted across to take cover in the tangle of bushes surrounding the lake.

He could see them clearly now as they walked tentatively around the muddy slope towards a platform originally meant to accommodate the anglers who had long ago given up on it.

Easing himself down in the bushes, he settled. And waited.

'I'm not sitting there!' Linda exclaimed, wrinkling her nose in distaste at the dirty wooden shelf jutting out to the water's edge. Barely visible, overshadowed as it was by the trees and bushes behind, she felt sure it would be infested with something nasty.

'Don't sit down, Jas!' she ordered her friend then. 'We're not stopping here to get bum rot!'

'Stop whingeing!' Andy gibed. 'We come here all the time, don't we, Ste?'

Nodding, Steve sat down and patted the boards beside

him. 'It's all right, Lin, honest. Come and sit with me.'

Arms folded, Linda considered it for a moment, then gave in. 'All right. But I'm warning you now, if I catch anything I'll do you!'

'That a promise?' Steve asked, leering as he snatched at her inviting tits.

Pushing his hand away, she said, 'Oi, you! I'm not that easy! And where's this draw you promised us?'

'Give us the skins, mate,' Steve said, clicking his fingers at Andy. 'And hurry up, 'cos I want me shag.'

'And who said you're getting one?' Linda squawked indignantly.

'That was the deal.' Steve laughed. 'You won the scrap – you get the prize!'

Sitting down, Jasmine snorted softly. 'Well rates himself, don't he?'

'Mmmm,' Linda muttered. 'You can say that again.'

Grinning with the confidence of one who knew he was getting his rocks off come what might, Steve rolled his spliff.

Shuffling across the boards to sit beside Jasmine, Andy said, 'So, what we gonna do while they're at it? You wouldn't sit here and see me deprived, would you?'

'I'd sit here and see you drowned!' she retorted sharply.

Steve laughed. 'Yeah, that's right, Jas! You tell 'im!'

'What the fuck was that?' Linda squealed as something splashed in the water just inches from the platform. Pulling her feet up to her backside, she peered at the dark ripples as they gently lapped against the wood, then subsided.

'It's probably a rat,' Andy said, picking up a stone and hurling it into the lake. 'There's loads of the fuckers down here at night.'

'*Rats?*' Linda and Jasmine squawked in unison, scrambling to their feet.

Kicking Andy in the leg, Linda said, 'Why the fuck didn't you tell us, you dozy bastard?'

Reaching up, Steve grabbed her hand and pulled her back down.

'Don't be soft. They're only water rats, they won't come near you. Here.' He handed the spliff to her. 'Have a pull on that and calm yourself down.'

Snatching her hand away when Andy reached for it, Jasmine sat back down, muttering, 'You'd better be right. I'll go mental if I see a rat!'

Undeterred, Andy made a lunge for her. 'Don't worry, I'll protect you!'

'Fuck off!'

'You got anything?' Linda asked Steve, handing the spliff to Andy without looking at him.

'Like what?'

'*Duh!* Like a joey?'

'Oh, here we go!' muttered Jasmine.

Linda shot her a bad look. 'Shut it, you! No one asked you to listen.'

Laughing, Steve said, 'Have I *fuck* got a joey! I'm a bareback rider, me.'

Linda snorted indignantly. 'Oh, well, you can forget that, then. I ain't doing nowt without!'

'Is that right?' Steve grinned, getting to his knees.

'Yeah.'

'*Yeah?*' He undid his fly.

'Yeah!'

As Steve fell on top of a none-too-reluctant Linda and proceeded to wrestle her skirt up around her waist, Jasmine tutted.

'Oh, great! They're gonna do it right in front of us!'

'We could always join in!' Andy suggested hopefully.

Disgusted, Jasmine leaped to her feet, telling him curtly, 'You can if you want, but I'm off! See you tomorrow, Lin.' With that, she scrambled out the way they'd come.

Peering over Steve's shoulder, Linda laughed at Andy's dejected expression.

'Ahh, look at his face, the little gooseberry! Has she pissed off and left you with a stiffie, eh?'

Turning, Steve winked at his friend. 'Don't worry about it, mate. You can have a go of this when I'm done.'

'Fuck off!' Linda yelped indignantly, slapping Steve none too gently on the shoulder.

'Now, now!' Steve laughed. 'That's not very nice, is it? He's me mate, and you know what they say about sharing with your mates . . . If *he* can't –' he pulled back from her slightly '– *I* won't. Your choice?'

'Oh, all right!' Linda tutted, then pointed at Andy accusingly. 'But you'd better be quick – and don't try to neck me or I'll spit in your gob!'

Sam pushed his plate away with a satisfied burp. Across the table, Elsa smiled tightly – well used to if not overly fond of these Arabic manners her husband refused to drop.

'That was great,' he said, rubbing at his straining gut. 'Delicious.'

'Thank you.'

Standing up, she reached for his spotlessly clean plate – careful to avoid knocking the crystal vase displaying the bouquet he had bought for her. Gathering together the rest of the dishes, she carried them through to the kitchen and put them into the dishwasher before joining Sam in the living room.

He was relaxing on the couch now, his shoeless feet stretched out before him, holding a glass of cognac in one hand as he air-conducted a Stravinsky CD with the other.

Sitting at the far end of the couch, Elsa reached for the glass of sherry he'd poured for her and took a delicate sip before asking, 'Did you manage to see your clients?'

It was safe to talk now that dinner was out of the way. Eating was a sacred event for Samir – one not to be sullied with small talk.

Smiling mysteriously as he urged his invisible orchestra towards a crescendo, Sam said, 'Yes, thank you. It was very . . . *fulfilling*.'

Elsa gave him a puzzled look. He really did say the strangest things sometimes. Surely he meant *profitable*? But she'd long ago given up trying to correct his English. It frustrated him – made him think she was patronizing him, which he particularly hated.

'Do you like the flowers?' he asked then.

Smiling, she glanced back at them over her shoulder. They were beautiful. A riot of contrasting colours that somehow blended without clashing. Purples and blues, oranges and lemons, all softened by strands of wistful baby's breath. And all immaculately arranged in perfect symmetry – her one bugbear with cut flowers. She couldn't abide the thrown-together modern nonsense.

'I love them. Thank you, they're really gorgeous.'

'And thank *you* for a great meal,' Sam said, sighing contentedly – glad to be home, relaxing in the warm, clean, comforting atmosphere.

And he *was* relaxed, now that his balls were empty – for a short while, anyway.

Raising her glass when the track came to an end, Elsa said softly, 'Happy anniversary.'

Sam clinked his own glass against hers, then got up, remembering his second gift. He had thought to save it, to present it when her parents were there. But there was no harm in doing it now. Just the two of them.

'I've got something for you,' he said, heading into the hall for his jacket. Moments later he came back with a package in his hands. 'Close your eyes. And keep them closed until I tell you to open them.'

'What is it?' Elsa asked excitedly – the dancing light in her eyes reminding Sam of the sweet young girl she had been all those years ago.

All those years . . .

'Close them!' he ordered playfully. Then, as soon as she did, he said, 'Open!'

Looking down at the small velvet box as Sam slowly pulled back the lid, Elsa gasped when she saw the necklace. It was a delicately filigreed gold crucifix, studded with nine glittering rubies that sparkled like fire in the lamp light.

'Oh, it's gorgeous,' she cried, taking it from him and holding it up to examine it. 'Are they real?'

'Of course!'

'But it must have cost a fortune!'

'Ah, but you're worth every penny.'

'Thank you so much!'

In an uncharacteristic display of emotion, Elsa threw her arms about Sam's neck and kissed him full on the lips. Seizing the unexpected opportunity, he slipped his arms around her and hugged her to him, breathing in her expensive soapy scent.

Given her reaction, he considered it neither wise nor necessary to mention the enormous discount he'd received from his jeweller client. The sweet young girl Sam had 'imported' from back home had obviously pleased the incredibly ugly, astonishingly wealthy diamond merchant well.

And the results had in turn pleased Elsa well.

'Do you want to go to bed early tonight?' Elsa suddenly whispered into his neck – so quietly Sam almost didn't hear her.

Pulling back, he gazed at her uncertainly. 'Really?'

'Really.'

'Are you sure?' Rising, he pulled her gently up with him.

Standing in front of him with the necklace clutched to her breast, Elsa's eyes were wide and dark as she said, 'I'd like to try.'

Afraid that any hesitation would bring her to her senses, Sam wasted no more time on talk. Taking her hand, he led her up the stairs.

Elsa undressed quickly, prudishly, with her back to Sam so that he wouldn't see her unsightly, floppy excuse of a stretch-marked stomach as she peeled her tights down. No man should be subjected to that, in her opinion. And sometimes – only sometimes, but the thought was there nevertheless – she wished she'd never had children, for their arrival had marked the beginning of the end of her body.

Her only salvation during this process of physical deterioration had been her strict Catholic upbringing, which gave her the perfect excuse not to flaunt herself.

God does not permit good Catholics to expose their bodies sinfully, Samir . . . And you wouldn't condemn me to eternal hellfire for the sake of your lust, now would you?

Saying a hurried silent prayer to her God, Elsa leaped into the bed and pulled the fresh sheets up around her throat – averting her eyes from Samir's manhood as he released it from its Y-fronted prison. Believing that his erection was due to the prolonged abstinence she'd inflicted upon him, she felt a twinge of guilt for the regrets she was having right now about having suggested this.

But she *had* suggested it, so she had no choice but to let him get on with it. Gritting her teeth tightly, she asked him to turn the light off.

Obliging reluctantly, Sam joined his wife beneath the sheets. He wished she'd let him leave the light on for once – but at least she was *willing*, for once. It made all the difference in the world to take her with her permission.

And if only she'd permit him more often, he wouldn't need to seek the company of women like Pat, he thought as he rolled on top of her. But then again, need and desire were different beasts entirely.

Much grunting and thrusting later, he rolled onto his back and stared up at the ceiling for the second time that night. This time, however, he was not sweating.

'I'm sorry,' Elsa murmured beside him. 'I really thought this time—'

Sam shook his head. 'Ssshh. It doesn't matter. Go to sleep. We're both tired, that's all. Roll over – you know you prefer to sleep that way.'

'Goodnight, Samir.' Sighing, she rolled onto her side with her back to him.

Sam lay perfectly still, staring up at a thin strip of light coming through the gap at the top of the curtains until he was sure that Elsa was asleep. Then, easing the quilt back, he climbed carefully out of the bed and padded softly across the carpet.

Expert at feigning the heavy, evenly spaced breathing of deep slumber, Elsa let out a tiny, juddering sigh of relief when he left the room. Seconds later she heard his office door along the landing gently closing and, not for the first time, thanked God for the day Samir had bought the computer. The hours he spent on it each night keeping up with the news from back home had given him something other than the physical side of their relationship to focus his attentions on – which he'd been so obsessed with before he got the machine.

Smiling the smile of a reprieved woman, she allowed herself to relax into a real sleep.

It was just gone eleven when his patience was rewarded.

He watched as the boys got to their feet, quickly followed by the fat girl. She was still trying to straighten her clothes as the boys set off around the slope, and that she wasn't at all pleased was evident in her raucous yelling.

'Don't just take off, y' pair of bastards! Wait for me!'

'No can do!' *the first boy shouted back over his shoulder.* 'We've got to see a man about a dog!'

'Yeah,' *added the second nastily.* 'And *what* a fuckin' dog – ruff ruff, ruff ruff!'

'Cunts!' *the fat girl screeched as the boys hopped over the fence and began to run towards the gate – both of them barking and howling now.* 'BASTARDS!'

He gritted his teeth as the girl clumsily navigated the fence, muttering a string of obscenities under her breath.

Half expecting her to do the sensible thing and follow the boys to the gate, he was surprised when she didn't. Instead, once fully on the path, she turned and headed even deeper into the park.

He was almost disappointed. This would be altogether too easy. Was there no end to the stupidity of the female species?

Taking the hood from his pocket, he slipped it over his head, then pulled the latex gloves over his hands. That done, he slid out from the cover of the bushes and stealthily followed the fat girl as she began her last walk home.

7

Seddon woke with a start when the phone jangled beside him. Snatching it up before it woke his wife, he was already sitting as he said quietly, 'DI Seddon.'

The digital clock beside the phone showed that it was still only four forty-five a.m. A sure omen of disaster.

'Sergeant Banks,' the caller announced, adding ominously, 'You're needed down at Alex Park ASAP, sir. There's been another.'

Seddon ran his hand through his rapidly thinning hair.

Another? So soon? This couldn't be happening. It was a nightmare.

'Sir . . . ?'

'Yes, all right, Banks. I'm on my way. Whereabouts in the park?'

'Just past the lake, near the bushes behind the Playgroup,' Banks told him. 'There's a unit setting up there now.'

Seddon yawned deeply, then shook his head to clear the fog.

'Has Ms Wilde been notified?'

'Yes, sir. She's on her way.'

'Right, thanks.'

Hanging up, Seddon sat for a moment with his elbows

on his knees, grinding the sleep grit from his eyes with the balls of his thumbs.

'Who was that?' Pauline murmured behind him.

'The station,' he told her quietly. 'I've got to go out. Go back to sleep.'

Reaching out, Pauline gave his spreading waistline a gentle squeeze.

'Make me a coffee before you go?'

'I can't, love.' Still sitting, he reached for the trousers draped across the bedside chair. 'There's been another murder, and I've got to get down there as soon as. Anyway, we finished the milk last night.'

Pulling herself upright, Pauline leaned across to his side of the bed to switch the lamp on. He shivered as her naked breasts grazed his bare back, scorching his flesh with their feathery softness.

But this was not the time!

Resolutely pulling his trousers on, he stood up to button the fly and gazed down at his wife's unselfconscious nudity. She never ceased to amaze him. She looked as good to him today as when they'd met, sixteen years earlier. It was *he* who wore the visible marks of the passing years – he on whom time had taken its toll for the both of them.

'Is someone coming for you?' she asked, yawning.

Pulling his shirt on, he said, 'No, I'm driving. Why?'

She stretched languidly. 'I thought I'd take a drive down to the garage and pick up some milk. But if you're taking the car, I suppose I'll have to walk, won't I?'

A vision of her lovely body mutilated beyond repair assailed his mind's eye.

'I'll bring some back!' he snapped. 'Don't go out.'

'Ex*cuse* me?'

Releasing a heavy sigh, he said, 'Sorry, love. It's this case. If you'd seen what this beast is doing to these women, you'd . . .' Pausing, he shook his head. 'Well, you wouldn't go out on your own again, let's put it that way.'

Pauline regarded him with concern. She'd never seen him react so strongly to a case before. It was affecting him badly. She just hoped they caught this man soon.

Pulling his jacket on, Seddon leaned down to kiss her goodbye. Peering deeply into her pale grey eyes with his haunted brown ones, he said, 'Promise you'll wait for me to bring the milk back?'

'Okay,' she replied softly. 'But only if you promise to hurry up – and not worry about me. I'm a big girl now, remember?'

'Deal!' he agreed, grinning. 'See you later.'

'Er, you can get your butt back and turn the lamp off before you go, matey,' Pauline said as he reached the door. 'If I'm under house arrest, I might as well go back to sleep.'

Lynne Wilde was in solemn conference with one of her technicians on the pavement outside the small gate at the Demesne Road side of Moss Side's notorious Alexandra Park. When Seddon pulled up at the kerb in front of the forensics van, she cut the conversation and went to him.

'Morning, Ken. Hope you haven't had breakfast?'

'That bad, huh?'

'Worse,' she said, then looked over his shoulder with a flicker of irritation as one of her team emerged from

148

the back of the van with a body bag. Excusing herself, she barked, '*No!* I don't want that yet, I'm nowhere near finished. And where the hell are the goddamn slip-ons I asked for ten minutes ago?'

Seddon raised a surprised eyebrow at the uncharacteristic sharpness of her tone. A consummate professional in every respect, Lynne had a reputation for never raising her voice.

At least he wasn't the only one this was getting to – as if that were any consolation.

Ramming her feet into the elastic edged slip-on shoe-covers, Lynne set off into the park with Seddon in tow.

'He's a fucking animal, Ken!' she spat as she waded through the wet grass, mindless of the dog crap lurking beneath. 'The worst kind of bastard imaginable! She can't be a day over fourteen! And what the bloody hell was a child of that age doing in *this* park at that time of night, anyway? Where the hell were her bloody parents, that's what I'd like to know?'

Seddon felt his stomach churn. *Oh, God, no! Not a child!*

'And there have been no children reported missing,' she went on venomously. 'Can you *believe* that? I checked . . . Not a single bloody one! How *could* they not know that she hadn't come home, for God's sake? What's *wrong* with the people round here?'

Seddon shook his head as Lynne gave him a questioning glare, but he didn't answer. Seasoned though she was at handling the carnage she encountered day after day, right now she was reacting as any decent mother would when faced with the wanton destruction of a child. Lynne would no more dream of letting a child of her own roam these streets at night than she would think of drowning it at birth, and couldn't understand *any* parent not knowing where their child was at any given moment.

A canvas screen had already been erected around the crime scene. A set of bright arc lights blazed down into it from above, illuminating the faces of those present and making them look even more sickened than they already felt. From the young police officers standing guard outside the tent, to those combing the grass around the park for clues, to the forensics team – without exception, they looked green around the gills.

And the silence was eerie. An unspoken agreement existed in matters such as this, where the victim was a child. There was none of the banter – the grave-humour comments usually bandied about to alleviate the horror of the business at hand.

The young couple who had made the gruesome discovery were sitting in the back of an ambulance that had been parked on the Playgroup Centre yard. Its doors were wide open and Seddon could see that the woman was crying hysterically, while her partner patted dazedly at her hand, his own face white with shock.

Seddon would speak to them later – when he'd seen for himself what they had seen.

Lynne was carefully removing a tiny fold-down mobile phone from the dead girl's inside jacket pocket when Seddon came through the screen opening behind her. Dropping the phone into a clear plastic evidence bag, she handed it to him.

'We should be able to ID her from that,' she muttered, adding through clenched teeth, 'Assuming her parents came by it legitimately and had her registered as its owner.'

Putting the bag in his pocket, he said, 'I'll get it checked.' Then, flicking a quick, all-over glance at the corpse, he asked, 'How long's she been here?'

Lynne shrugged. 'Four to five hours, at a rough guess. Certainly no more than that.'

'Done here, you reckon?'

'Definitely. Her weight would have made quite an impression if she'd been dragged here through the wet grass, but there's no evidence of that. You'll have to excuse me a second, Ken,' she said then. 'I just need to . . .' Her voice tailed off; words were unnecessary for the routine physical examination she had begun to perform.

Doing his level best to ignore the intimate cavity-probing, Seddon squatted down and gazed properly now at the mutilated torso. He was immediately filled with a mixture of deep, deep sadness for the child herself, and deepest, darkest hatred for the man who had done this to her.

As he peered at the lacerations, it occurred to him that something wasn't quite right. Although he had no doubt whatsoever that the same man they were already looking for was responsible for this latest atrocity, there was something different about this one – something he couldn't quite put his finger on.

Frowning, he narrowed his eyes and looked harder, willing his eyes to make sense of what his intuition was telling him. Suddenly, he saw it.

This victim had been massacred in exactly the same way as the others: an inverted cross – bottom to top, west to east. Yet strangely, instead of being neat to the point of clinical brilliance as the previous morning's find had been, the wounds inflicted on this body were more like those found on the first and second victims.

This girl had been subjected to a furious hacking, which just didn't hold with the 'progression of expertise through practice' theory. But if proof were needed that the same hand had produced these results, there was always the ever-present forget-me-not to confirm this was their man's work.

Averting his eyes from the limp petals just visible amongst the flayed innards, Seddon pondered the possible reasons behind this apparent deterioration of the quality of the incisions.

She must have struggled, he decided, and fiercely enough to have proven a threat to the assailant, giving him little alternative but to slash her at random. She certainly looked tough enough to have defended herself violently. She was large, and young enough to be fighting fit – unlike the skinny junkie prostitutes the killer had targeted so far: they would have been relatively easy to overpower, particularly given the element of surprise the murderer obviously employed. The reports clearly showed that the knife was always inserted from behind.

But why had he chosen this young girl instead of the usual prostitutes? Surely he hadn't thought she was a working girl? But then, maybe he had – given her build, and the fact that she was alone in the park at such an hour.

Seddon felt a sudden chill of apprehension as he thought what the press would do once this got out.

The public could tolerate the slaying of prostitutes, but a child was something else altogether. They would be outraged, and would demand to know why the police weren't working harder – why they hadn't caught the monster before this terrible tragedy occurred? And then they would demand to know how the police proposed to prevent another, even younger child being tortured, raped and murdered.

And Seddon would have no words of assurance to give. For how could he expect them to believe that the attacker had given them nothing to work on? Nothing but these devastated corpses to bury.

'Oh . . . my . . . *God*!' Lynne murmured beside him, snapping him out of his reverie.

'What is it?' he asked.

She turned to him, a gleam in her eye. 'There's semen!'

'*What*?' he gasped, hardly able to take in what she had said.

'Semen!' she repeated gleefully. 'Honest-to-God DNA-providing sperm!'

Seddon rocked back on his heels, a perplexed look on his face. Much as he'd have loved to believe the semen had come from their man, it just didn't fit. The killer had never left a single trace before, not a single solitary cell of himself – no hair, no fibre, *nothing*. Why would he slip up so badly this time?

'It's not his,' he stated with absolute certainty a moment later.

Lynne refused to let go of the possibility.

'I know it's incredibly unlikely,' she conceded, 'but there are definite indications that this attack went wrong in some way. It's feasible he could have slipped up for once, isn't it?'

Seddon gave her a weary smile. 'We both know it's pretty fucking improbable, Lynne, but we'll give it the max, just in case.'

'Do you carry your rain cloud around with you, or just attract one to you wherever you go?' Lynne asked, a small, defeated smile curling her lips. 'A more cynical man I've never met!'

'Me?' he grinned. 'I'm a born optimist, me. And on that optimistic note, I predict that we'll catch this bastard – with or without his cooperation!'

'Well, just make it soon,' Lynne said quietly. 'Before he nets himself another child.'

8

At eight-fifteen on Wednesday morning, Debbie closed her front door and walked slowly along the landing towards Lisa's place with a sick feeling of panic churning her stomach. She was dreading having to knock in case Pat answered, but she knew she had to get it over with if she ever hoped to sort things out with Lisa.

Pat woke up on the second knock.

'Lisa! Get the door!' she bellowed through the wall. Snuggling back beneath the quilt, she muttered, 'Can't get no bleedin' peace round here!'

Knowing full well who it would be, Lisa took her own sweet time going down the stairs.

'Oh, it's you, is it?' she said when she finally opened the door. 'You've got a cheek, coming here after what you did!'

Debbie took a deep breath. Grovelling, first thing on a cold Wednesday morning, really went against the grain. But it had to be done.

'Look, Lisa, I didn't come to argue. I just wanted to say I'm sorry.'

Lisa raised an eyebrow and folded her arms. 'Oh yeah?'

'Yeah. I felt terrible last night.'

'So how d'y' think *I* felt?'

Debbie winced, praying that Pat wouldn't come rushing out to see why Lisa was shouting.

'Look, I'm really sorry,' she said again, almost whispering now. 'I don't even know why I did it . . . but I never meant to hurt you, I swear I didn't! You know I wouldn't do something like that on purpose.'

Lisa felt like laughing in Debbie's worried little face – telling her that she really didn't give a shit about Jamie any more because she'd got herself a *real* man now. A really *gorgeous* man, at that! Instead, she said nothing. The bitch needed to be taught a lesson for doing the dirty like that. Why let her off easy? She deserved to feel bad.

'Lisa . . . ?'

'What?'

'You don't hate me, do you?'

Lisa shrugged, 'Dunno. Ain't decided yet.'

Debbie's face fell, tears stinging at the back of her eyes. She didn't want to lose Lisa over a stupid kiss – *four* stupid kisses, actually, but that wasn't the point.

'Look, I've decided not to see him again, if that makes it any better?'

'Please yourself.' Shrugging, Lisa examined her nails nonchalantly.

Debbie frowned. 'But I thought—'

'Ah, but you *didn't* think, did you?' Lisa cut her off angrily. ''Cos if you had you wouldn't have done it, would you?'

A spark of defiance flared in Debbie's gut. Lisa was being unreasonable when, in truth, she had no right to say *anything* about what had happened – certainly no right to make Debbie feel like she'd done something wrong.

'If you hadn't gone off with Linda in the first place and left me on my own,' she snapped, 'none of this would have happened!'

Lisa's nostrils flared. 'Oh, I like *that*! You do the dirty on me, then blame *me* for it! What's up? You jealous 'cos Linda likes me better than you, or something?'

'No!' Debbie retorted, almost blushing at the partial truth of Lisa's accusation. She'd got it the wrong way round, that was all. Debbie *was* jealous, but not about Linda liking Lisa more than her. It was about *Lisa* seeming to like *Linda* more. But she knew if she said this, Lisa would laugh and say she was being pathetic. And perhaps she was?

'Anyway, you did it,' Lisa stated flatly. 'So there's no point going over it again, is there?'

'Okay, I'll go, then,' Debbie said sadly. 'But I meant what I said – I *am* sorry.'

As Debbie began to walk away with her head bowed, Lisa rolled her eyes and called out, 'Come here, you daft cow!'

Debbie turned back with a hopeful look on her face.

'Yeah, you,' Lisa said. 'Get your arse in here while I get dressed. You can feed Monty for me.'

Debbie ran back but hesitated at the door, unsure of the reception she'd receive inside. It was all very well Lisa forgiving her, but Pat might have other ideas.

'Where's your mum?' she asked nervously.

'In bed. And what you whispering for?'

'Isn't she – you know – pissed off with me?'

'What for?'

'Last night?'

Lisa gave her a puzzled look. 'What's that got to do with her?'

'Didn't you tell her?'

'Course not!' Lisa snorted. 'What d'y' think I am? I can fight me own battles, thanks.'

Breathing a sigh of relief, Debbie followed her inside, going straight into the kitchen to feed Monty as Lisa started up the stairs.

Halfway up, Lisa stopped and looked back at Debbie through the stair rail.

'So what's he snog like?' she asked, smiling slyly.

Debbie's stomach did a flip as she remembered the feel of Jamie's soft lips . . . The sweet taste of his tongue . . . The exotic scent of Lynx on his skin.

'Not that good, actually,' she said, wrinkling up her nose to make the lie more convincing. 'And he's got bad breath.'

Lisa knew full well that Debbie was bullshitting but decided not to challenge her about it. Far better to make her suffer by forcing her to sustain the lie out of a sense of guilt.

'Good job you've chucked him, then, isn't it?' Lisa said. 'Tell you what, we'll just completely ignore him every time we see him from now on! That'll be a laugh, won't it?'

Smiling smugly, she turned and ran up the stairs to the bathroom, where, too lazy to be bothered boiling the kettle for a proper wash, she gave her face a quick splash of cold water and rubbed a finger of toothpaste around her teeth. There was no one to impress in school now, so there was no point going overboard, was there? Anyway, she was only going in today to make sure Debbie really had jacked Jamie in – and she didn't need to be clean to do that.

Drying her mouth on a scrap of toilet tissue, she suddenly remembered the trip to Tatton Park. She'd had no intention of going, but now this had happened she thought it might just be a laugh after all. A chance to make Debbie really pay for hurting her like that.

The only problem was, Debbie had said she'd have to take the money in this morning or there would be no seats left. She just hoped Sam had been more generous with her mum than he'd been with her.

Leaning over the banister, she called down to Debbie in a loud whisper, 'How much did you say that trip was?'

'I didn't,' Debbie whispered back. 'But it's two-fifty. You coming, then?'

'Might as well. Won't be a minute.'

Easing open her mum's bedroom door, Lisa popped her head inside. 'You awake, Mum?'

'No! Whaddyawant?'

'I need a fiver for the school trip.'

'Shoe,' Pat grunted, pulling the quilt up around her head to deter any further attempts at communication.

Lisa found the shoe and took out the wad of money stuffed inside it, raising an eyebrow as she saw how much there was. There had to be a couple of hundred quid at least. Peeling two ten-pound notes off the top, she stuck the rest back into the shoe and crept out, closing the door quietly behind her.

Her mum would never notice how much she'd taken

– and if she did, Lisa would deny it till the day she died.

Mrs Kent was pleasantly surprised when Lisa strolled up to her desk with the money for the trip that morning. Despite Lisa's often rude manner and habitual defiance, she felt sorry for her and secretly believed that her academic and social failings were more than a little attributable to neglect on the home front.

If the rumours were true – and from the one and only time she had ever seen Pat Noone set foot inside this school, she had no doubt that they were! – Lisa's mother was not only a battler of the first degree, she was also a prostitute. And although Mrs Kent – happily married herself – liked to think she empathized with single mothers and the disadvantaged in general, she believed there to be no excuse on God's green Earth for a woman to sell her flesh. Or to neglect her child – the gift from God she herself would never receive.

'I'm so glad you've decided to come, Lisa,' she said, taking the money. 'And you're better now?'

'Better?'

'Yes, Debbie told me you weren't feeling too well yesterday. Still, there's nothing quite like a good rest to see off sickness, is there?'

Lisa wanted to laugh but, not wanting to drop Debbie in it for lying, she resisted the urge, saying instead, 'Yeah, I felt dead rough all day, but I'm all right now. So, can I definitely go on the trip?' she asked then.

Mrs Kent opened her drawer to take out the paying-in book.

'Yes, I should think so. But you're lucky. If you hadn't brought this today . . .'

'Yeah, I know, I wouldn't have got a seat. Debbie said.'

'Well, there we are, then.' Mrs Kent wrote Lisa's name in the book, then put it back in the drawer and smiled. 'Glad to have you on board, Lisa.'

'My pleasure,' Lisa replied, smirking.

'Don't forget to bring a packed lunch,' Mrs Kent called out as Lisa walked away. 'And some sensible shoes.'

Joining Debbie at the back of the class, Lisa said, 'Thanks for covering for me. She didn't even ask me for a note, which is good 'cos it's murder getting me mum to write them. She always leaves it till she's pissed, then they can't read her writing and think I've forged it.'

'It's okay,' Debbie said, feeling she'd redeemed herself a little for the whole Jamie thing.

She still didn't know how she was going to handle seeing him, though. The problem being that he had no idea that Lisa fancied him, and wouldn't understand if Debbie told him she had to stop seeing him because of her. It was a mess, but at least she had until lunchtime to think of a good excuse.

Taking out their books, the girls fell silent as the morning's lessons began, although neither was able to really concentrate as they were both too wrapped up in thoughts of the lunchtime confrontation.

Before they knew it, the morning was over.

As soon as the lunch bell began to ring, Lisa jumped to her feet. Stuffing her books into her bag, she grabbed her jacket from the back of the chair and hassled Debbie to get a move on. She couldn't wait to get to the canteen. She was dying to see Debbie squirm when she had to tell Jamie to get lost.

Debbie, however, was truly dreading it. Dragging her feet as Lisa hustled her along the corridor, she wished she could be anywhere else but here right now. She even tried to pretend she felt a bit sick and didn't really want to eat anything, but Lisa kept a determined grip on her arm and practically ran her into the canteen. Fortunately, Jamie was nowhere in sight.

Zoë Clayton was in front of them in the dinner queue. Nudging Debbie, Lisa whispered, 'Watch this!'

Tapping Zoë on the shoulder, she said, 'All right, Zoë? How you feeling today?'

Turning quickly, Zoë gave her a nasty glare – the effect of which was somewhat lessened by a fierce black eye.

'Is that supposed to be funny?'

Lisa shrugged nonchalantly. 'It made *me* laugh.'

'What was all that about?' Debbie asked when Zoë stomped away with her dinner tray.

'Linda kicked the shit out of her in the loos last night,' Lisa explained, adding snidely, 'But you missed it, 'cos you were too busy with Mr Stinky Gob!'

Blushing, Debbie reached into the cabinet and snatched up a sandwich she hadn't intended to choose.

'What's up?' Lisa asked innocently.

'Nothing. I just felt sick remembering it, that's all.'

Lisa smirked. *Oh, the joy!*

'That must be what's up with your gut, eh? Why you said you didn't want to eat?'

'Mmmm.'

Handing in their dinner tickets, they took their trays over to a table by the window opposite the door – at Lisa's insistence as, yet again, she didn't want to miss Jamie when he came in.

A few minutes later, Jasmine Kelly joined them. She shrugged when Lisa asked where Linda was.

'Dunno. She didn't answer when I called for her this morning. She probably kipped round at Steve's,' she added with a sly grin.

Lisa was on instant gossip alert. 'What d'y' mean?' she demanded.

Smirking, Jasmine leaned towards them across the table, whispering conspiratorially, 'Don't tell her I told you, but when I left them last night, he was just about *up* her!'

'You what?' Lisa's mouth gaped. 'No way, man!'

Jasmine nodded authoritatively. '*Way*! But you'd better not tell her I said it or she'll kill me!'

'Course I won't! But, wow! I can't believe it! I knew she was after him, but *shagging* him? Shit, man!'

'What about protection?' Debbie interjected prissily, then blushed as they both gave her a disparaging look.

'Don't make it sound like she *planned* it, like some sort of slag, or something,' Jasmine hissed. 'She'd break your fucking neck for that.'

'I didn't mean that,' Debbie protested.

Kissing her teeth, Jasmine said, 'Yeah, *right*!' Then, blatantly cutting Debbie out of the conversation by turning her shoulder, she proceeded to tell Lisa all about the night before. Just as she finished, the two heroes themselves turned up.

'*Wha'suuuup?*' Steve drawled in a bad American accent,

imitating his favourite TV commercial. Plonking his tray down, he straddled a chair and shuffled it up to the table.

Andy followed suit, wedging himself in between Debbie and Jasmine – his two favourite ladies.

'Where's your mate?' Lisa asked, glancing at Debbie to see her reaction.

Shrugging, Steve said, 'Am I my brother's keeper?'

'You're not brothers!' jeered Andy.

Clipping him around the ear, Steve said, 'And you ain't the brightest bulb in the lamp, but I don't hold it against you, do I?'

'You ain't holding nowt against me, mate!' Andy cackled. 'Anyone'd think you was turning batty boy!'

'Shut it, numpty!' Steve shook his head in despair, then turned back to Lisa. 'Anyhow, since you're so interested, Jamie ain't in today. He's pulling a sicky.'

'Yeah,' Andy chipped in, grinning at Debbie. 'Reckons he's got some sort of throat infection.'

Blushing again, Debbie looked down at her suddenly tasteless sandwich.

'Talking of sickies,' Lisa said, ignoring Jasmine's warning glare. 'Have youse seen Linda?'

Exchanging a sly smile with Andy, Steve said, 'Nah. Not since last night.'

'Hmm,' Lisa murmured curiously. 'Well, she's not in school. I hope she didn't knacker herself out with all that *scrapping* at the youthy last night.'

'More like all the shaggin' after!' said Andy. 'She's like a bleedin' rabbit when she gets going, isn't she, Ste?'

'Ugh! Don't remind me!' Steve screwed his face up

in distaste. 'Shit, man, I knew she was built, but I didn't think she was *that* fat! I ain't seen an arse that big since I went to the elephant house at Chester zoo.'

'You tight gets!' Jasmine snapped at them angrily. 'You wasn't so fussy last night, was you? You make me sick!' Gathering her things together, she got up and marched away from the table.

'What's up with her?' Steve said, genuinely surprised at her reaction.

'Lin's her best mate and youse are slagging her off,' Lisa said. 'What did you expect?'

Before he could answer, the school's ancient Tannoy system crackled to life and the secretary's nasal voice blared out: '*Steven Lunt, come to the office, please . . . Steven Lunt, to the office.*'

Lisa grinned. 'Oh, aye? You been a naughty boy then?'

Frowning, Steve said, 'Nah, I ain't done nothing – I don't think?' He turned to Andy then, puzzled. 'I haven't, have I?'

'Don't think so.' Andy said. Then: 'Oh, hang about . . . what about that thing in the gym?'

Steve considered this, then shook his head. 'Can't be that. Dingbat's already pulled me for that, remember?'

'What did you do in the gym?' Lisa quizzed him.

Taking a bite out of his burger, Steve mumbled, 'Nowt much.'

'Yeah, right!' Andy snorted. 'Just wedgied some little git and ruptured his arsehole! Nowt much, eh?'

The Tannoy sparked to life again, but it wasn't the secretary this time, it was the Head.

'*Steven Lunt, come to the office immediately. Steven Lunt – to the office!*'

'Shit! What does that wanker want?' Pushing himself up from the chair, Steve wiped a smear of ketchup from his chin and stuck his fingers up at the speakers hanging from the rafters above their heads.

'Better go,' Lisa teased. 'He'll get the cane out if you wind him up. And you don't want us to see you crying when he batters the arse off you!'

'I'd like to see him try!' Steve retorted. Grabbing a handful of chips from his plate, he motioned Andy to get up. 'Come on, mate. Let's go and kick his head in for disturbin' our dinner!'

'Wonder what that's about?' Debbie said when they'd gone.

'Linda's mum's probably getting him nicked for shagging a minor,' Lisa suggested with a smirk.

Debbie frowned. 'They can't do him for that, can they? Not if they're both under sixteen?'

Giving her a pitying look, Lisa said, 'You're getting just like your mum, you – a right little moany-hole!'

Steve rapped sharply on the Head's door, then swaggered inside when the Head called him in.

He stopped in his tracks when he saw the uniformed copper standing stiff-backed against the wall, but any trace of bravado he still possessed completely evaporated when he then noticed the sombre-looking plain-clothes guy sitting sideways on to the equally grim-faced Head's desk. Whatever this was about, it was heavy shit. Plain-clothes officers didn't get involved with wedgie jobs.

'Sit down, Steven,' the Head ordered, his voice brooking no argument. 'This gentleman would like to speak to you.'

Steve obeyed without a murmur.

'Steven Lunt?' Seddon asked. Steve nodded. 'I'm Detective Inspector Seddon,' he went on. 'I'd just like to ask you some questions about your relationship with Linda Parry.'

Steve felt the world turn beneath his feet. Oh, no *way* had she landed him in it for shagging her? And then a really awful thought occurred to him: what if she'd said they'd *forced* her because they'd legged it straight after? He flicked a questioning glance at the Head, but Mr Lennox just peered back at him, giving nothing away.

'I, er, don't know what you mean, sir,' he replied at last – sounding small and frightened to his own ears. 'I haven't got a relationship with her.'

'But you do know her?'

'Well, yeah . . . sort of. I mean, I've seen her around, like. But I don't really *know* her.'

Seddon clicked his fingers at the uniformed constable and held out his hand for the list of numbers Linda's mobile phone company had faxed to him that morning.

'Then maybe you could explain why she had your name and number in her phone menu? And why she called *you* most regularly of all the numbers she had listed.' Pausing, Seddon traced a finger down the list. '*If*, as you say –' he looked up sharply, frightening Steve with the intensity of his glare '– you "don't really know her"?'

Steve shrugged in what he hoped was an innocent way. 'I don't know. She must have got my number off someone. She did, well, she *did* call me a couple of times,' he admitted then. 'But we're just, you know – mates.'

'She called you last night at approximately seven-fifteen?'

Steve blanched, his mind working overtime. He considered saying he hadn't answered his phone last night and hadn't known she'd called. But what if the copper had details of the *length* of Linda's calls? If he did, he'd know that they were connected for a good few minutes. Stupid bitch!

'Well?' Seddon asked impatiently.

'Yeah,' Steve admitted quietly. 'But she was only asking if I was going to the disco.'

'And were you?'

'Yeah, me and me mates. We always go – everyone does.'

'And you saw Miss Parry there?'

Steve folded his arms and chewed at his bottom lip. 'Yeah.'

'Speak up, please. I didn't quite catch that.'

'Yes!' Steve squirmed in his seat. 'I saw her – but that's all.'

Seddon peered at the boy for a long time. He was undoubtedly hiding something, but what – and why? And then it occurred to him.

'Did you have a sexual relationship with Linda Parry?' he asked bluntly.

'*No!*' Steve blurted out – too quickly, causing Seddon to raise an eyebrow. 'No, I didn't,' he said again, making a conscious effort to sound less defensive. 'And if she says different, she's lying!'

Seddon didn't believe a word of it.

'*Did* you have a sexual relationship with Linda Parry?' he asked again, slowly, giving the boy a chance to redeem himself with the truth.

Steve blushed to the roots of his hair, and again vehemently denied the accusation.

Seddon changed tack.

'Okay, these mates of yours. What are their names?'

'Why do you want to know that?' Steve asked nervously.

'Just answer the question, Lunt,' Mr Lennox cut in sharply.

Steve gave the Head a hooded but decidedly dirty look, before saying grudgingly, 'Jamie Butterworth and Andy Green.'

'*Thank* you,' Seddon said sarcastically as he marked the possible co-conspirators' names down in his book. He would speak to both of these boys.

'Can I go now?' Steve half rose from his seat.

'Just one more thing,' Seddon said, waiting until Steve had slumped back down before continuing. 'What time did you see Linda at the disco?'

Steve shrugged. 'Dunno. I wasn't exactly watching the clock, was I?'

'Lunt!' Mr Lennox reprimanded him sternly.

Steve shrugged again, looking down at his hands now. 'About half-seven – eight?'

'And that was just in passing, was it?'

'Yeah.'

'And you didn't see her again after that time?'

'No.'

'So you didn't see her when you left the disco?'

Steve faltered with the denial ready on his tongue. This copper *had* to know. Maybe someone had seen them leaving the youth club together? Maybe even seen them going into the park?

'All right, yeah,' he admitted at last. 'I *did* see her again. We just walked her and her mate down Alexandra Road, then we left.'

'We?'

'Yeah, me and Andy. Her and her mate, Jas, were walking the same way as us, that's all.'

'So you walked them along Alexandra Road, then left them?'

'Yeah, I just said.'

'And you didn't enter Alexandra Park with them?'

Steve knew they had him – knew there was no point denying it.

'Yes,' he muttered, looking down.

'Louder, please?'

'Yeah, all right! We went in the park with them,' Steve snapped, adding defensively, 'But she's lying if she says we forced her. She was well up for it!'

'Did you have sex with her?'

Steve's head sank further onto his chest, and Seddon suddenly understood what was worrying him – the boy was afraid he was being charged with rape.

'Steven,' he said quietly. 'You are not in trouble for having sex with Linda, but your honesty is vital, do you understand?'

Steve looked up at this, his confusion evident in his eyes. Of course he didn't understand. What was he being asked all these questions for if it wasn't because he was in trouble for that?

Sighing heavily, Seddon leaned forward, choosing his next words carefully.

'Listen to me, Steven. This is not some trivial little matter that will go away if you make evasive answers to my questions and try to double-guess my reasons for asking them. It's a murder inquiry, and it's quite possible that you may be one of the last people to have seen Linda Parry alive. Now do you understand why I need your full and honest cooperation?'

Steve stared at him, his mouth a gaping hole of shock.

'I never *touched* her!' he gasped when he finally found his tongue. 'Not like *that*! We was just messing about!'

'But you *did* have sex with her?'

'Y-yeah, me *and* Andy – but we never did nothing bad. We didn't *hurt* her or nothing.'

Seddon nodded, taking on board the admission that this boy's friend had also participated in the sexual act, probably making *his* the second distinct sperm 'signature' Lynne Wilde had found inside the dead girl – not, as they had hoped, the killer's.

'I don't suppose either of you used a condom?' he asked, with just a sliver of hope that the answer would not be as he expected.

Steve shook his head, guiltily avoiding Mr Lennox's disapproving stare.

Haven't we taught you anything here at Birch High, Steven?

Seddon turned to Lennox. 'Is this Andy Green in school today?' Then, looking back at Steve: 'And this other girl . . . ?'

'Jasmine Kelly, sir.'

'And Jasmine Kelly.'

'I'll check if Green's in,' Mr Lennox said, picking up the internal phone to call the secretary. 'And I'll have Jasmine brought up. I know she's in, I saw her this morning.'

'Andy's outside, sir,' Steve whispered. 'He's waiting for me.'

Seddon motioned to the uniform. 'Go and tell Green to stay put. I'll speak to him when we've finished with this one.'

'Have Jasmine Kelly brought up to my office, please, Sheila,' Mr Lennox said into the phone. 'In fact, go and get her yourself, would you?'

Seddon turned back to a very sick-looking Steve and asked if he was all right.

'Yeah,' Steve murmured. 'It's just . . .'

'A shock?' Seddon said kindly. Steve nodded. 'But you're all right to go on?' Another nod. 'Good. Now think clearly about this, Steven, because it's vital. Did you see anybody else in the park last night?'

Steve shook his head. 'No, it was de—' The word died on his lips. *Dead*. Like Linda. He began to cry then, his shoulders shaking softly as tears streamed down his cheeks. 'I'm sorry,' he gulped. 'Sorry . . . I just . . . I . . .'

Feeling sick to the pit of his stomach for putting the boy through this, Seddon turned to the Head.

'Do you think we could get him a cup of tea?'

Mr Lennox stood up. 'Certainly. I'll get it myself.'

'Make it sweet,' Seddon called as the Head hurried from the room.

While they waited for the tea, Seddon went over to

the window. Not an insensitive man, he wanted to give the boy a chance to recover without the humiliation of being watched as he snivelled. This was a difficult enough ordeal without having his blossoming teenage pride bruised.

When Mr Lennox had given Steve the tea and he'd drunk half of it and was under control, Seddon resumed the interview. There was no doubt in his mind that the boy was in no way connected to this killing or to any of the previous murders, but the questions had to be asked nevertheless.

Picking up where he'd left off, he said, 'So, you saw nobody at the park? No unusual sounds? Nobody out walking a dog? Nobody walking along the road when you were going in or coming out?'

Steve answered 'No' to everything, until Seddon asked what time they had all left the park.

'We took off right after,' he admitted guiltily. 'We just left her in there by – by herself.'

Seddon raised an eyebrow at this. 'You, Andy and Jasmine?'

Steve shook his head. 'No. Jas left before . . . you know.'

Seddon noted down what he'd said, then asked, 'Where were you on Monday night, Steven?'

Steve brightened a little. That was easy.

'At home,' he said. 'Me and Andy set up my little brother's PlayStation, and then we stayed on it all night.'

'Can anybody verify this?'

Steve grinned sheepishly. 'Yeah, me mum, 'cos she had to keep coming in to stop the fighting.'

'Fighting?'

'Yeah. Lee – my brother – he wanted to get on it 'cos he'd only just got it for his birthday, yeah? But we wouldn't let him have a go, so he had a fit and I . . . well, I gave him a couple of licks to shut him up, like.' Steve shrugged guiltily. 'I know it was tight, but he fell asleep in the end anyhow, so we just carried on playing.'

'Until what time?'

'All night. Andy was staying over anyway, so we just didn't bother going to bed.'

'Did you leave the house at any point?'

'No way!' Steve almost laughed. 'My mum would have gone mad.'

'If she'd *known*,' Seddon said pointedly.

Steve snorted softly. 'She'd have known, all right. We've got one of them mega alarm systems – once you set it off it won't stop till you ring the security firm and tell them it's okay.'

'Which firm is that?' Seddon asked, pen poised.

Steve shrugged. 'No idea.'

'But I suppose you *do* know the code?'

Steve saw what Seddon was driving at and shook his head. 'I know it, yeah, but we couldn't have sneaked out and got away with it. Me mum would have gone ape! She was already in a right nark – kept telling us to turn it down 'cos she couldn't get to sleep with all the noise. You can ask her if you want.'

'Thank you, Steven.' Seddon closed his pad to let him know the ordeal was over. 'I think that will be all for now.'

'Are you fit to go back to your lessons?' Mr Lennox

asked, displaying uncharacteristic compassion. 'You could take the rest of the day off if you'd rather?'

Steve shook his head. 'No, thanks, sir. I'll be all right now.'

Andy gave Steve a questioning look as his mate came out of the office, but he couldn't ask what was going on as the copper was already calling him in for his turn.

Andy went in, nervous as hell after seeing the expression on Steve's face. Whatever was going on, it looked like they were in deep shit!

Steve dropped the bombshell to just one person when he got back to his class – but that was enough. The news spread like wildfire – made all the more dramatic when Jasmine Kelly, who was far too distraught to walk after hearing what had happened, was driven home in the police car.

It was afternoon break by then, and every pupil in the school was in the yard to witness as, crying hysterically, Jasmine was escorted down the path between the police officers. If there had been any doubts about the rumours, this sight made it one hundred per cent true.

Linda Parry had been murdered!

And Jasmine Kelly, Steve Lunt and Andy Green were involved somehow. They had to be – why else would the police have come to school to question them?

Throughout the remainder of the day, the rumours were discussed, spread and distorted, until it was 'common knowledge' that Steve and Andy were murderers. Guilty not only of forcing the newly deified Saint Linda to have sex against her will, but also of pushing her into the lake and refusing to help her out – even though everyone knew she couldn't swim. And worse – they had gone back later and held her head under the water to drown her, just in case she was rescued and told on them.

Jasmine, it was decided, must have got away before it happened, so her only crime was of abandoning Linda. But she couldn't have known what they were going to do, so that wasn't really her fault.

To make matters even worse, Lisa decided to tell anyone who'd listen about Steve and Andy's attack on *her* outside the youth club – although in her version, it was attempted rape and she'd single-handedly fought them off. This served as absolute proof that they had already been looking for a girl to rape, thus condemning them further.

They were a pair of rapist bastards!

When the home-time bell finally rang, there was such an air of suppressed violence about the school that Mr Lennox ordered his staff to keep the pupils locked inside the classrooms until Steve and Andy had safely left. But this only served to pour petrol onto the smouldering flame, confirming to the already convinced pupils that Steve and Andy must have something to hide.

Guilty!

The instant they were released, a large vigilante gang, consisting mainly of aggressive girls, set off in search of the rapists – hell-bent on ripping their balls off. Powerless to do anything to stop them, Mr Lennox called the police. And so, within seconds of the gang arriving on Steve's road, they were forced to scatter in smaller groups when two police vans screeched around the corner, lights and sirens on full alert.

Lisa and Debbie's group ran into the small park at the end of Steve's road and took over the kiddies' play area to discuss what they were going to do to the bastards when they got their hands on them.

They ranted in complete agreement, until one of the girls made the mistake of saying that Jamie Butterworth must be involved as well, at which point Lisa and Debbie vehemently jumped to his defence, and only the intervention of another girl who had seen Jamie walking home by himself on the night of the murder stopped it becoming a full-blown battle.

So Jamie was innocent, it was finally agreed.

But as for the other two . . .

Walking home a short while later, Debbie mulled over what had happened. Watching as she frowned and pursed her lips, Lisa wondered what was going through her mind.

'What's up with you?' she asked eventually.

'You!' Debbie snapped.

'*Me*? What have I done?'

'I thought you couldn't stand him?' Debbie blurted out accusingly. 'So how come you nearly ended up scrapping over him?'

'So did you,' Lisa counter-accused. 'And you said you was never gonna speak to him again.'

'I haven't!'

'Only 'cos he wasn't in school!'

Debbie sighed heavily, suddenly overwhelmed by the events of the day.

'All right, shut up, Lisa,' she muttered. 'I don't want to talk about him any more.'

Lisa gave her a hard look. 'Don't tell *me* to shut up, Debbie Morgan! I'll kick your bleedin' head in!'

'Lisa!' Debbie stopped short, forcing Lisa to stop too. 'Just pack it in, will you? I can't take it – not today. We've just found out Linda's *dead*, and all you want to do is argue about a stupid lad! Don't you *care*?'

Lisa frowned. She'd always been the one to tell Debbie what to do, what to say, when to shut up. She didn't like being on the receiving end at all. But she couldn't argue with what Debbie had said because, for once, she had to admit that Debbie was right. They *shouldn't* be arguing over Jamie at a time like this.

'Okay!' Lisa held her hands up. 'You're right. Let's just agree not to mention him again, yeah?'

Debbie knew the climbdown must have been difficult, but she felt a little too smug at having heard Lisa admit she was wrong to let it go at that. Folding her arms to show she meant business, she said, 'All right, but I just want to say one more thing about him first.'

'Oh yeah?' Lisa said, striking an aggressive pose.

Debbie faltered, wondering if Lisa was going to hit her. Then she thought *To hell with it!* If she did, she'd get it right back!

'Yeah,' she said firmly. 'I don't like the way *you've* decided that *I* can't talk to him any more. I like him!'

'No kidding?' Lisa's voice was low and menacing, but Debbie carried on anyway.

'There's no point being nasty about it, Lisa. I'm only telling you what I think. I won't go out with him because I don't want to hurt you, but I'm *not* going to ignore him!'

There, she'd said it! It was up to Lisa what she wanted to make of it now.

Lisa curled her lips in a nasty half-smile. 'Finished?'

'Yeah.'

'Good, 'cos I've got a few things of me own to say. First, I thought you were my best mate, but obviously you don't care that much about me – going off with Jamie when you knew I liked him!'

'That's not true!' Debbie spluttered. 'And you're not the only one who's liked him for ages, you know, so there!'

'But *I* told *you*,' Lisa shouted angrily. 'You never said a word! How was I supposed to know if you didn't tell me?'

'You never *let* me,' Debbie shouted back. 'And it wouldn't have made any difference if I had, 'cos you *still* would have thought you had dibs on him. You're the only one alive in the whole bleedin' world when you get started!'

Lisa was about to answer, but laughed instead. 'I'm not that bad, am I?'

Debbie snorted incredulously, then grinned. 'Yeah, actually, you are.' She held her hands to her heart then, mimicking Lisa: 'Oh, I'm *so* hard done by! Poor little me!'

Still laughing, Lisa shoved Debbie's shoulder. 'Pack it in! I don't sound like that. Anyhow,' she went on with a secretive smile, 'I'm not even bothered about him no more, so you don't need to worry.'

'What do you mean by that?' Debbie demanded, frowning.

'I mean I'm over him,' Lisa said, examining her finger nails, still smiling.

'Who . . . Jamie?'

'Duh! *No!* Prince bleedin' William!'

Debbie narrowed her eyes, suspicious of this sudden change.

'I don't get that. How can you be over him so fast?'

Grinning smugly, Lisa began to walk away, humming softly.

'Tell me?' Debbie demanded, trotting after her.

'Can't. It's a secret.'

'But we always tell each other our secrets.'

'Nah. You might get jealous.'

'*Jealous?* Of what?'

Lisa looked at her, still grinning slyly. 'I've got a new fella.'

'You have *not!*' Debbie gasped. 'Don't lie.'

Shrugging, Lisa said, 'Please yourself if you don't believe me.'

'All right, who?' asked Debbie. 'And when . . . And *how?*'

'Remember last night?' Lisa said. 'When you got off with *Jamie?*' It was only a mock admonition, but Debbie blushed anyway. 'Well, it was then. He walked me home, actually.'

Debbie's mouth gaped. 'He never!'

Lisa nodded, smirking with satisfaction. 'Did so.'

'So come on, then – who is it? Do I know him? Is he at our school? Was he at the disco . . . ?' Debbie pulled her head back as a thought occurred to her. 'It's not Steve, is it?' she asked, adding with a grimace: 'Or *Andy?*'

'Behave!' Lisa snapped. 'I wouldn't touch them rapists with someone *else*'s barge pole!'

'Who, then?'

Lisa smiled, her eyes gleaming at the thought of the

new love of her life. 'All right. He's called Benny, he's about twenty, and he's *well* fit!'

'Twenty?' Debbie was shocked. 'He's too old, Lisa.'

'No, he's not. He's gorgeous.'

'Yeah, but . . . *twenty*?'

'So I like older men?' Lisa shrugged. 'And he likes me, so there!'

Debbie frowned. This wasn't good. What would a man that age want with a girl not yet thirteen?

'What does your mum think about it?' she asked.

'I've not told her,' Lisa said, adding darkly, 'and I'm not gonna, so *you*'d better not, neither – especially not to your gobby cow of a mum!'

Debbie didn't bother responding to this. Lisa had been saying things like that about her mum for so long now, she probably didn't consider there was anything wrong in it.

'So, how did you . . . you know, get off with him, then?' she asked instead.

Lisa smiled dreamily – and lied her head off.

'He just came up and asked if I fancied going out with him. Said he'd seen me a while back and thought I was dead pretty, and that he's wanted to ask me out for ages, but he didn't have the nerve. Anyhow, I said I'd have to think about it, but then he said he'd loved me from the minute he laid eyes on m—'

'You're lying!' Debbie cut her off sharply. 'I don't believe a word of it.'

Turning on her angrily, Lisa said, 'No, I'm not! You're just jealous!'

Debbie shook her head. 'I'm not, Lisa. I just think you're making it up, and that's sad.'

'I'm *not* lying!' Lisa insisted, her mouth pursed into an angry little pucker.

Debbie gave her a disbelieving look. 'If you *say* so.'

'All right,' Lisa admitted. 'So he never said that about *loving* me – but the rest is true!'

'Tell me what really happened then?' Debbie said, willing to give her the benefit of the doubt.

Lisa began to relate the real version of events, and Debbie almost believed her – until she started talking about how Benny had rescued her from Steve and Andy when they'd tried to 'rape' her. That rang a bell, and Debbie suddenly remembered what had been niggling her ever since Lisa had told everyone her earlier version.

'About that,' she said, interrupting Lisa mid-Benny-praise. 'How come if they attacked you like that you never mentioned it in the canteen when they came over? How come you were laughing and joking with them like everything was all right?'

Lisa couldn't answer this. It hadn't actually occurred to her to be angry with them, but now that Debbie was saying it, she realized it did look iffy. Maybe there was something wrong with her? Or maybe it was just that she knew she'd grossly exaggerated the reality, making what she honestly saw as them just messing about sound like a serious sexual assault. Whatever it was, Debbie had picked up on it, and consequently probably wouldn't believe her about the rest of it. Lisa could hardly blame her, but then again it wasn't a total lie, and it pissed her off to have her word doubted.

'So what was that about?' Debbie persisted.

Shrugging, Lisa said, 'You know I don't hold grudges for long. Anyhow, I didn't think they were being that serious at the time. It was only after we heard about Linda it sort of fell into place, like.'

Debbie mulled this over for a moment and decided it was feasible enough.

'All right,' she said, linking her arm through Lisa's. 'Forget them. What about this Benny bloke – did you *really* meet him, then?'

'Yeah, honest.'

'And now you're going out with him?'

In the new spirit of honesty, Lisa grinned sheepishly.

'All right, not exactly,' she admitted. 'But he *is* well fit.'

Debbie shook her head. 'You're a right one, you! So come on, tell me what *really* happened.'

Lisa told her everything then – right up to losing Benny at the chippy.

'I wish I knew where he lived,' she finished with a groan. 'But I haven't got a clue.'

'But you told him where we live?'

'Where *I* live!' Lisa said, laughing as she added, 'And don't think you're getting your hands on *this* one, 'cos I really *would* kick your face in!'

'I wouldn't want him!' Debbie snorted. 'He's well too old.'

'Bet you wouldn't say that if you saw him.'

'But I'm not going to, am I? And neither will you again, by the sound of it.'

We'll see, Lisa thought, but didn't bother saying.

Friends again, they went home. Debbie, glad she had Lisa all to herself again. Lisa, sure she would see Benny again – whatever Debbie thought.

★   ★   ★

A rare sight greeted them when they reached their block: their mums standing together outside Lisa's front door. Debbie immediately felt sick. It had to be trouble – there could be no other reason for their mums to be talking. They were hardly the best of mates.

'Oh, God,' she moaned, unlinking her arm from Lisa's. 'I wonder what's going on.'

Lisa shrugged – safe in the knowledge that whatever it was, her mum would send Sue Morgan packing rather than give her the satisfaction of seeing her punish Lisa for whatever she might have done.

Debbie's mum rushed towards them as they came through the upper landing door, her face a mask of anguish. Throwing her arms around Debbie, she said, 'Are you all right, sweetheart?'

'I'm fine,' Debbie answered warily. 'Why?'

Sue glanced worriedly at Pat, then Lisa, then back to Debbie.

'Haven't you heard?' she said after a moment. 'About your friend . . . Linda?'

Debbie sighed sadly. 'Yeah. They told us in school.'

Sue's eyes filled with tears. 'Oh, my poor baby. Come on, let's go home, eh?'

'She doesn't half go overboard, that Sue,' Pat announced with a derisive snort as she watched Sue bundle Debbie away. 'Coming in, love?'

Lisa stood for a moment, watching as Debbie and her mother went inside with their arms around each other. Having witnessed the tenderness between them – a tenderness she rarely, if ever, got from her own mum – she felt a strange tugging sensation in her heart.

Not fully understanding the feeling, she shrugged it

away and followed her mum inside, pausing in the hall to stroke Monty who, as if aware that something sad was happening, didn't leap all over her for once.

'It's been on the news all day,' Pat said, sinking down onto the couch and lighting herself a cigarette. 'Showed her picture and everything. Didn't half give me a shock, I can tell you. She came here once, didn't she?'

'Yeah,' Lisa said, sighing as she slumped down beside her. 'A few months back.'

'Thought I recognized her,' Pat said. 'So what was she up to, then?'

'What do you mean?' Lisa asked, frowning.

Pat snorted softly. 'Oh, come on. In Alex Park, at *that* time? Don't tell me she wasn't up to nowt.'

'She wasn't!' Lisa said, annoyed by the implication.

Shaking her head, Pat gave a wry grin and said, 'I wouldn't be so sure, if I was you. You could tell by looking at her she knew the score.'

Lisa stared at her mum in disbelief. 'That's a horrible thing to say,' she gasped. 'She wasn't like that.'

'The size of the tits on her, an' all!' Pat went on, chuckling. 'It's a wonder she didn't have three kiddies already! Here . . . what's up, love?'

Lisa swiped at the tears that had begun to rain down her cheeks.

'Linda wasn't like that,' she snapped. 'She was dead nice. And it wasn't her fault she had big tits. She was my mate!'

Reaching across, Pat gave her hand a squeeze. 'Aw, look, I'm sorry, pet. I didn't mean nothing, but you know me. Never keep me gob shut when I should, do I? It's just the shock of it, that's all. And, well, you've got to admit it's funny, seeing as the bastard's only done pros so far . . .'

She left the rest unsaid, but Lisa knew full well what she was getting at.

'Yeah? . . . Well, he should have stuck to them, shouldn't he?' she shouted, snatching her hand away and leaping to her feet. 'Linda would never have gone with a bloke for money! She thought it was disgusting – and so do I!'

'Oi!' Pat warned. 'Watch it!

'Oh, leave me alone!' Sobbing now, Lisa ran from the room.

'Where you going?' Pat shouted after her, but she was already thundering up the stairs to her bedroom.

Stubbing out her cigarette, Pat reached down the side of her cushion for the bottle of vodka she'd stashed when Sue Morgan had come hammering on the door.

'Cheeky little cow,' she muttered, unscrewing the cap. 'Wouldn't even *have* a bedroom to storm up to if I didn't work my backside off for her! And what thanks do I get? *None!* Disgusting, indeed! I'll give her bleedin' disgusting if she ever talks to me like that again – dead friend or no dead friend!'

Lying face down on her bed, Lisa sobbed into the pillow. It had finally sunk in that Linda was dead, and the knowledge hurt. Even more so after hearing her mum's thoughts because no doubt everyone else would be drawing the same conclusion, and that just wasn't fair.

Just because Linda had looked older than she was, and had acted so . . . well, truth be told, a bit slaggy. That was no reason to say stuff like that about her, was it?

And it *was* only an act. Lisa knew full well Linda would only have slept with Steve because she loved him. And as for going with Andy as well, Linda would only have done that to keep Steve happy, she was sure.

That pair of bastards had a lot to answer for! Doing the dirty on Linda was one thing, but they'd pissed off straight after – and left her to get murdered.

And despite all the talk at school, she knew deep in her heart that Steve and Andy had been telling the truth about that. They *had* left Linda on her own in the park. And because of that, she was dead. Murdered by the prozzie-killer. Steve and Andy might not have done it themselves, but as far as Lisa was concerned, they were to blame and she'd never forgive them.

9

When school began on Thursday morning, Lisa's class were informed that the Tatton Park trip was cancelled and their money was refunded. No one was bothered. A trip was the last thing on any of their minds right now. They were all still reeling with shock over Linda's death and, along with the rest of the school, still blaming Steve and Andy.

Jamie was absent again, having contracted a genuine throat infection – nothing to do with Debbie, but she still felt guilty when she heard about it. Steve and Andy were also absent. Mr Lennox had thought it best in the circumstances, at least until the real killer was caught. And Jasmine Kelly was still too upset and doped up to leave her bed.

Lisa had gone in, more to keep up with the latest gossip than anything else. By lunchtime, however, she was itching to escape. The atmosphere was too weird – subdued, despite the rampant gossiping and speculation, and heavy with the loss of one of their own. Linda might not have been the most popular girl in the school, but she had had enough friends to make the sadness pervading the air all too real.

'I can't take this,' she told Debbie as they headed for the canteen. 'I'm getting off as soon as I've had me dinner.'

Instead of protesting, as Lisa had expected, Debbie nodded her agreement and said, 'I think I'll come with you. It's doing my head in, too. I keep thinking I can see her out of the corner of my eye, but when I look properly, she's not there.'

Lisa shuddered. 'Ugh. Pack it in.'

'Sorry.'

'It's all right, I'm just a bit . . .' Pausing, Lisa shrugged, unable to put a word to how she felt.

'Upset?' Debbie suggested simply.

'Yeah.' Lisa sighed heavily. 'It doesn't seem real, does it? I mean, I know it *is*, but I can't believe it. Shit, man – we were only with her the other night!'

'Drinking her cider,' added Debbie sadly, despite not having had any herself. 'Sharing smokes with her.'

'Watching her kick the crap out of Zoë . . . Oh, sorry – you missed that, didn't you?'

Recognizing the dig, Debbie blushed and looked down.

'I can't believe we'll never see her again,' she said after a moment, her voice breaking slightly as tears stung her eyes.

Lisa sniffed loudly, an unfamiliar wobble distorting her chin.

'Yeah, it just feels like she's on holiday or something, doesn't it?' Rooting through the papers in her pocket to cover her emotion, she managed to pull herself together. 'Here, I wouldn't put it past her though, would you?'

'What?' asked Debbie.

'To come back and haunt us,' said Lisa, grinning. 'She'd love that, Linda – scaring the shit out of us all.'

'Oh, don't!' Debbie wrapped her arms tight around

herself. 'I didn't get to sleep last night for thinking about her. I don't want to be imagining her sitting on my bleedin' bed as well!'

'Come off it!' Lisa giggled. 'What would she want with *your* bed when she could be in Steve's? Here, that'd be a laugh,' she said then. 'Can you imagine his face if she turned up in the middle of the night? She could do anything she wanted. Chop his dick off – anything! I bleedin' would!'

Debbie frowned. 'He'd deserve it, the bastard!'

'Well, I never!' Lisa snorted softly. 'And you so nice usually.'

Reaching the canteen doors, Debbie hesitated. Looking in through the glass pane, her stomach tightened when she saw how crowded it was. Turning to Lisa, she said, 'Look, I don't really fancy going in there and listening to any more crap about Linda. Can we just go?'

'Yeah,' Lisa agreed, linking her arm through Debbie's. 'We'll go to the park, eh?'

'Not *Alex* Park?' Debbie looked fearful. 'I don't want to see where . . . Well, you know.'

'Neither do I,' said Lisa, pulling Debbie quickly behind a group of lockers to avoid an approaching teacher. 'But I don't reckon we'd see anything, anyway. It'll be swarming with dibble. Come on,' she said when the teacher had passed them by. 'Leg it!'

Debbie felt strange, wandering the streets in school time, and she was glad when Lisa suggested going to the Addy – the old adventure playground at the end of City Road furthest from their houses. No one lived up that end now, so at least they wouldn't be seen and reported. The

Lantern pub was still open, but beyond that, everything was due for demolition – including the Addy. And hardly anyone used the subway now either, even though it was the quickest route to town. The risk of being attacked was so much greater in the midst of the deserted buildings – lots of places for muggers and sex attackers to hide, and routes for them to escape.

Not naturally rebellious, Debbie was already beginning to regret wagging it. Lisa had no problem with it at all, and seemed to almost relish the danger of being caught. But the exposure just made Debbie feel panicky. Every time a car passed them by she squeezed her eyes shut, convinced it was the police, or the Head – or, worse, her mum!

'I don't know why you like doing this so much,' she complained, scuttling along beside Lisa. 'I'm crapping myself! I keep expecting to get arrested, or something.'

'Give over!' Lisa snorted. 'You don't half wind yourself up. I've never been pulled, and if I was, I'd just say I was off ill, or something. Gawd, I couldn't half do with a fag,' she said then. 'Don't suppose you've got any?'

Shaking her head, Debbie said, 'What would your mum say, though? If you got dragged home in a cop car?'

Lisa laughed. 'She'd back me up, stupid! You don't reckon she'd let a copper near our door without giving him shit, do you? She hates them, and so do I 'cos they're all wankers.'

'That one that came to see my mum after she got mugged was nice,' Debbie said. 'Dead kind, and all. He told her to ring him any time if she got worried, and that.'

'Young?' Lisa asked with a knowing smirk.

Debbie frowned, thinking. 'No, I don't think so. Clark, I think.'

'Not his *name*, stupid! Was *he* young?'

'Oh, I see. Em, yeah, I suppose so. Well, younger than my mum, anyway. About thirty-ish I reckon.'

'So, did she ring him?'

'I don't know? Why?'

'I bet she did!'

'So what if she did?' Debbie demanded huffily. 'What you getting at?'

Lisa gave a casual shrug. 'Nowt.'

'Yeah, you are,' Debbie persisted irritably, following as Lisa climbed the fence into the Addy. 'You're trying to say she fancied him, aren't you?'

'Well, she probably did,' Lisa retorted, making for the ramshackle set of rope-and-tyre swings – only one tyre of which had survived the attentions of the yobbish local kids. 'She ain't exactly got a lot of choice, has she?'

'Meaning?'

'*Meaning*,' said Lisa as she straddled the precariously supported tyre, 'that she'd jump at the chance of a legover – even if it was with a filthy pig!'

'You really piss me off sometimes!' Debbie snapped, glaring at her angrily.

Lisa laughed, pushing herself higher.

'Oh, stop getting your knickers in a twist. You think she's some sort of saint, but she ain't. She gets horny, just like everyone normal.'

'Oh, you mean like *your* mum?' Debbie sniped, too upset by Lisa's remarks and the events of the past few days to keep her mouth shut. 'She just *loves* it, her, doesn't she? Can't get enough of it, my mum reckons. And she ain't too fussy who *with*, neither – so long as they keep the booze flowing!'

Lisa leaped down from the tyre, a furious look on her face. Debbie knew she'd gone too far but she stood her ground, too annoyed to back down.

'You'd better take that back!' Lisa growled, grabbing her by the front of her neat school jumper.

'Get off me,' Debbie hissed, tugging at Lisa's hands. 'You think you can say what you want about my mum, but she's miles better than yours! At least she doesn't spend all day in bed – and she cleans up, and makes dinner, and that. Yours just gets pissed and shouts at everyone. And people say things about her, so there!'

'Like what?' demanded Lisa.

She had to know how much Debbie knew, because if *she* knew the truth, her mum must too, and there would be hell to pay.

'I said like *what*?' she said again, grabbing a handful of Debbie's hair now.

Debbie cried out in surprise and pain as Lisa gave her hair a vicious tug.

'Stop it, Lisa!' she squealed. 'You're hurting me!'

'Tell me what you meant, then?'

'Nothing. I didn't mean nothing!'

'Yes, you did. Now tell me – or I'll rip your fucking hair out!'

'Just what – what I already said,' cried Debbie. 'That she sleeps around, and doesn't care who with as long as they bring her a bottle. That she's got a free bed, and anyone's welcome in it!'

Lisa almost laughed out loud.

'So they reckon she lets fellas into her bed, yeah?'

'Yeah.'

'And *"they"* would be your mum and Betty bleedin' King, I suppose? *Well?*' Lisa gave Debbie's hair another short, sharp tug.

'*Yes!*' Debbie yelped. 'Please, Lisa . . .'

'And have you ever seen a man come in our flat?'

'Yeah. *Owwww* . . .' Debbie squealed again as Lisa tugged even harder. 'I *have*, Lisa! That wotsisface – Sam!'

'Anyone else?'

'No!'

'That's *right*,' Lisa hissed. 'And that's 'cos he's her *boyfriend*! So what's wrong with that, eh?'

'Nothing,' Debbie muttered tearfully. 'I was only saying what I was told.'

Lisa pulled Debbie's head back and hissed into her face, 'Well let me tell you . . . my mum ain't no slag – *got* that?'

Debbie nodded. 'Yeah, okay!'

'And if I so much as hear a *peep* that your nasty bitch of a mum has said anything like that about her again,' Lisa went on, 'I'll tell *my* mum, and then see what she gets!' With that, she let go of Debbie and stalked away to the climbing frame.

Debbie stayed where she was, pulling loose clumps of hair free and dropping them to the patchy grass as tears slid down her cheeks. She didn't know what to do now. She couldn't go home, because then she'd have to tell her mum why she was in such a state – and knowing her mum, she'd take it into her head to go and confront Lisa's mum, which would be awful because Pat Noone was quite capable of kicking the shit out of anyone who criticized Lisa.

She couldn't go back to school either, because they'd want to know why she'd skipped out in the first place, and then Lisa would get into trouble as well. But one thing was for sure, she couldn't stay here. Lisa definitely wouldn't let this drop just like that. And in a way, Debbie could understand that, because she had gone way over the top this time and she knew it. She should never have said what she had. Lisa's remarks about Debbie's mum had been nowhere near as bad as Debbie's had been about Pat. She doubted Lisa would ever forgive her.

Weighed down with guilt, but too proud to crawl to Lisa and say she was sorry, she headed out of the Addy, set for a lonely afternoon's hiding.

Lisa watched Debbie go, glad that she hadn't tried to make it up because the way Lisa was feeling right now, she'd have probably finished the job properly if she had. The cheeky bitch!

At least Debbie hadn't known what Lisa's mum *really* did with men, or there would be ructions. Sue Morgan was more than capable of phoning the social services and reporting her for that – and where would that leave Lisa? In a home, that was where!

Climbing to the top of a domed metal spider's web frame, Lisa hooked her legs through the bars and let herself drop back so that she was swinging upside down. Pulling free a couple of strands of Debbie's long hair that were trapped beneath her nails, she watched them as they drifted to the ground and thought about the consequences of the fight. If 'fight' was what you could call it, because she hadn't actually *hit* Debbie. But knowing

Sue Morgan, she'd call it a severe beating and get Lisa done for assault, or something stupid like that.

'Shit!' Gritting her teeth, she closed her eyes and muttered the word over and over: 'Shit, shit, shit, shit . . .'

'That's not very ladylike, is it?'

Lisa almost fell of the bar with shock when she heard the laughing voice.

'What you doing here?' she squawked, scrabbling to get upright.

'Just passing through on my way to town,' Benny said, his eyes twinkling as he watched her disentangle herself with difficulty. 'What are *you* doing here, more like? Why aren't you in school, young lady?'

Regaining her seat at the top of the frame, Lisa looked down at him and was taken aback by how gorgeous he looked in the bright light of day. He was wearing the same black leather jacket he'd been wearing the other night, but it looked even better on him now. In fact, everything about him looked better than she'd remembered – and that was some achievement. His hair was so dark it almost looked as if it had a blue sheen. And his skin was so pale and soft-looking. But his eyes, now that she could see them clearly, were astonishing. They were a vivid blue – like sapphires, twinkling in the weak sunlight. She felt her stomach do an involuntary little flip.

'Well?' he asked again, giving a tiny laugh. 'School?'

'Oh, I was there this morning,' she said, shrugging to cover her embarrassment. 'But they let us out early, 'cos . . . well, they just did.'

Pulling his head back, Benny gave her a disbelieving look.

'I've never heard of schools letting you out early for no reason.'

'Oh yeah,' she lied. 'They do it all the time at ours – teachers' training days, and that. Have you got any fags?' she asked then, blushing at her own cheek as the words left her mouth.

Benny snorted softly. 'Yes, I have, but considering you told me you're only twelve, I don't really think I should give you one.'

'Aw, please,' she begged. 'I'm gasping. I haven't had one all day.'

He shook his head, still laughing at her with his eyes.

'You shouldn't be smoking at all. You're far too young for nasty habits like that.'

'Please yourself,' she said sulkily. 'Though I don't see why not, seeing as you gave me one the other night *after* I told you my age. And I reckon you owe me one anyway, for taking off like that.'

'My, my,' he admonished playfully. 'We *are* in a strop, aren't we? Okay,' he relented, 'I suppose you've got me bang to rights on that!'

Taking a pack of cigarettes from his pocket, he lit two and held one out towards her.

'Here – and don't say I never give you anything!'

'Ta!' Reaching down, Lisa grabbed the cigarette and sucked on it as if her life depended on it. 'I really needed that!'

'Hark at the old woman!' he laughed.

'Oi!' she flipped back. 'You're the old one, not me!'

'Oh well, if you're going to be rude . . .' Turning, he started to walk away.

Lisa's heart thudded in her chest. Shit! Now she'd

gone and offended him. Jumping down from the frame, she ran after him.

'Benny, wait! I'm sorry . . . I was only joking.'

When she caught up with him, Benny was chuckling quietly to himself.

'I knew that,' he said.

'Well, thanks for making me run!' she scolded.

He shrugged. 'Do you good, a bit of exercise – make up for the gym lesson you're probably missing right about now.'

Tilting her head back, Lisa stared up at him suspiciously.

'How did you know we have gym on Thursdays?'

'Ah, but I know everything, don't you know?'

'Bollocks! No one knows everything!'

'Language!' Benny chided softly. 'And *I* do.'

Still puzzled by his knowledge of the lesson she was missing, Lisa followed him as he made his way to the old bench set in the far corner of the playground. Leaning unhealthily against the fence, it was almost obscured from view by overhanging trees and knee-high grass.

Perching beside him as he sat down, she said, 'All right, if you're so clever, what's my mum's name?'

'Hmm, let's see now.' Pursing his lips, he narrowed his eyes as if in deep concentration. 'Pat!' he declared after a minute.

'No way!' she gasped. 'How did you know that?'

'Like I said – I know everything.'

'No, really – how did you know?'

Benny smiled secretively. 'Ask me another.'

'All right,' she said, thinking hard. 'Er . . . What's my dog's name?'

'Hmm,' he murmured. 'It's slightly more difficult to tap into the animal cosmos.'

'You what?'

'Just a technical term. Let's see now . . . Prince?'

Lisa grinned smugly. 'Wrong!'

'How about . . . Rover!'

'Uh-*uh*! You *are* the weakest link!'

'Jasper?'

'No.'

'Nero?'

'Nope.'

'Fang?'

'No. You're never gonna guess.'

'Ssshhh!' Benny had his eyes shut now. 'I'm tuning in. Sam?'

Lisa giggled. 'Closer than you think, but no.'

'Oh?'

'Just a friend of me mum's,' she said. 'Guess again.'

'Ah, well.' Opening his eyes, Benny shrugged. 'Guess I'm not meant to play this game today.'

'Ha!' Lisa was triumphant. 'I knew you wouldn't get it! Know everything, my arse!'

Benny frowned. 'Will you *please* stop swearing?'

'I didn't.'

'You did, you said *arse*, and before that, *bollocks*. And when I got here, you were saying *shit, shit, shit*!'

Lisa giggled. 'You don't half sound funny saying that.'

'That's because I don't *like* saying it,' Benny said. 'And I don't like *hearing* it, either – especially not from the mouths of pretty little girls.'

Lisa blushed, not sure whether to be pleased at the 'pretty', or annoyed at the 'little'. Looking down at the long-dead cigarette she was still clutching by the tips of her fingers, she said, 'Don't suppose I could have another one?'

Sighing heavily, Benny reached into his pocket. 'All right, but it's your last one. And that's another reason you shouldn't be smoking – you can't afford it!'

'Do you work?' she asked after lighting up.

'Not now.'

'But you did?'

'Once,' he admitted, shifting his position on the bench and changing the subject. 'So, what about school, then? They didn't really let you out early, did they? You can tell me,' he said, smiling conspiratorially. 'I don't grass on my friends.'

'Are we?' she asked.

'Are we what?'

'Friends, stupid!'

Benny's face darkened immediately. 'Don't call me that!' he hissed.

Lisa's bubble of euphoria of a moment ago burst.

'I – I'm sorry,' she gabbled. 'I didn't mean anything by it. It's just something you say – a joke, like.'

'Well, I don't find it funny,' he snapped. 'Not at all! It's rude and insulting, and I don't ever want to hear you saying it again!'

'I won't, I swear! And I *am* sorry, Benny. I didn't mean to upset you.'

After a moment, he gave her a tight smile.

'All right, apology accepted. And I didn't mean to snap, but I hate that word. *Stupid*!' he repeated it bitterly. 'An inane, meaningless word, used by the ignorant to label those they don't understand!'

Lisa raised an eyebrow at his angry tone, but didn't question it. It was a bit too weird for her, but then, he *was* a lot older.

'Truth?' he suddenly said.

Lisa was confused. 'You what?'

'Tell me the truth about school.'

'Oh, that.' She tutted. 'Okay, but only if you tell me how you knew when we have gym today, and how you knew me mum's name? And no more of that bullsh – *rubbish* about knowing everything, all right?'

Benny gave her a lopsided grin. 'Okay. The second is easy. I knew your mum's name because I heard those boys teasing you about her the other night, remember?'

'Mmmm,' Lisa murmured darkly, remembering only too well what Steve and Andy had said. At least now they were in disgrace, no one would believe them if they tried to spread it around.

'The first,' he went on, 'I guessed.'

'How?'

He laughed. 'I'll let you into a secret. I used to go to your school, and gym was always on a Thursday, rain or shine. Can't say I went very often either, but there you go.'

'You *never* went to my school?' Lisa gasped, then narrowed her eyes suspiciously. 'Hang about . . . how do you know what school I go to?'

Looking at her with exaggerated patience, Benny said, 'See that tie wrapped around your cheeky little neck? Well, I've got one exactly the same at my flat.'

'You've never kept your school tie all this time?'

'Excuse me, *child*,' he snorted. 'Exactly how ancient do you think I am?'

'Don't know?' She grinned. 'Forty? Fifty?'

'Impudent wretch!'

'Now, now! No name-calling. It's rude – *remember*?'

'Me – forget?' He placed a hand on his chest. '*Never*! I'm like the proverbial elephant!'

'Eh?'

'Never mind. And stop changing the subject . . . Why aren't you—'

'At school?' Lisa cut him off in a bored voice. 'All right, I came out 'cos I was upset.'

'Oh?'

Pulling hard on the cigarette, she blew out a smoke ring, then said, 'Me mate got killed the other night.'

'Oh.' Benny nodded sympathetically.

'Yeah,' Lisa went on, warming to her theme. 'You know that bloke what's been murdering all the pros? Well, they reckon it was him.'

Benny was thoughtful for a moment, then nodded again.

'Oh, right. I think I saw it on the news. Linda something-or-other?'

'Parry,' Lisa said. 'Linda Parry. She was my mate.'

'I see.'

'She was dead nice, you know.'

'Mmmm.' Glancing surreptitiously at his watch, Benny gasped. 'Ten past three already!' Dropping his spent cigarette, he jumped up.

'You going?' Lisa asked, disappointed.

''Fraid so,' he said. 'And I'm late now after spending all this time with you – when you should have been in *school*,' he added pointedly.

'Where you going? Can I come?'

Benny shook his head. 'Sorry, no. I'll have to run as it is.'

'Where to?' she persisted, adding hopefully, 'I can run.'

'Not fast enough,' he said, grinning. 'Anyway, I'm sure we'll see each other again, so . . . look after yourself, yeah?'

'When?' she called after him as he ran towards the subway, but he didn't answer, just waved back at her over his shoulder.

Lisa watched as Benny dipped under the fence and disappeared into the mouth of the subway. Slumping back on the bench, she sighed. Now what was she going to do? She didn't know where he lived, how to find him, anything. Was she going to have to wait for him to find her every time she wanted to see him? Just hang about in the Addy on the off chance?

Still, he'd said they'd see each other again. She'd just have to be patient until then.

Getting up, she set off for home, grinning to herself as she went over their conversation in minute detail. He definitely liked her, she had no doubts about that. It was just a pity Debbie hadn't seen them together – she'd have been well jealous. Especially when Benny had said they'd see each other again – *and* when he'd said she was pretty!

'So stick that in your pipe and smoke it, Debbie Morgan!' she said out loud, giggling to herself.

By the time Lisa reached home, she was completely happy with the world – and ready to forgive Debbie for the fight. Doing something she would usually rather die than do, she knocked at Debbie's on the way past and apologized. Well, she had to tell *someone* about Benny, and Debbie was a great listener. A great friend altogether, she had to admit.

And Debbie was so grateful to Lisa for coming round to make things right, she didn't even tell her that she didn't believe a word she had said.

10

Sam left his client's house at just after four, pleased that the meeting hadn't taken nearly as long as anticipated – and thoroughly satisfied with the agreement they had reached. His bank balance was looking healthier by the day!

He was almost as pleased about the deal he had just struck as he had been the previous night upon hearing that the dreaded in-laws were to be delayed yet again. They wouldn't be arriving now until midnight tonight. Two whole days late! Two days knocked off the week! Fantastic! And with them coming so late, he would have plenty of time to relax after work without Mother Conroy fussing and criticizing her way around his house.

Climbing into his car, smiling the smile of a lucky man, Sam realized he still had time to fit in another prospective client before finishing for the day. Not as potentially rewarding as the grateful man he'd just left, but lucrative nonetheless. All of his dealings were, or he wouldn't have bothered. The risks he faced should the true nature of his business be discovered were just too great to justify otherwise.

Searching in vain for the client's phone number in his inside pocket, he realized he had left it in the suit he had been wearing when he last saw Pat. He'd just have to get it from Jessica instead.

Tapping out the office number on his mobile, he was irritated to hear the answering engaged tone. When a second try a few minutes later was equally fruitless, he knew he'd have to disturb Elsa – who would undoubtedly be rushing around like a headless chicken at this very moment, making last-minute adjustments and alterations to the guest room, the food, the lounge cushions, etc., etc.

Elsa sounded out of breath when she eventually answered, but vigorously rejected his suggestion that she should take a break.

'I enjoy being busy, Samir, as you well know. Now what was it? I'm right in the middle of basting the duck.'

'Sorry, dear,' he apologized, 'but I need you to find something for me.'

Elsa sighed heavily into his ear. 'Can't it wait? I'm really busy.'

'It's just a phone number,' he said. 'It's in my black suit – the one I was wearing on Tuesday. It's in the wardrobe.'

'Really!' She tutted. 'You'd forget your head if I didn't twist it the right way in the morning! I'll go and look.'

He heard the phone go down, and knew she'd call him back from the bedroom extension when she'd found the number. He tapped his nails on the steering wheel as the minute became two, then three, then five. What the bloody hell was she doing?

Irritably, he pressed redial. His home number rang ten times, then the answerphone kicked in.

'Shit!' Cutting the connection, he angrily stabbed in the office number again, muttering, 'Bloody stupid woman!' as it began to ring.

'Rashid Imports, Jessica spe—'

'About time!' Sam cut his secretary short. 'I don't pay you to gossip to your friends on my phone!'

Hearing an all too familiar clicking sound, he bellowed, 'AND DON'T BLOODY *TUT* AT ME!'

'AND DON'T YOU BLOODY WELL *SHOUT* AT ME!' Jessica yelled back furiously. 'I *didn't* tut, for your information! And if I *did*, it's *my* business! Now, did you ring just to have a go at me, or did you want something?'

Taken aback by her outburst, Sam blustered for a moment, then forced himself to calm down. The last thing he needed was for Jessica to walk out – and from the way she'd sworn at him just now, he'd obviously pushed her fairly close to the edge.

'*Well?*' she demanded shortly.

Sam cleared his throat, modulating his voice to one of mere indignation before answering. It never did to let a woman think she had you all the way under!

'Hmph, well, yes, I did want something actually.'

'And that would be?'

'Mr Ishtar's phone number.'

'Just a moment, please.'

Sam rolled his eyes as, for the second time, he was placed on hold – only this time, with the annoying piped abortion of Streisand's greatest hits that Jessica had ordered for the office flooding his ear. She'd insisted it would be just as good as the real thing. As if!

Finally: 'Have you got a pen?'

Taking his Parker pen from his breast pocket, Sam said, 'Yes, go on.'

When she'd read the number out and he'd jotted it down, he said, 'Thank you, Jessica. I'll, er, I'll . . .'

'See you in the morning,' she said – more kindly now that she'd had a chance to calm down and could also hear the apology in his voice. 'Bright and early, with –' she added pointedly '– a *smile!*'

'Yes. Thank you.'

Disconnecting, Sam leaned his head back on the seat. *Women!* Why did they always manage to make men feel like such shits?

Tapping out the number Jessica had given him, he started the engine and began to roll away from the kerb just as the client answered.

'Ah, Mr Ishtar . . . Samir Rashid here . . . Wonderful news . . . I have a last-minute cancellation.'

Elsa's shoulders sagged as she sat on her bed staring at the garment lying on the floor at her feet where she'd dropped it just minutes before.

A pair of women's panties – worn, and most *definitely* not hers! She would *never* wear such lewd, disgusting underwear. Only a woman without morals or decency would entertain the idea of wearing such a thing – let alone buy it in a public place!

So whose were they? And why were they stashed in her husband's inside pocket like some sort of hoarded treasure?

In a numb void of disbelief, she stared at the soiled evidence of Samir's betrayal – for what else could it be? She'd already considered – and dismissed – the possibility that he could be a secret cross-dresser. Even were the preposterous notion of her vehemently homophobic husband being 'that way inclined' remotely possible, he would never get this minuscule thong on over even *one* of his meaty thighs – never mind both of them *and* his enormous rear!

Shocked by the phone ringing again beside her, Elsa came to with a start. Oh, God! Not him again? She couldn't speak to him right now. She needed to get her head together; assume a calm she was far from feeling – for the sake of the children, if nothing else.

And then there was the problem of her parents. They were due tonight, and there was no way she was prepared to let them see her in such a state. Hers was one of the only truly 'happy' marriages in their family, and she wasn't about to lose that status – at least, not until she'd learned the facts . . . however hard they might be to swallow. Anyway, she'd fought too hard for her family's acceptance to lose it all now.

Devout Catholics – such as the members of her entire family – simply did *not* get married outside their denomination, especially not to *foreigners* of such radical persuasions. But Elsa had felt a compulsion to defy this age-old status quo and, rather than choose from the local pool of eligible Catholic bachelors as she had been raised to do, she had set out to net the first exotic, mysterious foreigner she had laid eyes on. And Samir Rashid had been it. It was coincidental that she had then fallen hopelessly in love with him. He'd had all his hair in those days and had weighed a good deal less than he did now, and Elsa had found him irresistibly attractive. Once the deed had been done, her family had had to accept it, although

Elsa knew that deep down they still harboured hopes that she would one day be widowed, enabling her to marry 'properly'. God forbid she should divorce! After the dust had settled her parents had seemed almost to warm to Sam, and Elsa had been so grateful for their 'almost' approval that she forgave them the years of criticism she'd endured at their hands.

Shaking her head to clear it of all the unwanted thoughts when she heard the answerphone clicking in, she pushed herself up from the bed. If it *was* Samir, he might well decide to come home for the number he'd wanted, and she mustn't let him see her like this if he did. He'd know something was wrong and would try to wheedle it out of her, which would just result in an almighty row. And she wasn't ready for that. He was far too crafty when cornered, and she herself was too volatile not to blurt out what she suspected – giving him the perfect opportunity to blame her outburst on the menopause whilst coming up with some feasible excuse for having the panties.

No. If she wanted to find out the truth, she'd have to catch him red-handed – if indeed he were guilty of anything. She'd just have to hide the evidence and play the waiting game.

Swooping on the panties with renewed determination, she held them between fingertip and thumb and deposited them in the empty laundry bag hanging from a hook on the back of the bedroom door. Then, folding the bundle into as small a ball as possible, she looped the drawstring around it, then climbed up on the dressing-table stool to stash it in one if the old hatboxes she kept on the top shelf. Samir never bothered with her boxes.

The panties would be safe there until she had reason to bring them out again – either to use as evidence against him, or to dispose of should he prove to be innocent. And she sincerely hoped the latter would be the case. She was too old and settled to think about the consequences to the family should her husband be exposed as a cheat.

Climbing back down from the stool, Elsa put everything back in its place and went to the bathroom to clean her hands thoroughly before continuing with her work. She would tell Samir that she had accidentally unplugged the upstairs phone whilst cleaning and hadn't heard the answerphone. He would accept that.

Now she just had this week to get through before she would get a chance to begin digging up his dirt. She just hoped she survived that long without giving way to the rage already building in her heart.

11

O n Monday morning, almost a week after she was killed, Linda Parry was finally laid to rest. And it couldn't have been a worse day. During the night, the sky had opened its great dirty mouth to spew a torrent of rain onto Southern Cemetery, making the freshly dug plot a mud slide of epic proportions. And it was still raining now – a fine, insistent drizzle that soaked everyone to the skin in seconds.

The pall-bearers slipped and almost dropped the expensive mahogany coffin head first into its final resting place. Reverend Vine actually skidded to a halt at the graveside, almost preceding his charge into the care of their mutual master. And the huge congregation of family, school friends, police officers and ghoulish gatecrashers trampled more than a few respectfully laid wreaths in their attempts to reach the grave upright.

'This is not just a time of great sorrow,' Reverend Vine began when, at last, everyone was ready, 'but also of great joy. For we do not leave this world without first having fulfilled the plan our Lord designed truly with us in mind.

'We that are left behind to suffer the enormous pain of loss,' he went on, 'must remember, as our tears fall, that beyond our loved one lives on in the joy and care of the greatest Father of them all – our Lord, Jesus Christ.

'Linda Melissa Parry was, and is, a special young soul. Her purpose here on Earth may not have been apparent to everyone she knew, and yet she was as important to our lives as the rain we are, as I speak, receiving unto our heads is to the grass on which we *try* to stand . . .' Pausing, he smiled modestly as a slight murmur of amusement passed through the sodden congregation.

Linda's mother was not in the slightest bit amused.

'He's taking the piss!' she complained bitterly through her tears. 'He's 'aving a laugh at my Linda's funeral! I'm gonna get him struck off!'

'That's doctors, Gwen,' Linda's dad said, trying to comfort his former wife as best he could – given the handcuffs that attached him to the guard-dog prison officer. 'He's doing all right, love. Our Lin would've laughed her bollocks off at this. She liked a good laugh, did our Lin.'

Gwen Parry was having none of it.

'And you can shut it!' she howled, shoving him away. 'If you wasn't such a bad bastard, she'd be at home now, with me! You ruined her life!'

'Gawd, it's better than the pictures, this,' Lisa hissed under her breath to Debbie. 'Bet Lin's up there now, telling her mum to stick the boot in!'

'Don't,' Debbie moaned, swiping her tears away. 'I can't stand this. Don't they care that she's gone? Why are they arguing, today of all days? It's horrible!'

Lisa put her arm around Debbie's shoulders as she sobbed.

'Will you *stop* that!' Linda's aunt bellowed at the

arguing parents as they looked set to scuffle. 'You're a damn disgrace, the pair of you! That's my niece in there . . .' Pointing at the coffin, she burst into tears and had to be led away.

The prison officer tried – and failed – to remove his charge. Bob Parry wasn't going anywhere until he'd seen his daughter laid safely to rest.

Worried for his own safety at the hands of such an obviously rough family, Reverend Vine cut out the jokes and got down to the serious business of burying the poor child at a rush – sure that the sooner he got her soul away from the blighted life she'd obviously had to endure here on Earth, the better off she'd be.

'And so we relinquish her soul into the care of our Lord, Jesus Christ. Ashes to ashes . . . Dust to dust . . .'

'I'm gonna report you!' Gwen Parry shrieked as she was led away past the vicar. 'You didn't even *know* her!'

'Only because *she* never introduced them!' Jasmine remarked bitterly to Lisa and a calmer Debbie as they left the graveside – all three clinging to each other so as not to slip. 'Linda never got taken to church *once* in her whole life! Can you imagine that?'

Lisa gave her a strange look. 'You religious, Jas?'

Jasmine shook her head quickly. 'Don't be soft. But it wasn't for lack of me mum and dad trying. At least they *cared* about my immortal bleeding soul!' This last was said loudly as they filed past the funeral car that Linda's mum was being helped into. 'All *she* cared about when Linda was alive was using all the social on herself! Going out to the blues, picking all sorts up! Lin hated her, you know.'

'Sshh!' Debbie hissed. 'She'll hear you.'

'I don't care!' wailed Jasmine. 'She was my best mate! *I* cared about her!' she screeched back at the car.

'You saying I didn't, you fuckin' little bitch?' Gwen Parry retaliated furiously, trying to climb back out of the car to get at Jasmine.

As quickly as they could, Lisa and Debbie bundled Jasmine away before she could do any more damage.

Hiding amongst a thick group of trees in the neglected older section of the cemetery, he watched as the girls made their way towards the main gates. Under cover of the hulking angel headstones so favoured in earlier years, he shadowed their progress – the welcome rain rendering him invisible to those mourners who were still straggling from the graveside, their heads down as they walked.

This same rain, however, also made it impossible for him to gauge if his *girl was crying. The other two obviously were, but that was a far simpler matter. Theirs was the primitive wailing of the child who's lost its playmate. But was* she, *too, indulging in the self-serving act? Or was her wet face simply a result of the rain?*

He hoped, in a way, that she was *crying, for that would mean that she cared. Not about the worthless life he'd taken on her behalf – the physical symbol of his efforts. But that she cared about – no,* understood – *the enormity of his love for her. His willingness to eradicate all who stood in their path as he led her to purity. As* he *now understood, so her tears would indicate her own understanding.*

In this holiest of places, he gave silent thanks to his Master for leading him so quickly to this state of absolute knowledge. In the previous months, he had not fully comprehended the meaning behind the orders he had obeyed without question. It could never be said that he had failed in his duties, although, until now, he had had scant idea as to the real significance of those orders.

Until the night he had chanced upon – no, not chanced upon, been led *to – the girl.*

And now that he did *know the purpose of it all, he would pursue his mission with gladness.*

He would have to wait a while, however, to seal the fate of the thing in the freshly dug grave they were all now deserting. That was unfinished business – but caution must be employed to successfully execute the plan he'd been inspired by just last night.

He had waited so patiently for this next revelation, fearing with each silent day that he had somehow failed in his duties – and angered his Master, causing Him to remain silent. It had been so hard not to continue as before without a sign, but he had had the faith to wait. And his patience and belief had at last been rewarded.

The first sign had been the notice in the local evening newspaper, declaring the time and place of the debacle he had just witnessed.

The second had come as he prayed in the depths of night. As soon as he had heard the sweet words, he had known that it was absolutely the right next step to take. And he had not been enlightened earlier, he now realized, because the others had not been personal to him. They had merely been stepping stones to the one he was really intended to find.

The girl.

It was so logical, he wondered how he had missed it in the first place. But then, was it not arrogance to presume that this sudden understanding was attributable to himself? Of

course he understood now – now that he had been shown.
If he hadn't been, he would still have been as much in the
dark as the rest of them were.

And before too long, she *too would bathe in the light of*
eternal wisdom.

Saddened by the whole affair – and a little more understanding of Gwen Parry's despair than those in the
congregation he'd heard muttering accusations against
her – Seddon approached the funeral car just before
the door closed. Bending low, he spoke to the grieving
mother in respectful tones.

'Mrs Parry, I would like to offer my sincere con-
dolences on behalf of the Greater Manchester Con-
stabulary . . . And I'd like to assure you that we are
doing everything in our power to—'

Gwen Parry let out a screech of rage. 'Get away from
me, you bastard!' Spittle foamed at the corners of her
mouth as her sister and father physically restrained her
from getting at Seddon. 'My Linda wouldn't be dead if
you'd done your fucking jobs right! Useless, no-good,
dirty wankers! You didn't give a shit about them pros,
and now my Linda's gone because of it! I'll kill you if
you come near me again – I swear to God I will!'

'You'd better just go,' Linda's grandfather told Seddon
in a voice as grey as his complexion. 'This hasn't been
easy for her – for any of us.'

'I'm so sorry,' Seddon muttered lamely, backing away
quickly to save the family any further heartache.

He strode quickly to his car without once looking at any
of the mourners still making their way towards the gates,
so great was his guilt and shame. Unlocking the vehicles,

he jumped inside, pulling the door to behind him. Eyes closed, he rested his head against the seat's back.

Gwen Parry had every right to be angry, but it didn't make Seddon feel any less responsible. He felt the entire weight of her accusations lay firmly on his shoulders. *He* was leading the investigation. It was *his* duty to find the man responsible for killing her daughter. *His* fault that the maniac hadn't been caught before he got to Linda.

'Damn!' Slamming his fist down onto the steering wheel with frustration, he jumped when the horn issued a sharp blast. Glancing around the car park to see if anyone had noticed, he was glad to see that it was now almost deserted.

Letting out a long, painful sigh, he fired up the engine and was just about to pull out when a tap on the passenger side window stopped him. Looking up, he saw Lynne Wilde peering in at him, her hair straggling from its usual neat bun to hang limply down her wet cheeks. Leaning across, he opened the door. She climbed in, shivering in a thin jacket.

'Gracious, it's cold,' she complained, blowing on her fingers.

'Where's your car?' he asked, turning the heater up a notch.

'Back at the office,' she told him, holding her hands up to the heater vents. 'We were doing a pick-up in the van and we passed by the gates, so I had them drop me off. How did it go?'

Seddon shrugged. 'As well as can be expected, as they say. You want a lift back?'

'If you're going that way,' she said, then frowned,

looking at him with concern. 'You okay, Ken? You look a bit off-colour.'

'Nah, I'm fine.' Forcing a smile, he pulled out onto the path, waving as they passed the vicar.

'Reverend Vine,' Lynne said. 'Did he do the service?'

'Mmmm. Damn near started a riot, too.'

'Oh?'

'I'll tell you later. Don't suppose you fancy a coffee?'

Lynne checked her watch.

'Yes, okay, but it'll have to be a quick one. I really should be back already. We've got so many stiffs stacked up in the fridge at the moment, it'll be standing room only soon.'

Seddon shook his head, grinning. 'You've got such a way with words.'

Fifteen minutes later, dry and warm in a window seat at Café-au-Lait, he told Lynne about the fiasco of a funeral.

'I can't say I'm surprised,' she remarked when he'd finished. 'Reverend Vine's not exactly known for his tact.'

Frowning, Seddon sighed heavily. 'Yeah, but when it's a child, you'd have thought he could be a bit more sensitive.'

Lynne watched as the Detective Inspector gripped his cup, swirling the dregs until they lapped out onto his fingers. Passing him a tissue, she wondered at his distress. It wasn't just the funeral that was agitating him, she was sure – or even the vicar's crude attempts at humour. More likely it was the mother's outburst, but even that was par for the course in their profession and shouldn't be troubling him to this extent.

'Do you want to talk about it?' she asked quietly, glancing surreptitiously at her watch.

'What? No, no, I'm fine, really,' Seddon replied, pulling himself together. 'I was just . . .' Pausing, he shrugged.

'Feeling guilty?' she ventured.

'I guess so,' he admitted. 'More than you could imagine actually, and not just about this case.'

Lynne waited, sure he would elaborate if he wanted to.

'Do you mind?' He pulled a cigarette from his pocket.

'No, go ahead.'

Lighting it, he released the smoke loudly.

'It's Pauline,' he said after a moment. 'I'm disturbing her.'

'What do you mean, *disturbing* her?' Having met Pauline twice – albeit briefly – Lynne knew that she adored her husband, and would be concerned *for* him rather than disturbed *by* him.

'She thinks I'm withdrawing from her,' Seddon admitted, smiling sadly. 'Says she can't get two words out of me without twisting the thumbscrews, and that I'm snappy when I do speak. And she reckons I'm trying to make her a prisoner in her own home,' he added guiltily. 'But I can't help it, Lynne.' Looking up at her, his eyes were dark with embarrassment. 'It's not her, it's this damn case. Every time I look at her, I think about that kid and what that maniac did to her. I see *her* ripped to pieces, then I start worrying it's going to happen to Pauline if I don't protect her. But how am I supposed to do that when I can't get a single sodding thing on the bastard?'

Slamming his fist down on the table, he knocked his cup over, spilling what was left of his coffee. Lynne reached across and mopped it up with a tissue.

'Why now?' she asked. 'What's so different about this case that it should affect you like this? Don't get me wrong,' she went on quickly. 'It's not that I don't understand the emotion. I'm a mother, after all, and you should hear my kids complain about my over-protectiveness. But why now with Pauline, as opposed to all those other cases?'

'I don't know.' Seddon shrugged. 'I really don't.'

'I think you do,' Lynne ventured gently. 'I think you've just said it. You feel powerless because you haven't caught the man. Guilty for your ineffectiveness, and therefore worthless in Pauline's eyes. She's supposed to see you as the all-conquering hero, and you've failed.'

Seddon looked up with a grin. 'You train for psychiatry, or something?'

'Just stating the obvious,' Lynne said. 'And if that *is* the truth of it, Ken, then recognize it and let it go before you smother her with fear. Intelligent women don't take kindly to being locked away from the outside world. And for God's sake, talk to her about how you're feeling. She'll understand.'

Seddon nodded. 'You're right. I'm being unfair.'

Lynne smiled. 'No, you're being a typical man. Now, how about that lift? You can tell me any new developments on the way.'

'Fat chance of that,' he snorted, standing up.

'By the way,' she said, smiling as he held the door open for her. 'I always respond well to flowers.'

Seddon gave a mock-shocked gasp. 'I can't buy you flowers! I'm a married man!'

'Shut up!' Lynne grinned, knowing full well that he knew what she'd meant.

Arriving at the Coroner's offices a little while later, Lynne thanked Seddon for the lift and climbed out. Looking back at him before she closed the door, she said, 'Don't forget the flowers.'

Grinning, he saluted. 'Yes, ma'am.'

Pauline was standing on a stool, changing the lounge nets, when she saw her husband pulling up outside the house. He left the car at the kerb, obviously not intending to stay long, but that was hardly surprising given that he wasn't actually due back until later tonight. It was more surprising that he was here at all, and she hoped he wasn't just making sure she'd stayed in. It was becoming a struggle to accommodate his increasing paranoia, without completely losing her independence by humouring him. It wasn't even a full week since he'd been called out to Alexandra Park to deal with the murdered girl, but it already felt like a year.

'Pauline, I just came to—'

'Not to check up on me, I hope?' she interrupted firmly. 'Because I can't—'

'No!' Interrupting her now, Seddon shook his head. 'To give you these, actually.' He pulled a small, pretty bunch of flowers from behind his back and held them out to her. 'Not much, I know, but I got them from a bucket at the garage. I, er, just wanted to tell you I'm sorry. I've been behaving like a complete idiot for the past few days, but I'm all right now.'

Stepping down from the stool, Pauline accepted the flowers with a smile.

'Thanks, they're lovely. I'll put them in a vase. So, why the change of heart?'

'I talked to Lynne Wilde,' he said, following her through to the kitchen. 'Remember her?'

Pauline smiled. 'Oh, yes?'

'Yeah. Told her I was doing your nut in worrying about this case, and she said I should tell you what's going through my head and let you get on with your life. Actually, she said you were far too intelligent to put up with my caveman tactics,' he added with a sheepish grin.

Pauline cocked an eyebrow. 'Smart lady. We'll have to invite her for dinner.'

'Mmmm,' Seddon murmured, coming up behind her as she filled the vase at the sink. 'But not tonight. I want you all to myself tonight. No work, no colleagues – no clothes!'

'Sounds good to me. Now, how about a nice cup of coffee?'

'God, you know the way to a man's heart!'

Pauline smiled and pushed him firmly onto a kitchen chair. She put the flowers into the vase, then made the coffee.

'All right,' she said, joining him at the table. 'Talk to me. Tell me exactly what's worrying you, and let's get it sorted once and for all.'

Driving back to the station twenty minutes later, Seddon felt a new determination to solve the case – and not to allow the hopelessness of it to affect him again. Any clue, however slight, however insignificant, he would pounce on it and rag it until it yielded something further. And he wouldn't stop until he had the bastard behind bars where he belonged.

Lisa, Debbie and Jasmine entered Alexander Park in a huddle of linked arms – each dreading seeing the spot where Linda had been killed, but in absolute agreement that they had to do this. Now – today.

Stopping just inside the gates, they looked at each other fearfully, shivering despite the sunshine that had begun to struggle through since the rain had stopped ten minutes earlier.

'Rizlas?' Lisa said.

'Here.' Jasmine reached into her pocket and pulled the pack of papers out. 'Cig?'

'Here.' Lisa held up the cigarette she'd been clutching – now bent, and soggy from the sweat on her palm. 'I've got the draw as well.'

'I've got the matches.' Debbie shook the small box.

'You roll best, Lisa,' said Jasmine. 'You take it.'

Clutching the paraphernalia tightly, Lisa took a deep breath. 'Let's go, then.'

Making their way to the lake, they climbed over the low fence and stepped gingerly around the water's edge to the fishing platform.

'We were sitting here,' Jasmine said, pointing out the exact spot. 'I was here, and L-Linda was th-there.'

'Ah, don't cry, Jas, come here.' Going to Jasmine, Debbie put her arms around her and hugged her while she sobbed.

Blinking back her own tears, Lisa sat down on the wet

boards and began to roll the spliff they were to smoke in Linda's memory. Debbie and Jasmine joined her when their sobbing had subsided.

Slipping the roach in, Lisa lit the smoke and took a deep pull on it before passing it to Debbie. Debbie took her pull and passed it to Jasmine. Taking it back, Lisa held it up to the sky.

'To Linda,' she said.

'To Linda!' the others chorused, tears streaming down their cheeks.

12

In the days following Linda Parry's funeral, Seddon and his team spent every waking moment poring over the documentation relating to all the murders, hoping in vain to find anything they might have overlooked that would give them a lead. Day after fruitless day, they traipsed over each murder site, searching for a new angle. They found nothing, but Seddon would not give up. He contacted Lynne Wilde daily – both to update her as to the *nothing* he still had, and to beg her to miraculously find them something to work with.

The only consolation he could draw from his futile efforts was that no more murders had been committed in the meantime. But while he hoped it was the high police presence that was keeping their killer off the streets, he secretly feared that the man was simply biding his time.

And, all too soon, his fears were realized.

As Friday bled into Saturday, a three a.m. call woke him from a restless sleep. As if his body had been expecting it, he found himself pulling his trousers on even as he answered the ringing phone.

Five minutes later, he was on his way out of the door.

Arriving at Southern Cemetery, he looked about him

in utter disbelief, saying to nobody in particular: 'I do not fucking *believe* this! This has got to be a fucking joke?'

In the glare of the hastily erected arc lights, the plundered grave looked for all the world like it belonged on the set of a 'Hammer House of Horrors' movie.

The mound of earth he had witnessed being shovelled in to cover the coffin just days ago was now back in its original pile beside the grave.

The piles of respectfully laid flowers and wreaths were scattered all over the place.

The coffin he had seen interred – so lovingly chosen, and *bolted* – was now back up top, *open*.

But worst of all, Linda Parry's corpse had been *arranged* within it.

Naked now, stripped of the name-brand clothes her mother had barely managed to afford in which to send her child into God's care, her arms and legs had been draped over the sides of the casket. Her mouth had been forced open and moulded into a silent 'O' that was as wide as her unseeing eyes now were, giving her the gruesome appearance of a rubber sex doll waiting to be used.

Swallowing down a surge of nausea, Seddon turned on the assembled squad of officers and barked, 'Somebody cover her up, for God's sake!'

'We were told to leave it, sir,' a green-faced PC told him.

'Well, now I'm telling you to cover *her* up!'

Turning from the macabre scene, Seddon marched back to his car and snatched up the pack of cigarettes he'd left on the seat. Lighting one with wildly shaking fingers, he began to pace the car park in tight, furious circles.

In all his days, he'd never seen anything like this. This wasn't your normal run-of-the-mill grave-robbing. This was far more sinister. This was calculated. There were some sick bastards in this world, but this defied belief. Digging the poor cow up and undressing and *fiddling* with her! What kind of monster pulled shit like this?

Turning at the sound of the approaching Forensics van, he stopped his pacing and waited for Lynne Wilde to emerge. When she did, she looked frazzled and sleep-dazed.

With only the light from the interior of the van where it streamed through the vehicle's open doors illuminating their faces, they peered at each other and shook their heads simultaneously – each unable to find anything remotely suitable to the occasion to say.

Lynne finally broke the silence as they made their way to the grave.

'Who reported it?'

Seddon shrugged, his shoulders a mass of knotted muscle.

'I'm not sure. I didn't take it all in at the time. Something about a courting couple, I think?'

'Nice end to a romantic Friday evening,' she muttered grimly.

'Mmmm,' he murmured, adding ominously, 'I just hope theirs was the *only* romantic evening being enjoyed here tonight.'

Understanding the implication, Lynne let a breath hiss out between her teeth. 'We'll soon know if it wasn't.'

He stayed down behind the wall of the florist's shop on the corner opposite the cemetery. When the Forensics van had passed through the gates and disgorged its crew, he climbed stealthily back up to his viewing perch. Shielded by the branches of a huge overhanging yew tree that was rooted in the smaller pet cemetery behind him, he rested his binoculars on the flat ledge of the wall and resumed his surveillance.

It was almost ten minutes before he saw the flurry of activity and knew that they had discovered the truth. Smiling, he lowered himself back down, satisfied that they now – at last – were beginning to realize what they were dealing with.

Not just any old ordinary sicko – oh, no! They had now witnessed the awesome power of the only truly chosen one.

And now that his duties were almost completed, he could go home and prepare for the next stage.

The forget-me-not was inside the vagina this time. Extracting it with a pair of tweezers, Lynne slipped it delicately into the evidence bag.

'You absolute fucking *bastard*!' she hissed.

'Has he?' Seddon demanded through gritted teeth.

Nodding, Lynne closed her eyes.

'Bad?' he asked.

Snapping her eyes open again, she stared up at him in amazement.

'How could it *not* be bad, for Christ's sake? I can't think of anything *more* bad, can you?'

'Oh, *fuck*!' he bellowed, reaching up and actually pulling at his own hair in frustration and disgust. 'Fuck fuck *fuck*!'

'Er, sir . . .' A young PC tapped his shoulder. 'I think you'd better see this.'

'*What?*' Turning to see what the PC was pointing at, Seddon saw a local independent TV company news truck rolling up to the gates, closely followed by a jeep bearing the *Southern Herald* newspaper logo.

'Aw shit! Who the fucking hell told *them?*' he snapped. Then, turning back to the PC, he bellowed, 'You'd better get the fuck over there, son, 'cos I'm telling you now, if one of those vultures sets foot through that gate, I'll personally rip your bollocks off and stick 'em up your arse!'

'Yes, sir!'

'Bring that screen around,' Lynne ordered her team. 'I don't want so much as a hair on this girl's head on the front pages tomorrow!'

Barred from entering as the PC hurriedly closed the gates, the *Herald* photographer climbed onto the roof of the jeep and pointed his infra-red telescopic lens towards the scene within – snapping for all he was worth as the screen was hurriedly closed in around the open coffin.

Going one better, the TV crew hydraulically hoisted their cameraman up above the level of the gates. The driver radioed in for the eye-in-the-sky helicopter to be deployed as the smarmy presenter tried in vain to interview the PC through the gates.

Composing himself to a state of mere simmering fury, Seddon finally made his way over to give a brief account of the situation. There was no point trying to keep this quiet but with luck he could at least minimize the effect the news was going to have not only on Linda Parry's grieving family but on the population of Manchester as a whole – who already suspected that the police were doing nothing to catch the killer.

'Can you tell us what's happened, Inspector?' The presenter thrust his microphone through the gate as Seddon approached. He was instantly joined by the *Herald* reporter.

'Yeah . . . can you confirm that Linda Parry's grave has been vandalized?'

'Inspector . . . is it true that a couple—'

Seddon held his hands up until they ceased their questioning.

'It's DI Seddon,' he told them, 'and no, I can't confirm or deny *anything* at this stage – as you well know. I would, however, be very interested to know where you got your information from? And don't do that!' he snapped as the *Herald* photographer jumped down from the jeep and trained his lens on Seddon's face.

'He's only doing his job, Mr Seddon,' the reporter said, smiling greasily. 'And on the point of how we found out,' he went on, 'that's confidential, as *you* well know. Now we can do this with your official sanction, or we can report exactly what we *believe* to be true . . . Which would you rather?'

Seddon bit back an urge to scream at them all to go fuck themselves. Instead, returning a tight smile, he said as reasonably as possible, 'Nobody's saying you won't get your pound of flesh, gentlemen, but obviously it is too early to give you a detailed account at this time. Whatever you *do* report, however, I'm sure I don't need to remind you that it would be totally irresponsible of you to go by what you might have heard from *whatever* source without waiting for the full facts. That, of course, would be detrimental to our efforts to find the killer before—'

'So, you *are* telling us this has something to do with

the prostitute-killer?' the presenter cut in, pouncing on the inadvertent slip.

Mentally kicking himself, Seddon ground out between his teeth, 'No, of course I'm not saying that this is connected to those murders. I'm simply stating that any news relating to the deceased girl right now is likely to add fuel to the wrong sort of fires – and we *all* know the damage that could do, don't we, *gentlemen?*'

'I don't see how?' the reporter replied evenly. 'Facts are facts.'

'And hysteria is destructive,' Seddon shot back. 'And that is exactly what we'll get if you present this irresponsibly.'

'Well, then,' the presenter interjected, smiling. 'Perhaps you'd like to tell us what you *want* us to say?'

Lighting a candle, he placed it carefully in the centre of the altar, then laid his latest trophy down in front of this and reverently smoothed the creases from them.

How unlike the first pair he had taken from the fat girl these panties were. How very virginal *did the flowery cotton seem in comparison with the black-silk sluttishness of the first pair.*

So very indicative of the soul-cleansing he had administered.

Kneeling now, he joined his hands together and rested his forehead on the thumbs.

The heat of his exertions began to seep from his brow into the flesh of his hands. It travelled slowly up his arms, spreading out across his shoulders, then down into his chest and back. As the warmth suffused his entire body, he held his breath for a moment, afraid of dulling the sensation with conscious thought.

Eyes tightly closed, he began to breathe deeply, willing his mind to clear of the pictures stored there – and the sensual pleasure they brought. The very earthly pleasures he must never indulge in this of all places.

The grave . . . The digging with his bare' hands . . . The coffin . . . The prised-open lid . . . The whore within . . .

'It is done,' he said.

Even spoken softly, the words seemed to reverberate around the small room. He felt a moment's irritation at his lack of control, then reminded himself that there was no longer anyone on the other side of the wall to hear him.

The previous tenant of the flat next door had taken a particular dislike to his choice of music. A large, sweaty bully of a man, the previous tenant had made a pathetic attempt at intimidation, threatening all manner of nonsense. All of which had gained the man nothing but the onset of some pretty potent mind games. It hadn't taken very long at all before the troublesome lout took flight. But then, how could anybody escape the awesome power of the Master – let alone such a vacuous coward as that tenant had been?

Clearing his mind of the multitudinous thoughts at last, he finally heard what he had been waiting for.

Tomorrow.

Satisfied, he rose to his feet and turned to the huge, gilt-edged mirror standing against the opposite wall. He regarded his candlelit nudity with pride, eyes riveted to this mirror-self as he stroked his hands along the length of his engorged member – thrilling in its history, proud of its impartial abilities.

A lesser man could not hope to possess, nor yet provide

the stamina to raise and sustain this glorious testament to manhood. Nor could a lesser man ever hope to fulfil the requirements of this most demanding of tasks. For it took far more than mere testosterone to plunge oneself into the Devil's abyss time after time – even when one was aware of the rewards.

'I do believe I will succeed . . . I do believe I will succeed . . . I do believe . . .'

The chant began as softly as a feather floating to the ground from a great height, and rose in volume and intensity with each masturbatory stroke until, with a final victorious yell, he climaxed – turning as he did so to spray the room with gloriously unfettered seed.

And only then, when he was completely sated, did he succumb to the sleep of the truly blessed.

13

Lisa woke early on Saturday – thanks to Monty, who she'd coaxed into her room the night before for comfort, scraping at the door.

'Pack it in,' she moaned. 'I don't wanna get up yet.'

Whining, Monty ran across to the bed and nudged her with his wet snout before returning to the door for a renewed bout of carpet digging.

'All right, you little shit!' she said when she couldn't stand it any longer. 'All right!'

Getting up, she shivered in the cold air. Reaching for her dressing gown, she threw it on, then yanked the door open and followed the galloping dog down the stairs.

Letting him out onto the landing for his early-morning pee, she left the door slightly ajar and wandered into the kitchen to put the kettle on, muttering under her breath the whole time: 'Stupid dog should learn how to hold it in! And *she* should get the bleeding heating fixed before we freeze to bleeding death! And as for that bitch, Debbie bleeding Morgan, she should shrivel up and die, the two-faced cow!'

Kicking the front door shut when Monty came back in, Lisa carried her tea through to the living room and plonked herself down on the couch with a face of sheer misery.

Yeah, it was shit that Linda had been murdered, but

that didn't give Jasmine the right to nick Debbie off her, did it? But that's exactly what she *had* done. But that Debbie had gone along with it quite willingly, was what pissed her off the most. And that Debbie's mum thought Jasmine was just *great*. That was the ultimate kick in the teeth, that was! Jasmine was always round there these days, having her tea or staying over. It made Lisa sick – and really, really angry.

It had all started on the day of the funeral. In the park they'd been a team, smoking the spliff and crying for Linda. But when it came time to go home, Lisa had got a real shock. She'd hugged Jasmine and said goodbye, then she'd stupidly waited for Debbie to do the same. Instead, Debbie had hugged and said goodbye to *Lisa*.

'Aren't you walking back with me?' Lisa had asked.

And Debbie had said, 'No . . . Didn't I tell you? I'm going to Jas's for dinner. She asked me the other day.'

And that had been that. They'd linked arms and gone one way; Lisa had sulked and gone the other. And they'd barely crossed paths since. Apart from the other day when she'd seen them dashing into Debbie's flat as she was calling Monty in. And she knew full well they *had* seen her, the bitches, no matter how much Debbie denied it the next day – just before setting off to meet Jasmine at the baths!

Well, sack 'em! She didn't need either of them!

'Right, Monts!' she said angrily, causing the dog's ears to twitch with trepidation as he wondered what he'd done wrong now. 'I've had enough of this shit! I'm gonna wash me hair, then I'm going for a walk, and I'm staying out till I find Benny! *He*'s still me friend, even if them cows have abandoned me!'

That decided, Lisa went back to the kitchen and refilled the kettle. Leaning back against the sink as she waited for it to boil, she almost jumped out of her skin when someone rapped sharply on the window behind her.

'What the hell did you do that for?' she demanded, wrenching the door open, making both Debbie and Jasmine start. 'You nearly gave me a heart attack!'

'Sorry,' Debbie spluttered, 'but you've got to see this.'

'See what?' Lisa asked coldly, giving Jasmine a dirty look.

'Show her,' Jasmine said, pushing Debbie forward.

'Show me what?'

'This.' Debbie held a newspaper out towards her.

'A paper,' Lisa sneered, folding her arms. 'So?'

Opening it, Debbie held it in front of Lisa so that the headline screamed into her face: '*Murder Victim's Grave Ransacked!*'

'What the hell is this?' Lisa demanded, snatching it from Debbie's hand.

'You've got to read it,' Jasmine said. 'It's awful.'

Staring at the paper, Lisa stepped back. 'You'd better come in.'

Sitting on the couch with Debbie and Jasmine on either side of her, she read the report, her lips moving soundlessly over each word.

Murdered schoolgirl Linda Parry's grave was ransacked last night in what police are describing as a 'sick new twist' in the recent spate of rape/murders occurring in Manchester.

Linda, who was only thirteen years old, was murdered

almost two weeks ago in Moss Side's Alexander Park. Police still haven't managed to trace her killer, believed to be the same man responsible for the murder of five prostitutes in recent months, all within a five-mile radius of Alexander Park.

We received a call to our Incident Hotline in the early hours of this morning from a man claiming to have seen the culprit responsible for this latest atrocity. The 42-year-old man, who wishes to remain anonymous, told our reporter Mitch Lee that he had been cutting through the Cemetery with a female friend when they saw a man behaving suspiciously near one of the graves. The man fled when he realized he'd been seen and despite a chase he got away, leaving behind Linda Parry's ransacked grave.

When asked to comment, Detective Inspector Ken Seddon of Greater Manchester Police would only say that somebody had 'tampered' with the grave, but refused to give further details.

Our reporter didn't leave it there. Go to page three for exclusive pictures of the devastating scene.

'Oh, God!' Lisa moaned after going to page three and seeing the grainy aerial shots of Linda's grave, partially concealed by the scene-of-crime screen. 'How could anyone *do* that?'

'That's not the worst of it,' Jasmine said, leaning towards her to point something out. 'Look behind that screen thing . . . See the coffin?'

'What?' Lisa peered but couldn't see what she was getting at.

'It's open!' Debbie explained. 'The lid's off!'

'No way!'

'*Way*!'

'Oh my God! It is, as well!'

'Told you!'

'We'll have to go and see it,' Lisa declared after a moment. 'Make sure it's all been put back right.'

Debbie and Jasmine exchanged a glance. 'You can't get in,' Debbie said quietly.

Lisa glared at them, eyes narrowed. 'You've already been, haven't you?' she accused.

Debbie nodded and looked down guiltily.

'Well, it's closer to my house,' Jasmine said. 'We thought we might as well go on our way here, didn't we, Deb'?'

'Yeah,' Debbie admitted, adding quickly, 'but we *were* coming to tell you, Lisa.'

'Yeah, but only *after*,' Lisa snapped. 'So how come you was at hers so early, anyway?' she asked, shooting a poisonous look at Jasmine.

Debbie blushed. 'I stayed there last night,' she admitted guiltily.

'Oh, surprise, surprise!' Lisa said angrily. 'All right, well, you've told me now, so youse can piss off, can't you?'

'Aw, Lisa . . . don't be like that.'

'Just get lost,' Lisa hissed. 'I've had enough of you two.'

'Come on, Debs.' Jumping to her feet, Jasmine peered pointedly around the messy room. 'We don't have to stay in this stinking dump. Anyway, Jamie and Steve are waiting for us!'

Lisa leaped up at this final insult and went for Jasmine.

Managing to get between them, Debbie pushed Jasmine towards the door – afraid not only of what Lisa would do to Jasmine, but what Pat would do to Debbie if she heard the commotion and came downstairs.

Herding Jasmine out, she said, 'I'm sorry, Lisa, I didn't mean to upset you. I'll come round later, yeah?'

'Go and fuck yourself!' Lisa screeched, sending them both scurrying out.

When they'd gone, Lisa rooted down the cushions of the couch for a cigarette. Even a dimp would do – anything to quieten the screaming anger in her belly. Finding a crushed Regal King Size, she smoothed it out and took it to the window. Lighting it, she leaned her head and shoulders right out of the window, puffing on it quickly – knowing that her mum would kill her if she walked in and caught her at it.

A couple of minutes later, she saw Debbie and Jasmine emerge from the side of the block. Huddled together, arms linked like a pair of old women, they headed over City Road and disappeared onto the estate. Obviously going to meet the lads at the market, Lisa surmised, scowling. That was where *she* and Debbie used to go on Saturday mornings – before Jasmine stuck her rotten oar in and ruined everything.

She still didn't understand quite how it had happened. When Linda had still been alive Jasmine had taken the piss out of Debbie all the time. And *now* look at them!

Throwing her dimp down into the garden below, she slammed the window shut in disgust. Well, *let* them push her out – see if she cared. When they saw her with Benny they'd be sorry!

Rushing upstairs, Lisa had a quick wash and brushed

her teeth, then got dressed and ran a comb through her still-greasy hair. Washing it would have to wait.

Today was the day she would meet up with Benny again, she vowed – even if she had to hang around the Addy till it was too dark to see her own hand in front of her nose!

Pat woke up with a pounding head and a mouth full of saliva. Feeling an all-too-familiar churning in her bowels, she immediately knew that the King Prawn Special she'd indulged in the night before had been a terrible mistake.

Cursing herself for going to the dingy Chinese take-away she usually avoided like the plague, she reached for the bottle of vodka on the bedside table – hoping to cure the head if not the stomach. Draining the final inch from it, she stuck her tongue inside to catch the last drips. But it wasn't enough. She needed another bottle.

Hearing Lisa going down the stairs, she croaked, 'Lisa? . . . Come here a minute, will you?'

Lisa didn't answer, and seconds later Pat heard the front door clicking shut.

'You selfish little bitch!' she yelled, slumping back against the pillow.

When her stomach began to spasm, Pat forced herself up and rushed to the toilet – for the first trip on what she knew from experience would be a day-long ticket to ride.

Crossing over Bonsall Street, Benny picked his way across the rubble that was all that remained of the flats he had lived his early life in.

Once upon a time, when he'd still had a mother.

Coming to the half-destroyed chain-link fence, he scrambled over it, then forced his way through the dense, overgrown bushes on the other side until he reached the wooden fence encircling the Addy. Hoisting himself up onto this, he smiled when he saw the familiar figure sitting on the bench just a couple of feet away. He'd known she would be here today.

Jumping down silently, he crept up on her.

'Well, well! I thought I'd find you here.'

Lisa jumped when she heard his voice. She'd been here twenty minutes, and had already mentally given up on him appearing – *almost*.

'Shit! You scared me half to death!' she scolded him, patting her thudding ribcage – as if it were the shock of his creeping up on her that had made her heart race, and not the excitement of seeing him again.

Hopping easily over the back of the bench, Benny sat down beside her, stretching his long legs out before him.

'Sorry, couldn't resist. So, were you waiting for me, or what?'

'Pfft!' Lisa snorted. 'As if!'

'Wouldn't mind if you were,' he said, taking two cigarettes from his pack. Lighting them both, he handed one to Lisa. 'I've been thinking about you, actually.'

'Have you?' she gasped, almost choking on the smoke she'd just inhaled.

'Yeah. I saw it in the paper about that girl, and I remembered you saying she was your friend. Did you see it?'

'Yeah.' Lisa nodded sadly. '*Debbie* brought it round this morning.'

'Oh?' Benny raised a questioning eyebrow at the way she had spat out her friend's name. 'Fallen out again, have you?'

'Huh! You could say that.'

'I don't know!' Sighing, he shook his head. 'You girls and your silly arguments.'

'It's not *my* fault,' Lisa protested. '*She*'s the one who's pissed off with someone else.'

'Language.'

'Sorry. But it *is* her fault. She's supposed to be my best mate, but ever since Linda got done in she's been hanging about with *her* best mate. I hardly ever see her no more, and when I do, they're always together, like they've been bleedin' super-glued or something! They make me sick!'

'I see.'

'And not only that,' she went on, turning right around on the bench now, scowling with indignation. 'Remember that night when I met you? . . . How me and her had fallen out 'cos she got off with my boyfriend?'

'*Your* boyfriend?' he said softly.

Lisa blushed, then flapped her hand, saying, 'Yeah, well, you know what I mean – the lad I'd liked for ages!'

'I remember.' He nodded, suppressing a smile at her animated indignation.

'Well, she's only got off with him *again*!' she went on, her voice rising with outrage. 'I told them to get lost, so then Jasmine tells her to hurry up 'cos *he*'d be waiting for them! Don't you think that's well cheeky?'

Benny stared off into the distance for a moment, then said, 'Know what I think?'

'What?'

'Sounds to me like you need a new friend.'

'Huh, no kidding!' Lisa muttered, pursing her mouth.

'Mmmm,' he murmured, nodding thoughtfully. 'A new friend to show her that you don't need her any more. That you don't care *who* she sees, or who she goes out with. That's guaranteed to make her jealous.'

'You reckon?'

'Oh, yeah!' He nodded wisely. 'That never fails. And I'll tell you what . . .' Pausing, he looked at her for a while, eyes narrowed as he struggled with his thoughts. Then, suddenly, he shook his head and said, 'Then again, no. Maybe that's not such a good idea.'

'What?' she demanded. 'Tell me?'

'No, nothing. Forget I said anything. It was just some stupid idea.'

'Aw, please. I hate it when people do that.'

Looking back at her, Benny shrugged. 'Okay, why not? It can't do any harm, can it?'

'*What*?' Lisa squawked, feeling she'd burst if he didn't tell her. '*Benny!*'

'All right!' He laughed. 'I was just thinking . . . If you want, we could hang about together for a bit. Let them see us together, show them you don't need them.'

'Wow, yeah!' she squealed. 'That'd be so cool! They'd shit a brick!'

'Language.'

'Sorry. But, God, *yeah!*' Half rising from her seat, she looked at him eagerly. 'Can we go now? They'll probably be at the market.'

Benny looked at his watch and pursed his lips. 'Bit difficult right this minute, actually. Tell you what, I just need to go back to my flat to pick something up, then I'll meet you down the market in say . . . twenty minutes?'

'Aw, can't I come with you?'

Benny frowned. 'Oh, I don't know about that. What if someone saw us and got the wrong idea?'

'Like what?' Lisa asked.

He gave her an indulgent smile. 'And I thought you were smart.'

'I don't see what's so wrong about us walking down the street together,' she retorted sulkily.

'*You* know there's nothing wrong with it, and so do I,' Benny stated patiently. 'But other people might think I'm doing something wrong.'

'But you're not!' Blushing, Lisa looked down at her feet, unable to meet his eye in case he saw the wishes lodged there.

Benny laughed, then said, 'You know what, Lisa? You're right! We're doing nothing wrong. But just to be on the safe side,' he went on more seriously, 'how about if we don't walk there together? How about you follow me? I'll leave my door open when I get there, and you come in a few minutes after me, okay?'

'Cool!' Lisa said, grinning widely.

Benny jumped to his feet.

'Come on then, Shadow, my friend . . . *Shadow* me!'

Lisa could hardly keep the grin off her face as she followed Benny at a discreet distance. She had to trot a couple of times to catch up with him when he disappeared around a corner, but this just added to the fun. She felt like a spy – or, better yet, a private detective trailing a suspect. But it was the thought of Debbie seeing her with Benny that was really exciting her. She couldn't wait to see Debbie's face when she copped a load of him!

Having walked around every little back street in Hulme – including a few she'd never known existed, despite having lived there all her life – Lisa expected to end up somewhere miles out. She was surprised to find herself still in Hulme when Benny finally stopped. And on a road she knew very well – the road she walked along every day to get to school.

On one side of the road it was wall-to-wall blocks of shabby council flats – where all the misfits were shoved to keep them away from the 'decent people', according to Sue Morgan, who had told Debbie, who'd duly told Lisa. On the other side, the row of shops Lisa and her mates regularly shoplifted from on their way home from school. Hairy Man's was their favourite. The owner – a fat, Greek man with a welcome-mat of grey hair sprouting right up and over the neck of his grubby, sweat-stained T-shirt – was the easiest gimp in the world to wind up. He lived above his stinky little empire, and spent every waking moment stacking and re-stacking the shelves – when he wasn't bossing his fat, moustachioed wife about, or chasing Lisa and her mates with the big stick he kept under the counter.

Hearing a quick, shrill whistle, Lisa looked across the road and saw Benny opening the ground-floor door of Linton Court – the block of flats directly opposite Hairy Man's shop. She smiled to herself, pleased to know that they had this shared territory in common.

When he'd gone inside, she strolled along to the junk shop two units down from Hairy Man's and pretended to study the array of haphazardly jumbled rubbish displayed in the window. A couple of minutes later, she turned casually and crossed the road.

It was dark and cold inside Benny's block. Lisa wrinkled her nose as the stench of something putrid festering unseen assailed her nostrils.

'Up here,' Benny hissed.

Looking up, she saw him leaning over the metal banister rail a couple of flights up. He had a finger to his lips, cautioning silence. Tiptoeing across the stained concrete, Lisa started up the stairs.

When she reached Benny's floor, he was waiting in the open doorway to his flat. Quickly ushering her inside, he closed the door firmly behind them.

'Whew!' Grinning widely, he wiped imaginary sweat from his brow. 'Thought we'd never make it.'

'Me too!' Lisa giggled, casting a furtive glance around the small hall with its three closed doors.

'Welcome to my humble abode,' he said then and, stepping aside, he pushed open the centre door and waved her inside with a theatrical bow. 'After you, my lady.'

Lisa went through into what was obviously the living room – although it was difficult to tell as it was so dark, the window completely obscured by a heavy pair of floor-length brown curtains. Coming in behind her, Benny switched on the overhead light.

'Would Madam care to take a seat?' he asked, slipping his jacket off and draping it across the back of an old orange and brown couch.

'Thanks.' Lisa smiled, feeling suddenly shy as she perched on the edge of the couch and looked about her.

In the stark glare of the unshaded bulb, she saw that the room was neat and stark. Apart from the couch and one matching armchair – both of which had seen better days – there was only the barest minimum of furniture.

Against the far wall, beside a door which, she noticed with a spark of curiosity, had an enormous padlock securing it, there stood a dangerous-looking electric fire – its flex so frayed in places that the inner wires were visible. To the right of this, an ancient TV set dominated the corner, on top of which sat a large, paint-splattered ghetto blaster with a neat pile of cassette tapes stacked against it. And beside this, beneath the shielded window, stood a small, spindly-legged orange-wood table. There was nothing else – no pictures, ornaments, books or papers. Nothing at all to suggest that someone actually lived here.

Placing his cigarettes and lighter on the table, Benny rubbed his hands together.

'It's not too cold for you, is it? I could put the heating on for a bit if you want?'

Lisa thought it an odd suggestion when they were only supposed to be here for a few minutes, but she nodded anyway – hoping that if they stayed a while they'd get too settled to leave.

Now that she'd managed to gain entry into Benny's private space, the thought of going to the market seemed less important somehow. There would be plenty of opportunities to rub Benny in Debbie's face. Right now, she was more interested in seeing how he lived – *and* in making her presence felt in his home.

'Do you want a drink?' Benny asked, after turning

both the dry-air heating and the fire on. 'I've got tea. Or I could nip out and get some juice, or something?'

'Tea's fine, thanks.'

Sitting back as Benny made his way into the small kitchenette to her left, Lisa craned her neck to see into the room as he switched the light on. It too was neat and free of clutter. An old but incredibly clean electric cooker and a small, chipped fridge were the only pieces of furniture, as far as she could see. There were no gadgets other than a kettle on the single worktop and, surprisingly, no dishes or cutlery littering the shiny draining board.

Boy, it was nothing like her house, that was for sure! You couldn't move in there for dirty pots and mouldy plates.

'Do you take sugar?' Benny called over his shoulder as he filled the kettle.

'Erm, yeah . . . three, please.'

Turning to look at her, Benny shook his head. '*Three*? That's disgusting! You'll have two!'

Lisa grinned. 'All right, but I won't like it.'

'Yes, you will.'

'Benny?' Lisa called after a minute. Getting no answer, she tried again, a little louder. '*Benny?*'

This time he turned around.

'Sorry? Did you say something?'

'Yeah, I just wondered . . .' She pointed towards the table. 'Could I have one of your fags, please?'

'Sure, help yourself.' He waved a hand, then turned back to spoon loose tea into a pot he'd taken from the cupboard.

'Have you got an ashtray?' she asked then.

'On the window ledge. But don't open the curtains!'

'I won't,' she said, then asked, 'How come you've got them shut this early, anyhow?'

'I don't like people looking in on my life,' Benny said – thrilling her with the revelation that she must be one of the few to have seen, let alone *been inside* his kingdom.

Smiling at her privileged status, she eased her hand behind the curtain and tapped her fingers along the ledge until she found the ashtray.

'Here we are, then,' Benny said, coming back into the room carrying two steaming cups.

'Thanks.' Taking one from him, Lisa sat back down on the couch, wincing as the heat scalded her fingers.

Benny sat on the chair and gulped at his tea as though his mouth were made of asbestos.

'Drink up,' he said after a moment when she still hadn't tasted hers.

'It's a bit too hot,' she said.

'Best way to drink it,' he said. 'Just sip it, you'll soon get used to it.'

Lisa's nostrils twitched as the strange, aromatic steam drifted up her nose. Not wanting to appear ungrateful with Benny watching her, she took a tentative sip – grimacing when the bitter liquid scorched her tongue. It tasted absolutely disgusting.

Benny laughed out loud. 'Bit weird, huh?'

She grinned sheepishly. 'Just a bit.'

'It's my favourite,' he said. 'Bit of an acquired taste, admittedly, but you soon get used to it. And it's actually really good for you.'

'Yeah?' she asked doubtfully, wondering how anything that tasted so foul could possibly be good for you.

'Oh, yes.' He nodded knowledgeably. 'It's called Pershong-Lai. It's the fennel that makes it taste a bit weird, but it's great for the circulation. And the Lai bit is a really effective blood-cleanser.'

Lisa was impressed – even if she wasn't sure she needed anything to cleanse her blood or aid her circulation. She took another sip anyway, eager to show that she too could be sophisticated. Her twisted expression of disgust made Benny laugh again.

'Here's a tip,' he said. 'Just hold your nose and pour it in. You won't taste it, and you'll feel great in no time.'

Taking a deep breath, she did as he'd said, and found to her relief that it really worked. Not wanting to prolong the agony, she waited a minute, then downed the whole lot in one.

'Good girl!' Benny said when she triumphantly displayed the empty cup. 'You see if that doesn't make you feel wonderful. Now, how about some music?'

'Yeah, sure. You got any Britney?'

'Any *what*?'

Lisa smirked at his ignorance. 'Britney Spears? Oh, never mind. What about Robbie? I love him.'

'*Robbie* . . . ?'

'Williams?'

'Sorry.' He shrugged.

'Oh, yeah, I forgot,' she quipped, relaxing more by the second. 'You're too *old* for stuff like that! So what *have* you got, then? No, don't tell me,' she went on facetiously. 'Frank Sinatra? Lulu?'

Giving her a mock-hooded look, Benny stood up.

'Don't be so cheeky! I'll have you know I've got good taste in music.'

Placing a tape in the machine, he pressed 'play' and pushed the volume control up, then sat back down, tapping his fingers on the arm of his chair in time to the raucous rock music now flooding the room.

Lisa screwed her eyes up as the sheer volume rattled the teeth in her head.

'Gawd, what *is* this?' she shouted over the noise.

'Whitesnake. Great, isn't it?'

'If you say so!' She grimaced. 'I prefer something a bit more souly, myself.'

A look of irritation flickered across Benny's face. Standing up, he switched the racket off and slotted another tape in. Pressing 'play' again, he sat back down, giving Lisa a glance that seemed to say: '*Satisfied?*'

This time the music was just plain weird. Eerie synthesized strings rolling around a deep, ethereal bass line, all driven along by a hypnotic phased drum loop, interspersed with screeching noises that sounded to Lisa like a dolphin trapped in a womb.

As the music insinuated itself into Lisa's brain, she began to feel hot and sticky.

'Why don't you take your jacket off?' Benny suggested as she began to fidget.

Peeling it away from her shoulders, she found she didn't have the energy to do anything but let it fall behind her. Slumping back, she inhaled deeply, trying to draw a little oxygen from the stifling air.

Across the room, the electric fire seemed to be glowing brighter and brighter – the heat shimmering hazily around the bars almost as if it were a living, breathing thing, advancing towards her across the brown cord carpet.

'So . . .' Benny's voice came to her across the vast desert plains. 'Who are you, then?'

'Eh?' Lisa struggled to understand his words. She felt strange, weightless – and so, so hot. 'I, er . . . Lisa!' she managed with effort.

'*Yes*,' the nomad went on, his voice low, and smooth as liquid gold. 'But who exactly *is* Lisa?'

'Just . . . *me*,' she murmured, struggling to get the words out over her dry, swollen tongue.

'Lisa . . . Lisa . . .' the camel-driver sing-songed. 'Tell me all your secrets, Lisa.'

He watched as sleep captured her, rendering her free of her conscious sins. When her eyes finally rolled back on themselves and her head fell forward onto her chest, his lips quivered in a tiny smile.

How innocent in sleep was this child in need.

Taking the empty cups into the kitchen, he whistled softly as he cleansed them of their germs.

After drying and replacing them in the cupboard – handles facing west in absolute symmetry – he went back to check on his angel.

Kneeling beside her, he put his ear to her chest and listened to her deep, even breathing for a moment. Then, checking his watch, he stood up.

Time was running on, and there was still so much to do before night staked its claim.

14

'Samir . . . Are you listening?'

Sam looked up dazedly. 'Uh, what?'

Slumped in his chair with his face embedded in the knuckles of his fist, he hadn't heard a word that his prattling wife and mother-in-law had been saying. He had been contemplating if not murder then at least suicide . . . Anything to escape the hell this week had been. In fact, it was more than a week. But why had he thought they would go home on the originally appointed day? Just because they were a couple of days late didn't mean they would stick to the rules and go home on time. He should have known they would punish *him* and not the rail service for messing up their plans!

Shifting to relieve the unrelenting pressure that had been building in his neglected balls throughout the week, he said, 'Sorry, dear . . . I was just thinking. What did you say?'

'I said we should take Mummy and Daddy out to dinner before they go.' Elsa's voice was shrewish as she tried not to show her irritation in front of her mother.

She'd been battling the urge to tear Sam to pieces ever since she had found the panties in his pocket. But it wasn't only that discovery that was making her want to kill him, it was because he had been so damn miserable the whole time her parents had been here. Slouching in his chair night after night, refusing to engage in the family conversations – refusing even to *feign* interest.

Her parents had noticed, of course, and this, more than anything, infuriated Elsa. That her loving husband should provide her mother with the perfect opportunity to use 'the look' on her. And *how* she'd used it. That look she'd employed when Elsa was a child, that said: *'You really are a pathetic creature, but I suppose I must try to tolerate you somehow.'*

'If it's too much trouble, dear,' her mother was saying now, her tone imperious and affronted, 'we could always get something from the buffet car. Not that it will be satisfactory for Daddy, of course,' she went on with a sigh. 'But needs must, and all that.'

'Of course it's no trouble,' Elsa snapped, throwing Sam a couple of hundred eye-daggers. '*Is* it, Samir?'

'No, no . . . of course not.' Sam forced himself to smile.

At least they were leaving. He could surely sit through a final meal, knowing they'd soon be gone.

And then maybe the strange atmosphere that had hung over the entire house all week would disperse. He couldn't put his finger on it, but there was definitely something amiss. Elsa was her usual efficient self, Mother and Father Conroy their usual boring, interfering selves. And he himself had done nothing untoward, he was sure. But still the air stank of suppressed *something* about to explode.

He *had* wondered if Elsa had somehow found out about his yen for prostitutes, but he had immediately dismissed that notion. How could she have? She never ventured into 'that part of town', and certainly didn't associate with anybody else who did. And if she'd even suspected him, surely the fact that he had stayed in night after night playing the dutiful husband would have allayed those fears?

Maybe Pat had been right after all. Maybe Elsa *was* going through 'the change'. He certainly hoped that was all it was, because this new sharpness of hers was a very uncomfortable table mate.

'Well, I'll just freshen up.' Sighing, Mother Conroy pushed herself up from her chair with the resigned air of a queen whose subjects were not being as attentive as they ought. 'I'll tell Daddy to bring the bags down,' she added, with one raised eyebrow. 'Although how he'll manage, with *his* back . . . ?'

The remonstration was clearly aimed at Samir for not leaping to his feet to take on the task. When he still didn't move, she pursed her prissy lips, gave Elsa 'the look', and walked haughtily from the room.

'What is *wrong* with you?' Elsa demanded in a hiss when they were alone.

Sam looked at her, frowning. 'I was just wondering the same about you, actually.'

'*Me?*'

'Yes, you.' Leaning forward, Sam pointed at his wife. 'All week you've been treating me as though I've done something wrong, and it's very bloody annoying.'

'*Oh?*' Elsa gave him an incredulous look, the anger she'd so valiantly kept under wraps all week, simmering to the surface. '*I'm* annoying *you*, am I? . . . Because *you've* done nothing wrong?'

'Exactly!' Sam sat back triumphantly. 'I mean, what

more could I have *done* to make them welcome? I paid a fortune for flowers for your mother . . .' He waved a hand towards the basket sitting regally beside Elsa's own bouquet on the dining-room table, each now beginning to show signs of wilting. 'And I gave your father the most bloody expensive whisky and cigars to see him through this God-awful week!'

'*God-awful*?' Elsa interrupted.

'Yes, bloody *God-awful*!' he repeated. 'You don't think men actually *enjoy* listening to women gossip, do you? Good God, woman, it's a wonder you and your mother can still speak at *all*, the amount of yakking you've done this week!'

'Well, I'm very sorry you feel like that,' Elsa replied coldly. 'I'm sure we never meant to *bore* you.'

'I'm sure you didn't,' he muttered tersely. Then, 'Well, look, I'll let it go *this* time, because I know you've been under pressure having them here. But when they've gone, I want you to understand that I won't tolerate this irritability of yours any longer.'

'Oh, you won't?' Elsa was smiling now – a small, malicious smile that tightened something in Sam's gut. 'Well, fine, Samir. We'll see what we'll see, won't we?'

'What's that supposed to mean?'

'Oh, nothing.' Standing, she smoothed her skirt, then moved around the room, fussily rearranging and plumping the cushions.

'I hope you're ready when it's time to go,' she said after a minute, her voice back to its normal, reasonable tone. 'You know Mummy hates to be kept waiting.'

Mummy can go and fuck herself till she bleeds! Sam

thought, but didn't say. Instead, he stood up and headed for the door.

Oh, he'd be ready all right. He'd look the perfect picture of the handsome executive he truly believed himself to be. And he'd lavish attention on Elsa and her pompous parents for all he was worth.

And then he'd drop them all off a cliff and go get himself some relief!

It had been a mistake taking the children to the restaurant. Sam had known it would be from the off, and knew it was probably his suggestion that they stay behind that had made Elsa so determined to drag them along. Well, he'd bet a year's salary she was regretting it now.

They were bored, and playing up in the tiresome, unignorable way only children could successfully pull off. They didn't like the 'rotten food' . . . And no, they didn't want to sample Nan's, or Grandad's or Mum's or Dad's. Nothing would be any good here in this dump, where even the water smelled funny and the Coke wasn't real and the waiters were weird-looking . . . All of it said loudly enough for people at the neighbouring tables to hear and look disapproving about.

'You really should learn to discipline them,' Mother Conroy intoned like a mantra each time the brats opened their mouths, making Elsa's jaw clench as she suppressed the urge to batter her beloved children senseless there and then.

Sam knew he should do something to keep them in line but, quite frankly, he was enjoying the disruption. It would cut down the time spent on dinner and give him a chance to escape. The sooner he off-loaded the whole bloody lot of them, the sooner he could go and fuck the guts out of Pat.

He only had to wait a further twenty minutes before he would get his wish.

'No, I don't think I want a dessert,' Mother Conroy declared as the dinner plates were removed, her face a picture of pained tolerance. 'No, no coffee either. In fact, I think it would be better if we just went straight along to the station. The children are about ready for bed, wouldn't you say?'

'Couldn't agree more!' Sam said, thrusting his platinum card at the hovering waiter with a silent cheer.

After a whirlwind drop-off at Piccadilly Station – which consisted of him roaring up to the entrance, leaping out and practically flinging the suitcases onto the concourse before hustling Elsa and the children home – Sam was on his way to Hulme, foot to the floor, anticipation coursing through his groin.

He hoped Pat was in. If she wasn't, he'd have no choice but to go down to the Lane to look for her. And if she wasn't there either, he'd have all the hassle of having to find one of the more 'suitable' girls to give him the relief he so desperately needed. He certainly wouldn't risk trying out a new one. There was no telling what you'd pick up with all the drugs they were doing these days.

In his haste, Sam forgot to leave the car out of sight around the corner and drove into Pat's street, pulling up right outside the main door at her end of the block. Leaping out, he ran all the way up the stairs.

Pat was in, but she wasn't in the best of moods. After spending almost the entire day running between bed and toilet, she had finally stopped leaking from every orifice and was just dressing to go out for some much-needed booze and a packet of cigarettes when she heard the frantic knocking at the front door. It really pissed her off. The last thing she needed was some idiot delaying her now.

Throwing the bedroom window open, she barked rudely down at the unseen visitor: '*Whaddya want?*'

Stepping back, Sam grinned up at her, waving the bottle of brandy he'd stopped off to buy on the way.

'Oh, it's you, is it?' she snapped, still annoyed with him for running out without paying last time. 'You got my money?'

'Ssshh!' he hissed, glancing around nervously. 'Let me in!'

'Only if you've got my money. Otherwise, you can piss off back where you crawled from!'

'All right, I've got it!' he said. 'Now stop messing about and let me in!'

'Here, catch.' Throwing a huge bunch of keys down, she slammed the window shut.

'Pat?' he called up the stairs when he finally managed to find the right key and get in. 'Where are you?'

'Up here, stupid!' she called back, tutting her irritation as she undressed. *Where was she*, indeed! He'd just bloody well seen her up here, hadn't he?

'Where's Lisa?' Sam whispered, creeping into her room moments later with a couple of glasses he'd collected from the kitchen *en route* – thoroughly relieved not to have encountered the dog from hell.

Shrugging, Pat climbed back into the messy bed.

'She isn't here, the little cow. Pissed off out earlier,

didn't she? Left me to fend for myself, and I've been sick as a dog all day! Not that *you*'d give a damn!' she added peevishly.

'Well, I'm here now,' Sam said, putting her keys down on the bedside table before gathering together the heap of clothes, magazines, and used tissues that were scattered all over the bed. 'I'll look after you.'

'Yeah, *right*!' she snorted. 'And don't start cleaning up! I *hate* it when you do that. Just get the bloody drinks poured and give me a fag.'

Putting the pile down on the floor, Sam tossed his cigarettes to her. Then he poured the drinks before undressing and clambering in beside her.

'Ugh, what's that smell?' he asked, wrinkling his nose.

'Probably me,' she told him unconcernedly. 'I did tell you I'd been sick all day.'

He shook his head. 'No, it can't just be that . . . It smells like . . . Has the dog done something?'

'Are you just gonna moan?' she snapped. ''Cos if you are, you can just give us me money and piss off!'

Sam gave her a hurt look. This wasn't the welcome he'd expected after a week of torturous abstinence.

Draining her glass, Pat thrust it towards him.

'Fill that up, if you've nowt better to do. And don't bother giving me them sad eyes, 'cos I'm in no mood for that shit!'

Without a word, Sam poured her another drink. And then another. And, finally, she allowed him to do what he'd come for.

As he heaved and grunted on top of her, Pat lay as limp as a week-dead fish beneath him, refusing to participate in any way – to teach him a lesson. In his desperation to relieve his aching desire, he didn't even notice.

Rolling off when he'd finished, gasping for breath and dripping with sweat, he gave her an enormous grin.

'Sorry it was so quick, but you don't know how long I've been waiting for that!'

Lighting two cigarettes, he passed one to her and lay back against the pillows with a contented sigh.

'All week I've thought of nothing else.'

'Bet that pleased wifey,' Pat snorted.

'Huh!' he grunted. 'She's been far too busy to notice me.'

'*Ah*, you *poor* thing.'

Completely missing the sarcasm, Sam nodded his agreement and launched into an account of his in-laws' hellish visit. When he confided that Elsa had been behaving oddly, Pat suddenly remembered her little gift, and wondered if the stupid cow had found it.

In a way, she hoped not – not now that she'd had a chance to consider the possible consequences. What if Elsa decided to boot Sam out, and he turned up here with his suitcases? What was she supposed to do then? It wasn't like she really wanted him or anything. She didn't! It was too much hassle by far, putting up with a man on a permanent basis.

On the other hand, she kind of hoped the bitch *had* found them. Wouldn't that just shake her smug, secure little world to the core!

'Anyway, I practically shoved them on the train,' Sam was saying now. 'And I can't tell you how glad I was to see the back of them. If I never had to see them again, I'd be a very happy man. So . . .' He turned to her. 'What have *you* been doing all week?'

'Oh, you know.' She shrugged. 'All sorts. Been down the boozer a couple of times. Went to the pictures with me mate the other night. Got that curry last night and ended up—'

'*Mate?*' Sam interrupted, pouncing on her previous comment. 'Which mate?'

'Just Kim,' she replied casually. 'Anyhow, like I was sa—'

'Do I know her? I don't think I've heard that name before.'

Turning, Pat looked him full in the face.

'*And?*'

'And what?' He sniffed – a sure sign that he was feeling put out. 'I'm just saying I don't know that name. It *is* a woman, I presume?'

'You *what?*'

'Well, is it?'

'Yes, it bloody well is, actually,' Pat snapped, furious that he should feel entitled to cop an attitude about her seeing *anyone*. 'Not that it's any of *your* sodding business!'

Sam's hand trembled as he took a slug of his drink. He just couldn't stem the tide of jealousy he always suffered when he thought about Pat with another man. And it wasn't exclusive to her – he felt this way about *all* the girls he 'visited'. It was a man thing.

'Who *else* have you seen while I've been stuck at home?' he asked, more waspishly than he could help.

'Oh, that *does* it!' Pat bellowed, the stress of his questioning stirring her bowels and reigniting the flame she thought she'd extinguished. Pushing the quilt aside, she grabbed her dressing gown from the floor and yanked it on.

'Where are you going?' he demanded. 'Don't run away when we're talking!'

'Talk to your fucking self!' she roared. 'And piss off back to your wife while you're at it! I can't be doing with all this jealousy shit!'

'I'm *not* jealous!' he shouted back at her. 'A man's got the right to know what his women are doing behind his back!'

'*Women*?' she screeched incredulously. 'I'm not one of your harem bitches, you stupid bastard! I'm a bleedin' independent pro, making me own money! You've got no rights with me, so get that into your thick head and piss off!'

'Stop shouting,' he hissed, glancing nervously at the wall.

'Don't tell me what to do in me own *house*!' she screamed, picking up his clothes and flinging them at him. 'Get out! And leave the money you owe me or I'll be sending Mrs Frigid the bill!'

Storming out, Pat marched into the bathroom, slamming the door so hard behind her that it rocked the mirror balanced on the ledge above the sink.

Shaken by her threat, Sam quickly pulled on his trousers and vest and went after her. Tapping on the door, he tried to coax her out in the hope of calming her down before she did something stupid. After being told three times to 'go and fuck himself!', he gave up.

Angrily dragging the rest of his clothes on, muttering under his breath the whole time about the injustices heaped upon men by ungrateful women, he pulled his wallet out and threw all the paper money he had on the bed.

If Pat wanted to treat him like so much dirt beneath her feet, let her! But she needn't think he'd be coming back for more. There were plenty more whores in the sea!

As Sam let himself out of the front door minutes later, Ada Baker peered at him through a crack in her bedroom curtains.

So it was *the Paki one!* She congratulated herself for having recognized his voice. And another fine carry-on they'd had, too! Shouting and screaming at each other like a pair of old dockers. Disgraceful! Any normal couple would keep it down at this time of night – respecting their neighbours' right to a good night's sleep. But not that tart next door! Oh, no . . . that madam didn't give a damn that it was going on for eleven!

And as for dropping her keys out of the window, that just about summed her morals up, that did. What kind of woman did that? Not the respectable kind, that was for sure.

Watching until the *Paki one* had exited through the door below and climbed into his big poncey car, Ada let the curtain drop, then clambered back into bed, smirking with satisfaction the whole time because there was *nothing* went on in this street she didn't know about. Nothing!

Seconds later, she was fast asleep.

15

Lisa came to with a groan. Her head was stuffy, and her mouth felt as though it were full of dry cotton wool. As she forced her eyes open, an icy hand of panic gripped and twisted her insides when she found she couldn't see a thing. The absolute darkness petrified her. It felt as though it were advancing on her from all sides, pressing into her flesh and seeping into her nostrils and mouth like a living thing.

Shivering with terror and cold, she drew her legs up to her chest and buried her face in her knees, willing her sluggish brain to start working and tell her where she was. As the fog gradually lifted, she began to remember fragments of the day.

Debbie . . . Jasmine . . . A newspaper . . . The adventure playground . . . Benny . . .

BENNY!

She'd gone to Benny's flat with him. He'd given her something disgusting to drink . . .

But what then?

Nothing.

Except . . .

Getting hot. Feeling sleepy.

Had she fallen asleep? Had Benny put her to bed?

Oh, God! What if he'd . . .

Panicking, she felt around her body, relaxing when she found that all her clothing was in place.

'As if he'd do that!' she muttered to herself croakily, scolding herself for even *thinking* someone as lovely as Benny would take advantage of her.

Reaching out, she gingerly tapped a hand around her in a circle, hoping to get a clue from her fingertips if not from her eyes as to where she was.

She was undoubtedly on a mattress. There was no sheet but a thin blanket was bunched up around her feet. Benny must have placed it over her, she realized with a warm tingle, and she must have kicked it off in her sleep. She must remember to thank him.

But first she had to get up and find the door. Let him know she was awake.

Reaching up, she felt for the curtain to pull it back and give herself light. But there was no curtain, just a board of wood where it should have been. *Strange*, she thought, then shrugged. People were always breaking windows and boarding them up round here.

Hearing a key turning in a lock a few feet to her left, she frowned. Was she locked in? Surely not.

Seconds later, the door slowly opened and she had to squint her eyes against the light coming in from the hall. And then it dimmed as a figure appeared in the doorway.

'B-Benny?' she whispered, her voice husky with uncertainty.

'Who else did you expect?' he replied, his own voice sounding strange and cold. 'Or are you used to finding men in your bedroom in the middle of the night?'

'W-what?' she stuttered, completely thrown. 'I d-don't know what you mean?'

'What I *mean* is . . .' He came slowly into the room. 'Are you a slut, like your *mother*? A harlot . . . a strumpet!'

'*What?*' Lisa shook her head, sure it must be a dream – or, rather, a *nightmare*.

'Never mind!' he said then, seeming to shake himself free of whatever had annoyed him. 'That's all by-the-by for now. I just wanted to make sure you were all right before I went out . . . And to give you this.'

'You're going out?' Lisa gasped, the panic returning with a vengeance as she clumsily accepted the hot cup he was holding out to her. 'You're not leaving me here, are you? I don't feel right, Benny! Please don't go . . .'

'Hush, hush,' he said in a soft sing-song voice. 'I have work to do. But first, be a good girl and drink your tea.'

One whiff of the strange aroma brought back the full memory of the disgusting taste.

'I, er . . . thanks, but I don't want it,' she said.

'Well, *I* want you to have it.' He stepped back as she tried to hand the cup back to him. 'For me.'

'But I don't like it,' she whined. 'Honest, Benny . . .'

'Maybe not, but you do like *me*, don't you?'

'Yes, but—'

'No buts!' he cut her off gently. 'If you like me, you'll drink it. You want me to like you too, don't you?'

'Yes,' she admitted, glad of the dark to cover her blushes. 'But—'

'Ssshh . . . Just drink. You need it to make you better.'

'But I'm all right,' she protested weakly. 'Honest.'

'Don't you remember feeling ill?' he asked, as if he were talking to a very young child.

Lisa frowned in the dark, trying to remember how she'd felt before waking in this room. All she could remember was the gross tea, the heat, and the weird music.

'Drink up,' he insisted. 'It'll make you better, I promise.'

Tears trickling down her cheeks, Lisa raised the foul-smelling tea to her lips.

'Good girl.' Taking the cup from her when she'd finished, Benny reached out to stroke her hair gently. 'Now lie down and get some sleep. I'll be back before you know it.'

'Please don't go,' she moaned, lying down. 'I don't want to be on my own.'

'I won't let anything hurt you,' he told her, pulling the blanket up around her shoulders. 'But you must stay here and rest, or I won't be able to protect you.'

'I don't understand,' she whimpered.

With a smile in his voice, he said, 'Ah, but you do. You just don't realize it yet . . . But you will. Now, promise you'll be quiet?'

'Can't I come with you?' she pleaded, reaching for his hand. 'Please, Benny . . . don't leave me on my own.'

'Ssshhh!' Withdrawing his hand from her grasp, he patted her shoulder. 'I have to do this without interference, but I promise we'll talk when I get back.'

As he backed out of the room, closing the door behind him, Lisa found herself plunged into darkness once more. She heard the key turning in the lock, but it didn't register as clearly as it had the first time. She was feeling sleepy again.

Ever so . . .
Sleepy . . .

Pressing his ear to the door, he waited until he heard the deep breathing of sleep before moving away, safe in the knowledge that she would sleep for hours, giving him all the time he needed to complete his work.

In his room, he allowed himself an extra few minutes to light the candle and give thanks for the ease of his journey. This done, he checked he had everything he needed, then left, making absolutely sure that the padlock was firmly in place.

Switching the radio on to a continuous-play music station, he set the volume at a level loud enough to mask her cries should she wake before he got back – but not so loud that it would disturb the nosy old bitch in the flat below.

Double-locking the front door, he checked it twice, then moved off down the stairs, as dark and stealthy as a hunting panther.

Preparation was the key to success, and he prided himself on his abilities in that department. And this time he had excelled himself. He had prepared everything in minute detail, leaving nothing to chance, for chance was the left-handed tool of the right-handed imbecile.

Outside, he slipped easily into the shadows and made his way to his destination without encountering a soul. If he had been seen, he would have known that the time was not right. But, as he had expected, there were no obstacles.

How could there be, when the Master had decreed that it should be tonight?

Smiling, he fingered the keys in his right pocket, tracing the large 'L' that was the key ring with his thumb. In his left, he lightly held the small plastic bag.

With a sudden inspiration, he pulled out both articles and cupped his hands together so that the two were joined as one.

'Oh, yes,' he sighed as the heat suffused his hands and travelled up his arms. 'This is so right . . .'

16

Pat stayed in the bathroom until she was sure that Sam had left. Going back to the bedroom, she was more than a little pleased to see that he'd left money on the bed – especially so when she counted it and found that it came to one hundred and twenty-five pounds. That would do nicely – as would the cigarettes, lighter, and half-full bottle of brandy he'd also left behind.

Jumping happily back beneath the quilt, she lit one of the cigarettes and set about finishing the booze in record time. Her stomach was still a bit iffy, but she knew she'd soon forget about that when she got well and truly plastered.

Holding her glass aloft, she toasted Sam.

'Thanks, dickhead! At least you're good for something!'

Incensed by Pat's attitude, Sam was sitting in his car down below, watching her front door, sure that she would appear at any minute and go looking for another man like the whore she was! If she did, he'd know once and for all that she wasn't worth his time. Not that he didn't already know that, but sometimes it took a cold hard slap in the face to make one face up to the truth of a situation.

When, after half an hour, she still hadn't come out, he decided to go home – with a little detour to the Lane *en route*, just to see who was around . . .

Standing in the dark beside the huge communal wheelie bin at the side of the block opposite Lisa's, he watched the man in the car, who, in turn, appeared to be watching Lisa's front door. If this were so, it could be a sign to leave his plans for another time.

When the man suddenly started his engine and left, he decided he must have been mistaken. It was so easy to become paranoid about the people encountered during these most intense periods of concentration. Those blessed enough to be as attuned to their surroundings as he was recognized this, and used it as protection against the unforeseen.

Settling back against the wall as the car disappeared around the corner, he prepared for the wait that he knew he must bear patiently if he were to succeed.

The majority of the flats on Lisa's block showed at least one light glowing. As he waited, these were extinguished one by one, until all but one flat was in complete darkness. The one remaining was Lisa's own, and its light was only the blue flickering strobe of a TV in the upstairs front bedroom.

The whore must be watching TV in bed, he decided. All the better if she were, as it would give him more cover. He would gain access without being heard and, should she get a chance to open that foul mouth of hers, he could simply turn the volume up and drown her out.

Darting across the road when he felt he had given her neighbours sufficient time to settle in their beds, he eased himself in through the main door and ran silently up the stairs – key in one leather gloved hand, large chunk of 'treated' beef in the other – a necessary precaution when dealing with animals . . . particularly large, potentially dangerous dogs.

Trapped behind the living-room door, Monty whined when he heard the key in the lock. Hoping it was Lisa come to release and feed him, he sniffed at the crack below the door. Hackles rising as he sensed an unfamiliar scent, he began to growl, then to bark in short, sharp warning bursts intended to dissuade the intruder from entering.

Growling again as the intruder approached the door, he rose slowly to his feet and backed away from the door, giving himself plenty of room to pounce should it open.

'*Montyyy*,' a strange, sing-song voice whispered through the door. '*Good boy, Monty . . . Look what I've brought for you . . .*'

Stiffening in readiness as the handle slowly turned, Monty's snout quivered above his fangs. He sprang forward as the door opened a fraction, slamming into it with his full weight.

When the door had closed as quickly as it had opened, the dog found himself staring down at a large chunk of meat on the carpet. Sniffing it suspiciously, his hunger overrode his urge to protect. Snatching up his find, he carried it to the far side of the room – ignoring the sounds of the stranger going about his business on the other side of the door.

With the dog almost certainly due to be out of commission for the next few hours, he started up the stairs. Peeling his leather gloves off as he went, he replaced them with latex surgical gloves, then pulled the mask on over his head, tucking it neatly inside his collar.

The first door he came to turned out to be the bathroom. Uninterested, he moved on to the next.

This was obviously Lisa's room. In the doorway, he peered around at the display of childish mess with dismay. Obviously the mother's negligence extended to every area of the poor child's life. But she would pay for this crime – just as she would pay for her crimes of the flesh.

Closing Lisa's door, he moved on to the third door, behind which he could hear the strains of a late-night television talk show. Pressing his ear to the wood, he was gratified to hear that it was one of the louder American shows, where screaming, shouting women were the norm. The perfect cover should the whore be awake.

Hearing a deep, rumbling snore, he hesitated. Was it the whore, or did she have a man in there? It was hard to tell.

But he was prepared – whatever the situation.

Easing the knife from his pocket, he slowly opened the door – just enough to be able to see what lay in wait.

The whore was alone, and in a deep sleep. Sprawled across the bed, half in, half out of the quilt, her barely covered chest rising and falling as her wide-open mouth spewed forth its snores.

Stepping inside, he watched the whore with care as he quickly scanned the rest of the room for anyone who might be hiding. When he was absolutely sure that they were alone, he closed the door behind him and moved towards the bed.

*   *   *

Pat began to wake as soon as she felt the edge of the bed subsiding. Squinting up through gunk-glued eyes, she couldn't make out the face of the dark figure hovering over her.

'That you, Lisha?' she slurred groggily.

Getting no answer, it occurred to her that it was probably Sam. He must have carried her keys out by mistake and had now come back to try and persuade her not to contact his wife. Well, sod him, if that was all he cared about!

'Sam?' she snapped angrily. 'I hope you haven't—'

'*Shut up!*'

'You *what?*' Furious, she struggled to sit up. 'Don't try coming that wi— *Aaagh!*'

Hitting her full in the face with the back of his fist, he leaped onto the bed and dragged her up by her hair. Flinging her over onto her stomach, he forced her face into the pillows and straddled her, holding the back of her head firmly in place as she struggled for breath.

'*Forgive her, Father,*' he hissed as he forced her gaping mouth into the suffocating linen. '*For she has sinned . . . plentifully and unashamedly!*'

Unable to hear the voice clearly, Pat still thought it was Sam's. Assuming that he was trying to scare her so badly that she would never reveal his dirty secrets to his wife, she was shocked to the core when she felt the tip of a blade piercing the flesh above her pubic hair.

Her life flashed in front of her eyes as she realized that this was no joke. Writhing fiercely, she freed one of her hands from the quilt in which they were entangled and lashed out with her nails. If he meant to silence her like this, she'd make damn sure he was marked for life!

As the knife wrenched up through the hanging folds of her stomach, she knew she was fighting for her life. Twisting herself violently beneath him, she managed to free her mouth of its pillow gag and, drawing in a great lungful of air, screamed for all she was worth: '*SAAAMMM . . . NOOOOO!*'

A heavy blow to the back of her head silenced her.

Satisfied that he had done all that he could, he thrust his signature-mark into the bloody mess and leaped from the bed.

Disgusted that she had been wearing no panties for him to retain, he considered taking a pair from her drawer. But a quick assessment of the heaps of filthy clothes strewn all around the floor changed his mind. He'd already broken one ritual by entering the demon's lair so it would not harm him to leave empty-handed for once. Anyway, he had a much more precious gift from this whore waiting for him at home.

Quickly tidying himself, he scrutinized the area for anything he might have mistakenly dropped, then made a hasty retreat.

Clutching the blanket to her throat, Ada Baker strained to hear through the wall.

God, but the tart had excelled herself this time! Screaming like that, then all that banging and thumping. It was enough to wake the dead! It had certainly woken Ada, and that was some achievement once she got her head down for the night.

Still, despite the annoyance of being disturbed, there was something about it all that just didn't sit right with

Ada. Why had the Paki come back so soon after leaving? And what had they been fighting about to make the tart scream out like that? And then him running out like he had the Devil at his heels. It didn't make sense.

Unless he'd done something bad.

Hearing nothing more above the noise of the TV still playing through the wall, Ada lay back down, her face a mask of worry lines. Much as she would have loved to say that the tart had asked for a good hiding, she still thought there was something odd about it all. After a fight like that, why wasn't Pat Noone screaming blue murder now? She wasn't the sort to take a bloke belting her lying down. And just say that for once she'd *taken* rather than given the worst of it, why wasn't she crying, then? Hard as Pat Noone was, surely even *she* would be sobbing if she'd had a really good hiding.

Unable to rest for the awful sense that something was wrong, Ada eventually got up and pulled on her dressing gown. Taking her teeth from the glass on the table, she slipped them in and made her way downstairs, listening the whole time for signs of movement next door.

At her own front door, she hesitated. It was gone twelve. If she went outside, anything could happen. But then something already *could* have happened next door. And if it had, she'd be the only one who knew – the only one who could do something if the tart needed help.

Peering as far as possible along the landing outside through the spyhole, she saw that it was deserted and decided to risk opening the door. All she needed to do was knock and check if Pat was all right. More likely than not she'd get her head bitten off for her trouble, but she had to know or she'd never get back to sleep.

Getting no answer to her third knock, she frowned. Why wasn't the dog barking like before? And why wasn't Pat screaming at her to piss off and mind her own business?

And what if the Paki came back for another row and caught her here?

Wrapping the dressing gown tighter around herself, Ada scuttled along the landing to Sue Morgan's flat. She knew Sue and Pat didn't really get on, but their daughters were friends. She'd be the best one to help her find out if something was wrong in there.

Sue was in bed but still awake, having decided to finish a book she'd been reading. When she heard the knocking at her front door, she glanced at her alarm clock and was annoyed to see that it was ten past twelve. Who the hell would be calling at this time of night?

Pulling on her dressing gown, she went downstairs and put the chain on the door before opening it and peering out through the narrow gap. She was more than a little surprised to see a worried-looking Ada on her doorstep. She didn't think she'd ever seen her outside after eight p.m.

'What is it, Ada?' Reaching behind herself she turned the hall light on, then took the chain off the door. 'Is something wrong?'

'I'm not sure,' Ada said, hugging herself against the chill night air. 'You'll probably think I'm just a nosy old cow, but I didn't know who else to mention it to.'

Reaching out, Sue took the old lady's arm and pulled her into the hall.

'Come into the warm, love. I'll make us a cup of tea, then you can tell me what's up.'

Taking her through to the living room, Sue turned on a lamp and sat her down. Bringing a pot of tea in a few minutes later, she sat down and listened as Ada explained what had happened.

'And the door only went once,' Ada finished. 'So I know Pat didn't go out after he'd gone. And that's what's worrying me. Why won't she answer the door now?'

Sue raised her eyebrows and sighed. 'Well, you know what she's like, Ada. If she doesn't want to speak to you, she's quite capable of ignoring the door.'

Ada shook her head. 'I know what you're saying, but she's more likely to open it to give me what for, isn't she? It's not right.'

'What do you want to do?' Sue asked, hoping against hope that Ada wasn't about to suggest that *she* go and knock.

'I'm wondering if we should call the bobbies?' Ada said.

Sue frowned. 'Do you really think that's necessary?'

Ada shrugged helplessly. 'I don't know, love, but something's wrong. I can feel it in me water.'

'All right!' Sue nodded decisively. 'I'll call them – but only after we've tried giving it another knock. And God help us if she's in,' she added with a grin. 'Just give me a minute to get my coat.'

Making their way along the landing a couple of minutes later, Sua and Ada stood shoulder to shoulder at Pat's door for mutual support. Taking a deep breath, Sue knocked, then stepped back to the railing – out of reach should Pat come out all guns blazing. When nothing happened, she knocked again. Then again.

After five minutes, she gave up.

Agreeing that it was strange that the dog hadn't barked even once – everyone knew how noisy Monty was! – Sue finally called the police.

The two shivering women then waited on the landing outside Sue's flat until the police arrived, some twenty minutes later.

PCs Quinn and Bates saw the women waving at them before they got out of the car. They sighed simultaneously. Neither was thrilled at being sent to this non-event.

'Another action-packed night in Hulme,' Bates quipped, switching the engine off.

Quinn tutted. 'What happened to all the violent busts we were promised, eh?'

'Suppose we have to get through the Mothercare stage first,' Bates replied, glancing up at the women. 'Still, I never thought I'd end up spending all me time calming nosy old bints down.'

Grinning, they got out of the car and strolled up to the second-floor maisonettes to have a chat with the women. After hearing the gabbled story about the neighbour who wouldn't answer her door, Quinn and Bates were more convinced than ever that their earlier assessment had been dead right. There was nothing wrong here – just two nosy women with nothing better to do than spy on a neighbour and jump to all sorts of conclusions. Still, they were here now, so they supposed they'd better 'investigate' the complaint.

'What should we do?' Quinn asked when they too received no answer, after some seriously hefty cop-style knocking.

Bates shrugged. 'Sack it off. She's obviously gone out.'

'No, she hasn't,' Ada interrupted, having gradually edged her way along the landing despite being told to wait at Sue's. 'I'd have heard the door, and I'm telling you now, no one else come out after he legged it! Now, what are you going to do about it?'

Bates and Quinn looked at each other and shrugged. They obviously weren't going to get out of here without a fight from the old bird.

'I'll radio in for advice,' Bates eventually decided.

As his colleague moved a few feet away to make the call, Quinn took out his notepad. Unlikely though it was that there was something amiss, he should at least *look* as though he'd made an effort should it come to anything.

'So, you say the man you saw entering Mrs Noone's flat was Asian?' he asked.

'Yeah, that's right,' Ada said. 'Something like that, anyway. That kind of look about him.'

'And he had a car?'

'Yeah . . . a big, posh job.'

'Could you identify the make?'

'No idea.' She shrugged. 'Wouldn't know one from another, me. It was big and dark, that's all I can tell you.'

'Dark?' Quinn said, suppressing a yawn. 'Black, blue, green?'

'Sorry, no idea.'

'But you're sure it was him who came back?'

'I reckon,' Ada replied uncertainly. 'I mean, I didn't see him or nothing the second time, but I reckon it was him all the same. Anyway, she screamed his name out, didn't she?'

'Oh? And that would be . . . ?'

'Sam, I think. Yeah, definitely Sam.'

'Oh, I think I've heard the girls mentioning someone called Sam,' Sue cut in.

Quinn turned to her. 'The girls?'

'Yes, my daughter Debbie is a friend of Pat's daughter, Lisa.'

Quinn jotted all of this down, then asked, 'Would Lisa be at home tonight?'

Sue shrugged. 'I would have thought so. I don't think she has many friends. She's a bit too much like her mother for her own good, that one . . .' She tailed off as she became aware of Quinn's questioning look. She was saved from having to elaborate by his colleague motioning him aside.

'The Sarge says to boot the door in.'

Quinn frowned. 'Are you sure?'

Bates shrugged. 'That's what he said. Apparently, our Mrs Noone here is a regular old pro. The Sarge reckons she's either topped herself, or that nutter's had her. Says we should just boot it in and let him know the good news.'

Craning to hear what they were saying, Sue and Ada exchanged looks of disbelief.

Regular old pro? . . . Topped herself? . . . Had by the nutter?

'Would you mind stepping back, ladies?'

Puffed up with the importance of their task, Bates and Quinn shooed Sue and Ada out of the way, then took it in turns to aim kicks at Pat's door. Four kicks later, it gave. Taking their batons out from their weighty belts, they strutted inside, closing the door firmly behind them.

Inside, Bates shoved the kitchen door open and took a quick peek inside, giving only a cursory glance around the small, dark area. Quinn did likewise with the living room, then they started up the stairs – each sure, from the absolute stillness of the house, that they were right and the nosy women outside wrong. There was no one here.

'Oh, *Pat*?' Quinn crooned, going before Bates. 'Are you here, Pat?'

'Couple of gentlemen callers to see you!' added Bates with a snigger. 'Come out, come out, wherever you are.'

'Boo!' Quinn said, bursting into the bathroom.

'Sshh!' Bates hushed him, laughing. 'Them two out there will report us if they think we're messing about!'

Pushing open Lisa's door with his hands joined before him as if holding a pistol, Quinn slipped his head in, then back out, hissing in an American accent: 'Ain't no one here, Bate-man. Take a look-see in there.' He nodded towards Pat's closed bedroom door.

Grinning, Bates pushed it open . . .

On the landing outside, Sue and Ada huddled together, sure that at any minute they would hear Pat kicking off inside. They both jumped when they heard a loud exclamation from the bedroom above, then footsteps thundering down the stairs. Stepping back as the door opened and PC Quinn came flying out, they grabbed at each other in alarm.

'What's up?' Ada managed at last. 'What've you found?'

Ignoring her, Quinn sparked his radio to crackling life.

'We need someone down here, sarge – ASAP! He's done it again!'

'What's going on?' demanded Sue. 'Is Pat all right . . . ? Where's Lisa?'

'Not now, ladies.'

'Is the child all right?' Ada was panicking now. The tart might have deserved whatever she'd got, but not the child – cheeky though she was.

'This child,' said Quinn, a little calmer now that he'd summoned the higher powers. 'How old is she?'

'Twelve,' Sue told him. 'Same as my Debbie. Oh, God . . . don't tell me something's happened to her?'

'Not as far as I'm aware,' Quinn assured her. 'She doesn't appear to be here. Only the . . . only the mother. Now, you're sure you've no idea where the girl might have gone?'

'I'll ask Debbie,' Sue said and, turning, she ran back to her own house.

'I'll have to ask you to stay here, Mrs . . . ?' Quinn checked his notes and cursed himself for not taking down such a basic detail as her name. From here on in, every detail, no matter how small, had to be treated as vital information.

'Baker,' Ada supplied croakily. 'Ada Baker. I live next door, so I won't be going nowhere. What's happened, love?' she asked then, fearful of his answer.

'She's been attacked,' was all he said.

Ada gasped. 'Aw, no! She's not . . . you know?'

Without answering, Quinn looked away as the distant strains of a siren reached him, coming closer by the second.

'My Debbie says she should be at home.' Sue came running back, holding a piece of paper. 'But this is a list of their friends' names and addresses in case she's stopping over somewhere.'

'Thanks.'

Slotting the paper into his notepad, Quinn suggested that they should go home now, but asked that they stay up so that the detective in charge could speak to them when he arrived.

'It's something bad, isn't it?' Sue asked quietly.

'I can't discuss it,' he said. 'Sorry.'

Knowing in her heart that someone, probably Pat, was dead inside the flat, Sue took Ada's arm and began to lead her back down the landing.

'Come on, love, we're in the way here. Come to mine, eh? Wait for them there.'

Ada nodded, her face haggard. 'Yeah . . . thanks, love.'

'Could you make sure your daughter's available?' Quinn called after them. 'The girl could be all right, but we need to make sure . . . under the circumstances.'

'Of course.' Turning, Sue nodded, saddened by the thought that something bad might also have happened to Lisa. She might not like her, but she didn't want to see her come to any harm. Debbie would be devastated if something happened to Lisa so soon after their friend had been murdered.

A sudden chill gripped her heart. Turning back again, she called out to Quinn.

'Excuse me, officer . . . I don't know if this is relevant, but . . .'

17

'Lisa? . . . Wake up, there's a good girl.' Kneeling beside the mattress, Benny shook Lisa's arm gently. 'Lisa, come on . . . I've got news . . . about your mother.'

As the words penetrated the fog clouding her brain, Lisa groaned, forcing herself to rise above the stupor.

'Me mum,' she croaked through dry lips. 'What about me mum?'

'Don't worry,' Benny told her with a smile. 'There's nothing to worry about. She's safe now, in the arms of the One who truly loves her.'

'What – what does that mean?'

'Never mind that now.' Lifting her gently, he held a cup of water to her parched lips. 'Drink this. Come on, I'll help you. And when you're properly awake we'll talk about the next stage of the plan.'

Sipping at the cool water as Benny trickled it onto her tongue, Lisa felt her senses returning.

'What did you mean about my mum?' she asked when he moved the cup away.

'Later.' Hooking an arm beneath her back, he helped her to her feet. 'First, you need a bath. It's all ready and waiting.'

'But I don't want a bath,' she protested. 'I just want

to go home and see me mum. How long have I been here? She'll be worried.'

Benny smiled down indulgently on her worried face. 'Silly girl . . . she's not *worried*. Didn't I just tell you she's fine now?'

Lisa shook her head as if to try and make sense of what he was saying.

'I don't get it. What are you going on about? She was fine before.'

'No, she wasn't,' Benny told her firmly. 'That was just part of the delusion.'

'*What?*'

He gave her another indulgent smile, saying, 'This is precisely why I told you to wait until you'd woken up properly before we could talk. How can you hope to understand the complexities of our entwined fates when you're still dazed by sleep? Now, come and get your bath.'

Confused, Lisa said nothing as he led her along the short hallway into the bathroom. The bath had been drawn to half its capacity, and a faded green towel was folded neatly over the lip of the sink.

'Get undressed and pop yourself in,' he said, motioning towards the bath as he straightened the toilet roll on top of the cistern.

She flapped her hands at her sides, unsure if he expected her to do this in front of him.

'Y-you're not staying, are you?' she asked. 'Only I can't just . . . you know . . .'

Benny gave her a strange look. 'Of course not! I just wanted to tidy up for you. I'll be waiting in the front room – don't be long.' With that he turned and left her alone, closing the door behind him.

Lisa ran across to lock it but found that the original bolt had been removed, leaving just holes where the screws had been and a small, square patch of unpainted wood against the gloss white of the door.

Glancing towards the bath with its steaming water, she knew she couldn't undress and climb into it if there was even a chance of Benny walking in. She was far too shy for that. She decided she'd best just have a wash instead. If she took off her shoes and socks she could stand in the bath and make splashing sounds. That way Benny would think she'd done as he'd asked – and for some reason, she knew this would please him.

As she sat on the toilet seat to take off her shoes, there was a tapping at the door.

'Yeah?' she called out.

'I forgot to tell you to pass your clothes out when you're undressed,' Benny called back. 'I want to clean them.'

Lisa's heart jerked in her chest. She couldn't go back out there without her clothes, and it would take ages to wash and dry them.

'I – I can't,' she said after a moment. 'I've nothing else to put on.'

Laughing softly, he said, 'It's all right, I'm leaving something out here for you.'

Undressing quickly, she wrapped the towel around herself and tentatively peeped outside. True to his word, Benny had left a bundle of clothes on the floor beside the door. Pulling them towards herself, she placed her own where the others had been and shut the door again.

The bundle turned out to be an old Adidas tracksuit. Large – obviously meant for a man. Realizing it must be Benny's own, Lisa smiled to herself, then sniffed the jacket in the hopes of catching his scent, but it smelled of nothing. Not aftershave, nor sweat, nor even washing powder. Just nothing.

Disappointed, she laid the tracksuit pants flat along the floor at the base of the door – to jam it should Benny think she was finished and try to enter. It was a trick her mum often used to keep Lisa out of her bedroom when she was entertaining Sam. Not that Lisa had ever tried to walk in on them, but her mum had said it was just in case she came home one night and didn't realize he was there.

Climbing into the bath, she sank down into the deliciously hot water and felt herself begin to relax.

As her head cleared, she pondered how strange everything had been since she came here. If this were any other man's flat she would be terrified by now, and yet she didn't feel as though she was in danger with Benny. How could she be? He was her friend. Hadn't he taken care of her when she got ill so suddenly? Funny that she couldn't remember anything about that, but she supposed that was just part of the illness – like being delirious when you've had alcohol poisoning. And she'd seen her mum like that often enough to know your memory was the first thing to get fucked up.

Looking around the bathroom, which was as clean and bare as the other rooms in the flat that she'd seen so far, she wondered why Benny harboured none of the clutter most of the men she'd ever encountered did. Her mum's last serious boyfriend, for example – *a short-lived, violent affair that had been!* – had kept more bottles of aftershave, jars of hair gels and tubes of moustache-blackening crap in their bathroom than the stuff that both Lisa and her mum together kept. But then, he'd been a right ponce! Nothing at all like Benny.

And that was another thing . . . Benny was so good-looking, and obviously not vain and poncey, so why did he live alone? Most men of his age had a woman and a couple of kids by now. But then again, maybe he did have?

Closing her eyes, she imagined the scenario.

In his last year at school – or maybe just after he left – Benny had met and fallen in love with a totally gorgeous girl. She'd loved him too, and they'd vowed to stay together for ever. A few months later, they had moved into this very flat and, within a year, they'd had two brilliant kids – a boy that looked just like Benny, and a blonde little girl, just like the mum. Benny had been so pleased with his family, he had given his girlfriend everything a woman could possibly want . . . never guessing for one minute that she'd turn into a completely selfish bitch and dump him the minute someone richer came along!

Shaking her head at the injustice of it all, Lisa vowed to herself that she would make up for everything Benny had been through. She'd treat him really, really well – to compensate for the fantasy girlfriend's inadequacies. She'd make sure he felt extra special, by showing him that not all girls were out for what they could get. And maybe one day – when she was fifteen or sixteen – Benny would realize that Lisa was the only woman capable of loving him as much as he deserved to be loved. And when he did, he'd go and ask her mum if he could marry her, and—

'Lisa?' Benny tapped on the door, shocking her out of her daydream. 'Are you all right in there?'

'Yeah, I'm fine, thanks.' She sank down beneath the water, covering her barely sprouting breasts with one arm, her hairless modesty with the other. 'I was just getting out. Won't be a minute.'

'Okay, well, hurry up. I need you out here.'

Getting dressed after a quick towel-dry, Lisa zipped up the tracksuit jacket, then went through to the living room with the towel wound around her hair.

Benny was kneeling on the floor with her clothes laid out in front of him as though they contained a spreadeagled body. Looking up at her, he smiled.

'Ah, good, you're ready. Sit there.' He pointed to the carpet where the headless neck of her jumper gaped.

'What are you doing?' she asked, kneeling down. 'I thought you said you were washing them?'

'And no doubt they could do with a good scrubbing,' he responded softly. 'But first, we need to *cleanse* them.'

Lisa pulled a what-on-earth-are-you-talking-about face, causing Benny to roll his eyes ceilingward in mock frustration.

'Oh dear, you do ask a lot of questions,' he said, although she hadn't. 'You just won't open your mind and admit what you already know, will you? But never mind that now.' He flapped a dismissive hand. 'All in good time. Now, what I want you to do is close your eyes and concentrate while I start the ceremony.'

Lisa frowned. 'What ceremony? What are you doing?'

'*We*,' Benny said, emphasizing the word with a conspiratorial smile, 'are cleansing your garments of the negativity they have accumulated. Bad impulses and negative attitudes cling to clothes like you wouldn't believe, which is why we have to do this . . . now . . . before you can *hope* to move ahead without your blind-fold.'

'I haven't got a blindfold,' Lisa said, wondering if he was tripping out, or something. Drugs could do that – make you talk a load of rubbish. It would certainly explain the weird things he'd said. Which reminded her . . .

'Benny? You know that stuff you said about me mum?'

'Not *now*!' Closing his eyes, Benny held his hands over her legless jeans as though he were a priest performing absolution. Looking up a second later, he saw that she was still watching him and frowned. 'What are you doing?' he asked.

'What do you mean? I'm not doing anything.'

'Exactly! But you're *supposed* to be, aren't you?'

Lisa shrugged. 'Dunno. Like what?'

With all the patience he could muster, Benny said slowly, 'Close your eyes so that we can begin.'

Lisa sighed exaggeratedly. 'All right, but it's stupid, if you ask me . . . And I *still* want to know what's going on.'

Bringing his hands down to his thighs with a slap, he glared at her with narrowed eyes.

'Don't defy me, Lisa,' he said, his voice low and dark. 'I won't tolerate defiance!'

'What you talking about?' she snapped, unable to mask her irritation at the absurdity of the situation. 'I haven't done nothing!'

'Meaning that you *have*,' he retorted arrogantly.

'*What*?'

'Is that all you can say?' he snarled. '*What* . . . ?' he mimicked cruelly. 'What what what what *what*? Have you nothing more intelligent to offer? Hmm? Maybe you should go to school regularly, have you thought about that? . . . Instead of hanging about the streets all day, picking up strange men! How do you hope to reach your salvation if you persist in defying your Master?'

Lisa eyed Benny nervously as he ranted. Spittle was bubbling from the corners of his mouth, and his eyes were so dark they appeared to be all pupil. She knew instinctively it would be unwise to retaliate against his unfair attack. He was obviously off the planet right now, and anything she said was likely to inflame him further. It always did when her mum was in one like this.

'So what are you prepared to do about it?' he demanded at last.

'About wh—' she started, but stopped herself before the dreaded word came out. 'I don't understand the question,' she said instead, as evenly as possible despite her hammering heart.

Benny's nostrils flared as he fought an urge to slap her insolent face. Breathing deeply until the storm began to pass, he said: 'I asked what you were prepared to do about your salvation? It's hardly fair of you to leave it all to me, is it? I've already done more than my fair share on your behalf. The least you can do is participate with sincerity, instead of mocking me for my efforts. Now close your eyes and do it properly!'

Fearful of the consequences should she refuse to play along, Lisa closed her eyes and waited.

Satisfied with her show of obedience, Benny closed his own eyes once more, and resumed his position.

'Master, we gather here today to ask Your divine forgiveness for the sins of this child . . . Lisa . . .'

Lisa opened her eyes when he said her name, thinking he was addressing her. She shut them again quickly when she saw that he was in the full throes of fervent prayer.

Bloody weird, if you ask me – but he obviously wasn't going to. He was in a world of his own, and the best she could do was keep quiet until he'd finished – and hope he would go back to normal then and tell her what was going on.

'In Your infinite wisdom, You brought her to me,' Benny went on, his voice thick with gratitude that he should have been blessed with such a responsibility. 'Master, You have *seen* my endeavours . . . You have *known* my desire to complete Your most worthy of causes . . . But now we need a manifestation of Your presence, Master . . . We need Your absolute might to cleanse the evil from this wayward child and her belongings . . .'

'*Ahhh!*' Lisa squealed with shock as Benny's hands suddenly came down on her shoulders like claws. 'Benny, *please* . . . you're hurting me!'

'Hear the protestations!' His voice rose in intensity as his fingers dug deep into her writhing shoulders. 'Feel her resistance! See how desperately we need Your almighty power to fend off the forces surrounding us at this time? . . . Save her, Master . . . *Save* her . . .'

'Let *go!*' Pushing at his hands, Lisa tried desperately to get free. 'You're frightening me, Benny. Stop it!'

Muttering a mantra under his breath, Benny held on with brute force for what seemed an age. Then, suddenly, like the breaking of a dam, he let go and settled back on his haunches with a sweet smile.

'Thank you, Master,' he said with a blissful sigh. Then, turning his smile on Lisa, he said, 'Thank your Saviour.'

Looking up at him through her tears, Lisa was shocked to see that his eyes too were glistening. It made her feel strange inside – scared, yet curious. Why had he said all that stuff about saving her? Did he really think she was bad? Or was he just one of those Bible-bashing nutters who thought it was his job to save her soul? Did he really *care* about her? she wondered, then decided that he must do to go to all this trouble for her.

But did he have to be so *mad* about it?

'Say it!' he demanded, still smiling.

'Thank you,' she murmured, blushing with the sheer embarrassment of it all. She'd never been to church in her life; had actively mocked the tiny core of Christian kids at school for their goody-goody behaviour and divvy clothes. No one *normal* did this sort of shit. What would her mates say if they found out? It didn't bear thinking about!

'*And . . . ?*' Benny was saying now, as if prompting a small child to remember its manners.

She gave a tiny shrug. 'And what?'

'Ah ah ah!' he scolded with a wagging finger. 'Who are you thanking?'

'Thank you, *Master*,' she said, getting his drift at last and complying to get it over with.

Sighing, Benny looked at her fondly.

'There . . . that wasn't so difficult, was it? You can go and get dressed in your room now,' he told her then, gathering her clothes together and handing them to her. 'I'll make us something to eat.'

'I'm not hungry,' she said, getting unsteadily to her feet. 'I think I'd better just go home.'

'You *are* home,' he told her. 'Now be a good girl and get dressed. I'll put some toast on.'

Lisa stood in the middle of the floor, clutching her clothes to her breast as Benny went into the kitchen. What did he mean, she *was* home? Surely he didn't expect her to move in here with him? He knew she was too young to leave home.

Her eyes flicked every which way around the room as she pondered the situation. The only thing she knew for sure was that she had to go home. She'd already been out for ages. Her mum would slaughter her when she got hold of her.

It suddenly occurred to her that she didn't even know how long she *had* been out. Getting ill and falling asleep like that had knocked her off kilter. She didn't even know whether it was day or night. And with the curtains still drawn, there was no way of finding out.

She contemplated pulling the curtain back a little to check, but thought better of it. She didn't want to risk annoying Benny again. He might decide that his stupid ritual hadn't worked properly and start it all over again.

'What are you thinking?' Benny was watching her from the kitchen doorway, his head cocked questioningly to one side.

'I, er, was just wondering what time it is,' she said.

'Why?'

Lisa frowned. 'Well, er, because I don't know how long I've been out. If I'm too late back, me mum will get worried.'

Benny shook his head. 'Silly girl. I've already told you she's better now.'

'But I don't understand what you mean by that?' Lisa said. 'She wasn't ill or nothing. And she *will* get worried if I don't go home, Benny, honest!'

'No, she won't,' he stated calmly. 'She's free of all worries now.'

Fear clutched at Lisa's stomach like a hand, squeezing the breath out of her. In that instant, she knew something had happened to her mum – something bad.

'What's wrong with her?' she asked, mumbling around her tongue, which suddenly felt as if it had swollen to twice its normal size.

A flicker of irritation flashed across Benny's face.

'Get dressed,' he told her sharply. 'I've better things to do than stand here going over the same old ground. Go to your room – *now!*'

Scuttling past him as he looked set to explode again, Lisa dashed into 'her' room. Benny's voice followed her as she closed the door.

'And don't try anything with the front door because it's locked, and I've got the keys!'

Leaning back against the door, her heart thudded noisily in her ears as she began to realize that all was not as it seemed in Benny's kingdom.

He'd said she'd been taken ill and fallen asleep. Well, she couldn't remember that, but she supposed it was feasible, given that she *had* been asleep. Okay, so maybe that was true, she decided. But why, if he was only trying to help her, had he locked her in after carrying her to bed? And why was he being so weird with her – shouting at her like that and hurting her? And that stuff he'd said about her mum . . . It didn't make any sense.

'Lisa?' Benny suddenly shouted, sounding for all the world as if he were calling his little sister in for tea. 'The toast's getting cold. Hurry up in there!'

Dressing as quickly as possible, Lisa came to the conclusion that whatever was going on here, it would be best if she just played along with a smile. Then, the second she got a chance, she'd be off!

18

S eddon stood back as the paramedics gently loaded
Pat Noone onto the stretcher and manoeuvred her
out through the door. It had taken them the better part
of an hour to revive and stabilize her, but she'd stand
little chance of surviving if they didn't get her to hospital
for immediate surgery. They had already radioed ahead
with a description of her injuries, and a specialized theatre
team was assembling even now at the Manchester Royal
Infirmary.

It had come as a shock to everyone when Seddon
had discovered that Pat wasn't dead. Not least Seddon
himself, who would never have imagined that anyone
could have survived such a brutal attack. But he should
have known that a battler like Pat Noone wouldn't allow
herself to be taken out so easily.

He just thanked Christ he'd managed to get there so
fast. If he'd arrived after the forensics team, he'd have
been barred from touching anything and would have
been denied the opportunity to check her pulse – which,
in fact, he almost hadn't bothered doing, given the gruesome slashes he'd come to know so well criss-crossing
her stomach. An instinct had told him to do it, however,
and if he hadn't followed it, she might well have slipped
away unnoticed while they stood around waiting for the

body bag. As it was, she was only holding on by a bare thread. He only hoped she would rally round enough to tell them what had happened and, with luck, give them a description of her attacker.

Anything from a survivor of the Forget-me-not Killer would be better than the nothing they had now.

And Seddon knew it was his man that had created this carnage. All the signs were there – the cross-cuts, the gift. The only things that were different about it were that this time the victim had lived, and that the attack had taken place indoors.

Strange that the keys were here though, he thought, looking at the bunch they'd found on the bedside table – now secured in an evidence bag. The neighbour had told the greenhorns that Pat had thrown them down to her attacker. But then, Seddon supposed, if the attacker had used them to regain entry, he could have left them behind – either by mistake, or because he no longer needed them. Whatever! The important thing was to check them for prints.

'Well, this is a turn-up, isn't it?' Lynne Wilde had arrived.

Seddon was glad to see her.

'You can say that again,' he said. 'I don't know who was more shocked – me, or the greenhorns who found her? Have you been filled in, by the way?'

Lynne nodded. 'Briefly, but I want to have a good look around before we let the team loose in here. Did the constables disturb anything, do you know?'

Seddon gave her a weary look. 'Well, obviously they didn't expect to walk into a murder scene – or rather, an *attempted*.' He shrugged. 'I think they did their best, but there's no telling if they waded in a bit less than carefully. By the way, that—' he pointed to a pile of vomit in the corner '—is one of theirs.'

'Nice,' she murmured, pulling her gloves on as she surveyed the room with a critical eye. 'Let's see what we've got, then.'

She, like Seddon, had a burning desire to find the *anything* that would lead them to their man. And she was more likely than he to spot it. They both knew this.

'Who examined her?' she asked, peering closely at the bloodsoaked bed for hairs and fibres.

'The parameds. When I got the pulse, I got them here ASAP.'

'Good call,' Lynne murmured. 'From the looks of this blood, a minute later and she'd have gone. Did they find the—'

'Yeah,' he cut her off, knowing she meant the flower. 'Right where it always is. And she'd been done very recently.'

'Sperm?'

'Yep.' He shrugged. 'Still, it'll probably turn out like the last girl, I suppose. I mean, she isn't exactly a virgin, our Pat.'

'You know her?'

Seddon gave a soft snort. 'Oh, yeah. We go *way* back, me and Pat. She's been tomming for – what – fifteen years at least. I've pulled her in God knows how many times, and she's a right one, I can tell you! Rip your face off as soon as look at you. But she's all right, if you know what I mean. Dead against drugs, and kids getting into the life.'

Lynne raised an eyebrow. 'Sounds like a regular saint.'

'Hardly,' he chuckled. 'But you know where you are with the Pats of this world. Leave them alone and they don't do anyone any damage. She had a kid, by the way. A girl, about twelve.'

'Oh? And where is she? She didn't . . . ?'

Seddon shook his head. 'There's no sign of her. Hers is the room next to this, and it doesn't look like the bed's been slept in tonight. Mind, it's hard to tell,' he added with a grin. 'The state of the place.'

'Mmmm,' Lynne murmured, glancing around at the accumulated junk littering Pat's room. 'Doesn't look like it's seen a Hoover for a while, does it? Oh, and what's this about a dog?' she asked then.

'Oh, yeah. The greenhorns found an Alsatian in the front room downstairs. Out cold, poor sod. The dog handler had it away just before you got here. They're taking it for analysis, find out why it's so zonked.'

'Do you think it's been drugged?'

'Can't think of anything else that would knock a big dog like that out without leaving marks.'

'No blood down there?' she asked hopefully. 'Nothing to suggest it might have had a go at the bastard?'

'Unfortunately not.'

Lynne looked thoughtful for a moment, then said, 'You think she knew him?'

'What do you mean?'

'No forced entry,' she said, repeating what she'd been told already. 'A guard dog laid low without being injured by or, apparently, injuring whoever was in here. It all adds up to familiarity, doesn't it?'

'I suppose so. We'll have to wait and see what Pat's saying when she comes round.'

'*If*,' Lynne murmured.

'Yeah, if,' Seddon conceded with a sigh. 'Be an absolute shame if she doesn't. She's the best chance we've got of getting anything on the freak.'

'What about the child? Do you know where she's staying?'

'Not yet,' he admitted, looking at his watch. 'I'd better get down to have a word with the informants, actually. One of them has a daughter the same age who knows all the same people.'

'Good luck.'

'Thanks. See you later.'

Making his way outside,. Seddon decided to check something out before going to see the women who'd made the call.

Stepping back to the railing, he looked up at Pat's bedroom window, then averted his gaze to the next-door one. On both there was an overhang of some twenty inches or so protruding out above the front door. The neighbour had said that she'd seen the man entering and leaving, but Seddon wondered if it would be possible to see someone clearly if they were standing directly below this lip.

He made a mental note to check it out later. He would go into the neighbour's room and have one of the PCs stand outside Pat's door. That way he could see for himself how much was visible, to assess the validity of the neighbour's claim.

For now, though, he had a child to locate.

Sue and Ada were waiting on the couch in Sue's front room. A WPC watched over them from the doorway.

Walking in, Seddon saw that both women were

exhausted, but the older of the two looked quite ill – her face an unhealthy shade of grey, and her mouth hanging open loosely as if she couldn't get quite enough oxygen. The shock of the situation had obviously caught up with them both. Motioning the WPC into the kitchen to make a pot of tea, he sat down.

'I'm Detective Inspector Seddon,' he said, using his full title since it tended to have a calming effect on shocked witnesses. 'I'll be taking your statements, but first I need to ask if you're feeling up to it?'

Sue nodded, then asked in a whisper, 'Is she really . . . you know . . . *gone*? I mean, that poor policeman, he looked so shocked.'

'I can't believe it,' Ada moaned beside her. 'I can't believe she's gone. I mean, I know I slagged her off, but she didn't deserve *that*.'

Sue squeezed Ada's arm. 'I know, Ada, I did the same myself. It's just—'

'Ladies,' Seddon cut them off gently. 'She's not dead.'

'She's *not*?' They both gasped, wide-eyed with surprise.

'No,' he assured them. 'Very severely wounded, but she's still alive.'

'Well, where is she?' Sue demanded, her voice stronger now. 'What are you doing for her?'

'She's on her way to the MRI,' Seddon told her, glancing at his watch. 'In fact, she should be there already. There's a skilled team waiting for her there,' he went on reassuringly. 'She'll get the best possible treatment, so there's no need to worry.'

'Thank God for that!' Sue sank back with obvious relief.

Seddon raised a mental eyebrow. He knew from the greenhorns' account that there was no love lost between this woman and Pat Noone. He wondered if her sudden concern was a measure of her guilt for the way she'd treated her. People were funny like that. They could hate someone, use every opportunity to bad-mouth them, but the minute something rotten happened, they went on a major guilt trip and behaved as if they'd been the best of friends.

'Mrs Baker, are you all right?' he asked Ada who was now fanning her face with her hand. 'Do you want me to get a doctor to take a look at you?'

'No, no . . . I'll be fine,' Ada said. 'It's just the shock of it all. Go on, love,' she motioned with a nod towards his notepad. 'Get on with the statements, eh?'

'Would you like a cup, sir?' The WPC came back with a tea tray.

'Um, yeah, thanks.' Taking one, he pointed at the sugar bowl. 'Put a couple of big ones in Mrs Baker's, eh?'

After a quick drink of the weak tea, Seddon placed his cup on the floor and began to take down the informal statements. He soon found himself running out of sheets in his pad. Revived by the sweet tea, Ada Baker had a lot to say about the comings and goings of the area. He knew it was going to be a ball-ache, sifting through it all later to weed out the relevant stuff from the gossip, but she was the sort of woman you had to give rein to. The real old-school type of nosy. Let them run off at the mouth, and you were sure to catch more than one fish.

'So this man,' he asked, when she started to circle back on herself. 'He's Asian, you say?'

'Yeah.' Ada nodded emphatically. 'A Paki.' Pausing, she had the grace to look sheepish at her vehement use of the word. 'I'm not prejudiced, or nothing,' she told him. 'It's just that I've got an axe to grind with that lot. They stole my baby!'

'Sorry?' He was confused. 'They *stole* your baby?'

'My *Sheila*,' Ada said, looking at him as though he were an idiot for not knowing this momentous news already. 'She got hooked up with one of them, didn't she? Bloody brainwashed the silly cow, they did. Got her wearing one of them stupid long dress thingies and changed her bloody name to summat daft . . . Ashrina, or something. Then they shipped her off to their bleedin' country, and I ain't never seen her since. *Stole* her – like I said!'

'I see.'

'Yeah,' she went on, calming a little. 'So that's why I say it like that. Not 'cos I'm against all Pakis – just *them* ones!'

'Mmmm, well . . .' Seddon cleared his throat. 'So this *Asian* man. You've seen him before his visit tonight?'

'Oh, yeah. He's a regular, him.'

'And are there any other regular callers?'

Ada thought about it for a moment, then shook her head – almost regretfully, Seddon thought. As if, now that she knew Pat Noone was still alive, she was back in bad-mouth mode, and would like nothing better than to be able to say that there was a constant stream of men calling at the house of ill repute.

'No,' she admitted at last. 'Only him, that I've noticed. Comes once, maybe twice a week.'

'But you say last night was different somehow?'

'Yeah. Usually Pat lets him in – or Lisa, if she's there. But last night, Pat throws him the keys out the window, like. Then they have this big barney, and he come storming out again.'

'How long after he'd arrived would that have been?' Seddon asked.

Ada shrugged, pursing her wrinkled mouth as she made a mental assessment.

'Half an hour? An hour at most.'

'And then he came back?'

'Yeah, not long after. I'm not too sure how long, 'cos I'd switched the telly off and dozed off by then.'

'But you're sure it was him?'

'Well, who else could it have been? Letting himself in with keys, and all. He must have still had them from when she threw them down, mustn't he?'

'And you say you saw his car tonight?' Seddon asked, steering her away from speculation and trying to hook her into the facts. 'A large, dark car, you said?'

'Yeah, that's right. He don't usually bring it onto the street, but he did tonight. He sat in it for a while after they had the row, and he must have been pretty buggered off, if you ask me – the racket he made when he took off.'

'And you heard him come back?'

'Not the car, no,' she admitted. 'Like I said, I was dozing by then.'

'So it could have been someone else entering the second time?'

Ada didn't answer this, just gave Seddon a look as if to say he couldn't really be *that* stupid. Anyone with an ounce of common sense would know it must have been the same man.

'All right. Well, thank you for that,' Seddon said, concluding her part of the interview for now. 'We'll arrange for you to come down to the station at some point to look through the books. See if we can't get lucky and find this Asian man, eh? And I'll have someone get together some pictures of cars, see if we can't identify that, too.'

Ada smiled self-importantly. 'Any time. But send someone for me, if you would? Only I can't walk too good these days, and buses are a nightmare with my back.'

'No problem,' Seddon told her, returning the smile.

'Now, Mrs Morgan.' He turned to Sue. 'Do you think I could have a word with your daughter?'

'Yes, of course. I'll go and wake her up.'

Debbie was already awake. She hadn't been able to even *think* about going back to sleep with all the police activity going on outside. But, mainly, she was really worried about Lisa. They'd said she wasn't there, but Debbie couldn't think of anyone Lisa had ever stayed with. For some reason, most of their friends' mothers were like her own when it came to Lisa. It seemed they all had a problem with Pat, and tarred Lisa with the same brush. Debbie had always thought this unfair, but Lisa seemed to brush it off.

'Hello, Debbie.' Seddon smiled as she came into the room. 'I'm Detective Inspector Seddon.'

'I know. I saw you at the funeral.'

'Oh?'

'Yeah, when Linda was . . .' She tailed off.

'Ah,' Seddon murmured. 'Linda Parry?'

'Yeah. We were friends.'

'I see,' he said gently. 'I'm very sorry. I didn't realize.'

'I did tell that policeman,' Sue interrupted. 'I thought it might mean something? . . . When he said about it being the same man. I just wondered if it might be linked?'

Debbie felt a chill run down her spine.

'He didn't get Lisa?' she gasped, tears springing into her eyes. 'No . . . *please* . . .'

'No!' Seddon told her quickly. 'He didn't get Lisa. She wasn't at home tonight, I promise.' He clicked his fingers at the WPC. 'Get her something to drink, would you?'

'I'm all right,' Debbie sniffled, comforted by her mother's protective arms. 'I . . . I just thought . . . What about her mum? She's not . . . ?'

'No, she's not,' Seddon reassured her. 'She's been injured, but she's at the hospital being well looked after.'

'So where's Lisa?' she wailed. 'I want to see her. She's my best f-friend.'

'Well, that's why I need to speak to you,' Seddon said, gently but firmly. 'We need your help, Debbie. Now, do you think you'll be okay to go on?'

Swiping at her tears with the back of her hand, Debbie nodded. 'Yeah.'

'Good. Okay, well, first I'll need you to tell me anyone you think she may be visiting tonight.'

'I've already given the policeman a list,' Sue said, frowning now at the obvious incompetence of the police force in general.

Seddon also frowned – at the obvious incompetence of the greenhorns.

'I'm sorry,' he apologized. 'Everything's a bit confused down there at the moment. I'll get onto it when we've finished here.' Turning back to Debbie, he said, 'Now, your mother said you might know Lisa's mum's boyfriend?'

'Sam,' said Debbie. 'Yeah.. Well, not really *know* him, but I've seen him a few times, and Lisa talks about him.'

'In what way?'

'Just that he's her mum's boyfriend,' she said, adding with a blush, 'And that he's a bit tight.'

'Tight?'

'Yeah.' Debbie flicked a nervous glance at her mum, afraid she might be annoyed to learn that she and Lisa discussed men in such a way. 'She tries to get a bit of spends off him sometimes, but he always says he's skint.'

Sue Morgan's eyebrows shot up at this.

'I hope you don't try the same thing?' she demanded, scandalized at the very thought.

'No, Mum,' Debbie protested. 'I've never even *spoken* to him.'

'Do you know what kind of car he drives?' Seddon interrupted. 'Mrs Baker says it's a large, dark car. But we need to ascertain what make and model it is.'

'I think Lisa said it was a . . .' Debbie paused, her young face screwed up as she tried to remember the word Lisa had used. 'A *Lester*?' she offered after a moment. 'Something like that, anyway.'

Lester . . . Lester . . . Seddon racked his brains. Then it came to him.

'Could it have been a Lexus?'

'Yeah, that's it! . . . I *think*?'

'Colour?'

'I don't know. Sorry.'

'No, don't worry, that's fine.' Seddon smiled. 'You've given us the most important bit. Now, his name? Sam, you say?'

'Yeah. That's what Lisa calls him, anyway. I think it's

short for something foreign, though. She calls him an Arab ponce.' Debbie cast another nervous glance at her mother. 'Only when she's annoyed, though.'

Seddon wrote it all down, then said, 'Just one more thing. Do you know where Lisa's father is?'

'She ain't got one,' Ada interjected croakily, surfacing from a light doze. 'Poor lass hasn't seen hide nor hair of that sod for years. Bad lot, he was. Didn't half put them two through it when he was around.'

'You knew him, then?'

'More's the pity!' Ada sniffed her disapproval. 'Everyone knew Lenny Noone. Right little arsehole, he was!'

Seddon knew the name, but couldn't remember why at the moment. He'd look into it when he got back to the station.

'Does Lisa have any contact with her father?' he asked Debbie.

'No.' She shook her head firmly. 'She definitely doesn't. She hates him for leaving them, and for never coming back to see her, not even on her birthday, and that.'

'And she wouldn't have gone to stay with Sam?'

'No way!' Debbie half-smiled at the suggestion. 'She doesn't know him *that* well. She'd have said.'

'Anyone else you might have missed out on the list your mother gave to the officer?'

Debbie thought hard, then shook her head. 'I don't think so.'

'Right, well, I think that'll be enough for now,' Seddon said, standing up.

'Oh, hang about,' Debbie said suddenly. 'There *is* someone she's been talking about.'

'Oh?'

'Yeah, some lad called Benny . . . well, a man, really. She reckons he's about twenty.'

'Who's this?' Sue demanded, frowning. 'Not someone *you*'ve been hanging about with, I hope?'

'No, Mum,' Debbie told her patiently. 'I've never even seen him. It's someone Lisa met at the youth club.'

'A twenty-year-old man at the youth club?' Sue exclaimed. 'I hope he's not one of the adults supposed to be supervising you? I'll have something to say if I find out the workers are fraternizing with the children! You won't be going again, that's for—'

'Mum!' Debbie cut her off with an exasperated sigh. 'He's not *from* the youthy, she met him outside. Well, she *said* she did.'

'But you don't believe that?' asked Seddon.

Debbie shrugged, then shook her head guiltily.

'No, not really. We'd fallen out over a lad we both liked, and I think she made it up 'cos he asked me out, not her.'

'And what did she say about this Benny?'

'Only that he was about twenty, like I said. That he was absolutely gorgeous, and that he'd said he'd fancied her for ages.'

'Huh!' Sue snorted softly. 'Well, it's got to be a lie then, hasn't it?'

'Why's that, Mrs Morgan?' Seddon asked.

Sue blushed. 'Well, she's not exactly a . . . *pretty* girl, if you know what I mean?'

'Poor little cow,' Ada chipped in. 'Ugly as her dad, she is. Can't see no *man* falling for her.'

'Exactly,' said Sue, smiling sadly.

'Well, I didn't believe her,' Debbie said, adding defensively, 'But not 'cos she's too ugly! *I* think she's pretty when she washes her hair and puts make-up on!'

'Well, thank you for your help.' Seddon smiled at Debbie. He silently applauded her loyalty to her friend, but his instincts were telling him that she was probably right about Lisa inventing the man-friend to cover up her embarrassment at being rejected. The last thing he needed to do now was start looking for fictitious boyfriends when he had a very real man to check out.

'Thank you, ladies,' he said to Sue and Ada then. 'I'll be in touch to let you know what's happening.'

'Do you think you could get in touch with the hospital and ask after Pat?' Sue asked as he reached the door. 'Only they won't tell you anything if you're not related, will they?'

Seddon nodded. 'I'll let you know as soon as I get a chance.'

Back outside, he checked his watch and sighed when he saw that it was only three a.m. He had a busy night ahead of him and, most likely, a busy day to follow. He couldn't afford to slacken in the slightest now that he had a lead – however tenuous it might be. But the priority right now was finding the girl and making sure she was all right.

Radioing in for a check on foreign Lexus owners, he made a beeline for one of the greenhorns.

'Come here, you . . . I believe you've got a list you should have told me about . . . ?'

19

Lisa was scared – *seriously* scared. Sitting on the couch as Benny paced the floor in front of her, she felt like she was about to faint. Her head was buzzing as if there was a swarm of bees inside it, and her mouth was dry and foul-tasting. Her eyes stung from the tears she'd cried – and those she'd been forced to hold back.

Benny had had a complete shit fit when she wouldn't stop crying. He'd screamed at her to stop it or he'd kill her, and then he'd dragged her from 'her' room by her hair and thrown her down on the couch with such force that she thought he'd broken one of her ribs.

'You didn't even *try* to understand!' he was saying now, his teeth clenched, his hands balled into fierce-looking fists as he paced just inches from her. 'Did you? *DID . . . YOU?*'

Lisa gulped back a scream of terror as he thrust his livid face towards her. Tears streamed silently down her cheeks as he abruptly moved away again.

'You're just an ungrateful little *bitch*! After everything I've *done* for you! Oh, Benny, *save* me!' he mimicked. 'Take me to your flat and make me *clean*! And what thanks do I get? NONE! Shut . . . *UUUPPP!*'

Running across to her as she let out an involuntary

sob, he caught hold of her hair and banged her head against the back of the couch.

'*SHUT . . . UP! . . . SHUT . . . UP!*'

'Benny, *please . . .*' she sobbed. '*Don't!*'

'*Benny, please!*' he mimicked, grabbing her cheeks with the steely fingers of one hand and bringing his face right down to hers. '*Oh, Benny, please . . . Benny, please!* . . . Please *what?*' he snarled then. 'What exactly are you trying to make me do, devil's spawn? Mmmm? Mmmm? What are you trying to tempt me with now, Satan's daughter? *These?*' Grabbing at her breasts with his free hand, he fondled them roughly beneath her jumper.

'*THIS?*' He thrust the hand between her legs, rubbing cruelly.

'Oh, yes!' he hissed. 'That's what you want, isn't it? The same as your *mother*! Slut . . . Whore . . . *JEZEBEL!* Is *this* what you're after?' Still holding her face in his vicelike grip, he unzipped his jeans.

'NO!' Lisa sobbed as he thrust himself towards her mouth. 'Benny, *please . . .*'

Laughing evilly, he pulled back slightly and said, 'Oh no! You won't make me fall for *that*, child of Satan!' Taking a small packet from his back pocket, he threw it at her. 'Put it on me!'

'Wh-what is it?' she sobbed, unable to see anything with her head forced back.

Benny laughed again. 'Oh, he's got you well trained, hasn't he? The innocence of a child? Am I supposed to *believe* that? Put it *on*! NOW!'

Snatching up the packet, he tore it open and thrust the condom into Lisa's hands. Waiting patiently, he hummed one note over and over as she fumbled with the unfamiliar sheath.

She couldn't believe it was happening. One minute he was talking about God and about doing the right things in life. The next he was telling her he'd killed her mum – and all the other whores. And now he was making her put this condom on him so that he could do awful things to her. And even though she didn't believe for one minute that he had really killed her mum, she was sure he would hurt her seriously if she didn't do what he wanted – as sure as she knew her own name.

'Good girl,' he hissed when she'd finally managed to get the condom over his rigid manhood. 'Now, *lick* it!'

'Please don't,' she pleaded, looking up at him, tears streaming freely down her face. 'I've never—'

'LIAR!' he screeched, dragging her head down and forcing himself into her mouth, making her gag uncontrollably.

Covering her muffled choking sounds, he chanted the word rhythmically with each thrust: 'LIAR . . . LIAR . . . LIAR . . . LIAR . . .'

20

S eddon climbed into his car with a defeated sigh.
He'd just left the last house on Debbie Morgan's
list, and here, as with all the others, he'd met an unspoken
hostility at the mere *idea* of Lisa Noone being an over-
night guest. It would have been easy to assume that
she was a terrible, evil child, given all these so-called
respectable adults' reactions to her. But he guessed it was
fundamentally due to Pat that her daughter enjoyed such
notoriety. Debbie's had been the only heartfelt positive
opinion of her. Hers, and Ada Baker's rougher version.
Lisa was a little sod in Ada's eyes, but the old woman
obviously pitied rather than despised the girl.

He started the engine just as his radio crackled.

'Seddon,' he answered, manoeuvring out of the parking bay one handed.

'PC Hunt, sir,' a voice replied. 'Got a possible ID
on the Arab, sir. I'm with a tom who reckons he was
a regular of hers. She says she knows more, but she
wants to see you personally.'

'Where are you?'

'Corner of Westy Lane, sir.'

'Right, keep her there. I'll be about ten minutes.'

Doing a U-turn, Seddon put his foot down and headed
for Westy Lane.

✱   ✱   ✱

The tom turned out to be Gloria Witherspoon – another face Seddon knew well. She'd been a nice girl once upon a time, when Seddon first came across her, but the intervening years had seen her decline, and she now bore the trademark stoop and caved-in face of the seasoned junkie. A thief and a liar, Seddon knew she'd sell a man's dick if he left it in her long enough, then swear he'd donated it to medical research.

'Hiya, Mr S.' Gloria sniffed as Seddon got out of his car. 'He's just been telling me about Pat.' Nodding towards PC Hunt, she hugged herself deeper into her jacket.

'Has he now?' Seddon shot a look at Hunt that clearly warned that he'd better not have given any details out.

'Just told her about the assault,' Hunt muttered.

'Terrible, that, isn't it, Mr S?' Gloria shook her head. 'We was only talking the other day about all the girls getting done in, and now she's got herself assaulted. Terrible.'

'Yeah, Gloria, it's terrible,' Seddon said, leaning back against his car. 'Now, about this Arab?'

'Yeah, Sam.' She sniffed again. 'Right poncey git! Jealous cunt, an' all. Once he's had you, he thinks you should *save* yourself for him. Wanker!'

'And he's a regular of Pat's?'

'Yeah. The only one she takes back to hers, an' all.'

'She must trust him, then?' said Seddon, picking at his nails as he waited for her to reveal why she'd wanted to see him personally. There was always a sting in the tail with the junkies.

Shrugging, Gloria said, 'He's all right, mostly – *if* you *treat* him right,' she added with heavy meaning.

Seddon looked up. 'In what way?'

Gloria licked her lips, reminding Seddon of a lizard. Hugging herself even tighter, she said, 'What's it worth, Mr S?'

'Depends what you've got?'

Smiling with all the warmth of a snake, she said, 'Good one, that, Mr S. Bet it works on some of 'em, an' all.'

Seddon shrugged. 'How am I supposed to gauge how much it's worth if I don't know what it is, Gloria? Be sensible.'

She looked at him hard for a few moments, then said, 'All right. I've got his full name, and I know whereabouts he lives. And I can tell you a few things that ain't quite *normal* about him, if you get me drift?'

He sighed. 'Not much is it, Gloria? Worth about, say . . .' Pausing, he pursed his lips as if debating a fortune. 'Twenty quid?'

'That all?'

'Take it or leave it.'

Gloria struggled with her greed for a moment, then gave in as a come-down shiver almost dislodged her spine from her pelvis.

'All right! He's called Samir Rashid, and he lives down West Didsbury way, in the big houses by the college. Don't know which one, but you'll suss it out.'

'What else have you got?' Seddon asked impatiently. Now he had the name, he just needed to know what she'd meant by *not normal*.

'He likes a bit of rough,' Gloria said. 'Carries all this weird shit about in his boot – clamps and wires, and stuff.'

Seddon and Hunt exchanged an amused glance.

'What's he do with them?' Seddon asked.

'Clamps your nipples up and wires you in to the lighter thingy in his car,' she explained, with a grimace of disgust. 'Thinks a bit of pain gives you pleasure, the fuckin' freak! Like we do this for the bleeding fun of it!'

Seddon raised an eyebrow. 'And I always thought you liked your work, Gloria?'

'Yeah, right!' she snorted.

'So why would Pat Noone put up with that sort of shit from a punter?' he asked.

'Oh, I doubt he tried it with *her*,' Gloria said. 'Everyone knows what *she*'s like. Mind, he probably got off on that, eh? The threat of having his head kicked in by a woman? Being treated like the worthless dog he is! It's all part of the same shit, isn't it? And what a turnabout, eh?' she went on, with a wry grin. 'Mixing it with us filthy-mouthed pros when he's got a raving Catholic missus at home doing the fucking rosary every time he farts!'

Seddon's ears literally twitched at this.

'His wife's a Catholic?'

'Shit, yeah. One of them proper holier-than-thou bitches. Why d'y' think he comes down here?'

'How do you know all this?'

'Pat knows everything about him,' she replied with a shrug. 'And everything punters tell us, we tell each other. You know how it is, Mr S. Got to have something to yak about when it's slow.'

'Have you seen him recently?'

'Yeah, he was round earlier. About twelve-ish, but I'm not too sure. Had a right bad-arse look on his mush, an' all. I thought he must have had a fight with his missus or something, but when he –' she pointed at Hunt '– started asking questions, I put two and two together, like. Mind, I'd be surprised if he's attacked Pat. I thought he was really soft on her. But you just can't trust blokes, can you?'

'Did he pick anyone up?' Seddon asked.

'Nah.' Gloria shook her head. 'There was no one here but me, and he knows better than to try that shit with me, so he fucked off. Had your money's worth yet?' she asked then, teeth chattering loudly. 'Only I need to get off. I think I'm coming down with something.'

Taking a twenty-pound note from his wallet, Seddon handed it to her, saying, 'You want to save the turkey for Christmas and put this towards a holiday, Glo. You look like you could do with one.'

Driving away a minute later, he radioed in to the station sergeant asking for an address, and anything else they had on Samir Rashid.

A few minutes later, the info came back.

Samir Ali Rashid. Age forty-five. Wife and two children. Resident at thirty-two Diddicott Avenue, West Didsbury. Registered owner of a bottle-green Lexus GS 300. MD of Rashid Imports/Exports based in Salford Quays. No known offences. Two complaints of racial harassment (complainant: Rashid) dropped before action taken.

Thanking the sergeant, Seddon told him to send a patrol car to meet him at Rashid's address.

* * *

Elsa stirred at the second knock.

'Samir,' she mumbled sleepily. 'Someone's at the door.'

When he didn't answer, she opened her eyes and saw that his side of the bed was empty. She wasn't worried. She knew exactly where he'd be: stuck in front of his computer.

Getting up, Elsa pulled on her dressing gown and peeped out of the window to see who could be calling at this time of night. She was shocked to see a police car and an unmarked car on the pavement outside the gate.

'Samir . . . the police are at the door!'

Sam jumped as Elsa ran into the room. Clicking his mouse with lightning speed, he cleared the images from the screen, then covered himself with his bathrobe before rounding on his wife angrily.

'Don't *ever* barge in here like that when I'm working!'

'I'm sorry,' Elsa said, glancing at the floating screen-saver suspiciously. *That was work?* 'It's just that the police are at the door. Will you answer it?'

Sam frowned. What on earth would the police want at this time of night? Then a liquid chill trickled through his chest. What if they'd found out about his *real* business interests? He could land up in jail – or worse, be deported back home, where he'd be in even deeper shit.

'You get it,' he said at last. 'I need to go to the toilet.'

'Your office might have been burgled,' Elsa said as he ushered her out of the room. 'I can't think of any other reason to come at this time, can you? Oh, no!' Pulling up short on the landing, her hand flew to her mouth. 'What if it's Mummy and Daddy? They might have been hurt.'

'Just stop imagining the worst and go and see what they want,' Sam snapped irritably, edging his way into the bathroom.

As Elsa went down the stairs, he cracked the door a little to listen.

'Mrs Rashid?' Seddon asked when she peered out at him with fearful eyes.

'Yes.'

'I'm Detective Inspector Seddon.' He flashed his ID badge. 'Is your husband home?'

'Samir? Um, yes, yes, he is. Is it about his office?'

'If we could just step inside?' Seddon said, moving forward even before she had stepped back.

Inside, he looked around the immaculate, expensively furnished living room, one eyebrow raised. Obviously Imports and Exports was an extremely lucrative business.

'What's this about?' Elsa asked, glancing nervously at the two PCs.

'If we could just speak to your husband?' Seddon asked, smiling.

'Yes, of course. He's in the toilet. I'll just get him.'

When she had gone, Seddon strolled around the room, stopping now and then to look at an ornament or to test the weight of one of the heavy crystal ashtrays.

The room was separated from the adjoining one by a pair of frosted-glass sliding doors. These were closed, but that didn't stop Seddon. Pulling them open, he stepped through into an equally immaculate dining room, half of which was taken up by a large eight-seater mahogany table.

An inveterate admirer of fine old furniture, he couldn't

resist stroking a hand over the deeply waxed and buffed wood. As he revelled in the satin-smooth finish, his gaze flicked over the arrangement of silver candlesticks and exactly placed mats and napkin rings adorning the table. This was a family that clearly enjoyed the finer things in life.

Something on the dresser against the far wall caught Seddon's eye. Turning, he saw a large vase of flowers and an over-full basket of smaller blooms. Each was beginning to show signs of wear, which was precisely the reason they'd been demoted from centre stage on the table – and the reason Elsa's mother had declined to take hers home when she left. Without knowing quite why they had sparked his interest, Seddon went over for a closer look.

'Detective Inspector?'

'Yes.' Seddon turned at the sound of the voice.

Sam stood in the doorway, his robe fastened tightly around his large gut. Elsa hovered behind him, nervously plucking at a tissue.

'Samir Rashid,' he said, extending his hand. 'I believe you wanted to speak to me? Is . . . is it about my office?'

Seddon wondered why the couple seemed so nervous. And why did they both think this visit was to do with Samir Rashid's office? Was there something dodgy about the business? He would be sure to look into that later.

'No, sir, this has nothing to do with your office,' he said, walking past the proffered hand into the living room, where the two PCs stood like a pair of guard dogs in front of the curtained window.

'What is it, then?' Elsa asked, sitting down and reaching

for a cigarette with shaking hands. She too had begun to fear the possibility that the real nature of Sam's business had somehow been uncovered. Not that she herself knew the full extent of what he did, but she did know it wasn't altogether above board. She'd always considered it best not to rock that particular boat by asking questions, however. The benefits were so great.

'If you don't mind,' Seddon replied, conscious of the fact that this was as yet just a routine questioning, but that it involved matters that would surely sour this seemingly perfect marriage should its nature be revealed to the wife. 'I would prefer to discuss this with Mr Rashid in private.'

'But I'm his wife,' Elsa protested. 'I want to stay!'

Sam shook his head. 'Go back to bed, Elsa. I'm sure that, whatever this is about, it won't take long.'

Grudgingly, she got up and left them to their illusion of privacy, knowing that every word they said would be audible from the bedroom above – if she stayed still and quiet enough.

'Mr Rashid,' Seddon began when he'd heard the door above closing. 'Could you tell us where you were tonight between the hours of ten and twelve?'

Sam frowned, wondering what this could have to do with his business. And then his spirits lifted. If it wasn't that, it couldn't be anything important. In all other respects he was a law-abiding citizen.

'Yes, of course,' he said, visibly relaxing. 'I was here.'

Seddon raised am eyebrow. 'Here?'

'Yes, here – with my wife and children.'

'And your wife would vouch for that?'

'Of course.'

'Does she know of your association with Patricia Noone and the other women who frequent Westy Lane?' Seddon asked, as casually as if he were talking to a friend about the weather.

Sam blanched and shot a nervous glance at the door.

'Wh-what? I don't know what you're talking about.'

'Oh, come now, Mr Rashid,' Seddon pressed on smoothly. 'We're all men of the world here.'

'No, really,' blustered Sam. 'I've done nothing wrong.'

That remains to be seen, Seddon thought.

'I'm sure you haven't,' he said. 'But until we obtain proof positive of your whereabouts tonight . . .' Pausing for effect, he shrugged, then said, 'I suppose I should really go with procedure and speak to your wife before we continue.'

'No!' Sam hissed, his face a sweating mess of guilt. 'All right, I do know Pat and the others . . . but it's not like you think. I've only met them briefly. In passing, you understand? I'm not guilty of anything.'

'Really?' Seddon asked with a sardonic smile. 'Now that's interesting, because I hear you're quite the regular down Westy Lane. And I also hear you're quite a regular visitor to Pat Noone's house.'

Sam's mouth opened and closed but nothing came out.

Seddon sat forward suddenly and put on his serious man-to-man face.

'Look, *Sam*, I'm not interested in your sexual preferences. I'm only interested in finding out who was responsible for the attack on Pat Noone tonight.'

'*Attack?*' Sam spluttered. 'Pat's been attacked? Where? When? Is she all right?'

'It was an extremely serious assault,' Seddon told him, watching his face carefully. 'We're treating it as attempted murder.'

'So, she's not—'

'Where were you between the hours of ten and twelve?' Seddon repeated his earlier question slowly.

Sam swiped at the beads of sweat rolling down his face.

'I, er, I was with . . . oh, shit!' Shoulders slumping, he put his face in his hands. 'I was with Pat for part of it,' he mumbled through his fingers. 'But I swear, on my family's lives, I didn't attack her.'

'We have a statement from a witness to the effect that you had an argument with her at her house. What was that about?'

Sam shook his head. 'It wasn't really an argument. We . . . we had a little row, that's all. She d-doesn't like it that I'm married. She wants me to leave Elsa, but I told her I'd never do that, and she was upset.'

'I see,' Seddon murmured, not at all convinced that a woman like Pat Noone would be upset over a married punter. 'The witness also states that you let yourself into Pat Noone's house tonight. Is that correct?'

'Yes. She'd been ill in bed all day and didn't want to get up, so she threw the keys down to me.'

'And when you left, you returned with the same keys some little time later?'

'What? . . . *No!*' Sam looked up now. 'I didn't go back. And I didn't take the keys when I went away. I left them on the table.'

'And would that have been the first or *second* time you used them to enter?'

'I only went in once,' Sam bleated. 'I told you this already.'

'All right. What *time* did you leave?'

Sam shrugged. 'I don't know. After eleven, I guess.'

'And what time did you return home?' Seddon asked then. 'And please remember that I may need to verify your answer with your wife.'

'About half one,' Sam admitted, knowing full well that Elsa wouldn't back him up in a lie if they told her what this was about. 'But I *swear* I didn't go back to Pat's.'

'So where *did* you go?'

'To Westy Lane,' Sam muttered guiltily.

'Did you get lucky?'

'Excuse me?'

'Did you pick anyone up?'

Seeing a way out of the mess, Sam seized it with both hands.

'Um, yes. Yes, I did.'

Seddon frowned suspiciously. 'On Westy Lane? You picked a girl up on Westy Lane, is that what you're telling me?'

'Yes,' Sam hissed. 'Okay?'

'Well, *no*, actually.' Sitting back, Seddon lit a cigarette. 'You see, we have another witness who says you didn't find anyone to your liking on Westy Lane tonight.'

'That's not true!' Sam protested, desperately aware of the need to cover himself. 'I met a – a new girl . . . on the corner. We went to the Arches. You can ask her.'

'Oh, I will,' Seddon said. 'Did you by any chance get her name?'

'Yes, of course,' Sam replied haughtily. 'I don't just

use them and cast them aside, you know. I like to get to know them a little, and—'

'What was it?' Seddon cut him off.

'Sorry?'

'Her *name*, Mr Rashid? If we're to verify your claim, then we'll need to locate this girl, won't we? So what's her name?'

Sam tried to come up with a name, but found to his despair that nothing would come other than Elsa, and his own sisters' names, none of which sounded remotely like the name of a young British prostitute.

'Well?' Seddon asked silkily. 'Was it April? . . . May? . . . June? . . . How about Lisa?'

Recognition of the name pushed a button in Sam's frantic mind.

'Yes! That's it!' he blurted out, then gulped as he remembered that Lisa was Pat's daughter's name.

'Where is she, Mr Rashid?' Seddon demanded, suddenly serious.

'What? . . . I – I don't know what you mean,' Sam said, flustered by the realization that he'd fallen into a trap.

'She's only *twelve years old*,' Seddon persisted. 'And she's missing from home – coincidentally, on the night her mother is savagely attacked, by *someone* with easy access to their home. I'm sure I don't need to spell out the penalties for having sex with a minor?'

'No!' Sam gasped. 'I'd never . . . that's horrible!'

'Is she here?'

'*No!*'

'Then you wouldn't mind if we took a look around for her?'

'But my children are asleep,' Sam spluttered. 'And

what about my wife? Look, please . . . I swear she isn't here.'

'I'm sorry, sir, but that's not good enough,' said Seddon. Motioning the PCs to the door with a nod, he said, 'Start out back. And don't leave a stone unturned!'

'No!' Jumping up, Sam attempted to bar the door. 'You can't just search my house. You need a warrant!'

'I'm afraid I don't,' Seddon told him calmly. 'When we have reason to believe a child may be in danger, we have absolute authority to enter and search any property with a connection to that child. Now if you wouldn't mind . . . ?'

'But what will I tell Elsa?' Sam moaned plaintively.

'That's not our concern, sir,' one of the PCs said, taking Sam by the shoulders and moving him aside.

'Very well,' Sam said, holding up his hands and slumping defeatedly down onto the couch. 'Search if you wish, but please try not to disturb my children.'

Staying with Sam while the PCs executed the search, Seddon came to the conclusion that he was probably telling the truth about Lisa not being here. He'd put up too little resistance to the search. But even if she wasn't here, that didn't mean Rashid didn't know where she was. He could easily have taken her and stashed her somewhere, intending to do God only knew what to her at his leisure.

But all that was just speculation, whereas the attack on Pat was something much more solid. Rashid was obviously lying about the 'new girl', just as he'd initially lied about his association with Pat. It could just be an attack of married-man guilt, but Seddon had enough of a reasonable doubt to merit questioning him further.

But more than that, he had an urgent need to locate Lisa Noone before any harm came to her – assuming it hadn't already. The sooner he got Rashid down to the station and under extreme pressure, the sooner they'd find Lisa, he was sure.

When the PCs came back, shaking their heads that they hadn't found any sign, Seddon stubbed his cigarette out in the crystal ashtray on the coffee table and stood up.

'Mr Rashid. I'm going to have to ask you to come to the station.'

'But why?' spluttered Sam. 'I haven't done anything. You can't arrest me for *nothing*.'

'Are you refusing to cooperate?' Seddon demanded coldly.

'No, no, of course not. But could I at least get dressed first?'

Seddon glanced at his watch. 'Yes, but be quick.'

Sam went to the door, then stopped, asking quietly, 'You won't tell my wife what this is about, will you?'

'No,' Seddon said. 'That shouldn't be necessary at this stage. Oh, by the way.' He pointed into the dining room. 'That basket of flowers . . . did *you* buy them?'

'Yes. Why?'

'Do you regularly buy flowers?'

'Well, yes, I suppose so,' Sam said, believing that it would make him appear more the devoted husband than he actually was. He knew how these English men paved the way to their women's hearts.

'You won't mind if we take them in for examination, will you?'

'Why on Earth would you want to do that?' Sam asked. 'And what will I tell my wife?'

Seddon shrugged. 'Tell her we're nicking you on suspicion of stealing flowers from the graveyard if you like. But whatever you decide, hurry up. I'm sure she's been disturbed enough for one night.'

Elsa sat on the bed after they'd left, mulling over everything she'd heard and comparing it to the lies Sam had told her. In his gabbled version he was a witness to a hit-and-run accident, and he was just going to help the police to try to identify the driver from mug shots. No explanation for the search of her home. Nor for the removal of her mother's flowers. All of which was a million miles away from the hushed conversation she'd actually heard.

She'd missed quite a lot of it, but the gist had been clear enough. Sam had been using prostitutes, and one of them had been attacked and the police thought Sam had done it. Why? . . . Because he'd been a *regular visitor* to the woman's house! Had been there *tonight*, in fact. And now the woman was in hospital in a serious condition, and her twelve-year-old daughter was missing.

Unable to verbalize the multitude of doubts assailing her, Elsa had mutely accepted Sam's pathetic excuses, and had even waved him off at the door as though he were doing someone a great service.

Sitting here now, alone, she began to put two and two together.

All the late-night appointments with clients.

All the showers as soon as he came in.

The panties she'd found in his pocket!

But was he really capable of hurting anyone? She couldn't for the life of her see it. He had a temper, yes, but it was only ever verbal, never physical. Still, they said the wife was always the last to know the truth.

A thought suddenly occurred to her. Maybe Sam had kept a computer diary? A lot of professionals did, she knew. And for someone like Sam, who couldn't function without a rigid schedule to keep him on track, it would be a godsend.

Getting up, Elsa made her way into Sam's office. She was surprised to find the machine still switched on, then she remembered that he'd been using it when the police arrived. Sitting down in his chair, she clicked the mouse to bring back the screen he'd been working on . . . And got the biggest shock of her life!

Filling the screen were some of the vilest images she'd ever seen. Men and women, all naked and aroused to the most disgusting degree, were rolling around on a huge bed doing unimaginable things to each other. Some were using *implements* on – and in – each other: whips, and enormous rubber penises. And one woman, dressed in a black PVC catsuit, with holes where the breasts and vagina should have been covered, was holding down a handcuffed girl, while a man forced himself into her from behind.

Shrinking away from the screen when she realized that this wasn't just a photograph but a moving picture, it dawned on Elsa that it must be coming direct from the Internet.

Snatching up the receiver of Sam's desk phone, the whirrings and clickings confirmed her suspicions. No *wonder* he'd insisted on a separate line! The filthy, abominable *bastard*!

Disconnecting it, she gave herself a moment to calm

down, then set about tracing the history of his calls. It read like a *Who's Who* of perversion. And, because he'd made the mistake of not creating a time-frame within which to delete the websites accessed, it was all there for her to see: dates, times, hours logged on – everything.

Determined to find out everything she could about the animal she had married, Elsa set about accessing each and every one of his files. The discoveries she made sent her head spinning. Not only did he have a prolific catalogue of deviant live-pornography sites, he'd also spent many nights 'talking' to girls in sex chat rooms – some as far away as Australia and America. And some of which he had managed to get a direct line to.

And all this while Elsa had slept in blissful ignorance on the other side of the wall!

As dawn began to cast its faint light into the room, she made an even more significant discovery: Samir had set himself up a separate bank account, from which he paid everything relating to his 'hobby'.

Unable to comprehend the lengths to which her husband's betrayal ran, she accessed the on-line account and read with astonishment the amount of money he had moved into and out of it. The Internet phone bill alone had reached almost three times the *yearly* amount for the house phone in just six months. And then there were the frequent – *very* frequent – withdrawals of fifty or one hundred pounds, all logged as having been withdrawn from a cashpoint machine in Chorlton.

By the time she switched off the computer, Elsa had no more illusions. But now that she knew everything, what was she to do about it? If she spoke to the priest, he would say that her sins of suspicion, and then her active snooping into her husband's private affairs, were as bad as, if not worse than, Sam's sins of infidelity and lewdness. And divorce would be an even worse sin, in the eyes of both the church and her family – a fall from grace from which she would never be redeemed.

But did she really want to reveal what she knew to *anyone* – let alone to her family? What would it do to the children if this became public knowledge? They would have to endure the rejection and taunts of the 'good' families they associated with.

And then there were the neighbours. Could she really run the gauntlet of their ridicule? Survive their incredulity at her ignorance? Have them snigger behind her back as they discussed her obvious inadequacies as a wife – that her husband should succumb to the temptations of every other female within reach!

But would she survive anyway, in a marriage that was clearly a punishment for going outside her faith? A good Catholic man would *never* have done this to her, but *she*'d had to be different. *She*'d had to rebel and marry the *foreigner* – despite all the warnings. Well, now she was paying the price!

Running a tired, shaking hand through her hair, Elsa pushed herself up from the chair. After all the soul-searching, she'd finally come to a decision. If this were a simple matter of Samir indulging his disgusting per-versions *visually* – albeit peppered with the occasional visit to a prostitute – then maybe, just *maybe*, she'd be able to swallow that knowledge for the sake of the family.

If, however, she found out that he really *was* guilty of

the attack for which he'd been taken away . . . Well, that was an altogether different matter.

And there was only one way to find out the truth.

21

L isa woke with a start. For a moment she didn't
have a clue where she was, but then it all came
back to her with a sickening rush. She was at Benny's . . .
In 'her' room . . . And he'd . . .

No! She didn't want to think about *that*. It was too
horrible! So horrible, in fact, that if she hadn't been
able to feel the evidence on her bruised mouth, she'd
have sworn it was a nightmare.

But it wasn't. It was the awful truth.

Staring into the gloom, she was immediately aware
of a difference. Instead of the previous pitch darkness,
there was now a silvery grey mistiness about the room.
Looking around, she saw a leaking-in of light from a tiny
gap at the bottom of the wood boarding the window. It
wasn't much, but it made her feel a little stronger –
as if she were still a part of the world outside, despite
being locked in here by the maniac she'd thought was
her friend.

The same maniac who claimed to have killed her mum,
and God only knew how many other women.

Listening for sounds of him moving about in the flat,
Lisa edged cautiously towards the window and traced her
hand lightly along the gap in the board. She eased a finger
beneath it. It was tight, but when she wiggled her finger

she found that she could get in up to the middle knuckle. Breathing shallowly, she pushed and pulled at the wood, trying to prise it away from the nails securing it.

After a few minutes, her finger felt as if it was going to break. The skin was raw and torn by splinters, but the wood hadn't budged even a centimetre. Aware that her finger was beginning to swell, she wrenched it free. She could just imagine what Benny would do if he came in and caught her trying to escape – and her too stuck to even *try* to defend herself.

Curling herself into a sitting ball, Lisa sucked on the swollen finger and eyed the door, waiting for his next visit. One way or another, she was going to have to do something if she wanted to get out of here alive. Quite what, she had no idea, but if she were smart, a chance would be sure to present itself eventually.

'Oh, Mum,' she moaned softly to herself. 'I wish you were here.'

Minutes later, the door flew open and Benny charged in with a cup in his hand and a manic grin on his face.

'Time for your drink, Lisa! Drink up . . . drink up! There's a good girl!'

Lisa flinched away from him, but he was too far gone to tolerate any kind of dissent. Dropping to his knees, he grabbed her hair and forced her head back. As he began to trickle the noxious liquid into her nose, leaving her no option but to open her mouth, he was almost singing as he said: 'Open up, there's a good girl. Open up for Uncle Benny!'

'Has she been conscious yet?' Seddon asked.

'Only briefly, a couple of hours ago,' the nurse told

him. 'But that's as good as we expected after the op she's had. Doctor Martindale will be able to tell you more. I'll let him know you're here.'

Thanking her, Seddon waited until she'd left the small room before sitting down on the visitor's chair beside the bed. Looking down on the woman he'd known for so long, he felt sad that she should have suffered this fate. He couldn't say he'd ever *liked* Pat, but he did have a grudging respect for her sense of morality – if such a word could be applied to an unrepentant prostitute. As he'd told Lynne Wilde, Pat was straight as a die in most respects.

She obviously liked a drink. Apart from the times she'd been brought into the station pissed as a dog, the prematurely broken veins visible on her nose and cheeks gave that one away. But she despised drugs and, even more so, the dealers who thrived on the misery they wrought. There were several good busts she could be credited for over the years. Just as she could be credited for taking out a local paedophile crew a couple of years back. That had taken guts, in Seddon's opinion, but she'd thrown herself into it with no thought for her personal safety, her only desire to protect the kids from the monsters.

And now look at her. Helpless. Hooked up to all sorts of bleeping machines, her face as swollen as her tortured body probably was beneath the bloodstained sheet. She was in a bad way, but Seddon knew she'd be a damn sight worse off in the mortuary some floors below. Thank God he'd had the foresight to check her pulse when he did.

'DI Seddon?'

'Hi, yeah.' Seddon stood up to shake the young doctor's hand. 'Doctor Martindale?'

'One and the same.' Dr Martindale laid the pile of files he was carrying down on the foot of the bed. 'I take it you know Mrs Noone?'

'Pat? Oh, yeah. We go way back.' Seddon gazed at Pat again.

Dr Martindale smiled politely. 'She looks a lot rougher than she actually is.'

'Really?' Seddon asked eagerly – his hopes of a good lead rising. 'I, er, I believe she's been awake?'

'Well, not quite *awake*,' Dr Martindale said. 'She *has* shown definite signs of consciousness, but she's not come round fully yet.'

Picking up one of the files, he glanced through it.

'Her vitals are remarkably good, considering,' he commented, more to himself than to Seddon. He wasn't too sure how much Seddon actually liked or cared about the woman, and didn't want to worry him unduly. 'Her stomach was a hell of a mess,' he went on gently. 'It took a lot longer than we anticipated sewing her up, but I can quite honestly say we did a great job.'

Seddon nodded. 'You kept her alive, doc, that's the main thing.'

Dr Martindale smiled. 'No small thanks to you, I believe?'

Seddon waved the compliment away. He'd done his job, that was all. What anyone would do, faced with the same situation.

'So what do you think of her chances?' he asked. 'Any idea how long before she regains consciousness?'

The doctor tipped his head to one side and shrugged.

'Anybody's guess, I'm afraid. Her chances are good physically, but there's no telling about her *mental* recovery, I'm afraid. She's suffered an enormous trauma. Not only the attack, but the operation too. It's amazing how shocking that can be to an already depleted system. Most of the recovery will be down to her own will-power and stamina.'

Seddon gave a tiny grin. 'If it's down to that, doc, she'll be up and running in a week.'

'Strong woman?'

'Balls enough for three men, that one.' Seddon looked at his watch. 'Look, I'm going to have to make a move. Do you think you could let me know if she starts coming round? I'll leave you my mobile number.'

'Yes, certainly. It might not be me because I'm due to go off in a couple of hours, but I'll let someone know to contact you immediately.'

Seddon gave him the number, then made his way to the door. Turning back, he said, 'One last thing, doc? Make sure no strangers get in here, eh? One of my men will stay outside, but as we don't know who we're looking for, they wouldn't know if he walked right past them wearing a tutu. Whereas you lot would spot someone different right off. Do you think you could do that?'

'No problem. I'll put everyone on the alert.'

'Thanks.'

Making his way outside, Seddon paused to light a cigarette in the doorway of the recently refurbished entrance to the MRI. Stepping aside to let a party of ageing wheelchair joyriders through, he squinted up at the bright morning sunshine and pondered again what he'd been mulling over all night: if Samir Rashid *had* taken Lisa, then where had he put her? And if not Rashid, then who the hell *did* have her?

Every line of inquiry had been checked thoroughly, to no avail. Every kid on Debbie Morgan's list had been visited. All the places Lisa might have run away to hide in had been checked. She was nowhere. She had disappeared into thin air.

But that was impossible. Everyone was *somewhere* – whether they wanted to be found or not. Seddon only hoped that wherever she was, she was still alive. He didn't relish the prospect of having to deal with another teenage girl's body turning up. Linda Parry had been more than enough for one lifetime.

Grinding the cigarette out, he made his way to his car. He wouldn't find Lisa by standing around here all day, and he wanted one last shot at Rashid before they had to let him go.

Having badgered Rashid intermittently throughout the night, Seddon's instincts told him that the man wasn't capable of committing these terrible crimes. But *was* he capable of starting something with a young girl? Had he preferred the innocent child to the jaded mother and begun something that had then spiralled out of control, resulting in the fight he'd reportedly had with Pat?

And had, by chance, the real killer come in to finish the job after Rashid left?

But no! That was just too far-fetched – too much of a coincidence. Where would the killer have got hold of the keys to let himself in? And why had Pat shouted out 'Sam', as the neighbour had said she did?

Whatever the truth of it, Samir Rashid was not as

squeaky clean as he made himself out to be. Precisely how dirty he was remained to be seen, but if he was responsible for hiding Lisa Noone away his bollocks were Seddon's – deep-fried!

'Lisa . . .' Pat mumbled, her fingers twitching as she reached for her child through the fog clouding her mind. 'Lisa . . .'

As Lisa receded into the black swirling mists, Pat reached out again, wanting to touch her child and pull her back to safety. There was something wrong. Lisa looked so frightened, her small plain face awash with tears. But she was gone before Pat could reach her.

'No!' she cried, forcing herself up into the light. '*NOOOOO!*'

'Excuse me?' DC Greene stood up and motioned to the nurse who'd been attending the patient all morning. 'I think she's waking up in there.'

Bustling past him into the room, the nurse automatically felt for Pat's pulse, saying, 'Hello, Pat . . . are you waking up, love?'

Pat's eyes twitched furiously as she tried to force them open. Growing concerned by her increasing pulse rate, the nurse reached across the bed and pressed the alarm button. Anxious seconds passed as Pat moaned and thrashed from side to side. The nurse was almost lying on the bed with her now, trying to hold her still, worried that she would tear open the terrible slashes to her stomach if she grew any more distressed.

'Mrs Noone?' the ward sister called, running into the room and taking instant control. 'Mrs Noone, wake up!' Issuing sharp little slaps to Pat's cheeks, she shouted down her ear. 'Come on, now . . . wakey, wakey . . . there's a good girl.'

Suddenly, Pat's eyes flew open.

'*Liiisssaaa* . . .' she screamed, tears streaming down her cheeks. 'I want my Lisa!'

'Hush, dear,' the sister said. 'Hush now . . . settle down!'

Pat looked around her wildly, then reached out to push the nurses away.

'Where am I? Where's my Lisa?'

'Who's Lisa?' the sister asked the nurse.

'I don't know.'

'Well, go and ask him out there,' the sister said, pushing her towards the door. 'Tell him to get this Lisa and bring her here before Mrs Noone does herself a damage!'

'Do you know who Lisa is?' the nurse asked DC Greene. 'Only Sister says can you please go and get her, because Mrs Noone's calling for her, and she's getting really upset. We're worried she'll do herself a real mischief.'

'I'll find out,' DC Greene said, pulling his radio free. 'Just give me a minute.'

'I'll be in here,' the nurse said, pulling her head back into Pat's room.

Greene radioed through to the station and left a message for DI Seddon to contact him immediately, making sure that the sergeant taking the call understood the urgency. Seddon had left implicit instructions that he was to be told if anything happened with the Noone woman.

A few minutes later, Seddon himself radioed Greene to find out what was wrong.

'She's calling for someone called Lisa,' Greene told him. 'And I thought I'd better let you know, because the nurse reckons she's in danger of doing herself a mischief. Is there any chance of locating this Lisa, sir?'

'That's what I've been trying to do all night,' Seddon replied curtly. 'Look, just tell them to calm her down as best they can. I'm coming over.'

Fifteen minutes later, Seddon marched through the doors at the far end of the corridor and strode towards Greene, a worried frown on his face.

'Is she okay? They haven't knocked her out again, have they?'

'No, not yet,' said the sister, coming towards him with a covered tray in her hands. 'But I'm about to.'

'Could you just hold off until I've had a chance to speak to her?' Seddon asked.

She shook her head. 'Sorry. I've already left it as long as possible. I'm concerned that she'll rupture her sutures, and I'm sure you'll appreciate the terrible consequences if that happens. Now if you'll excuse me . . . ?'

'Just give me one minute,' Seddon begged, following her into Pat's room.

'Mr Seddon,' Pat cried when she saw him. 'What's going on? Why won't they let me see my Lisa?'

'Calm down, Pat.' Seddon sat on the edge of her bed and tried to smile, but grimaced instead, genuinely saddened by Pat's condition and obvious distress. 'They're not keeping her out, love. They're just concerned about you getting yourself into a state.'

Pat reached for his hand and gripped it fiercely.

'There's something wrong,' she croaked hoarsely. 'I can feel it! There's something wrong. Where *is* she?'

'I don't know, love,' he admitted quietly. 'That's what I've been doing all night – trying to find her. Now, I need to ask you some questions.'

'What do you mean, trying to *find* her?' gasped Pat, even more blood draining from her already waxen face. 'Where is she? What's happened to her?'

'I'm really going to have to insist that you leave,' the sister told Seddon firmly. 'This is not doing my patient any good. Now don't make me have to complain to your superiors.'

'I need to ask you something, Pat,' Seddon said, ignoring the hovering sister. 'Can you tell me who did this to you?'

'Detective Inspector!' the sister barked.

'Please, Pat . . . it's important! Whoever did this to you may have taken Lisa somewhere. Was it Sam? Just tell me yes or no.'

'I'm warning you, Inspector . . .'

'Yes,' Pat whispered, making a huge effort to remember the blurred events of the night before. 'Yes, I think so . . . Oh, I don't *know*! It was too fast. I didn't get a proper look at him.'

'That's *enough*,' the sister said. 'Can't you see you're upsetting her?'

'Why did he come back?' Pat sobbed. 'Why did he do this to me? I wasn't going to tell the stupid cow . . .'

'Who, Pat? Tell who?'

'His bleedin' wife! We had a row and I threatened to send her the bill!'

'And that's when he did this?'

'Not then, no. He came back when I was asleep. Must've kept hold of the keys.'

'Nurse! Go and alert security. I want DI Seddon removed.'

'Yes, Sister.'

'Pat, this is important . . . Did you see Sam? When he came back, did you *see* him?'

'Only for . . . *No* . . . Yes . . . No . . . Oh, I don't know! He turned me over, and . . . God, why did he do it, Mr Seddon? What's he done to my Lisa? I know he didn't like her, but he wouldn't hurt her, would he?'

'He didn't like Lisa?'

'No, he thought she was too lippy. Stuck-up ponce! She's worth ten of him!'

Two burly security guards came in just then, with an anxious-looking DC Greene hovering behind.

'Get him out of here,' the sister ordered furiously. 'I've never seen such a disgraceful disregard for a patient's welfare in my entire time here! I shall report this, you mark my word, Inspector!'

Seddon got up to leave, but Pat clung to his hand.

'Find her, Mr Seddon,' she implored. 'Find my baby.'

22

S am was exhausted. After being dragged into the station in the middle of the night, he'd been questioned relentlessly until he could barely get another word past his parched lips. Finally, they'd given him a drink and put him in a cell to sleep. But sleep had been impossible.

How could he rest when he knew that they thought he had Pat's daughter hidden away somewhere? And why couldn't he make them believe that he would never, *never* hurt a child?

He'd tried to convince them by showing them the photographs he carried around of his own smiling, *safe* children. But their response had been to say they'd be contacting Social Services first thing in the morning to ensure that *his* children hadn't been tampered with. Did they really think he was such a sick, depraved man?

Apparently so, for it seemed that Gloria, the prostitute he would no longer entertain, had been running off at the mouth about his little . . . *foibles*.

He could have kicked himself for ever revealing what he considered to be his innocent little games to such a low-down dirty whore as her. But that had been before he'd realized how unsavoury she was. And by then, she already knew far too much.

They'd left him sweating it out in the cell for God

knew how long. Now they had him back in the interview room, and things were not looking good.

'So, Mr Rashid,' Seddon was saying, his hands folded on the table between them, his eyes burning an acid path through the wood into Sam's soul as he rapped his accusations out. 'Tell me about this problem you had with Pat Noone's daughter, Lisa? *Too lippy* – I believe that was the term used. Did she annoy you because she answered back? Is that why you got rid of her? Because she's not a nice, polite girl who knows her place? Is that why you took her from her mother? And is that why you tried to kill the mother, Mr Rashid? Because you couldn't control the situation? Because she was threatening to tell your wife what her husband is really like?'

'No!' Sam protested when Seddon finally paused for breath. 'I never touched Lisa – *or* Pat! You've got to believe me!'

'What I believe, Mr Rashid, is that you knew the game was up. You knew Pat Noone had had enough of you, and that she planned to contact your wife. "Send her the bill" was how she put it.'

Sam blanched at hearing Pat's exact words.

'How did you know she said that?'

Seddon smiled nastily. 'Surprised to hear that she's been talking, are you? Well, for your information, me and Pat go back a long way.' He leaned forward threateningly. 'And that's why this is personal, *Sam*. Pat may be a lot of things, but she's nobody's fool. She had you sussed, mate, and she was about to spill the beans.'

'She only said that because she was ill.' Sam swiped at the sweat dripping from his nose. 'She wouldn't have gone through with it.'

'But you couldn't be sure of that, could you? So you went back to make sure, didn't you?'

'No! I didn't go back. I told you!'

'Ah, yes!' Seddon sat back, still grinning. 'This is the bit about picking up an unknown girl called, *coincidentally*, Lisa! The girl no one but you saw or knows anything about. Is that correct?'

'Well, yes, I suppose so.'

'Bollocks!' spat Seddon. 'Now start again, Mr Rashid. You left Pat Noone's house at what time?'

'No, no, *no!*' Sam began to cry, small gulping sobs that racked his fat frame as tears rolled freely down his sweat-sodden cheeks. 'I didn't do anything to Pat. I – I care about her. And I've never touched a child in my life. Ask my wife . . . I swear on everything I own, that's the truth.'

'Oh, I intend to have a chat with your wife very soon,' Seddon told him coldly. 'In fact, I intend to investigate you very carefully, Mr Rashid. And I warn you now, I don't intend to let you get away with this.'

'Can . . . can I have my solicitor here?' Sam asked, brushing at the tears and forcing himself to regain some composure. This was way beyond him, and he was starting to realize that it wasn't as simple a matter as telling the truth and letting justice prevail.

Seddon peered at him narrow-eyed.

'And why would you want a solicitor, Mr Rashid? I thought you were innocent?'

'I am!'

'Then why the sudden need for a solicitor? Have you finally realized that you're up shit creek without a paddle?'

'I just don't know how to convince you that I didn't do it,' Sam replied quietly. 'And I can't do this alone. I need my solicitor. I thought that was my right?'

'Well, we do know a lot about our rights, don't we?' snapped Seddon sarcastically. 'For a man who never does any wrong! Okay.' He stood up abruptly. 'You can have your solicitor. We'll start this again later.' He looked at his watch. 'For the tape, this interview is terminated at ten forty-five a.m.'

Turning, he walked from the room.

Sergeant Banks called out to him just as he was about to leave the station.

'Ah, DI Seddon, glad I caught you. The Super wants to see you.'

Without breaking step, Seddon continued on out of the door, waving as he called back: 'You haven't seen me.'

If the Super wanted him, it could only mean one thing. He was going to get a bollocking because of the bad press. Well, sod that! The Super could get in line with the rest who thought he needed bringing down a peg or two. Seddon had more important things to do than stand around listening to political bullshit.

Like revisiting Pat's house to see if could pick up any clues from the kid's bedroom.

And paying Elsa Rashid a visit. He had a feeling a bit of a shake-up in that direction just might bring rewards.

Jumping into his car, he roared away from the station.

Just as he turned onto Pat's road, his mobile began to ring. Pulling into a parking space, he answered it.

'DI Seddon?' the caller said. 'Doctor Martindale here. Thought I'd better let you know there's been a complication with Pat Noone.'

Seddon had just begun to climb out of the car. Pulling his leg back in, he said, 'What kind of complication? Is she all right?'

'Well, we won't be sure about that until she's been back into theatre. We're just prepping her now. She seems to have suffered an abdominal haemorrhage.'

'And that's bad?'

'Under normal circumstances, yes. In this case, worse. Anyway, I'm letting you know now because she's been asking for you.'

'Has she said anything else?' asked Seddon, slamming the door and starting the engine. If he could get over there before she went under, he might get a chance to speak to her again – try to pin her down on Samir Rashid. A solid yes from her on that would give him all the time he needed to keep Rashid and bust through all the red tape that would otherwise see the fat bastard walking free later that day.

'Just one thing,' the doctor said. 'Something like "It wasn't him".'

'Damn!' Seddon hissed out a breath. 'Look, is she still awake?' he asked then. 'I should be there in, say—'

'I wouldn't rush, Mr Seddon. She's way beyond talking already. I'll give you another call if she pulls through.'

'*If?*'

There was a pregnant pause before the doctor replied.

'It's not looking too good, I'm afraid. Look, I'm sorry, but I've really got to go now.'

'Yeah, sure.' Seddon sighed. 'Thanks for that, doc. And do let me know how it goes.'

'I will. Oh, and one more thing.'

'Yeah?'

'A woman called the ward this morning, asking about Mrs Noone.'

'Did she leave a name?'

'No, she wouldn't. Just said she was a friend. Sorry I can't give you any more than that.'

'Sure. Well, thanks anyway.'

'No problem. Bye.'

'Yeah, bye.'

Disconnecting, Seddon sat and stared out of the window. This was just great! If Pat didn't make it, they had a snowball's chance in hell of pinning Rashid down. Then again, if the doctor was right, she was now saying it hadn't been Rashid after all. But could she be relied on in her condition? Maybe she was delirious? Or had she decided that her long-standing punter needed protecting?

But no! What the hell was he thinking? Pat knew full well that there was every chance her daughter had been kidnapped – or worse – by the man who'd attacked her. And Seddon knew that even if it turned out that Pat's own mother was the killer, Pat wouldn't protect her if she'd done something to Lisa.

One thing was for sure – Rashid was guilty of *something*. Seddon didn't know quite what yet, but he was buggered if he was going to reveal what Pat had reportedly said until he'd turned over the entire Rashid empire. And there was no better place to start than with Elsa Rashid.

Lisa Noone's bedroom would keep for now, he decided. He'd not get a better opportunity to take a crack at Elsa before Rashid was released.

Women, as Seddon had discovered numerous times, were a strange breed when in the presence of their menfolk: capable of overlooking the most dreadful of sins if it meant keeping home and hearth together. Alone, Elsa might be more amenable.

Setting off, he wondered about the woman caller Dr Martindale had mentioned. He concluded that it was probably Gloria Witherspoon, or one of the other pros – another strange breed. They would half kill each other over a five-pound punter, but if one of them was hurt, they closed ranks like a coven of blood sisters.

Elsa Rashid wasn't really surprised to see DI Seddon walking up her path. She'd expected someone from the police to call sooner or later, and had, in fact, been on the verge of contacting them herself. By now, even *she* had figured out that Sam was far deeper in the mire than she'd been led to believe.

'Please, come in,' she said, opening the door and ushering Seddon through to the lounge. 'Can I get you a drink? Coffee, tea? Or perhaps you'd prefer something cold?'

'Tea would be fine,' he said, sitting down on the sumptuous couch.

While she was out of the room getting the drinks, he took the opportunity to have another look around; surprised once more by the elegance and pricey comfort of the furnishings. The floor-length brocade curtains alone would cost a couple of grand – this he knew from Pauline's endless fascination with magazines chronicling the lives of the filthy rich. The twin entwined-lovers table lamps, which looked like hand-worked bronze, would also cost a fair portion of the National Debt. As would the ceiling light, which *had* to be pure crystal – no lead crystal ever twinkled with such clarity.

There was serious money in this house, but Seddon doubted that Rashid's imports/exports business had provided it legitimately. It was certainly a lucrative business, he knew that much, but this home had all the hallmarks of undeclared profits. More like a major drug dealer with class – and he'd seen a few of those in his time.

Elsa came back with a small silver tea tray. Placing it on the immaculately buffed walnut coffee table, she handed a cup to Seddon and carried her own to a chair.

'Can I take it you need more information about Samir's . . . *activities*?' she asked, taking Seddon completely by surprise.

'Well, I, er, did want to speak to you about him, yes.'

'You think he's guilty of attacking this prostitute – Pat Noone?'

'At this moment, we're still investigating,' Seddon replied carefully, unsure of how she knew Pat's name.

'But you do think he did it.' This was more statement than question. 'So do I,' she said then, stunning him even further.

'Oh?'

'I've been thinking about it all night,' she went on. 'And I just can't shake off the feeling that he's guilty. No matter how hard I try, I can't think of any other explanation for the way he's been behaving of late.'

Seddon remained silent, waiting for her to continue of her own accord. She seemed to be battling with her conscience, and he hoped the better part won. Moments of revelation were fragile if interrupted. And for such a woman as this – middle-class, upstanding, deeply committed mother and wife – verbalizing one single word about dissent within her castle was tantamount to social suicide.

'I've learned quite a lot about Samir recently,' she went on after a time. 'I heard what you said to him last night, you know? *And* how he reacted.' Smiling sadly, she shook her head. 'I suppose I should have guessed about his sexual urges a long time ago, but it's easy to gloss these things over, isn't it?' Pausing, she gave a sheepish shrug. 'Easier than putting yourself through hell night after night, anyway.'

'So you knew about his relationships with the other women?'

'Oh, I can't say I *knew*,' she replied – with startling honesty, Seddon thought. 'But I'd certainly suspected. But then, I suppose everyone suspects their partner at some time or other?'

'Mmmm.' Seddon nodded understandingly, although he'd never suspected Pauline of any such thing. Neither, he believed, had he ever given her cause to suspect him.

'Anyway,' Elsa went on with a heartfelt sigh, 'I knew for certain the other day.'

'Did something specific happen to make you think that?' he prompted gently.

She snorted softly. 'You could say that. I found an . . . *item* in his pocket that should not have been there.'

Raising a questioning eyebrow, Seddon waited.

'A pair of ladies' panties, to be exact – *worn* ones. In his inside pocket. Like a little *souvenir*,' she added bitterly. Leaning forward, she shook a cigarette out of an embossed leather case. 'You don't mind, do you?'

'It's your house, Mrs Rashid. Please go ahead.'

'I kept them, you know,' she said then, fixing Seddon with a disarming look. 'Because I thought I'd have need to produce them sooner or later. Although, to be honest, I didn't think it would be to the police. More likely to a divorce solicitor. I don't suppose they'd be of any use to you?'

Seddon felt a kick of excitement in his gut. If these knickers had been worn as she said, there was every chance they would turn up significant evidence. The Forget-me-not Killer always took the undergarments with him after the attack – it was as much a part of his ritual as leaving his gift was.

Pat Noone had been knickerless when they'd found her, but it had been assumed that she hadn't been wearing any at the time because she'd been at home in bed. What a turn-up it would be if these knickers proved to be hers.

'When did you say you found them?' he asked.

'Last week. The week of our anniversary, actually.'

'Oh.' Well, that ruled *that* out.

'But there are other things I discovered last night that I think you'd be interested in. Would you like to see?'

'Well, yes . . . if you think it'll be of use?'

Elsa looked at him with all the malice of a woman truly scorned – although Seddon was aware that it was not aimed at him.

'If it helps you decide that he *is* capable of what you're accusing him of, then I'm sure it will be,' she said.

Getting up, she led him upstairs to the computer room. Sitting primly, she booted up the machine and opened Sam's files, then stood and gave Seddon the chair.

'I'd rather not see this again, if you don't mind. I'll be downstairs when you've finished.' Reaching the door, she said, 'Incidentally, there are a few things you might like to know about his business. I'll be more than happy to disclose everything I know.'

It was almost an hour before a drained yet elated Seddon rejoined Elsa in the lounge. She had a glass of wine in her hand, and he hoped she wasn't drinking with remorse at having revealed so much. Still, even were she to do that age-old woman thing and withdraw what she had said, Seddon now had more than enough with what he'd seen upstairs to prove Rashid's *interest* – if not his active participation – in the darker aspects of the sexual underworld.

'I hope you don't mind,' he said, sitting down, 'but I've taken the liberty of ordering a unit to come and remove the computer equipment for the purpose of evidence.'

'Mind?' she snorted. 'I'd have probably smashed it to smithereens if you'd left it to mock me another night!'

Reaching into her pocket, she pulled out a small, clear plastic freezer bag and handed it to him.

'These are the . . . *panties*. I hope they prove useful.'

Taking the bag, Seddon stashed it in his inside pocket, saying, 'Thanks. I hope so, too.'

'She's going to die, isn't she?' Elsa said then. 'Pat Noone?'

Seddon looked at her hard, unsure how much he should tell her.

She smiled sadly. 'I thought so. The nurse asked if I was a relative, and from my experience, they only ask that when things are very bad.'

'It was you? You rang the hospital?'

'Yes,' she nodded. 'You see, I thought I'd reserve judgement on Samir until I'd had a chance to confront her. But after speaking to the nurse, I knew I probably wouldn't get a chance. That's what decided me, actually. You may not believe this, but I was actually contemplating contacting you when you arrived.'

Draining her glass, she put it down and sighed heavily. 'Now, about my *husband*'s business . . .'

23

Lisa stiffened when she heard the key in the lock. She'd been awake for hours, just waiting for this. Thankfully, most of the fog in her head had cleared now, but she still had a strange taste in her mouth. At least she'd finally figured out why. It was the tea – the foul, stinking tea that Benny had forced her to drink. And he must have given her an especially large dose last time, because she felt as if she'd been asleep for days.

Taking a deep breath as the door handle began to turn, she reminded herself what she had decided. That she would not touch a single thing he offered her to eat or drink. And that she had to stay calm – no matter what! No arguing. No winding him up. Just keep her gob shut like he'd told her, and let him say whatever he wanted to say. It was the only way she was going to suss him out – the only way she stood a chance of escaping.

Pushing the door open, Benny smiled to see her sitting up.

'Ah, good. You're awake. Did you have a good sleep? Feeling better now?'

Nodding, Lisa watched him warily as he came towards her.

'I've made you some breakfast.' He held his hand

out to help her up. 'Come and get it before it goes cold.'

She was about to say she didn't want anything to eat, but remembered again what she'd decided, and allowed him to take her hand.

'This is a great day,' he told her excitedly as he led her through to the living room and sat her down on the couch. 'It's Monday, you know? A new beginning for the week – and a new start for us. Now, are you comfortable?' he went on solicitously. 'No aches or pains?' He grinned sheepishly. 'I know that mattress isn't exactly the best that money can buy, but I'll change it when we've got our routine set up. What do you say to that?'

'It's fine as it is,' she replied in a tiny voice.

It seemed to please him.

'Oh, you're such a good girl,' he beamed, squatting down before her. 'Never complaining, always willing to sacrifice your comforts. A real lady in the making. And I'm here to see the butterfly emerge.' Reaching out, he gently moved her hair back behind her ear, his beautiful eyes sparkling with emotion. 'And it really is awesome to be party to that. Thank you, Lisa.'

Getting up abruptly, a move that made Lisa wince, he went to the kitchen to fetch the breakfast. She sat stock-still, completely unnerved by this sudden change in him. Had those awful things he'd done been some kind of horrible mistake? Was he regretting it now, and trying to make amends by being so nice?

Or was it another trick? Be nice, make her relax – then *squash* her like a bug as soon as she opened her mouth.

'Here you are, my lady. Toast and jam, and a nice hot

cup of tea. You eat up while I get this place shipshape. Then I'll show you my surprise.'

Taking the proffered plate and cup, Lisa balanced them delicately on her knee. She had to grit her teeth against the warm buttery aroma rising from the toast. She'd been so determined not to eat anything he gave her, but she was starving. Maybe just a tiny bite . . .

Before she knew it, she'd picked up a triangular slice and eaten it – then a second, and a third, until it was all gone. Feeling the knot in her stomach begin to loosen, she sniffed suspiciously at the contents of the cup. If it was that stuff he'd been giving her, she definitely wouldn't touch a drop! She was surprised to find that it smelled just like normal tea and, tentatively sipping at it, she was greatly relieved to find that it was exactly that.

Holding the empty plate and cup on her lap, she watched Benny as he moved about the room, spraying and polishing everything that had a surface. He whistled as he worked, seeming relaxed and happy.

'There,' he said when he'd finished. 'All brand new and purified.' Turning suddenly, he smiled at her. 'Just like you, my dear. And me, of course. All thanks to the greatest Leader there ever will be. Have you finished?'

'Yes, thanks.' Handing him the dishes, Lisa was careful not to give any hint of what she was really thinking: that she wished this 'leader' of his would tell him to lay off whatever he was taking! For he had to be on *something* to bring on these mad changes of personality. One minute nice as pie; the next, a dark, twisted maniac who'd almost raped her – twice. What he *had* done had been bad enough, but she didn't know what she'd do if he went that one step further.

No wonder her mum had threatened to beat the crap out of her if she even so much as *thought* about touching drugs. They obviously sent you round the bend and back!

'Now, about that special surprise,' Benny said when he'd taken the dishes to the kitchen and washed them. 'Do you want to guess what it is?'

She shook her head.

'Oh, come on.' He grinned, lighting himself a cigarette. 'Just one guess.'

She eyed the cigarette greedily. Maybe if she played along he'd let her have one. And God knew she could do with one after everything that had happened.

'I – I don't know, Benny,' she said, her voice husky with nicotine longing. 'Are we going somewhere?'

He laughed softly. 'Ah, Lisa, Lisa . . . 'tis too soon for that, I fear. Maybe later, when we've learned to trust each other completely. Guess again.'

She shrugged. 'I don't know. I can't think of anything.'

Sitting down on the chair, he grinned happily.

'I know your favourite colour.'

'Oh?'

'Yes . . . it's blue. And you've painted your walls in it, haven't you?'

'My walls?' she repeated numbly.

'In your bedroom,' he went on, grinning conspiratorially. 'Or should I say, your *former* bedroom. And, while we're on the subject –' he gave her a mock frown '– I was very surprised to find it such a mess! But no matter about that now. I'll soon have you doing the right things. It's surprisingly easy to keep things in order once you get a routine going.'

'How did you see my bedroom?' she asked. 'Me mum wouldn't have let you in. She doesn't even know you.'

'She does now,' he stated casually. 'Anyway, look.' Pulling Lisa's keys from his pocket, he dangled them before her triumphantly. 'I didn't even need to knock.'

Lisa felt the room spin around her. 'W-what have you done to my mum?' she asked, her mouth dry with fear of his answer.

Benny frowned, for real this time. 'I thought we'd got past all that small-talk nonsense? I thought we under-stood each other?'

'I just w-want to know what you've d-done,' she stammered, fear pressing down on her as his eyes took on the same strange gleam she'd seen each time he was about to flip out. 'Please, Benny . . . she's my mum. I need to know!'

'You already do!' he shouted. 'I told you . . . I *told* you!' Jumping up, he balled his fists and closed his eyes, muttering through gritted teeth, forcing himself to calm down.

Lisa watched him with growing dread. If he flipped out again, there was no telling what he would do.

'W-what special p-plans have you g-got for us?' she asked, hoping to bring him back to his earlier excitement with a show of interest.

Benny's eyes popped open as if powered by an inner explosion.

'Oh, that's good,' he hissed, looking down on her with a smirk. 'That's *really* good. Did *he* teach you that?'

'W-who?' she stammered, sinking back into the couch as he towered above her.

'Your thoroughly discredited Lord and Master.' He spat the words into her face, so close that his breath disturbed her hair. 'The fallen one with whom you enjoyed such depravity before I came along to save your miserable, desecrated soul!'

Lisa took a deep, shuddering breath.

'Benny, I don't know who you're talking about,' she whimpered. 'Honest, I don't. Please don't get mad again. I just want to know what we're going to do. You said you had something special planned.'

'Well, yeah,' he said grudgingly. 'I have. But I don't know if you're really ready yet.'

'I am,' she said, forcing her lips into a parody of a smile. 'Honest. I just want us to be friends again. We were dead good friends, weren't we?'

Benny looked at her hard, assessing whether or not to trust her. Finally, he nodded.

'All right,' he said, backing away. 'I'm sorry for shouting, but I didn't know if you were playing more games. Right.' Shaking his arms out as if to relieve the tension, he clapped his hands together and smiled. '*This* is what we're doing today . . .'

He swept his hand theatrically towards the corner of the room. Looking to where he was pointing, Lisa saw a large cardboard box, and wondered how she'd missed it when they came in. It had rolls of what looked like wallpaper sticking out of the top, and on the floor beside it was a stack of egg cartons – the big, flat, industrial kind.

'What's it for?' Lisa asked.

'That,' Benny said with a grin, 'is for your bedroom. Oh, and I've chosen a new favourite colour for you, so that you can have a really new beginning, just like I promised.'

Bounding over to the box, he pulled it into the centre of the room and dropped to his knees to pull everything out.

There were four rolls of light pink wallpaper, a large packet of paste, two paint brushes, a huge tin of glue, a small tin of white gloss paint, a box of nails and a hammer.

'Da da!' he announced, looking at her to see if she was as delighted as he.

Lisa forced herself to smile back, thinking more than ever that he wasn't right in the head. How could he think she'd be staying?

'What are the egg boxes for?' she asked.

'Ah *ha*!' Still on his knees, Benny turned and shuffled across the floor towards the stack.

While his back was turned, Lisa eyed the hammer sitting in the midst of the decorating paraphernalia. If she just eased her foot out, she might be able to . . .

'These are for soundproofing,' Benny told her proudly, dragging the stack across to the centre of the floor. 'When we've put these up, none of the infidels out there will be able to eavesdrop on our plans! I read about it in a magazine. People do this when they want to play extra-loud music, and what have you. But *we*,' he tapped the side of his nose, 'know why *we*'re doing it, don't we? Mmmm?'

'Er, yeah,' she replied confusedly. 'I suppose so.'

Benny looked at her long and hard, then nodded.

'You were sent to try me,' he murmured softly. 'But we've managed to scale the wall, haven't we?'

'Have we?'

'Oh, yes. I can see it in your eyes. You and I are becoming one. And it's a great privilege – you do understand that, don't you? *You*'ve been blessed with this second chance, despite the sins of your mother. Just as *I* have been blessed with the test you've presented. But enough of that for now . . . Let's get on with this, shall we?'

Scooping up the cartons, then piling the rolls of paper on top, Benny got to his feet and made for the door, calling back over his shoulder: 'You bring the other bits, there's a good girl.'

Lisa's breathing quickened as she watched him manoeuvre the door open with his foot. Keeping her gaze glued to him, she slowly began to push herself up from the floor, intending to make a grab for the hammer. But she was too late. Obviously the same thought had just occurred to Benny as he suddenly turned around and pounced back into the room.

'Oops! Silly me. Nearly left you with a temptation!' Dipping down, he picked up the hammer, grinning as he said, 'You're doing well, but not *that* well! Come on now . . . no time to waste. Chop chop!'

Gathering together the rest of the things with a sigh, Lisa followed him through to *her* room. Once there, she was surprised to see that he'd turned a light on. She glanced around for the switch.

'It's outside,' Benny said; with his back to her.

'How did you know what I was looking for?' she asked.

Turning, he grinned at her over his shoulder.

'How many times do I have to tell you before you believe me? *I know everything!* Now come here and put that stuff down.'

She went to him and placed what she was carrying on the floor. As he hunkered down to prise the lid off the paint tin, she noticed that he now had the hammer tucked securely through his belt.

'I thought we'd start by painting all the woodwork.' He motioned with a nod towards the brushes. 'You start on the door, I'll do the window. It'll look a lot nicer in here when it's done, won't it?'

'Mmmm,' she murmured, dipping one of the brushes into the paint tin. Holding her hand beneath it to stop the paint dripping, she went to the door and began to paint.

Behind her, Benny started on the window board. It took him no time at all, and he was soon pulling the mattress away from the wall, preparing to start on the skirting boards. He hummed while he worked, making the atmosphere in the small room much less tense – almost as if they were two friends working side by side with a common goal, rather than kidnapper and kidnapped preparing the latter's cell.

'Benny?' Lisa ventured after a while, lulled by the calmer air between them. 'Did you really see my bedroom?'

'Yup, I really did.'

'And me mum?'

'At peace. Now stop chattering and hurry up. We've all these boxes to glue up yet, and then we've got to put the paper over them.'

'When you say at peace,' Lisa persisted, going over for more paint, 'you mean she's *happy*, yeah?'

'No doubt she *will* be, when she shows true repentance to her Master,' Benny grunted. 'A hard task, given the depths of her depravity,' he went on piously. 'But she'll either buckle down and learn, or suffer eternal torment.'

'But she's still at home, yeah?'

'When I left her, she was.' Irritation was brewing in his voice. 'Now, are you going to finish your job – or will I have to make you? Mmmm?'

'I'm doing it.'

Moving back to the door, Lisa painted quickly, convincing herself with each stroke of the brush that her mum was all right. She must be if she was still at home. And all this talk of repentance – maybe Benny had preached to Pat about God? Made her agree to go to church, or something? Hard as it was to picture her mum in church, she had to cling to the image. If she contemplated the alternative, she'd never get through this.

They worked on in a silence broken only by Benny's strange humming. It was no time at all before the painting was completed and they were starting on the egg boxes.

Lisa had just smeared a liberal amount of glue onto the back of the first one when someone knocked on the front door. She almost jumped out of her skin. Looking around quickly, she saw that the bedroom door was still standing ajar – as Benny had instructed, to release the fumes. She had a perfect view of the front door, just feet away. She could make it if she ran . . .

As if reading her mind, Benny dropped the gluey egg box he was holding and pounced on her. Wrapping a steely arm around her, trapping her own arms, he slapped his other hand over her mouth to stifle the scream he knew she'd been about to release and fell onto the bed with her.

'Don't you make a sound!' he snarled into her ear. 'Not one sound, do you hear me?'

While they lay in their deadly embrace, there was another burst of knocking. Then, moments later, the letter flap was lifted.

'Peter?' A woman's voice trilled through the empty hall. 'Are you there, Peter? It's Mrs Thompson. Come on now, Peter. If you're there, open the door. I need to see you. If you don't let me in to see that you're all right, I'll have to report you. And you don't want me to do that, do you?'

The flap dropped down after a minute. There was no sound in the room now except for Benny's rapid panting.

Unable to breathe with his hand constricting the air to her nose as well as her mouth, and too tightly held to struggle, Lisa felt as if she would burst. A blackness crept over her eyes, and a thousand pins and needles began to dance through every nerve in her body.

Benny listened intently to the sounds outside the door. Suddenly, the flap went up again and this time a stern, unfamiliar male voice came through.

'Mr Webster, this is Gary Yale from Social Services. If you're in there, I suggest you open up immediately. You're under a supervision order, Mr Webster. You *have* to see us. Now open the door!'

Pushing Lisa's face into the pillow, Benny strained his head back to hear more clearly. But nothing more came. After a moment, he heard footsteps receding along the communal landing, then the clip-clop of female heels moving down the concrete stairs. Hearing the faint thud of the main door closing down below, he finally relaxed his grip on Lisa's mouth and pushed himself roughly away from her.

'You traitorous *bitch*!' he spat, punching her in the back. '*You* did that! And how did you manage it, eh? How did you know who to contact? Did *he* tell you?'

Unconscious already, Lisa's body jerked with each punch he rained upon it, her ears hearing none of the accusations he levelled at her.

'You've been snooping in my private things! I *trusted* you, you whore from hell, and this is how you repay me! Leading that – that devil *witch* to my new home to torment me! Do you know what they'll do to me if they get through the protective barriers? Do you? . . . *DO YOU?* They'll take away my powers . . . make me one of *them*! And it's all your fault!'

Getting no response from Lisa, he grabbed her with both hands and flipped her over onto her back, growling with rage.

'Don't just lie there, demon spew!' he screamed, pulling her up by her jumper and shaking her. 'Say you're sorry! Say you're sorry, and you'll never, *ever* deceive me like this again! *SAY IT!*'

Finally realizing that Lisa wasn't conscious, Benny threw her from him and let out an anguished howl. Tearing at his own hair he screamed at her prone body: 'No . . . *no*! You can't do this! We're supposed to be in this together! You promised! You've got to do it right or it won't work! Can't you see that, you stupid cow?'

★　　★　　★

Down below, Claire Thompson and her supervisor, Gary Yale, were deep in discussion as they made their way along the footpath towards her car.

'I'm going to have to report him,' Yale was saying. 'He's persistently violated the supervision order.'

'But we don't even know for sure that he's actually living here,' Claire argued.

'The tracker seemed pretty damn sure,' Yale countered tartly.

Claire made a tiny huffing sound. She had never approved the use of these so-called trackers the department retained to hunt absconders down. In her opinion, it smacked of police-state behaviour and violated the patients' human rights.

'Anyway,' Yale went on, 'I think it's time to alert the police and have the address thoroughly checked out. Webster was under specific orders not to relocate without informing us. And quite frankly, Claire, it beggars belief that you let him slip through your fingers in the first place.'

Claire bit back her response. It would do no good at all to remind him that, as her supervisor, he too bore some of the responsibility for Peter Webster's having gone awol. Wasn't he supposed to oversee her cases and take her to task when something was amiss – the disappearance of a potentially volatile patient, for example. But oh no, not Gary – super-smooth – Yale. He'd rather 'lunch' with fellow executives, bemoaning the state of their department whilst heaping more and more work onto his subordinates' heads.

Still, pointing these things out would only incense Yale, and would definitely *not* buy her the time she needed to put right what she, in all truth, did feel responsible for. Not only had she allowed a high-risk patient to abscond, she had subsequently let him slip to the back of her mind as more immediately pressing cases took priority.

'Will you let me try one last time?' she pleaded. 'I'll go back alone. You know he gets paranoid around men, but I can get through to him. If you report him now he'll be sectioned, and he's not that severe a case. He deserves a chance.'

Yale gave her the cool look he reserved for the incompetent liberals flooding the mental health arena these days, then glanced at his watch.

'No, it's too late. I've still got several appointments before finishing for the day, and you're driving, in case you've forgotten.'

'Please just give me a little more time?' Claire was begging now. 'I know him better than anyone. I'm sure he'll respond to me. He's been fine for almost a year. There have been no incidents—'

'That we *know* of,' Yale cut her short. Marching around to the passenger door, he peered at her over the roof of the car. 'All right, Claire, you have two days. But if you haven't seen him and assessed his medication in that time, I'll have no choice.'

'Thank you.' Claire breathed a sigh of relief and jumped into the car, leaning across to open the passenger door for him. 'I won't let you down, Gary, I promise.'

From his window, he watched them go – the interfering tools of the oppressive regime that dictated the lives of the fools upon this island of sin.

He knew they had somehow been summoned here by the succubus in the other room. How, he did not yet know, but he soon would. And when he did discover her means, he would take measures to disable her connections.

Dropping back the curtain, plunging his chamber once more into the necessary darkness, he lit the candle and knelt before the flame of his Master's heart.

'I almost failed,' he whispered repentantly. 'I didn't keep close enough watch. I foolishly allowed her time alone to set her evil schemes in motion, believing, in my ignorance, that her sleep was the sleep of the almost dead. I will not make such a mistake again . . .'

24

Jessica was dusting the filing cabinet when the door opened. Turning, her ready smile slipped when she saw the small crew of policemen entering.

'Ms Price?' Seddon stepped forward, extending a sheet of paper towards her. 'This is a warrant to search for and retain any and all business files, invoices, banking details and other such documentation relating to Rashid Imports.'

'What is this?' Jessica demanded, looking down at the warrant with alarm.

'I'm sure you understood me well enough,' Seddon said, nodding to the uniformed PCs to begin the search.

As they began to extract her neatly indexed files from the various cabinets and drawers around the room, Jessica felt a surge of panic rise in her chest.

'Don't do that!' she snapped, attempting to block their progress by running around shutting everything they had opened. 'Hey! That's my personal stuff!' she yelled, as one of the PCs rifled her desk drawers. 'You've no right to touch anything in my desk! Stop it – now!'

'Ms Price!' Seddon barked, forcing her attention back to himself. 'We are authorized to search every area of these premises, including the desk from which you conduct your work. Now, if you'll stop impeding my officers, I'd appreciate your co-operation.'

Accepting defeat, she gave him a pained look, then nodded.

'Of course. Mr . . . ?'

'Detective Inspector Seddon,' he said, then waved her towards the inner door with its polished-brass name-plate proclaiming it to belong to S. RASHID, Managing Director. 'If you wouldn't mind opening up?'

'What exactly are you looking for?' Jessica asked lamely as she unlocked the door to Sam's inner sanctum. 'Only, if you'd just tell me, I'm sure I could locate whatever it is you want without you having to turn everything inside out.'

'I'm sure we'll manage, thank you.' Blocking her way as she made to follow him in, Seddon motioned to one of the PCs. 'Find a space for Ms Price to sit down, will you? And get her a nice cup of tea while you take her details, eh?'

Back at the station, Sam was in a state of shock.

'How could she do this?' he asked his solicitor, Mike Hunter, for the fifth time since they'd heard the shocking news. 'She's my *wife*! She's a goddamned *Catholic*, for Christ's sake,' he added, shaking his head incredulously, as if betraying a loved one were the worst crime of all for a Catholic to commit.

'You've got to calm down,' Hunter told him in a hushed but sharp tone. 'You won't help yourself by getting hysterical, Sam. Now tell me everything so I can at least *try* to patch this up. And don't lie to me . . . I can't help you if you don't tell me the whole truth – no matter how sordid it is.'

Sam looked at the man in front of him as if the solicitor had two heads.

'How long have we known each other, Mike?' he hissed. 'You *know* everything there is to know!'

Leaning forward to prevent the microphone he was sure would be hidden somewhere in the room from picking up what he was saying, Hunter hissed back, 'Let's get this clear from the outset, Sam. I know *nothing*! I've handled your business dealings, and I've read through your contracts. That's *it*!'

Sam gasped with disbelief.

'How can you say that?' he demanded, his voice rising with anger. 'You've *drafted* most of those contracts, Mike! You've been a guest in my home when I've had difficult clients to handle. You've even given me help to legitimize some extremely sensitive situations. So don't start pretending you're not involved now.'

Hunter began to gather his papers together.

'I'm offended, Sam,' he said coldly as he stuffed them into his briefcase. 'I've never been anything but honest with you. All of the business you and I have done has been legitimate.'

Almost laughing, Sam looked around the room for the cameras.

'This is for them, I suppose? You want them to record that you disclaim all knowledge of my affairs, is that it?'

'Keep your voice down,' hissed Hunter. 'All I asked was that you tell me everything. And by that, I meant about this *woman* you're supposed to have half-killed, and her missing child! *That*'s what I'm trying to help you with, but you seem set on dragging me down with you. How can I help you if that's what you're trying to do?'

Standing now, Hunter looked down at Sam, his nostrils flaring with annoyance at having been placed in such an impossible situation.

'I suggest you retain a different solicitor, Sam. One you don't feel it necessary to condemn!'

'Sit down!' Sam said slowly.

'What?'

'I said sit down, Mike.'

Something in his tone made Hunter obey.

'Right, two minutes,' he said, looking pointedly at his watch as he tried to keep a professional edge to the situation. 'And then I'm due in court.'

'Do you trust me?' Sam asked.

Hunter regarded him for a moment, then said, 'I thought I could. But in light of what's just happened, I'm not so sure you can be relied upon to—'

'I didn't do it,' Sam cut in quietly. 'Do you believe that?'

Hunter shifted in his chair and folded his hands together in his lap.

'I can only judge on the facts.'

'The fact is, I . . . *didn't* . . . do it,' Sam said again, slowly to press the point home. 'I'm what you people like to call "a victim of circumstance". Yes, I was with Pat Noone on the night she was attacked. And yes, I did dislike her daughter. But that does *not* make me the kind of man who would almost murder a woman, or kidnap a child . . . *does* it?'

'Well, no, but—'

'But you no longer trust your own judgement?' said

Sam. 'You have known me for almost six years, Mike, yet you can honestly say that after all this time you believe me capable of these crimes?'

Sighing heavily, Hunter looked down at his folded hands.

'No,' he said after a moment. 'No, Sam, I would not have believed that you were capable of them.'

'And now?'

Hunter shook his head. 'No.'

'Thank you.' Nodding sadly, Sam let out a relieved breath. 'So I can count on you to represent me?'

'*If* you tell me *everything*,' Hunter said, coming back full circle. 'But it must be said, Sam, that Elsa's decision to hand you over lock, stock and barrel is a damning indication to the authorities. Maybe we should start there, and try to work out what could have made her do such a thing?'

At the house that was no longer a home, Elsa was well under way with her plans.

She had sent the children to her sister's house, where they would be staying until everything was organized.

She had transferred exactly half of the money in her and Sam's joint bank account into a new, sole account. She had left Sam's own private one untouched. The police would know all about that by now, and she didn't want to be classed as his accomplice by interfering with it.

Elsa had arranged an assured tenancy for a small, three-bed-roomed semi-detached house a couple of miles away. It was far enough from the house she'd shared with Samir for her to be out of the line of fire when the news exploded about his part in the murders, yet close enough for the children to stay on at their respective schools.

She had also arranged for a removals van to come to the house in the morning. Now all she had to do was pack what she wanted to take with her – which was almost everything. She deserved *some* recompense for the life of drudgery she'd been subjected to with Sam.

She would worry about the police after she had settled in the new house. She was well aware that when they knew the full extent of Samir's illegal business dealings they might attempt to confiscate everything that had been bought with the proceeds. Fortunately, her father had taken all of that in hand for her. She could quite safely sit back and allow him to sort out any trouble that might arise from her taking possession of the household things she so cherished.

The phone began to ring – as it had done repeatedly for the last hour or so. Convinced that it was Samir calling from the police station, she had so far ignored it – continuing with her wrapping, but speeding up each time, fearing that he would somehow manage to wangle bail and catch her before she'd had a chance to disappear.

And that was the last thing Elsa wanted now that she had made the decision to start divorce proceedings. What bliss to never have to set eyes on *him* again! Even the church would have to see she had no option but to divorce a murderer.

And if Samir thought she was going to allow her children to visit him in prison, he had another think coming!

*   *   *

At the ransacked office, Jessica slammed down the phone and sank her head into her hands, muttering, 'Where the bloody hell *are* you, Elsa?'

She didn't know what to do. The police had taken away all of the client files – the explicitly detailed files Sam had self-importantly ordered her to keep. Foolish, *foolish* man! And now, because of his obsessive need to record every transaction he made, Jessica was in *his* shit up to her neck!

Every single one of the files – those that Sam had assured her would never be discovered – was written in Jessica's own hand, or at least typed by her. DI Seddon had as good as told her that her involvement in Sam's business affairs made her an accomplice. Had she not known what she was writing? he had asked, knowing full well that one cannot set pen to paper or finger to keyboard without reading the results as they appeared.

And now she couldn't even reach Sam's stupid wife to find out what the hell was going on!

A sudden thought occurred to Jessica – a ray of sunshine in an otherwise stormy sky. Leaping from the chair, she kicked a path through the mess of papers littering the floor and ran into Sam's equally ransacked office. Grunting as she pushed his heavy desk aside, she peeled the carpet back from the corner until the floor beneath was fully exposed. Then, reaching down, she hooked a nail through the tiny inlaid brass handle and raised the trapdoor beneath which lay Sam's safe.

If only he'd taken her advice and kept his documents in here, he wouldn't be in this mess now. But, typically, he'd ignored the sense in her suggestion – too lazy to take the trouble to remove them and put them back each day.

All the safe contained, as far as she knew, was the money – two thousand pounds – that Sam liked to call his 'escape fund': money he would use to flee back home should the shit ever hit the fan in the UK.

Well, it had certainly done that now. But the money would be of no use to Sam if he was stuck in prison.

Lifting the small compact safe with difficulty from its hiding place, Jessica dropped it down onto the floor. Then she felt around beneath Sam's desk for the spare key.

Typical of a man to hide it in such an obvious place, she thought as she located it. Equally typical of the police*men* to have missed it.

With a flash of inspiration, she ran back to the outer office and locked the main door securely. All it would take was for the DI to pop back and catch her with her fingers in the safe. That would be *guaranteed* to place her firmly in the frame with Sam!

Back at the safe, she inserted the key into the lock, her fingers trembling wildly. Opening it up at last, she gasped with shock.

Inside, there was far more than two thousand pounds. It was more like ten, she estimated at a glance. Bundle upon bundle of neatly bound stacks of twenty-pound notes. And beneath it all, sparkling like the Crown Jewels, were several diamond rings, necklaces and ear-rings.

Rocking unsteadily back on her heels, Jessica stared open-mouthed at the contents of the safe. Then she quickly pulled herself together and began to empty everything into a large carrier bag.

★　　★　　★

'All right, let's cut the crap, shall we?' Seddon glared at Sam across the table. 'We know everything! Times, dates, names. We've got it all.'

Mike Hunter cleared his throat.

'With respect, DI Seddon, my client does not need to be subjected to such a full-on assault at this moment. You have given us no time in which to discuss your latest *findings*, and he has not, as yet, been allowed a meal – which, as I'm sure you'll agree, is already long overdue, given the length of his detention so far?'

Turning his wrath on the pompous solicitor, Seddon said, 'And I'm sure that even *you*'d agree that the life of a child is more important that the hunger pangs of your client?'

'Technically,' Hunter replied smoothly, 'you have no evidence to support your claim that my client is in any way connected to the disappearance of the child.'

'*Technically*,' Seddon countered sarcastically, 'I've got the word of the child's mother that your client is the man who attacked her, *and* that he had an active dislike for the child!'

'Ah . . .' Hunter held up his finger at this. 'Can I take it that this is the word of a woman who subsequently told the nurses and a doctor that, and I quote: "He didn't do it"? You see, DI Seddon,' he went on smugly, 'I too have pulled out all the stops to gather information.'

Seddon drew in a sharp breath. 'How clever, Mr Hunter. Unfortunately –' pausing momentarily, he smiled nastily '– certain other things have since come to light that preclude the need for the victim's word alone to incriminate your *client*.'

'Such as?' Hunter asked, battling to keep a neutral expression on his face.

'Such as,' Seddon said, leaning forward, 'a very nice import business, in which the main, if not *sole* commodity appears to be young girls – some, as young as thirteen years old – whom your client here appears to have been selling off as brides to a number of foreign businessmen residing in this country. Is that enough for now?' he asked then, the smile becoming more malicious by the second. 'Or would you like me to continue with the highly illegal data we have discovered on your client's personal computer? Or the flowers we confiscated from his house, which, believe me, are going to play a *major* part in this investigation?'

By now, Hunter had visibly paled.

'With respect,' he said croakily, 'I must insist that I be allowed to consult with my client about these new allegations.'

'Okay,' Seddon conceded happily. 'We'll give you a little time to consult. But please bear in mind that there is a twelve-year-old girl missing out there somewhere, and I believe your client is our only lead to finding her. I presume I can rely on you to impress the seriousness of this upon your client, and make him see the sense in cooperating with us?' He paused for a moment before adding ominously: 'Before it's too late!'

25

Sue Morgan was coming out of the kitchen when the morning newspaper landed on the mat. Picking it up, she carried it through to the living room, shouting up the stairs as she passed: 'Hurry up, Debbie. You'll be late for school.'

Minutes later, Debbie ran down the stairs and popped her head around the door to say goodbye. Her mother's expression stopped her in her tracks.

'What's wrong, Mum?' she asked, going to her with concern.

Wordlessly, Sue turned the paper towards her.

Debbie blanched as the headline screamed out at her in large letters: DAUGHTER OF LATEST VICTIM MISSING! POLICE FEAR WORST!

Beneath this, there was a picture of Lisa taken from an old school photograph.

'Oh, my God!' Debbie gasped, snatching the paper.

Getting up as Debbie read the article, Sue turned the TV on to the news channel. Within seconds, Lisa's picture was once more flashed before them as the newsreader solemnly intoned the story.

'Police have today confirmed that Mrs Patricia Anne Noone, who was attacked at her Hulme home on

Saturday night, was the intended sixth victim of the killer causing terror amongst the women of Manchester in recent months.

'A man is said to helping police with their inquiries in connection to this latest attack, and the five murders. His name has not yet been released, but he is believed to have been a client of Mrs Noone, who, it has been claimed, had been working as a prostitute for some time before the attack.

'Mrs Noone, who is still in a critical condition following a second life-saving operation at Manchester's Royal Infirmary, is the mother of missing Lisa Noone, whose picture we just showed.

'Lisa is twelve years old, and has been missing since her mother was discovered by neighbours in the early hours of Sunday morning. Police are appealing for anyone who knows her whereabouts to come forward. They stress that she may be in grave danger, and anybody having any information should contact their local police station urgently.

'We'll give you the number of the incident room dealing with Lisa's disappearance, and the Crimestoppers freephone number at the end of this broadcast.'

'Are you all right?' Sue asked Debbie, whose face was now wet with tears.

'Oh, Mum!' Debbie sobbed, throwing herself into her mother's comforting arms. 'I just want to see her!'

'Ssshhh,' Sue murmured, stroking her daughter's hair as tears slid from her own eyes. 'You will, sweetheart, you will. She'll be found, I promise. She'll be found, and everything will be all right.'

'But – but w-what if her mum d-dies?'

'Ssshhh . . . she won't.'

'But what if she d-does?' Debbie persisted. 'Lisa won't even know! She'll have no one.'

'She'll have us,' Sue said gently. 'She'll have us.'

They both jumped at a loud knocking on the front door. Seconds later the flap went back and a voice called through.

'Mrs Morgan? . . . Can we speak to you for a moment? We'd just like to ask you some questions about Pat and Lisa Noone.'

'Who on Earth is that?' Sue muttered, disentangling herself from Debbie as the knocking started up again.

Opening the front door, she found herself besieged by photographers. Camera flashbulbs exploded in her face as microphones were thrust towards her mouth and a barrage of questions flew at her.

'Is it true Pat Noone was a prostitute?'

'Can you confirm that Lisa Noone was about to follow in her mother's footsteps?'

'Mrs Morgan, is it true your daughter was Lisa Noone's best friend?'

Slamming the door shut, Sue felt her stomach turn over.

'What is it, Mum?' Debbie asked fearfully from the living room doorway.

'Stay in there!' Sue ordered before dashing up to the bathroom to be sick.

Seddon saw the mêlée of reporters outside Sue Morgan's door as soon as he turned the corner. He'd expected them to swoop when the news broke, but somehow he'd thought it would take them longer to suss out exactly who had discovered Pat – giving him time to check Lisa's room for clues in peace.

Driving to Pat's end of the block, he parked up and slipped across to the doorway, hoping to avoid being seen by keeping his head down. He should have known better. In the minute or so that it took him to get up the stairs, the reporters had regrouped to wait for him outside Pat's door.

Shoving his way through them, he used the duplicate set of keys he'd got the lab to cut from Pat's originals to let himself in and slammed the door behind him without having uttered a single word. The press would get their pound of flesh sooner or later, but Seddon had no intention of being the butcher supplying it.

In the hall, he stood for a moment, taking in the atmosphere. There was a strange smell in the air, and an eerie silence hanging over the entire place – despite the rabble still prattling amongst themselves on the other side of the door.

Avoiding the kitchen, through the window of which he'd be visible to the press – and wouldn't they just love to get a shot of him mooching through the victims' bin! – he wandered into the living room.

In here, the smell was even stronger. Going over to the closed curtains, he drew one back and opened the window to let in some air.

Looking around in the half-light, Seddon shook his head at the mess. No wonder it reeked, he thought. There were probably things lurking down the sides of the couch that had lived, died, and been reborn there in germ form.

Leaving this room behind, he made his way up the stairs – remembering, with each step, the last time he'd been here.

The shock of finding Pat Noone spread out on her own bed like a sacrifice – her stomach torn apart, and her blood surrounding her like a rich oil splash on a pastel watercolour.

And the bigger shock of discovering that she was still alive.

Passing the bathroom, he came to Lisa's closed bedroom door. Pausing there, he sighed from the heart. Beyond this door, a twelve-year-old girl had lived her life, dreamed her dreams, and fantasized about the unobtainable, whilst willing the years to accelerate her into adulthood when everything she hoped for would become obtainable. A normal twelve-year-old girl, with everything to live for.

And where was she now?

Pushing the door open, Seddon started to enter. Then he stopped in his tracks and stared open-mouthed around the room. Everything had changed. Since the night they had found Lisa's mother in the room next door, someone had been in here and *completely* changed it.

And he wasn't just imagining it. He *knew*, without a shadow of a doubt. Because that night, this room had been such a disgraceful mess he'd even joked with one of the young coppers about it. But now it was so clean and tidy that it actually looked as though it belonged in a different house. And not only that, but the furniture too had been rearranged.

The bed, which had been opposite the door when he first saw it, was now flush against the window wall.

The wardrobe, which had been behind the door, was now where the bed had once been.

The dressing table, which had been beneath the window – barely visible beneath a mess of unlidded make-up palettes, tipped-up bottles of nail polish and used tissues – was now behind the door, totally clean and polished to a shine.

And the carpet had been swept too – the heaps of clothes, shoes and magazines that had totally obscured it before were now out of sight.

Going into the room now, Seddon slowly turned and looked at everything in detail, unable to comprehend how this could be.

Unless . . .

Running back down the stairs, he let himself out, slamming the door firmly behind him. With the reporters – who had immediately picked up on his excitement – hot on his heels, he ran down the landing to the Morgans' house. Rapping urgently on the door, he pushed Sue back in when she answered and, following her into the hall, kicked the door shut behind him.

'Sorry about that,' he apologized, seeing the shock on her face. 'But I didn't want one of the vultures out there slipping in with me.'

'It's all right,' she said. 'They've been trying to trick me to open the door for the past hour. Would you like a cup of tea? I was just making one.'

'Yes, please. Do you mind if I go in here?' He motioned towards the living room.

'No, that's fine. Make yourself comfortable. Debbie . . . ?' Sue shouted then. 'Go up to your room for a bit, love. The detective wants to speak to me.'

'Actually,' Seddon said, 'it's Debbie I need to speak to.'

Sue frowned. 'Do you have to? She's really upset at the moment – what with the news, and them out there.'

'I'll go easy,' he promised. 'But I really must talk to her.'

Sue thought about it for a moment, then nodded and went into the kitchen to put the kettle on.

Going into the living room, Seddon sat down on the chair beside the couch where Debbie was lying, red-eyed from crying, a soggy tissue clutched in her hand.

'Debbie?' he said softly. 'Can we talk?'

'Yeah, sure.' Sitting up, Debbie wiped her nose with the tissue. 'Is it about Lisa?'

'Yes. I need to know about the last time you saw her. Do you remember when that was?'

Debbie nodded. 'Yeah, Saturday morning.' Her eyes filled to brimming again. 'Me and Jasmine went to see her, after . . . after Linda's grave got . . . you know?'

Seddon nodded sympathetically. 'Yes, I know.'

Licking a tear as it rolled down to her mouth, Debbie said, 'We showed Lisa the paper, and she said she wanted to g-go and s-see it for herself. But we'd already b-been, and she got dead upset.' The tears were rolling freely now.

Leaning forward, Seddon plucked a tissue from a box on the coffee table and passed it to her.

'What happened then, Debbie?'

'We fell out,' she admitted, her face awash with guilt. 'She told us to get lost, so we went.'

'And you didn't see her after this?'

'No.'

'Where did you and Jasmine go when you left?'

'We came back here for a minute, then went to the market.'

'And you're sure you didn't see Lisa again?'

'Positive. I went round to her place after Jasmine went home, but no one answered. I just wanted to say I was sorry, 'cos I felt dead tight about leaving her like that.'

'Because she was upset?'

'Yeah.' Debbie nodded miserably. 'Lisa was my best mate, and I took off with Jas. But I couldn't help it. Jas was dead upset about Linda.'

'Linda Parry?'

'Yeah. Her and Jas were best mates, till . . .'

'Is this really necessary?' Sue asked disapprovingly, coming in with the tea tray. 'You've asked her all this already. You're just raking it up again.'

'I'm sorry,' Seddon said, taking a cup from her. 'But I really do need to make absolutely sure Debbie hasn't seen Lisa since Saturday.'

'Of course she hasn't!' Sue snapped. 'We'd have told you if she had.'

'With the greatest respect,' Seddon said, 'there may be good reason why Debbie wouldn't tell any of us if she *had* seen Lisa.'

'What's that supposed to mean?'

'I haven't,' Debbie interjected. 'Honest.'

'Debbie,' Seddon said gently. 'I've reason to believe that Lisa may have been home since we took her mum to hospital. If you know anything about that, you *must* tell me. I can't stress enough how important this is.'

'She's been home?' Debbie asked, wide-eyed with surprise.

'How do you know this?' Sue demanded, sitting down beside Debbie.

Meeting her angry look with his level gaze, Seddon said, 'Because Lisa's room has been cleaned since we were here last.'

'Cleaned?' Debbie gasped incredulously. 'No way!'

Looking at her now, Seddon said, 'Why does that surprise you?'

Debbie snorted softly and almost smiled. 'Just, well, 'cos Lisa *never* cleans – ever! She hates it.'

'Takes after her mother,' muttered Sue.

'Are you sure, Debbie?'

'Yeah, dead sure,' Debbie said, with the emphatic tone of one who knows exactly what they are talking about. 'I even offered to do it for her once, but she said she likes it like that. Honest, she's never cleaned up in all the time I've known her, and I'm not lying. She doesn't do *anything* in her house, and neither does her mum. She just sticks everything behind the couch when it gets too messy, or in the cupboard under the stairs.'

Seddon mulled this information over. It certainly rang true, given the habitual neglect he'd seen throughout the rest of the house, and the mess he'd witnessed that first night in Lisa's room.

So, if it wasn't Lisa, then who the hell *had* been in that house since his last visit? And why had they only cleaned Lisa's room? And given that it was done to an almost professional standard, he could well believe that it wasn't Lisa who'd done it. Not if she *never* cleaned, as Debbie was claiming so adamantly.

'What does this mean?' Sue asked, more curious than aggressive now.

Seddon shook his head. 'I don't know, I honestly don't.'

Turning back to Debbie then, he said, 'Are you absolutely one hundred per cent certain that Lisa would not have cleaned her room?'

'I swear on my life,' Debbie said, crossing her heart with her tissue-clenching hand.

A short while later, on his way to the station to report his latest findings, Seddon detoured home to see Pauline. He saw precious little of her these days, and felt an overwhelming urge to talk to her now.

Over coffee in their comfortable – spotlessly clean – kitchen, he told her the latest developments.

'I can't make head nor tail of it,' he concluded. 'Why would she go on the run, then come home, find her mum's bed covered in blood, clean her own room like you wouldn't believe, then take off again?'

'Maybe *she* didn't,' Pauline suggested simply.

'Mmmm,' he murmured thoughtfully. 'But who else *could* it have been? No one had keys apart from Pat and Lisa. I know for a fact they weren't in the habit of leaving one with the neighbours. *We*'ve got Pat's, and I'm assuming Lisa's still got her own. But even supposing she'd lost them and someone had picked them up, Debbie says there was only a letter keyring attached to them, no address or anything.'

'And you've still no leads on possible places she could be staying?' Pauline asked. 'What about the estranged dad? Or any other family she might have gone to?'

'The dad's banged up in Sheffield on a four-to-six,' Seddon told her. 'And as far as we know, he's all the family she's got, apart from her mum. No one else has seen hide nor hair of her since Saturday.'

'And you're certain she couldn't have let herself in, got bored and tidied her room without looking in on her mum?'

'But that's just it,' Seddon said. 'This is not just a *tidying*, or even just a clean-up. It is *pristine*, Paul. And I doubt *any* child, no matter how well brought up – which Lisa certainly can't have been with Pat Noone for a mother – would be capable of cleaning to this degree.'

Mulling this over as she sipped her coffee, Pauline said after a moment, 'Supposing whoever she's staying with did it?'

Seddon frowned. 'Like who? We've tried everyone Debbie could think of.'

Shrugging, Pauline said, 'I'm just speculating, Ken. What about this boyfriend she was supposed to have told Debbie about?'

'I think we've established that he doesn't exist,' Seddon told her, smiling.

'Oh? And how can you be so sure?'

Now it was Seddon's turn to shrug.

'Well, because Debbie's convinced that Lisa made him up to get back at her for nicking the lad Lisa fancied,' he said, adding with a chuckle: 'You know what girls are like.'

'I know what *men* are like,' Pauline retorted, scolding him for his chauvinism with her single-raised-eyebrow look. 'Always willing to believe that we girls merely fantasize our lives away.'

'I thought you did?' Seddon grinned at her across the table.

'Only when appropriate,' Pauline said, then: 'Anyway, stop changing the subject. I've got a feeling about this.'

'Oh?'

'Yeah. Didn't you say Lisa told Debbie she'd met this man at the youth club the night they fell out over the boy?'

'So?'

Pauline gave him a pained look. 'So did you check it out?'

Seddon shrugged, then looked sheepishly down at the cup in his hands as he admitted, 'No. Not exactly.'

Pauline shook her head in mock despair. 'You know, for an intelligent man, you amaze me sometimes. If I was you, I'd have another little talk with Debbie and find out exactly what Lisa did say, because if she *did* meet this guy at the youth club, there's every chance someone could have seen him.'

'*If* he exists.'

'Well, you won't find out unless you start taking the possibility seriously, will you?'

Seddon shook his head fondly. 'You are something else, woman, do you know that?'

'I guess it takes a woman to point out the obvious, that's all,' Pauline replied. 'Now, isn't it time you got your butt back to work?'

'Yeah, I suppose so,' he agreed, sighing as he pushed himself away from the table. 'I just feel like I never see you lately.'

'Get a proper job, then.'

'Oh, yeah. I can just see me tossing burgers, can't you?'

'Not exactly,' she grinned. 'But I bet you'd make a

wicked stripagram – provided you can get hold of a uniform again.'

'Oh, so you liked me in uniform, did you?'

'Not specifically, no. But some of those *new* lads you're getting in these days . . .'

'Watch it!' Seddon scolded playfully, coming behind her and putting his arms around her. 'I could get a complex.'

Reaching up, Pauline pulled his face down and planted a quick peck on his cheek.

'On your bike, mate. You've a missing kid to find!'

'Slave-driver!'

Getting back into his car a few minutes later, Seddon knew that Pauline had been dead right. He *should* have checked out the story Lisa had told Debbie about the man at the youth club. And he would – later.

First, he had to go back to the station. He was due to take another pop at the suspect. If there was even the slightest chance that Rashid had anything to do with all this – although Seddon had to admit it was looking less and less likely – the only way Seddon was going to get it out of him was to keep on haranguing the increasingly nervous man.

26

Benny dragged Lisa from her room at six that evening. She didn't struggle, but still he felt the need to manhandle her. He was too excited to make even the smallest pretence of good manners today.

Although he hadn't stepped foot out of the door since Monday morning, when he'd taken a bus ride into town to choose the wallpaper to decorate Lisa's room, he knew that there had been news about his work. He had heard it for himself through the floor just that afternoon, during a session with his Master.

The old bitch down below had deliberately turned the volume of her TV up loud. At the time, it had infuriated him that she should attempt to sabotage his time of worship with her Earthly filth, and to show her that he knew exactly what she was trying to do, he had jumped up and down on the floor several times. But rather than turning the racket down, the old bitch had turned it up even more.

And that was when he had heard their names – the whore's, and her daughter's.

Dropping to his knees, he had put his ear to the floor just in time to hear the appeal for information about the missing girl.

It had gone on to something insignificant then, but he'd already got the message.

He was meant to wait for the girl to wake, then watch the local news bulletin with her. It was the next stage of the plan, and they were meant to witness it together – to signify their new beginning.

And so Benny had patiently sat out the rest of the day in silence, reading through the pathetic little diary he'd taken from Lisa's *former* bedroom during his last visit. It had made interesting reading – showed her for the depraved little slut she was already becoming before he'd rescued her.

As did the rest of the junk he had packed into the plastic bag and brought away with him: the teen magazines that gave extremely graphic descriptions of every sexual position imaginable – and then some; the school books that contained no work, just stupid little love-hearts with initials in each one ('L.N luvs J.B.', and, towards the end, 'Lisa 4 Benny 4 eva').

It had certainly entertained him while he'd waited for Lisa to wake up. And that, miraculously, had occurred at exactly five minutes to six. Five minutes before the news. A sure sign that his patience was finally to be rewarded.

'We're going to see something monumental,' he was telling her now, as he deposited her none too gently on the couch. 'You and I together are going to see the truth of our union in the eyes of the world.'

Lisa kept her mouth firmly closed as Benny dashed towards the TV and turned it on. She stayed stock-still when he came back and dropped down beside her on the couch. She forced herself not to flinch when he reached for her hand.

As the musical intro to the evening news came to an

end, she felt the excitement course through his hand into hers.

'This is it . . . This is it!'

The newsreader appeared, smiling grimly.

'Good evening. Tonight's main story is the worrying disappearance of schoolgirl Lisa Noone.'

Lisa gasped when her school photograph flashed up on the screen.

'So innocent,' Benny crooned beside her. 'So beautiful.'

'Lisa, who is just twelve years old, was last seen on Saturday morning. Later that night, her mother, Patricia Noone, was savagely attacked in the bedroom of their home in Southern Avenue, Hulme.'

A long shot of the front of Lisa's maisonette came up on the screen. Again she gasped – again Benny squeezed her hand.

'Lisa has been missing for three days now, and a spokesman from Greater Manchester Police said today that there are grave concerns for her safety. They are appealing to anyone with information to contact their local police station.

'Meanwhile, Patricia Noone is tonight recovering after a second life-saving operation at Manchester's Royal Infirmary—'

'No . . .' Benny gasped. 'Nooooo . . . !'

'Surgeons there say that she has now stabilized, although she remains in a critical condition. She has been placed under police protection while the investigation into her attack and the disappearance of her daughter is under way.

'Once again, we appeal to anyone who may have seen Lisa since Saturday to contact their local police station as a matter of urgency.

'Lisa is twelve years old, approximately five feet tall, slim, with mid-length dark blonde hair—'

Benny leaped up from the couch and raced across to the TV like a man possessed.

'You're lying!' he screamed into the presenter's face on the screen. 'Lying . . . lying . . . *lying!*'

Lisa cowered back into the couch as he proceeded to kick out at everything in a foam-mouthed rage. Screaming when he inevitably turned his fury on her, she threw her arms over her head to protect herself.

With an almighty roar, he leaped upon her and pinned her down as he fished down the sides of the cushions for the plastic bag he'd left there earlier after emptying it of Lisa's private papers.

Finding it at last, he pulled it out and tried to smother her with it, but Lisa struggled valiantly beneath him, causing him to almost fall from the couch. Furious, he punched her viciously in the face, silencing her and giving him enough time to throw the bag completely over her head.

As Lisa bucked under him with a strength Benny almost admired, he clung on determinedly, tightening his grip around the neck of the bag until at last she was still.

27

Seddon left the interview room more convinced than ever that Rashid wasn't guilty of attacking Pat Noone or kidnapping Lisa.

Rashid had finally crumbled and admitted his highly dodgy business dealings. He had even named names – a new case entirely, one that Seddon had every intention of cracking open like a walnut when this was over. He had, however, absolutely refused to admit that he knew his marriage brokering was illegal, or that he had known that any of the 'wives' involved were under age. But that too would be dealt with in due course. He had also adamantly denied knowing that the pornographic websites he had been accessing so frequently were in any way, shape or form illegal. But ignorance was not a defence in a case such as this.

As for the flowers, Seddon knew from Rashid's reaction that he didn't have a clue about them. He had been completely and utterly blank when told that the basket he had bought for his mother-in-law had contained forget-me-nots. He had shown not one flicker of worry or concern at this revelation – which, given the significance the killer obviously placed on this tiny flower, was enough to convince Seddon that Rashid could not be the one they were looking for.

In light of this, Seddon hadn't opposed Mike Hunter's demand for Rashid to be bailed pending charges for the stuff they *did* have on him.

But now he was back to square one. *Someone* out there had Lisa Noone and, once again, Seddon had no leads whatsoever.

Leaving the station, he paused to light himself a much-needed cigarette before setting off to speak to Debbie Morgan again.

And this time, he would take every little thing she said very seriously indeed.

Sue Morgan wasn't too pleased to see Seddon again, but she let him in anyway and called Debbie downstairs to repeat what she had already told him.

'This man Lisa said she met?' Seddon began.

'Yeah, Benny or something,' Debbie said.

'How did she describe the meeting?' Seddon asked, his pen poised above his notepad. 'And please try to remember *everything* she said.'

'Okay, I'll try.' Debbie shrugged, still sure it had been a figment of Lisa's bitter imagination.

'Well, she saw me with Jamie in the disco,' she began, tracing it back to the most memorable part for herself. 'She went totally off her head at me, then just stormed out. I came back here and watched out of my bedroom window for a bit to see if I could see her, but I didn't. Anyway, I didn't see her till the next morning, and that's when she told me about him. She didn't say till later – after you'd been to the school over Linda – but then she said Steve Lunt and Andy Green had been attacking her, and this man had come and chased them off. Then she said he walked her home, and that he said he'd seen her a while back and fancied her, and did she want to go out with him. That's about it . . . Oh, except that he was supposed to be dead gorgeous.'

'But you didn't believe her?' Seddon asked.

'Well, sort of, at first,' Debbie said. 'Until she started going on about how he'd said he loved her. I called her a liar then, 'cos I knew that was rubbish.'

'And what did she say to that?'

'Well, she admitted it.'

'That she was lying?' Seddon asked, feeling his slight hopes falling by the wayside once more.

'Well, that she was lying about him saying he loved her, yeah. But she still reckoned the rest was true. About him chasing Steve and Andy off, and that, and then him walking her home.'

'Steve Lunt and Andy Green from school?'

'Yeah.'

Seddon stood up. 'Okay, well, thanks very much for your help, Debbie.'

She smiled sadly. 'It's okay. I just want you to find Lisa.'

'We will,' he promised, hoping against hope that she would still be alive when they did.

Saying goodbye, he set off for Steve Lunt's address. Given what he knew of the lads, there was every chance they would both be there anyway, so he could kill two birds with one stone.

Sure enough, when he got to Steve's place there they were.

Sitting in the homely kitchen with the worried-faced boys, Seddon assured them that he was not here to reopen the wounds they'd received from the Linda Parry case, and apologized for the difficulties they had experienced after that last interview.

Now that things had calmed down and people had started to accept that they were not involved, the boys accepted the apology, but were still understandably anxious about his reasons for this latest visit.

'I need you to tell me everything you remember about a reported incident outside the youth club earlier that night,' Seddon told them. 'With Lisa Noone.'

Their faces instantly dropped at this – the blood draining from Steve's, as Andy's turned crimson. Their reactions excited Seddon.

'Nothing happened,' Andy said at last. 'I swear on me ma's life, we didn't really do anything.'

'All I want to ascertain,' Seddon said, 'is whether or not anyone else was involved. Was there another person outside the youth club with you at that time?'

Steve cleared his throat. 'Look, we were messing about with Lisa, yeah? And it got a bit, well . . . out of order, I suppose.'

'But we didn't do anything to her!' Andy insisted again.

'And what happened then?' Seddon persisted.

'Well, we were in this alcove giving her a light for a fag,' Steve went on, 'when this nutter grabs Andy by the throat.'

'Yeah,' Andy chipped in indignantly, rubbing at his throat as if it had only just happened. 'He was well out of order, man. I should have got him done – that was assault, that!'

'What happened then?' Seddon asked impatiently.

'Well, he let go after Lisa told him we wasn't doing nothing,' Steve said. 'And told us to do one.'

'Mad-eyed bastard!' Andy sneered, then blushed when he realized he'd sworn.

Ignoring the slip, Seddon asked them for a description of the man. They both shrugged and looked at each other.

'It was too dark to tell,' Steve said after a moment. 'All I know is he was bigger and older than us.'

'Yeah,' Andy cut in. 'Or we'd have kicked his head in!'

'Shut it, And,' Steve said, giving Seddon an apologetic look. 'He had black hair, I know that, and these mad starey eyes.'

'Yeah, like an alien – the freakozoid!'

'Can you describe what he was wearing?' Seddon asked.

'Yeah, a leather jacket . . . and gloves, I think.'

'Gloves?'

'Yeah,' Andy butted in again. 'Leather gloves! Nearly choked me to death with 'em!'

'How old would you say he was?'

Steve shrugged. 'In his twenties, I reckon.'

Leaving Steve's house, Seddon radioed through for a check on all local dark-haired males between the ages of nineteen and thirty-five, especially those with a history of violence. He then asked for a set of mug-book photographs of these men to be taken round to Steve Lunt's address for the boys to look through.

This done, he set off for the hospital to see Pat Noone, who had finally come round after her second op. He wanted to see if she was up to another chat, and to let her know the situation as it stood. Despite the doctor's concerns that he shouldn't tell her too much in case it upset her, Seddon knew that she would be more agonized if he didn't tell her.

When he was almost there, his mobile rang.

'Yo?' he barked into it, manoeuvring deftly around an out-going ambulance.

'It's Lynne,' the familiar voice announced. 'I've got something.'

Pulling sharply in to the kerb, he said, 'What?'

'Tissue belonging to Pat Noone's attacker – at least, I assume it's his,' Lynne said. 'I found a broken nail tangled in her sheets after she was taken to the hospital that night, and there was a tiny amount of skin stuck to it that I've had checked out very carefully. I've just had the results back, and get this – it's not hers *or* Rashid's.'

'So it can only be his?' Seddon croaked, his heart pounding a tattoo in his chest.

'Almost certainly,' Lynne said, a grin in her voice. 'I'm just about to cross-check the results with the National File. If he's on it, we've got him!'

'Lynne, you are a fucking star!'

'Oh, come now,' she chuckled modestly. 'A mere speck of celestial dust, surely!'

28

Claire Thompson climbed out of her car and looked up at the forbidding grey façade of Linton Court. She counted along the windows from the third-floor stairwell until she came to the one she had been told was Peter Webster's.

As when she had come earlier with Gary Yale, the window concerned was completely sealed against the light, the curtains drawn tight, giving not the slightest hint of a gap. She wondered for a moment if *anyone* was living there, never mind Peter. But she'd only find out by keeping calling until someone answered the door.

If she didn't find him, she was going to be in serious trouble. She should never have given him the opportunity to slip away from her. Should never have accepted his word that he had been taking his medication, or believed his show of normality. What she *should* have done was remember the cardinal rule: never believe what they say, only what the test results prove.

Reaching the main door of the block that she sincerely hoped contained Peter Webster's new home, Claire took a deep breath and pressed the security buzzer.

The security guard replied seconds later, asking her to state her business. Not wishing to stigmatize one of her cases by stating her true business, she said she was delivering a prescription. After being made to wait a good two minutes, the door-release buzzer finally sounded and she went inside.

Making her way up the stairs, she rounded the corner to the second level and almost bumped straight into an old woman who was hovering outside one of the two doors on that floor.

The woman was looking up the stairs towards the third floor, with her hands clutched to her chest as if in fear. Claire's compassionate nature wouldn't allow her to pass without asking if she were all right.

'It's not me,' the woman muttered, pointing a gnarly finger upwards. 'It's that bloody nutter, up there.' She peered at Claire suspiciously then. 'Here, you were here earlier, weren't you? With that black fella? Knocking on *his* door. You a friend of his, then?' This last was more an accusation than a question.

Shaking her head, Claire said, 'Not exactly, no.'

'A copper, then?'

'No.'

'Shame,' the woman muttered, folding her arms tightly. 'I thought someone had finally had the bottle to report the creep.'

Claire felt the hairs on the back of her neck bristle. If it was Peter up there and he was causing some sort of nuisance, it would do her no good at all if he was taken in by the police before she'd had a chance to see him.

'For what?' she asked.

''Cos he's a bloody maniac!' the woman said. 'Flaming racket he makes. All that mad singing and hopping about at all hours! I don't know what he gets up to in there, but I'll be glad when I get put in a home,

I can tell you. He's sending me round the bloody twist, he is.'

Claire's stomach was churning now. It had to be Peter. The singing and hopping about fitted in with his pre-medication behavioural pattern. And if he'd started it all up again, it could only mean that he'd stopped taking the medication, breaching a strict condition of his supervision order. It did not bode well.

'I don't suppose you could tell me what he looks like?' she asked. The chances of someone else having the same strange behaviour were slim, but just in case . . .

'Huh!' The woman snorted disparagingly. 'He's a looker, I'll give him that!'

'When you say a looker . . . ?'

The woman sighed with irritation.

'Yeah, all shiny black hair and bright blue eyes. Bit like that French bloke, Alan Delwotsit, but nicer, if you know what I mean? Still, no amount of good looks makes up for being a raving bloody loony, does it?'

Thanking the woman for her information, Claire continued up towards the flat, absolutely sure now that it *was* Peter Webster in there. Dreading what she would find, given what the old lady had said, she was fully aware that she was about to get into very hot water with her boss.

'Here,' the woman shouted after her. 'You'd best watch yourself, 'cos these last couple of days he's been worse than ever before. He might have gone quiet now, but he's not all there, that one! Screaming and shouting, then crying like a little girl. Off his bloody trolley, if you ask me!'

Getting absolutely no response from the flat, despite knocking on the door and shouting through the letter box for almost fifteen minutes, Claire finally admitted defeat. Knowing what she now knew, she realized that she couldn't hold off the inevitable. She had to report what she had learned, and let her superiors deal with Peter as they saw fit – whatever the professional consequences to herself.

After making sure that the would-be executor had gone, he dragged Lisa from the couch and across the floor into his chamber. She was still unconscious, but he wasn't concerned about that.

She should think herself lucky he had not gone the whole way and snuffed out her miserable, petty little life. She would certainly deserve it, the scheming harlot! But he had had to put his Master's plan before his own desires.

Laying her down on the bed, he hummed as he undressed her, feeling no desire as each intimate part of her body was revealed to him. His desire was fuelled by the knowledge of what was to be – not by the flesh of the female creatures soiling this Earth.

When her clothes were in a pile on the floor beside the bed, he positioned her as he had been ordered: her legs and arms spreadeagled, her hands palm up and open in readiness to receive the benediction.

And then he undressed himself before lighting the candle and kneeling in fervent prayer before the altar.

29

Seddon left Pat Noone weeping silently in her small private room. He knew he had been right to tell her everything. Obviously, she was extremely upset that Lisa had not as yet been found, but she had been relieved to be fully in the picture.

She had thanked him as he'd prepared to leave, telling him the decision she had made.

'When this is all over and you've found my Lisa, I'm getting out of this shit. We're packing up and going to see my sister in Birmingham.'

Seddon had been surprised to hear that she had family, but she explained that they'd fallen out over twenty years earlier. Now, though, she had decided to go and make peace, and give Lisa what she deserved in life – a loving family and a good, decent home. Seddon had wished her the very best of luck – and he had sincerely meant it.

Now he was on his way back to the station to see if Lynne Wilde's discovery had yielded fruit. But first he had to authorize Samir Rashid's release. Walking hurriedly into the room that housed the new mega-intelligence computer, Seddon found Lynne parked beside the operator, actively participating in the extensive database search.

'Do we know who it is yet?' he asked, dragging a stool up to sit beside her.

'Oh, yes . . . we know all right,' she said ominously. 'He is one Peter Webster. And he has a severe psychosis that seems to manifest itself in rather twisted religious beliefs, according to the data held by the Mental Health Authority.'

'It's got to be him!' Seddon declared gleefully. 'So what are we waiting for? . . . Let's go pick the bastard up!'

Lynne gave him a grim smile. 'Ah . . . therein we have a problem.'

'Which is?' he demanded, itching to get going now that they knew who they were looking for.

'We don't know where he is.'

'What do you mean, we don't know where he is?' Seddon was incredulous. 'I thought once they were on the nut register they had to be monitored closely.'

'In theory, they ought to be, yes. But it seems that he no longer lives at his registered address.'

'It's true,' Sergeant Banks, who was hovering behind, chipped in. 'We've had a unit down there already, checking the place out.'

'What the hell did you do that for?' Seddon demanded furiously. 'And why wasn't I informed? This *is* my fucking case!'

'They were only recce-ing,' Banks explained nervously. 'Super's orders.'

'Oh, I see,' Seddon spat, visibly bristling. 'So he's decided to take over now that we're getting somewhere, has he? We'll soon see about that!'

'Calm down, Ken,' Lynne said sharply, stopping him before he could go after the superintendent's blood. 'We're not going to find the girl if you carry on like a caveman, are we?'

Grudgingly, Seddon stayed put.

'All right, I'll calm down. But what are we going to do about this missing God freak? Just sit here twiddling our thumbs?'

'No, I'm going to speak to his caseworker,' Lynne said. 'Just as soon as I can get a number. Now relax, will you? You're giving me a headache.'

30

Running from the station, his bail note tucked in his pocket, Sam hailed a passing taxi and jumped in. Giving the driver his address, he slumped back in his seat and ran a sweaty hand across his exhausted face.

Closing his eyes, he let the breath he seemed to have been holding in since he was first arrested hiss out through his teeth. At least *one* of his nightmares was over, now that they had finally caught the real killer. He was free to go, they had said – but not to leave the country. He still had charges to face relating to his business. And he knew they would hammer him for that.

Thank God he had Elsa to support him through the trials yet to come. And she *would* stand by him, he was sure, now that he had been exonerated of any blame attached to the murders. He knew there were things he still had to face when he got home, but he had had plenty of time to consider what he would say.

According to the police, Elsa had not only found out about his relationships with Pat and the other whores, but she had also discovered his computer 'hobby'. Still, he was sure she would overlook these minor indiscretions once he had had a chance to talk to her – a chance to explain things from his point of view. And he knew exactly how he would handle it. He would weigh her down with guilt about her lack of affection towards him, and remind her of her sacred Catholic duties to honour and obey him. It was guaranteed to work.

Sure of his safe return to his wife's suddenly rather appealing bosom, Sam opened his eyes and looked out of the window. A feeling of apprehension assailed him as he gazed at the familiar streets all around him – the places he might not see for a few years once the detective inspector got to grips with him.

Forcing the dread from his mind as the taxi idled at a red light halfway down the Princess Parkway, he looked out of the window again and realized that the road to his left was where Jessica lived. It suddenly occurred to him to wonder how Jessica had fared when the police had raided his office?

He glanced towards her house, smiling as he imagined his loyal secretary giving the impossible DI hell. She wouldn't have stood for any of Seddon's nonsense. She would have made things as difficult as possible before bowing to the inevitable.

Given that he was just thinking about her, he was somewhat taken aback to see Jessica herself coming out of her front door. Even more so when she trotted down her garden path and hurried out of her gate, carrying a large suitcase. He wondered where she was going and hoped that, wherever it was, it was just for a short break. In the time he had left, he would need her help to sort out this mess he was in. If anyone could help him to build a convincing case to prove that he hadn't known his business was illegal or that some of the wives he imported were below the minimum marrying age, it was Jessica.

As she placed the case into the boot of her car, Sam's taxi began to move when the lights changed to green. Turning his head as they passed the road, he peered back at Jessica through the rear window until the sides of the houses blocked his view.

He would phone her in a couple of days, he decided. Arrange to take her out to dinner so that they could get their stories straight.

All Sam wanted to do right now was get home and have a bath. Then he would have his little chat with Elsa and smooth the waters. This done, he would gorge himself on one of her fine dinners, followed by a bottle of cognac. And then he would go to bed and sleep the sleep of the dead.

Turning along his road some ten minutes later, he could immediately see that something was amiss at his house. As the taxi drew closer, he realized what it was. There were no curtains at the windows. Maybe Elsa had taken them down to wash them? he wondered. Yes, that would be it. She must have decided to do a real spring-clean for his homecoming. What a woman!

But, pulling up outside his gate, he felt a thud in his gut as if he had been punched. Climbing from the taxi in a daze, he handed the driver a ten-pound note and told him to keep the change.

Standing on the pavement as the taxi pulled away with a honk of gratitude from the driver, Sam gazed at his house with mounting horror. Not only were there no curtains at the windows, there was nothing beyond those mocking panes but walls, floors and doors. The place was empty. Completely and utterly empty!

Elsa had done a spring-clean all right. She'd cleaned him right out!

31

Claire Thompson was sitting in Gary Yale's office, deep within the forbidding heart of the new Social Services building, less than ten minutes from the police station.

Yale was there, as was Callum McNeil, the head of the entire department. McNeil was pacing the floor agitatedly as Yale looked on – a little too smugly, Claire thought. Things were definitely *not* looking good.

'You should have told us sooner,' McNeil was saying accusingly. 'If you hadn't tried to cover Webster's disappearance he'd still be on the programme, and we'd all be in the clear. Now we have a major problem on our hands.'

'With respect, sir,' Claire said, 'he hasn't actually *done* anything.'

'Oh, come on, Claire, don't be so naive,' Yale interjected. 'He has violated the order in every way possible. Not only has he been allowed to slip through the net and find alternative accommodation without *your* knowledge,' he sniped, 'but he's quite patently not been taking his medication.'

'We don't know that for sure,' Claire protested lamely.

'This is ridiculous!' McNeil barked. 'You just told us yourself that the neighbour quite clearly described his social traits. If he's behaving like that again, then Lord only knows what he may have already done.'

'And this is not some harmless little Bible-basher we're talking about here,' Yale added churlishly. 'He's a potential danger to the public. He's a paranoid schizophrenic with a set of complicated psychoses, for God's sake!'

Before Claire could respond to this, the phone on Yale's desk began to ring. Snatching it up irritably, he demanded to know why he was being disturbed when he'd specifically left orders that he shouldn't be. Wasn't it bad enough that he'd had to come into the office out of hours for this hastily convened meeting without the night-switchboard operator disregarding his commands?

Stopped in the middle of his vitriolic rant by whatever the caller was saying, Yale listened for a moment, then handed the receiver across the desk to Claire.

'I think you'd better take this,' he said, his expression grim and loaded with accusation. 'It's the police. Apparently, they too are trying to locate Peter Webster. They think he's the one who's been murdering the prostitutes.'

Claire took the call, her heart sinking. After giving the police the information she had garnered about Peter Webster's new address and relating the conversation she'd had with his neighbour, she handed the phone back to Yale.

Standing then, she let out a shuddering breath and turned to McNeil.

'I'll hand in my resignation first thing in the morning, sir.'

Neither man objected as Claire made her lonely way out of the office.

32

L isa came to slowly. Vaguely aware of a low murmur coming from somewhere close by, she recognized the all-too-familiar sound of Benny in prayer mode and opened her eyes the barest fraction – just enough to see what was happening without alerting him that she was conscious.

It took a moment to adjust her eyes to the dim light cast by the low, flickering flame of the candle, but she was soon able to make out the unfamiliar shapes all around her. She guessed that she had finally made it into Benny's most private realm.

Feeling a sudden chill breeze across her stomach, Lisa glanced down at herself and was horrified to find that she was completely naked. Every instinct in her brain screamed at her to draw her spread legs together and cover herself up, but knowing that Benny would hear her if she moved, she forced herself to resist the urge.

Without moving a muscle, she peered around until she found exactly where Benny was. He too was naked, she saw. With his back to her, he was on his knees before what looked like a dressing table covered in black material. His head was bent forward onto his hands, which made his muffled mutterings sound even more sinister than usual.

Dragging her gaze away from him, Lisa looked around the room, hoping to spot something to use as a weapon. She almost cried out with shock and disgust when she saw the walls, but she just about managed to stop herself by biting down hard on the inside of her cheek.

All around her, plastered from ceiling to floor on every available wall space, were the crudest images she had ever seen. Photographs of naked men and women – there was even a dog in one of them – engaging in foul, perverted sex acts. All of the pictures seemed to have been altered in some way. Although most of the participants seemed to be partially clothed in some sort of rubber or leather gear, someone – most likely Benny, she decided, shuddering – had drawn extra *things* onto them all.

Most of the men were dominant in some way, standing threateningly over the women, evil intent on their faces. But, with Benny's help, they all now bore the horns and tail of the Devil. And they all had massively engorged penises and long, forked tongues – some of which were thrust into the women's open vaginas, whilst others were obviously intended to look as though they had caused the bloody gashes adorning the women's stomachs.

Lisa noticed that all of the women had been made to look as though they were dreadfully wounded. Most of them had graphically detailed, lovingly drawn cuts to the torso, but some had also been altered to look as if their vaginas had been torn apart, and others had had their breasts removed. Without exception, they all had writing scrawled across their faces, obliterating whatever features they might have had. Straining hard, Lisa could just about make out the words: Harlot, Whore and Jezebel.

And, without exception, they all had what looked like flowers stuck onto their wounds.

With a pounding heart, she forced herself back to her task of locating a weapon, knowing instinctively that Benny had not brought her into this chamber of horrors intending, to let her out again. Her desperately searching gaze finally came to rest on the hammer he had guarded so closely when decorating *her* room.

Obviously afraid to leave it lying around where she might get her hands on it, he had brought it in here and placed it on the floor behind the door. It was closer to her than it was to him, but she doubted she'd be able to reach it in time without alerting him.

Seconds ticked agonizingly by in the time-bomb clock of her psyche. Time was fast running out. Benny was engrossed in his prayers right now, but Lisa knew only too well that he wouldn't stay that way for much longer. He would be working to his agenda, as usual, and it would only be a matter of minutes before the mythical 'next part' came along.

Barely allowing herself to breathe in case she disturbed him, Lisa began to make her move. Slowly, cautiously, she inched her body in tiny increments towards the edge of the bed.

When at last she felt the sharp ridge of the mattress against her spine, she launched herself onto the floor with the force of sheer desperation, and rolled towards the hammer, reaching it just as Benny reacted.

'*Nooo!*' he screeched as Lisa leaped to her feet, clutching the hammer in both hands. '*NOOOOO!*'

33

Screeching to a halt at the blind side of Linton Court, Seddon threw the car door open and leaped out, barely manging to wrench the keys from the ignition as he did so.

Running across to the assembled units, he had a hurried discussion with the chief of the armed response team to bring him up to speed. Then, when everyone was sure of what they were potentially dealing with, the race to save Lisa Noone began in earnest.

Starting with gaining entry to the block of flats without the security guard alerting their man.

Which should have been easy enough, given that this was official police business, but Seddon knew from bitter experience that this one simple thing could blow them up. More often than not, the guards that the council hired to man the CCTV-style entryphones on these flats at night were as bent as could be, and made it their business to alert as many tenants as possible to impending police visits before they released the door.

If that happened now and any harm came to Lisa as a result, Seddon vowed that he personally would slam the security guard's head between the heavy steel lift-shaft doors that all these types of flats boasted, override the safety mechanism, press the button for the top floor, and cheerily hold the bastard down while his head was ripped from his shoulders by the rising lift-floor.

Fortunately for the guard, who was too engrossed in a Tyson title challenge to give more than a cursory glance at the screen to see who was at the door before pressing the release button, he didn't have to.

34

Lurching across the room, Benny threw himself at Lisa, knocking her totally off balance as he tried to wrestle the hammer from her desperately tight grip.

Winded, she clung onto her only hope of salvation for dear life and, kicking out at him wildly, managed to wriggle free.

Pushing herself across the uncarpeted floor with her feet, she felt a large splinter pierce the tender flesh of her naked backside. But she ignored the searing pain, thinking only of how to put as much distance as possible between herself and Benny as he scrabbled up onto his knees and came after her.

'Hell bitch!' he roared, flinging himself on top of her before she had a chance to swing the hammer and knocking her flat on her back. 'Spawn of thy Master's depravity!'

Seizing her by the hair, he slapped her hard across the face with his open palm, then again with the back of his hand. Then, pushing himself to his feet, he hauled her up with him.

He was aroused now, his desire to vanquish the demon controlling the body of his angel causing blood to rush into his Heavenly weapon.

'For what you are about to receive . . .' he hissed,

flinging Lisa's thin naked body down onto the bed, 'may Our Lord make you truly grateful . . .'

Screaming as Benny reached for her, Lisa used every last ounce of energy she possessed to kick him between his legs with the flat of her foot. As he buckled in agony, crumpling to his knees on the floor in front of her, she leaped up from the bed and, with a strength born of sheer terror, brought the hammer down on his bowed head with a sickening thud. And then another . . . and another . . . Each blow urged on by the hysterical screaming that Lisa could still hear but could no longer recognize as coming from her own mouth.

35

S eddon reached the door first, followed closely by
the heavily protected men of the armed response unit.

When the blood-curdling screams reached them, everyone who was crowded onto the narrow communal landing outside the suspect's flat froze.

Then all hell broke loose.

'Break it down!' Seddon ordered, not even attempting
to keep his voice low. '*NOW, goddamn it!*'

As the awful screaming went on and on, two officers
charged at the door with a large steel battering pole. It
took five attempts – four more than the average door
but, as they were soon to discover, the locks on this
door were of industrial strength, designed to keep an
army out. It wasn't the locks that gave way on the fifth
pounding; it was the door itself.

Charging through the flat in the direction of the
hysterical screaming, the first wave of armed officers
scattered into their positions, guns aimed at Benny's
bedroom door.

Scooting past them, a second wave grouped around
the door itself, while a third charged straight through
the middle, yelling: 'Armed Police! Stay exactly where
you are!' as they kicked the door clean off its hinges.

Dashing forward, Seddon pushed his way through

the men crowding the doorway. All he could think was that Lisa was still screaming, which meant she was still alive!

Finally getting inside the bedroom, he stopped dead in the midst of the unit men who were staring around themselves in open-mouthed disbelief.

Following their gazes, he too could barely believe what he was seeing. Every wall was totally covered with vile, violent, pornographic images. He felt as though he'd stepped into a medieval torture chamber, the blood-chilling effect of which was dramatically heightened by the guttering candle on the satanic altar that had once been a dressing table.

Not a single sound could be heard from the men who had just moments before been shouting and panting with adrenalin-fuelled exertion.

But the screams still rending the air shattered what would otherwise have been a total, stunned silence. The awful, gut-wrenchingly anguished screams of the girl-child standing naked in the midst of the blood, her feet and legs splattered with clinging lumps of gore and hair.

Finally regaining his power of movement, Seddon went towards the pitiful child. Taking off his jacket, he wrapped it gently around her violently shaking shoulders as he led her away from the gruesome mulch at her feet. Mulch that had once been a man's head.

'It's all right, Lisa,' he croaked, his voice breaking over the lump in his throat as tears flooded his eyes. 'It's all right, sweetheart . . . you're safe now. You're safe, I promise.'

36

P at jerked out of her light doze as the door to her room opened slowly. Her heart leaped into her mouth when Seddon's face appeared around it.

'What's happened?' she gasped fearfully, her face a mask of dread. 'Tell me, Mr Seddon, please . . . Whatever it is, just tell me?'

'Oi, less of that,' Seddon scolded softly as tears began to stream down her cheeks. 'I've got someone out here who wants to see you. But if you're just gonna carry on like that . . . ?'

'W-what?' So sure that he'd been about to tell her he'd found Lisa's mutilated body, Pat couldn't at first comprehend what he had said.

Pushing the door fully open, Seddon gently ushered Lisa in.

'LISA!' Pat cried, ignoring the pain racking her stomach as she tried to get to her precious child. 'Lisa . . . my Lisa . . .'

'Oh, Mum!' Lisa sobbed, running to the bed and throwing herself into her mum's open arms. 'I was so s-s-scared . . . He s-said he'd k-killed you!'

'It'd take more than that to see me off,' Pat sobbed, half crying, half laughing. 'Oh, Lisa, I've missed you so much!'

'I've m-missed you, too.'

Hearing all the noise, the ward sister bustled in to check on her patient. Giving Seddon a mock-stern look as she passed him, she tried unsuccessfully to remove Lisa from her mother's arms.

'Now, come along. Your mother is in no fit state to—'

'Give over, you dozy cow!' Pat said, clinging to Lisa. 'I ain't letting her out of my sight ever again!'

Throwing her hands in the air, the sister said, 'Okay – but be it on your own head if you burst something!'

Turning to leave the room, she narrowed her eyes as she looked at Seddon and, almost smiling, said, 'And you'd better not cause any more trouble, young man!'

'Young man, indeed!' Pat snorted when the sister had left the room. 'She needs glasses, that one, and no mistake!'

'Oi!' Seddon pointed a stern finger at her. 'I'm not that old, so just watch it!'

Gazing at him over Lisa's shoulder, Pat said softly, 'And you're not that bad either, Mr S. Not that bad at all. And I won't forget what you've done, you know?'

Seddon shrugged. 'Ah, I didn't do anything, Pat.' Nodding towards Lisa, who was now lying on the bed beside her mum, her arms wrapped tightly around her neck, he said, 'That's the one who did it all. That is one smart kid you've got there – and I hope you meant what you said?'

Pat's eyes filled up again as she returned Seddon's level gaze. Chin wobbling, she whispered, 'Oh, yeah, I meant it all right.'

Watching as Pat buried her wet face in her daughter's

hair and hugged Lisa for all she was worth, Seddon swiped at the tear that was trickling down his own cheek and backed silently from the room, pulling the door firmly to behind him.

MANDASUE HELLER

The Club

Are you in?

Jenna Lorde knows she's taking on a challenge when she inherits her dad's nightclub. But Zenith comes with a top class reputation and a location other clubs would kill for, so she reckons she's more than up for it.

Until she starts to realise that the dangers aren't just from other clubs. Beneath the glamour of the VIP lounge and the pumping music, sleaze and corruption are starting to creep in, and it'll take everything Jenna has to stop the rot.

The club's survival – and her own – depend on it.

HODDER

MANDASUE HELLER

The Front

Bad decision

When four old school friends decide to make some
easy money, they pick the wrong target. Very wrong.
Robbing a small supermarket on a Manchester estate
looks easy – but with one of them wounded and a dead
body on their hands, could things get worse?

Bad trouble

They could. The supermarket is merely the front for
something bigger. The friends are small fish who have
unwittingly plunged into a very big pond and now they
are swimming with the great white sharks of the
criminal underworld.

HODDER

MANDASUE HELLER

The Game

Hard times

When Mary's mother throws her out, the sassy teenager soon learns how tough life can be. Her new friend Lynne is older, more sophisticated. She has a taste for cocaine and isn't above walking the streets for extra cash to pay for it.

Hard men

Mary sticks to a straighter path, until the night Lynne brings Ali and Raiz back to their flat. The women don't know that their sexy new friends are small-time criminals, desperate for alibis for a drug-dealer's murder.

Hard drugs

All too soon, Mary is in more trouble than she can handle. Can her old friend Jane's risky scheme save Mary? Or has her fate been sealed by falling for the wrong man?

HODDER

MANDASUE HELLER

Tainted Lives

Three abandoned children

Sarah has been in care since she was seven, put there by her drug-addicted mother. Trying to live with the rejection is bad enough, but there is more pain to come.

Harry's mother locked him in a cupboard so she wouldn't have to look at his ugly face. When he and Sarah meet for the first time, they forge an instant friendship.

Then Vinnie comes into their lives. A good-looking, calculating thirteen-year-old, this is his last chance to change his ways.

Three tainted lives

As the years pass and they become adults, their lives take very different directions. But when their paths cross again, one of them will commit the worst crime of all . . .

HODDER

MANDASUE HELLER

The Charmer

It's too good to be true

Maria Price is a survivor of the care system who thought she would never have a family or security again. She's just inherited a house and a bank account.

He's too good to be true

Joel Parry – good-looking, charming and a wonderful lover – seems to know everyone who is anyone in Manchester. Joel just happens to need a place to stay. Before long he's moved into Maria's house and is helping her to spend her money.

But Joel isn't what he seems to be. He's deep in the drug scene, and his terrifying past is about to catch up with him - and the naïve girl who trusts him . . .

HODDER